League of Lies

Ellie Pool

Copyright © 2024 by Ellie Pool

All rights reserved. No portion of this book may be reproduced or transmitted in any form without written permission from the author.

This is a work of fiction in which pop culture and historical icons are used solely as artistic references. Names, characters, places, and incidents are purely the product of the author's imagination and are not to be construed as real. Any resemblance to actual persons, living or dead, or actual events is purely coincidental.

The entirety of this book was organically produced without the use of AI.

Creative contributor/Editing: AJ Adams

Cover design: Gayle Florence

Cover art: Michael McNab

Library and Archives Canada publication data: Pool, Ellie; League of Lies/ Ellie Pool

ISBN 978-1-7383157-0-3

10 9 8 7 6 5 4 3 2 1

Printed and bound in the Canada.

For Julian

Dedicated to the truth warriors:
You knew the risks and did it anyway.
Your sacrifices will never be forgotten.
With utmost gratitude,
God speed.

Preface

Have you ever wondered why we're taught to fear the witches and not the people who burned them alive at the stake? Who makes the rules? What is authority? As a child, these were the kind of thoughts that kept me up at night.

During her teen years, my Dutch mother lived through six years of godless, war-ravaged ruin and suffering at the hands of the Nazis. Her horror stories left me with an indelible curiosity about blind obedience to an evil regime or why people follow the rules when it's the wrong thing to do.

Conversely, I spent my blessed teenage years in a peaceful country with key democratic values and somewhat of a shared base reality. That was the setting in which I fostered my love of writing and in which I promised my 14-year-old self that one day I would write a novel. All things considered; the world seemed like an okay place back in the day.

One generation later, the free and cooperative society of the 1970s was a distant memory – a period in history unrecognizable through the eyes of the postmodern world. During those thirtyish years, Western culture experienced a creeping monumental shift that reminded me that I still needed to write a book. Alas, between real life challenges, a busy career, and an active family life, I barely had the energy to write a grocery list, much less a *novel*.

In the early 2000s, the calling grew louder. I watched in disbelief as people willingly surrendered their inalienable, God-given rights and freedoms to a global machine intent on installing an Orwellian one-world government. I spent the next twenty plus years researching history and social psychology – I needed to know why civil societies can act in such irrational ways. The insights I gained through my research are shared in the pages of this book.

At the beginning of 2020, we were facing a global crisis – neither the one you're thinking of *nor* that we ran out of toilet paper. We had a tyranny problem disguised as a medical emergency and leadership without a soul. Compliance to an evil regime was happening all over again but it was different now. *This* time, I had sufficient knowledge of humanity's dark side and how people fall for psychological operations.

As if God literally gave me a kick in the backside in the late spring of 2021, I injured my rib while I was surfing in Hawaii... or I may have tripped over my own two feet on the back deck. Regardless, I was forced to rest and... resting wasn't really my thing. Amid my self-pity, I started to write, foolishly allowing myself a year from first draft to publication. Almost three years later, I can safely say that turning an idea into a full-length novel is as hard as it sounds.

Finally, I can look into the naïve eyes of my teenage self and tell her I delivered on the promise I'd made: I did it!

----

*"Government is the coldest of all cold monsters.
Coldly, it lies; and this lie slips from its mouth: I, government, am the people.
Everything government says is a lie, and everything government has, it has stolen."*
~ Friedrich Nietzsche

Prologue

Massachusetts, April 18, 1775

With the rhythmic drum of horse hooves slamming to the ground, the revolutionary Sons of Liberty fervently rode through the cool, moonlight night. When clanging bells and blaring trumpets blasted a warning in the darkness, a sundry group of colonists awoke from their deep slumber.

From the towering steeple of Boston's Old North Church, two colonial lanterns glowed – the British Redcoats had arrived by sea to disarm the insurgents of their meager munitions at Concord.

Overtaxed, but without representation, the colonists had formed rebel militias out of humble, ordinary men: farmers, shoemakers, printers, saddlers and the like. Badly outnumbered by the seafaring invaders, these patriots boldly stared into the menacing face of the most powerful military in the world... and held the line.

When sunrise overtook the crisp morning air, the swelling group of minutemen forced the British army back to Lexington. A mystery shot rang out in the chaos – the shot heard around the world. In a conflict in which everything is at stake, the battle was on: life and death; freedom over servitude; neighbor against neighbor; and brother against brother.

With the howling of muskets and cannons booming throughout the day, putrid smoke filled the air. Crimson bayonets glinted in the sunlight, the fresh corpses forming murky pools of sacrificed blood on the battlefields. When the sun set on the grisly scene, one hundred and twenty-two men lay dead.

Fifty American patriots paid the ultimate price that day when they laid down their lives for liberty – an idea that a distant monarchy could never take away. The First American Revolution had begun.

Part I

Runaway

"The devil doesn't come dressed in a red cape and pointy horns. He comes as everything you ever wished for."
~ Tucker Max

Chapter 1

Dancing shadows kept time with the Gregorian chant as they cast a slow-motion hypnotic spell throughout the eerie church. The nearby statue of the Virgin Mary crashed to the shiny marble floor, shattering into a hundred pieces.

The thunder rolled.

Shimmering white light from a cluster of flickering candles reflected off drops of fresh blood on the darkened altar. A sudden flash of lightning revealed a bloodied crown of thorns on the dying man's head.

At once, a grotesque dark-green demon appeared in a thick blanket of black smoke and the repugnant odor of the underworld. A hooded cobra swayed beside him, his eyes as red as his keeper's.

Still on her weak knees in the first pew, the terrified young woman froze – unable to move and unable to scream.

"It doesn't matter what you do, Tessssa," the demon hissed with a growl, obstructing her view of the tabernacle. "We own your sssssoul."

Chapter 2

Sixteen years earlier

On an ordinary Tuesday morning rush hour in the Big Apple, an endless string of yellow taxis hauled wide-eyed tourists and weary locals along the shadowy boulevards. Amid a discordant symphony of obnoxious horns blaring, the foul odor of sour milk merged with exhaust fumes to permeate the bustling streets with a toxic odor. Times Square, aptly named for its keenly designed hourglass shape, was alive with the excitement of curious tourists in awe of humankind's evolution.

A short stroll away, Central Park was buzzing with children's laughter and the hum of people loving life. With the promise of a new day awakening, golden sunlight beamed down from the cobalt-blue sky, illuminating the specks of rust and coral in the fertile trees. A light breeze tantalized one's senses with its divine flirtation and the heavenly scent of tulips. It was the perfect setting against the iconic twin towers – a tranquil intertwining of nature and corporate America.

The Manhattan skyline came to life on the canvas in front of an attractive young woman as she worked her artistic magic under the shade of a picturesque red maple tree. Her long mahogany-brown hair was pulled in a high ponytail that danced in the morning light, the graceful movements complementing her tall, slender figure. She looked older than her sixteen years.

At 8:46 am, the magnificent cry of a red-tailed hawk injected a taste of wilderness into the endless New York noise. A low-flying passenger plane hummed above...

KABOOM!!

The north tower of the World Trade Center transformed into an amphitheater of hellfire, angry flames and dense black smoke. Act I – order, Act II – chaos.

Startled by the impact of the passenger jet crashing into an occupied building, the blossoming artist's paintbrush tumbled from her hand to the thick grass beneath her feet. On wobbly knees, she staggered toward the nearby park bench nestled in the shade of the vibrant maple tree.

With shattering glass and toppling steel barely drowning out the unearthly moans of the dying, survivors jumped to their certain deaths rather than burn alive. When the south tower was struck just seventeen minutes later, the mortified teenage beauty opened her mouth to scream but no sound came out. She squeezed her eyes shut to force away the anxiety welling up in her throat.

High-pitched shrieks punctuated the profanity while the crowds ran for cover. The surreal screech of emergency vehicles flew through the streets in the terror of the aftermath. This was no accident – the United States was *under attack*!

"Are you all right, luv?" A soothing, hypnotic voice with a London accent jolted the shaken young girl back to reality. It had come from the glowing silhouette sitting next to her.

"I..."

The angelic-sounding woman was in her mid-20s, rocking designer labels and stylish, cropped blond hair. She introduced herself as Diana, chuckling when she said she was sometimes mistaken for a Karen. "What's your name?"

"T...T...Tessaaa..." the young artist wailed.

"Tessa." Diana's regal smile and warm eyes radiated compassion, instantly gaining the young girl's trust. "Do you want to talk about it?"

Alone, traumatized, and two thousand miles from home, Tessa tried to steady her hands on the knees of her fashionably ripped jeans. "N...No." Her bottom lip trembled.

Diana glanced toward the twin towers – they'd been replaced by two thick columns of black smoke. "It's scary, isn't it?"

Tessa shook her head. "I...I'm..." Squeezing her eyes shut, she nodded. "I'm scared!" she sobbed, wiping her tear-drenched lips and dripping nose on the sleeve of her favorite royal blue sweater.

"Tessa, I know just what you need."

"You know how I can get *home*?" Tessa lifted her head to zero in on Diana's soft features.

"Come with me, luv."

Rubbing her bloodshot eyes, Tessa hesitated.

"Let's go get some tea. You'll feel better." Like a beacon in a raging storm, Diana guided Tessa off the bench by the forearm.

Avoiding eye contact with her new friend, the young, naïve Tessa packed up her art supplies and followed the stranger out of the park.

Chapter 3

Across the country in Western Wyoming, the Arem River Valley sparkled with an unparalleled natural beauty. Great blue herons soared over the white-water river as it thundered its way downstream over high falls and between thickets of lush forest. The sweet fragrance of golden rod wafted in the meadow among the sagebrush and rocky mountain maples.

In the shadows of the jagged, snow-capped peaks, the peaceful city of Dormin rested on the banks of the raging Arem River. In the early morning hours of September 11, the locals were buzzing – there'd been a shocking terrorist attack in New York City.

Gathering at the Come N' Go Saloon, the horrified citizens watched the drama unfold on the televisions mounted on every cedar wall. The old-west-style saloon was the community's favorite watering hole, recognizable by the familiar smell of whiskey past the second set of swinging doors.

At around three in the afternoon, when the citizens were too distracted to notice, Mayor Graham Maxwell Fisher III went missing from city hall.

As the east coast grieved, Dorminians grappled with their identity: contemporary riches and fabled days of yore. Rising from the roof of city hall, Old Glory, though tattered and torn, stood erect and vigilant over freedom won through bloodshed. Old Town Square, at the center of town, housed statues of the country's founders with their poignant words etched in stone beneath their feet. Wyoming folklore, Old Faithful, and the first state to elect a female governor way back in 1924. Life, liberty, and the pursuit of happiness.

The American spirit was alive and well in the Arem River Valley.

Chapter 4

While the rest of the country watched in horror, shell-shocked New Yorkers wrestled with the invisible weight pressing down on the entire city. As they came to terms with one of the worst terrorist attacks on American soil since the country's founding, Manhattanites moved robotically through the dusty city streets.

In a lavish penthouse suite on the Upper East Side, a prominent telecommunications businessman and billionaire was glued to the marathon news coverage. Jack Weber was struggling to understand as he watched the smoldering towers collapse at free-fall speed into a cloud of thick ash and budding suspicion.

The financial heart of America lay in a heap of rubble on the asbestos-covered, now spooky streets of America's biggest city, the haunting wail of sirens filling the deadened air. On top of the cinders and ash, a jihadist's passport landed, undamaged, its will to survive rivaled only by a cockroach in the apocalypse. Ghostly figures wandered the demolished area – too numb to think and too traumatized to speak.

First the towers. Later the pentagon. Somewhere in the confusion, an errant plane destined for the White House crashed in a farmer's field in Pennsylvania. Everyone was riveted to a moment in time when everything around them was crumbling, including Building 7 – which hadn't even been hit by a plane.

Amid the conspiracy theories and the fog of war, the headlines screamed: **ATTACK ON AMERICA! TERRORISTS! WAR!**

When Jack finally turned the TV off for dinner, the only thing he knew for certain was that the world had changed.

Chapter 5

Mature beyond her years, Tessa Ryan was only sixteen when she graduated high school a year early and had saved enough money to get out of small-town America. One cloudy July morning, she said goodbye to her unsuspecting parents, promising them she'd be back in a couple of weeks. Before the sun went down, Dormin was but a forgotten blur in her proverbial rearview mirror.

The eager young runaway landed at dusk in New York City, awestruck by the grand silhouette of the twin towers soaring above the skyline. The exotic images she'd only ever seen on television were now larger than life in the flashing marquis lights of Broadway and the magical ambiance of Times Square.

As Tessa adjusted to the big city, she put distance between herself and her roots by trading in her cowboy boots for an easel. From rodeo queen to Jackson Pollock. *I'm here, New York!* Sadly, she'd never realize her dream of opening her own upscale art gallery if she stayed in Wyoming; *cowboys just didn't have the cultivated taste for fine art.*

Unacquainted with the real world, Tessa was certain her artistic passion would be enough to sustain her through the hard times. So what if it meant going to bed hungry some days? She had no desire to be anything but an artist – starving or not. It wasn't like she was a prostitute trying to feed a heroin habit, and you can't put a price tag on peace of mind.

That peace came crashing down around her in the wreckage of 9/11. Tessa had been gone for a little less than two months, too rural-girl proud to ask her parents for help, and too big-city callow to tell them she needed it. Nobody was allowed to fly, anyway. She was stuck.

Then Diana appeared out of nowhere, the sweet English angel who introduced her to the worldly Aamon Della Rossi. At twenty-nine, he was thirteen years Tessa's senior – the classic tall, dark, and handsome Italian lover. The bewildered young girl was captivated by his clean-shaven good looks and the gentlemanly charm that reminded her so much of her first teenage love, Tyler.

Inheriting her father's stature, Tessa had been teased when she towered over her classmates back in the ninth grade. Flaming locks of mahogany brown hair cascaded past her slender shoulders to frame her delicate features and oval face. With her mother's stunning shade of olive skin and father's piercing blue eyes, she had grown into an alluring beauty evocative of Helen of Troy.

When an instant romance blossomed, Tessa was knocked off her feet by the incoming love bombing – a consistent shower of affection, expensive lingerie, and endless bouquets of deep-red, velvety roses. Why would someone so good-looking and successful want to go out with *her,* a small-town kid lost in all the glamour? Maybe she was just that special. *Maybe she had made it.*

In an eerily silent two-story house in Tessa's forgotten hometown, a mournful Cecilia Ryan was all alone. Tessa's father was out – presumably at the shop, but as the neighborhood drunkard, he could have been lured into the Come 'N Go Saloon for a barley sandwich.

With a sense of foreboding that unnerved her, Cecilia reached above her head to remove the family portrait from the faded wall in the hallway, her tiny frame supported by the tips of her toes. The image had been captured on the day of Tessa's High School graduation – a big deal in a small town. Her only child had left Dormin several days after the photo was taken, then never came back like she'd promised.

Taking her worn-out spot on the dated sofa, the frail woman zoomed in on the likeness of her beautiful daughter. She closed her eyes as she lit a cigarette and inhaled the noxious smoke. Wiping away sudden tears with her trembling palms, a sense of complete failure and horrible guilt overtook her troubled thoughts. *I'm sorry. Mama is sorry. Where are you? I'm sorry you were forced to grow up too fast. Mama loves you. Please come home.*

Why, oh *why* had she let her baby go?? It was a question she had repeated to herself over and over again, often through never-ending tears of sorrow, shame, and regret.

Chapter 6

Although the planes were back in the sky, it seemed the only thing flying by was time. Exactly two months earlier, all air traffic had ground to a screeching halt.

Tessa awoke to brilliant sunlight streaming into her tiny walk-up in Yorkville. The old window above the dated ceramic sink was the only natural light in the humble studio apartment, but it would have to do until she could afford something better. At least it had come with some cool retro furniture and the sofa-bed that she slept on.

As she savored the scent of brewing coffee throughout her tiny kitchen, Tessa gazed out the window to relish the scenery from the top floor of an old, five-story brownstone. On the other side of the boulevard, natural shrubs and grasses lined the banks of the East River, partially obstructing the view of the flowing water as it snaked through the city.

The tantalizing aroma of bacon wafting from her neighbor's apartment reminded Tessa that she hadn't eaten since the morning before. She opened the seldom-used fridge, silently praying that something had materialized overnight, or the law of attraction had conjured up a big old, thick, juicy Wyoming steak. *Nope.* Still one shriveled up radish and a partial jar of mustard. Her stomach growled again so she dipped the radish in the mustard and held her nose. She downed it in one bite and washed it down with a full glass of lukewarm water. *Yuck!*

With a bit too much force, Tessa closed the fridge. It was Veteran's Day – a perfect time for selling her art in the park to anyone with a few dollars in their pocket. At the end of the day, she could probably get a bargain on some day-old bread and overripe fruit before it hit the grocery store bins. Reaching for her tote bag, her mouth watered while she fantasized about that medium-rare ribeye.

Aamon was reading a daily tabloid when Tessa arrived at her spot in Central Park. He poked his head around the paper. "I knew you'd be here today."

Tessa wasn't in the mood to talk. "Hi."

"Rough morning?" Aamon leaned back to watch her quick, angry movements while she set up.

Even with the busy park noise in the background, Tessa's stomach rumbled loudly enough to startle them, drawing the attention of another couple within hearing distance. She instinctively tugged at the belt around her skinny waist to make sure it was still tight enough around her jeans.

"When's the last time you had something to eat, baby?"

"This morning," Tessa half-fibbed, turning her face until it was enveloped by the warmth of the late morning sun.

Unimpressed with being lied to, Aamon pointed at her waist. "Your stomach didn't get the memo." He winked while he folded the future birdcage liner.

Tessa stubbornly tore her eyes away, a gesture she hoped would make the hunger go away.

"Tessa, look," Aamon sighed. "I have a proposal for you. I want to help you until you can get on your feet." His voice was thick with emotion. "I love you, babe." He stood to take Tessa's hands and gaze affectionately into her eyes.

"No. I'm good." Tessa shook off Aamon's grasp and turned on her heel – she was going to make it on her own... one way or another.

Aamon was seated again, exaggerating his movements as he raised his ankle over his knee. "Fine." He shrugged. "But if it makes you feel better, you can pay me back."

Tessa dulled her senses to focus on her art. When her stomach growled again, she was forced to face reality – she was *literally* a starving artist! Staring up at the cloudy sky, she looked for answers in the scant contrails.

"*Caw...caw!*!" A nearby crow snapped Tessa back to the moment, as if taunting her.

A prim and proper woman walked by with a leashed Chihuahua on his default setting – an agitated little fella, nipping and yapping at everyone's ankles like he was trying to win a political argument online.

Turning around to face Aamon, Tessa's bony shoulders slumped in defeat. "Okay," she sighed. "As long as I can pay you back."

Aamon jumped up. "That's my girl!" With a grin, he gently tapped Tessa's backside with the palm of his hand. "Get your things."

"Whatever."

"Give me your portfolio," Aamon ordered. "I'll carry it."

With a knot in her stomach, the young artist surrendered her tote, unaware that she'd just handed over far more than her artwork.

When Tessa followed Aamon into the packed Parkside Café, she had a hollow, uneasy feeling inside caused by more than just hunger. Twenty minutes later, the mouthwatering taste and aroma of a hot breakfast and fresh-squeezed orange juice swept away any intrusive thoughts.

After breakfast, the bewildered young artist got a quick tour of the luxury apartment that Aamon had rented for her – a five-minute walk from her spot in the park and not far from the famous Plaza Hotel! The exterior of the apartment building was of classic architecture, reminiscent of a Scottish castle, the suite itself lavish and ultra-modern.

Over the next few weeks, Aamon showed the unworldly Tessa a side of New York that she never knew existed – exclusive parties and fine dining with the upper crust in grand ballrooms. With costly designer dresses and a professional stylist, the blossoming teenager felt so glamorous and grown up. Charming and smart, she had no trouble blending in or laughing at the shallow snobs' lame jokes. With her new circle of high-class friends, she was destined for great things.

On the last day of November, Aamon led the blindfolded Tessa to a storefront on the stately main floor of her apartment building. When the cloth fell off her face, she was standing in the middle of a beautiful studio that was located among high-end brand retailers and elegant bistros.

What?! An amazing apartment in an exciting, world-class city with her own beautiful, custom studio and a good-looking, loving boyfriend? Tessa covered her gaping mouth with both hands and threw her arms around Aamon's neck, grasping onto him like a life raft. "Thank you!" she wailed, tears of joy streaming from her innocent, love-sick eyes. She couldn't believe the perfection that was her life.

Two thousand miles away, the Stars and Stripes still flew at half-mast – a mournful reminder to Dormin that all was not well in America.

Longing for some sense of normalcy, eager citizens crowded Old Town Road for the annual Santa Claus Parade. It had already been a year since the missing mayor, affectionately known as old man Fisher, was perched atop the mayor's float puffing on his signature fat cigars. They recalled the ever-present ivory-white suit tightly hugging his portly frame and the ten-gallon hat covering his half-bald head. With his larger-than-life presence and his laughter ringing out all the way down the street, he'd tossed cheap candy down onto the eager spectators.

Now with a new mayor at the helm, festive Dorminians braved the elements after the disappointing parade, taking comfort in the familiarity of the traditional Christmas Tree Festival in Old Town Square. Combined with the December Fair, colorful ice sculptures would be featured on the front page of the Dormin Times, as always, with community spirit remaining an immense source of pride. Friendly chatter delighted the senses of the hungry citizens as they crowded around the fire pit to roast wieners on a stick. Full of laughter and steaming mugs of hot chocolate, all ages warmed up for the carols they would sing on the sleigh rides.

An obelisk, standing high above the Earth, stood at the very center of Old Town Square. Around its base was a ring of tentacles, fashioned like rays of the sun and reaching toward the strange deity carved of stone. Each of the tentacles was covered in multicolored lights. At dusk, the towering spruce trees transformed into twinkling red, white, and blue beacons, the glowing lights magically bouncing off the flagpole.

As it began to grow dark, the Dormin Community Choir belted out a rendition of The Star-Spangled Banner that could be heard for blocks, their breath vaporizing in the air above them. Later, a group of carolers spread out on the streets to bring the citizens tidings of comfort and joy. The customary red-and-green striped candy canes and blue-scarfed snowmen lined the boulevards.

Throughout the month of December, rural folk did what rural folk do best – they pulled together through the hard times. Places of worship served meals and gathered toys for children who would otherwise go without. Black Friday was of little interest to them. They chose instead to support the backbone of America: small, locally owned businesses where customers became friends. It was a reminder to the demoralized residents that when they took care of each other, something greater than them was always there – even when it didn't seem like it.

Chapter 7

Marseilles Mansion Estate was a little sliver of hedonistic heaven – a luxurious, sprawling private property in the French Riviera. The day after Tessa turned seventeen, she and Aamon boarded a first-class commercial flight destined for the exclusive resort where the rich and famous play.

Upon arriving at the seaside Paradise, Tessa found it strange that she was one of the oldest girls there. Some of the décor seemed odd, too – golden statues of ancient gods and a sundial perched on the edge of a rugged cliff. When the wind was just right, the hidden depths of the sea howled against the jutting rocks.

The couple returned home two days after Christmas, ready to take their relationship to the next level. Though Tessa had only known him for three months, a determined Aamon moved in with her. *How could she say no?* He was *paying* for the place. She knew practically nothing about his life outside their relationship but enjoyed basking in his star power and entertaining his cosmopolitan jetsetter friends.

With the willow trees reawakening in the early spring, the birds were returning after one of the snowiest winters on record. Ground Zero remained off limits while the crews continued to clean up all the asbestos-laden debris.

On an unseasonably warm March day, Tessa returned home from Central Park to a dark, sullen apartment. Full of excitement for a dreamy night out with her doting beau, she was thinking about which ensemble she would wear as she set her tote down on the spotless kitchen table. Startled by a sudden noise to her right, her heart thumped when she saw his angry face.

Aamon was brooding at the end of the black leather sectional, staring at the twinkling city lights in the fading twilight. He jumped up, his nostrils flaring. "Where were you!?" he shouted, striking her left cheek with all the force of his sudden, explosive rage.

Tessa gasped. "I wa –" The next punch was to the gut, and so hard that it knocked the wind out of her. She landed on her tailbone, struggling to breathe. The back of her head hit the hardwood floor with a sharp thud, white noise exploding in her eardrums.

With a gleam of darkness flashing across his eyes, Aamon grabbed the vase with the blood-red roses and fired them at her head. It narrowly missed, sending the flowers flying in a dozen different directions, the fragile glass shattering on the wall behind her.

Tessa scrambled to her feet, screaming as she ran for the door…everything went black.

When she regained consciousness, Tessa thought it strange that she was lying in bed. Aamon sat on the edge beside her, the soft glow from the lamp reflecting off his tears. He dabbed at the dried blood on her face with a warm washcloth, stopping to gently stroke her swollen cheek.

Curled up in a fetal position, Tessa touched the lump on her face, struggling to remember what happened.

"I'm… I'm so sorry I didn't protect you, baby." Aamon's voice cracked. "I didn't catch you when you fell – it all happened so fast." He dropped to his knees beside the bed, pleading forgiveness with his tear-filled eyes.

Struggling to control her nausea and dizziness, Tessa caught Aamon's loving gaze – she must have tripped on the rug. "Sorry for being such a klutz," she croaked.

"Learn to be more careful, sweetheart." Aamon smiled when he playfully tweaked her nose. "Be right back."

Tessa turned her aching face toward the clock radio in the dim, unnervingly silent room. 10:01! How long had she been out?

A minute later, Aamon came out of his closet donned in a waist-length, black leather trench coat and a gray fedora slanted to one side. The top three buttons on his white shirt were undone to reveal his muscular chest. He reeked of musky cologne and a hint of cigar smoke. "I've got business to take care of."

"Where are you going?" Tessa's whispered words rang hollow in the spacious room.

With his back to Tessa, Aamon took a square plastic packet out of his dresser drawer, discreetly slipping it into his pocket before he turned around. "Just business." He leaned down to peck her on the forehead. With a bit too much force, he used his thumb to caress the painful lump on her face. "Get some rest," he added, playfully mussing the top of her head.

After the front door closed, Tessa remained in a fetal position, pulling the light covers around her stiff neck. With her entire body aching, she cried herself to sleep.

Above the cursed city, a storm was brewing. Off in the distance, the thunder rolled.

Chapter 8

When day broke over gloomy New York City, heavy gray skies blended with an orange haze on the horizon. The storm had mostly missed them but was promising to make up for it.

Tessa fastened a giant burgundy bath towel around her chest in the steamy, fruit-scented bathroom, trying to rush the start of the day despite the pain. Shaking out her hair, she clicked on the hairdryer, startled when a shirtless Aamon appeared in the mirror. Making eye contact with his reflection, her heart skipped a beat. She clicked the blow dryer off.

A moment passed before Aamon spoke. "Tessa, everyone comes to New York to *'make it'*. Unless you're Andy frickin' Warhol, what are your chances?" The auburn of the early morning sunrise streaming into the room glowed off his face, drawing out the hardness in his darkened eyes.

With the sting of Aamon's words welling up in her throat, Tessa dropped her eyes, reluctant to face him. "What happened to you supporting my dreams?" she whispered.

"I'm just saying you're not exactly Pablo Picasso," Aamon sneered.

"I have my own art exhibit tomorrow," Tessa seethed through clenched teeth. "At a real gallery." She turned back toward the mirror, leaning forward to apply concealer to the bruised bump on her left cheek. Maybe he'd take the hint.

"My *buddy's* gallery," Aamon reminded her. "You'd be *nothing* without me." He turned to go. "I'll be waiting for you in the car."

In the early morning drizzle, the couple arrived at the Ebony & Ivory Art Studio, a gallery that had existed since the summer of 1967. Nestled in the heart of the warehouse district, the century-old, brown-brick building had retained all its character and none of its spookiness. Aamon parked his black luxury car right outside the main doors in the nearly empty, foggy parking lot.

The damp duo emerged from the foyer into the classy futuristic showroom where twenty-four of Tessa's best pieces were displayed on walls and easels. She was *so* excited to show the world the magical colors of her complex spirit and... her heart was pounding. Something was wrong. The paintings! *Gone?!*

The gallery owner was nearby, drenched, and visibly shaken. "I... I don't know what happened." He wiped the back of his hand across his pale forehead, sweating profusely. "The...spr... sprinklers..." He shrugged in disbelief. "They..."

Tessa watched in horror while the custodian swept her ruined works of art into a big heap with a wide push broom – her dreams were reduced to a pile of soggy rubble on the marble floor. She ran forward. "Nooooooooo!!!!!!!"

The gallery owner's high-pitched voice shook. "I'm so sorry, Ms. Ryan." He was limp-wristed and spoke with a lisp – often describing *himself* as the quintessential fag.

Tessa escaped Aamon's grasp. Defeated, she fell to her weak knees on the hard concrete floor, burying her face in her hands while violent sobs wracked her body.

Several minutes passed before a sturdy hand caressed Tessa's slumped shoulder. With tired, bloodshot eyes, she looked up to meet her boyfriend's loving gaze. Aamon guided her outside, turning ever so slightly to wink at the gallery owner as they spilled out onto the rainy parking lot. The owner replied with a knowing smile and a nod.

In an elegant Italian bistro several blocks away, Aamon led the shaking Tessa to a quiet corner booth. They waited in silence for Aamon's order – poached eggs on toast and a caramel latte.

Ignoring the food during the one-sided conversation, Tessa pretended to listen until Aamon's voice faded into white noise in the background.

"Hello." A big hand waved in front of Tessa's face. "Anyone home?"

Still sniffling, Tessa turned her pale, tear-stained face toward her companion. "What's up?" she asked flatly.

"I was saying I have a job for you." Aamon cut into the second piece of ketchup-smothered egg to slide a piece in his mouth. "Only if you're interested, of course." He set his utensils down to pick up his napkin.

"I'm listening." Hoping it was all a bad dream, Tessa avoided eye contact.

"I need a hostess at my club." Aamon concentrated on his meal again, nonchalant and confident.

Tessa didn't think about it long. She had no choice – she'd have to get a *real* job. Her high-school experience working at the Near and Far Café in Dormin would come in handy, after all.

The morning after Tessa's dreams were washed away, she started her new job, thankful that the timing worked out and Aamon had a vacancy for her. His private club was only accessed through a narrow alley that was full of garbage and exhaust fumes.

Once inside, it was clear that Club 23 was about as far from the weathered Near and Far Café as you could get. The latter was a mom-and-pop shop where the locals, mostly bored old men, gathered every morning to drink gallons of coffee and gossip. To add to the down-home feel, the owners served up heaping plates of delicious Wyoming beef with homemade gravy every day at lunchtime.

The ostentatious Mediterranean style of Aamon's club, on the other hand, was reminiscent of Old Vegas – dark and seedy, yet classy. Located below one of New York City's many pizza parlors, it was *literally* an underground establishment; it even had an elaborate system of polished concrete tunnels connecting it to other clandestine operations. In these hidden bowels, the spooky echo of footsteps and the cold, institutional lights played with one's imagination, sometimes conjuring up images of haunted old hospitals.

Scantily-clad servers and suave dealers in suit jackets moved to the background music – the smooth crooning of the stars that put Vegas on the map: Dean Martin, Sammy Davis Jr, Frank Sinatra, et al. The room was a buzz of conversations, dirty business deals, a few cheers, and sensuous laughter. A golden hookah pipe sat on a table in the corner, abandoned and emitting an enticing, mellow aroma. Near the smoking room, dozens of men in golf shirts and business suits were gathered around the gambling tables, boisterous and invigorated in the oxygen-rich environment.

Club 23 seemed like an ordinary business, so Tessa didn't notice anything was amiss at first. Still reeling from shock, the first several days passed by in a blur. After learning the leather and stiletto dress code, she trained for her role as a hostess – greeting customers with a full smile and showing as much cleavage as she legally could while seating them.

By the time the fog cleared, young Tessa realized she'd been watching some of the most recognizable people on the planet mingling with the worst elements that society had to offer. Full of dirty little secrets, Aamon's club was the cloak-and-dagger, invitation-only gambling version of Studio 54 – without the disco.

Several more days passed on autopilot while Tessa kept her head down, sticking to her mundane duties like her life depended on it. Then, by accident, everything changed.

Aamon was away on one of his frequent trips to Rome and Tessa's late shift had just ended. With the dining room closed for the day, the low hum and dim lights transformed the commercial kitchen into a creepy dungeon. Not used to being alone in the dark kitchen after hours, she got goosebumps when the surreal sound of her stilettos echoed in the hollow space. The wide, rust-colored ceramic tiles weren't yet dry after the kitchen staff had cleaned for the night, the overpowering scent of bleach still permeating everything.

Tessa stopped at the closet at the back of the room, quickly punching in her code so she could get out of there. Crouching down to open the safe, she carefully placed the envelope inside, the way Aamon liked it, and sprung to her feet. Or not. Losing her balance on her four-inch heels, she used the wall to her right to brace herself. It moved. The wall moved! *No way*!

Scrambling to her feet, Tessa frantically shoved the shoes and boots away. Intrigue – like she was starring in a suspense film! She pushed on the wall. Nothing. *Must have imagined it.*

Back on her feet now, ready to go home after a long day, Tessa sighed and kicked the wall. And there it was – it began to move! Behind it was a hidden door, locked and daring her to steal... um... *borrow* Aamon's keys.

A few minutes later, Tessa pushed the heavy slab open with her tense shoulder, stumbling across the door frame as her eyes adjusted to the dark. Removing her heels, she followed the hip-hop music down the hall on her tiptoes. When she reached the arched doorway, she was greeted by a scene she would never forget.

Chapter 9

Patrick and Cecilia Ryan hadn't heard from their adventurous daughter since she'd left, an ache filling their hearts with each passing day. As the one-year anniversary of her departure approached, they regretted that they couldn't always buy her the latest shoes or be at her soccer games, but they *never* expected her to be a runaway – she was the apple of her father's eye.

Cecilia's mind often wandered to her daughter as a precocious toddler – a curious child who loved to proudly hang her finger-painting masterpieces on the fridge, her chubby little cheeks blossoming into a smile while she did so. She glowed at the precious memory of a five-year-old Tessa surprising them with doughy pancakes one Christmas morning.

Disturbing images filled Cecilia's mind while she mourned the loss of her only child to the shiny, mean streets of New York. She awoke most nights, breathless and struggling to cope with horrible dreams about a young, faceless girl in danger.

Dr. Adamache, her psychiatrist, prescribed anti-psychotics and a sedative to quell her paranoia and anxiety. The pastor at St. Theresa's Roman Catholic church, Father Del Rosario, comforted Cecilia in the confessional and at church on Sundays, assuring her she was just grieving. Her daughter would come back, he said. She only needed to pray.

In New York City, a surreal scene played out in front of a horrified Tessa's eyes. Half-naked, aroused men gathered around a corner stage, cheering while they stuffed dollar bills into a young boy's G-string. No older than ten, the child drag-queen batted his false eyelashes and gyrated to their demonic jeers. The theme of the décor was light purple with yellow teddy bears and bright pink lights. And glamorous drag queens.

When the music stopped, the child dropped to his knees with fear in his eyes. Tessa gagged and turned away. At just seventeen years old, *nothing* could have prepared her for this. From somewhere else in the secret pitch-black maze, the sound of a child's nervous laughter reached her alert ears. Filled with morbid curiosity and unable to stop herself, she continued down the wide hall, pressing her back against the wall to find her way.

The laughter had come from a pastel-pink-and-blue room where the nightmare was about to be taken to a whole new level. Toys and teddy bears in bondage gear were abundant, as were children – probably between the ages of two and twelve – unable to hide from the rapacious stares of the grown men that surrounded them.

While Tessa watched from the dark shadows, a brown-haired little girl with an angelic face, who was *maybe* five years old, looked up from her coloring book with innocence twinkling in her eyes. An older, plump woman, who wouldn't look out of place in a grade school classroom, took the child by the hand and led her down the hall.

The little angel was whisked away through another prison-like barrier. Before the door closed, an eerie, bloodcurdling scream escaped. The surreal sound gripped Tessa's spine as it echoed through the shadowy halls. Still in her bare feet, she raced back to the kitchen, stopping just long enough to put her stilettos back on.

Afraid of what she might find there, Tessa fled to the employee restroom, well-lit, pleasantly smelling of expensive perfume. Thankfully, it was empty. Trying to catch a decent breath while her directionless thoughts raced like a coked-up mouse, she ducked into one of several marble stall doors. Struggling to stay conscious while cold pin pricks covered her entire clammy body, nausea struck. After a few dry heaves, she emptied the contents of her stomach.

Stepping out of the stall with her mind and soul on fire, the teenage escapee was bewildered at how fast her life had spiraled out of control. Suddenly, Dormin wasn't looking so bad. She washed her hands and splashed cold water on her pale face, pausing to look deep into her own eyes in the mirror. Her first inclination was to run. *Run?* To where? How? She had no money of her own – Aamon kept it all.

Needing some air to mull things over, Tessa returned Aamon's keys to his office, walking through the noisy poker room with her back erect and her head held high. She *had* to find a way out. Reaching the exit, she stumbled up the concrete steps to the alley and into the cool, dark night.

The dirty back streets were surrounded by tall, aging rust-and-gray-brick buildings that added to the sense of confinement. Above Tessa's head, dozens of crisscrossing power lines were arranged in a haphazard pattern like chemtrails. The alley was deserted except for some caged, snarling Dobermans – an irritation she chose to ignore while plotting her next move.

Shivering, Tessa studied the reflection of the full moon in the puddles. The traffic noise from the nearby busy streets was more obnoxious than normal, effortlessly matching the offensive odor of exhaust in the air. Leaning against the brick wall behind her, she noted the sign above the steel door to her left: A triangle spiral logo located to the left of the lettering: Club 22 Pizza – the joint above Club 23. *How original.* What was the basement of Club 23 called? Club 24?

The sudden movement of a fat rat scurrying out from under a disposal bin snapped Tessa back to the moment. The dogs had quieted down but continued to intently watch her while she longed for more innocent days. Trying to stay grounded, disjointed old memories of better times surfaced in a torrent of swirling thoughts.

"*Caw! Caw!*" A crow's annoying squawk prompted Tessa to duck back into the building to avoid the swooping predator. If she left, she'd have no money, no nice clothes, and no exotic trips. With no *real* friends in New York, the alternative was the street where she would starve. *Again*. She was trapped!

In good conscience, Tessa *couldn't* turn a blind eye to what she'd just seen, her own memories of childhood innocence making the scene that much more horrific. "Okay," she mumbled out loud as she slowly descended each step. "I need a plan." By the time she was back in the club, she had one: as soon as it was safe, she would notify the police, then get a one-way ticket out of this vile town.

Unprepared for the romance movie turned horror–flick when the dark side of Aamon showed its ugly face, Tessa felt lost, hopeless, and alone. Her poor parents *must* be worried by now. Yet... Aamon had done so much for her. Maybe she did owe him *something*.

Before Tessa got home, she had made up her mind. She would stay and earn her way out of this glamorous and glitzy hell with the pretty face. If she secretly saved her tip money for a few months, she'd have enough to get home.

Chapter 10

In a luxury penthouse on the Upper East Side of Manhattan, Jack Weber was lost in deep thought. On this beautiful spring night, he was on his expansive patio in his black bathrobe and plaid slippers, gazing at the city lights reflecting off the sea. His painfully introverted wife, Abby, was already asleep in their American Empire-themed master bedroom.

The Weber's housekeeper, Jenny, had also turned in for the night. With no kids of their own, they treated her more like a daughter than an employee; she'd moved with them from Malibu to Manhattan. An old spinster, she often blurred the lines between eccentric and just plain weird. As their trusted housekeeper, she was irreplaceable.

Jack's work in telecommunications had temporarily rendered him an unwilling resident of Manhattan – a curious alchemy of fascinating and stifling but a great place to do business. He was sickened by the side of the Big Apple that most people with influence ignored – a hotbed of human trafficking... especially children. The fashion industry protected predators, and the legal system protected criminals.

Though it was now several months after 9/11, the horrific images were still everywhere... all the time. Even when he closed his eyes, the traumatized Jack felt like he was watching it live. The devil dancing in the smoke underneath the watchful all-seeing eye of the sun. The fire roaring amid the broken glass and the haunting screams of the dying.

After the Patriot Act was signed in October 2001, Jack paid close attention as fundamental rights got incrementally stripped away with the stroke of a pen. One by one. Another law. One more decree. New legislation. He couldn't shake the feeling that it would be the death of the arguably already-anemic Constitution. As he predicted, a new era of heightened legal surveillance ushered in creeping government overreach that soon became the norm rather than the exception. Slowly... so as not to alert the citizens.

When Americans searched their wounded red, white, and blue souls for answers, *longing* for a savior, a display of American patriotism not seen since Pearl Harbor exploded. Millions of young men and women came forward to join the military. Citizens from coast to coast proudly displayed Old Glory in a show of national solidarity. Media, politicians and celebrities encouraged everyone to support the troops.

Darkness had struck terror in the hearts of men.

Chapter 11

Settling into a routine at the club, Tessa tried to close her mind and soul to what was going on behind that hidden kitchen door. Last time she counted the secret tip money, she had more than half of what she needed to buy a one-way ticket back to Dormin... only a few more weeks. The day Aamon found her stash in some expensive Italian lingerie, his anger turned to rage. How could she be so ungrateful?! It was time to teach her a lesson.

Tessa's schooling that day took place in the RJ Harbor General emergency room with blood gushing from a gash in her forehead. Her left eye was black, and her bloodied lips swollen to twice their regular size, making it difficult to form words and tell the medical staff what happened. While they treated her injuries, Aamon was there to explain away the accident, eager to settle the bill.

Before long, Tessa regularly showed up for work with bruises, doing her best to hide them with makeup and the little bit of clothing she was allowed to wear. She walked into a door. She fell. Whatever lie would work. *It was her own fault – he wouldn't hit her if she was a better girlfriend.* Besides, he was always so sorry afterward, lavishing her with gifts and telling her how much he loved her. Her job went from seductive hostess to classy call girl for Aamon's high-class associates – just business, he said.

Soon realizing that he Aamon had groomed her from the beginning, Tessa felt more degraded than ever. *How could she have been so stupid?*

An opportunity to escape her shackles came with the promise of greatness from one of Tessa's regular customers – a Broadway producer and owner of several shady businesses. She could be a dazzling star, destined for the marquis lights and beyond, if she would just ply her erotic trade dancing in his gentleman's clubs that lined the streets of Midtown Manhattan. With approval from her... boyfriend, that is. Aamon agreed – *if* she turned all the money over to him.

When Mr. Producer disappeared within days of her new gig, Tessa knew there would be no Broadway. No chauffeur-driven limousine. No name in lights. She would end up just another pretty face in the mosaic of broken dreams on the cutting room floor.

This cesspool of a city was the place that Tessa had longed to come to for so long, lapping up everything she could on TV, secretly planning on running away as soon as she got the chance. Manhattan, it turned out, was a fool's paradise, a witch's brew of glitter, plastic, and slime, a shallow world of abundant depravity and unchecked corruption – the side of New York that *didn't* get airtime, except for a little insider trading now and then.

One Monday evening after her day shift ended, Tessa waited in Aamon's office until he was done with work. The smooth sound of Frank Sinatra and the scent of rum with fruit juice filled the modest space.

When Aamon came back, he took the stemmed glass from Tessa's hand. When he removed the stilettos from her tired feet, she realized she was getting drowsy. Soon, she was lying on the poufy beige sofa at the back of the room; as she closed her eyes, a soft blanket tickled her exposed skin. With her head spinning, she drifted off.

The scene was a pulsating neon sensual bedroom where six nasty men brutally raped a frail young girl. The heart shaped bed was the color of blood. The mist in the room hid the faces... until... Tessa's heart thumped. It was *her* on the bed. *How did she get there? How was she going to get away?! Why couldn't she move her legs?* The light faded.

When Tessa woke up, she was in her own bed with intense spasms radiating from her lower body, barely able to walk to the bathroom on her own. By the time she returned to bed, Aamon was there with some pills – they would take away the pain, he said. He wasn't lying. The pain was gone, and she was strangely calm.

Within a few days, Tessa regained a clear head. That's when the flashbacks started. *Omigod.* The rape was real! Not a nightmare. She needed more pills to cope...

Aamon had something better, he said, as he tied a tourniquet around her arm. If she turned tricks, he would give her as much as she wanted. When the injection gave Tessa a euphoric rush, life as she knew it was over. All she could think about now was getting her next fix. One day turned into the next, the next, and then the next until her life was one, long, heroin-fueled haze.

With no money of her own and Aamon not always following through on his promise, Tessa sometimes ended up in flop houses and dark alleys willing to give oral sex to *anyone* for an instant jolt of the devil's gold coursing through your veins. She would do *anything* to stop the vomiting, the body aches and the shaking, ignoring the abscesses on her body where she'd injected too many times. She would lie to her boyfriend, steal from the customers at the club, and cheat whoever stood in her way. She would sleep on the street in the rain where passersby would toss coins in her jar.

The day the ambulance came, Tessa had been beaten, raped, and left for dead in the alley behind Club 23. When she woke up with tubes in her veins, she tried to get her bearings. It was dark out and the ward was quiet. She ripped the tubes out and left St. Mary's Hospital still wearing the white gown. The night was cool and the traffic was light. Somehow, she made it home, stopping just long enough to change her clothes.

In the same alley where she'd been rescued just a few days earlier, Tessa rushed to score some heroin... she had to stop the withdrawals. Presently, the sirens wailed... she had overdosed. With their emergency lights flashing off the brick walls in the dark alley, the paramedics rushed to save her life. Beside them was an overflowing disposal bin – the final resting place of a newborn infant just weeks earlier.

Ending up back at St. Mary's Hospital, but this time in Intensive Care, Tessa broke down and cried. Finally admitting she was a desperate junkie under the spell of a hideous demon called addiction, she'd reached the druggie's paradox: she couldn't keep using, and she couldn't quit. It was one of life's harsh lessons: Rock bottom has a basement.

A broken shell of the young, naïve country girl who'd arrived from Wyoming not even a year earlier, the life in Tessa's eyes faded. From starving artist to glamorous girlfriend to straight-up prostitute high on heroin to make it through the day. She forgot all about her opaque childhood, wide-eyed dreams, and Western Wyoming.

Chapter 12

In the Arem River valley, the heartbroken Fisher family continued to lament the disappearance of patriarch old man Fisher, beloved family man and county-wide popular politician. It was so odd how he disappeared without a trace, leaving his wife of over fifty years and his only son with no answers and no closure.

Max III's wife, Dorothy, began to die the day her husband went missing. Watching his mother transform from an energetic social butterfly to a despondent, depressed ghost of her former self within a few months, Max IV knew he had to do something.

That afternoon, the new Fisher patriarch looked like a haunted ghoul when he stared at the television cameras and pleaded for his father's safe return. That evening, he and his inner circle held a private service in the basement of St. Theresa's Roman Catholic Church; thought-provoking rumors circulated about what deity they were praying to.

Chapter 13

In New York City, Tessa bolted up in bed, panicked and drenched in perspiration from her recurring nightmare – the one about the gang rape. *In Club 23... a young woman's face... replaced with a spiraling heart. Six men laughing and mocking, ravaging her body as they took turns.* The horrific scene played over and over in the theater of her mind, during her waking hours and in her sleep.

Aamon's side of the bed was cold and empty.

Shaking and crying, Tessa swung her weak legs onto the floor to yank open the drawer of the nightstand. A whimpering sob escaped when she opened her pill bottle. *Only three left?!* She fell to her knees. "Please God! Please make it stop!" she screamed. Her whole body ached as she crawled across the hard vinyl floor in her black silk pajamas.

Feeling trapped, hopelessness had become Tessa's constant companion. When the pain overtook her ability to cope, part of her died... suicide was the only way out. She didn't care anymore. *She was a burden and a failure.* She was *so* tired.

Inside the bathroom, a sudden movement drew Tessa's attention to the full-length mirror across the room. She gasped – it was her as a child, giggling, chasing a butterfly. "Dear God!" Her voice shook as the guilt overtook her, the love for her innocent younger self coursing through her heroin-eaten blood. She couldn't go through with it *now*.

A howling shriek, seemingly from another dimension, reverberated in the shiny black-and-white room. Young Tessa now had glowing, neon-red eyes while she chased the butterfly, the innocence disappearing as she morphed into her beautiful British friend, Diana.

With her wicked laughter echoing, Diana shape-shifted into a haggard old witch with crimson shoes. "You're a walking skeleton with a dead spirit." She threw her head back when she cackled, releasing a swarm of horseflies from her twisted mouth.

Tessa put her hands over her ears and screamed. *Diana was part of it too?!* When she hesitantly looked back into the mirror, the old witch pointed at her with a warped index finger. Then she vanished.

In her place was a blood-red demon with a flickering forked tail and reptilian tongue. "Your beauty is *gone*. Nobody could ever love you, Tesssssa." The demon hissed with glee. "You're a burden and *nothing* else."

The closed bathroom door connected with the back of Tessa's skull.

"Get the scarf," the horned demon growled. "You killed Tyler."

Salty tears tickled Tessa's upper lip while her numb fingers struggled to form a slipknot in the ruby scarf – a gift from her mama. Sitting underneath the glass doorknob, shaped like a five-pointed star, she trembled as she fastened the noose around her neck.

A quick action in the mirror drew Tessa's attention back to the reflection. Tyler was there now, his blackened eyes searching for hers. Tyler, her high school sweetheart – her *dead* high school sweetheart whose suicide had been shocking and tragic. His extra-dimensional voice now seemed distant, yet his whisper was clear. "Don't do it, Tessa. It's a trick." He reached out his hand toward her.

Tessa crawled to the mirror to welcome Tyler's loving touch, her affection for him still overflowing within. She had barely touched his cold hand when he faded away into the endless darkness. "No! Don't leave me.... again!" she screamed. As if it would bring him back, she pounded on the glass until it cracked.

As if God were guiding her, Tessa cast the scarf away from her bloodied hand to break the vicious spell. Still on her knees, wild sobs wracked her whole body as her soul cried out for redemption. Making the sign of the cross out of reflex, she bowed her head. "I'm broken, Lord. I'm so broken," she wailed in agony. "I need you. I'm all alone."

Hunched over, Tessa's face collapsed into her hands. "God, help me. Please help me. Help me. Help me! I can't do this anymore! *Help me!* I *beg* you!"

As her desperate pleas rang out in the silence, Tessa stayed on her hands and knees for several more minutes while the angels and demons battled for her tortured soul. From somewhere in the inter-dimensional, psychedelic mist of chaos, a single, whispered word rang out in the hollow space. "Amen."

Staying in a fetal position on the bathroom floor for what seemed like an eternity, Tessa slowly rocked back and forth until all her energy was spent. Trembling, nauseated, and drenched in stress sweat, she dragged herself to the nightstand for her pills to quell the raging dope sickness. With the room spinning, she struggled to get the bottle open with her bloodied hand.

It was dark outside. In her confused state, Tessa didn't know if it was morning or night. After the shaking stopped, she went to bed hungry, by choice – yearning for the metaphorical bread of life. Tossing and turning, she eventually nodded off to a strange land where everything was hazy and mystical...

In a small, western, mountain town, the violet and magenta of both mysterious suns contrast with the teal storm clouds looming on the horizon. The football playoffs are about to start, and all the cool kids are at the tailgate party.

A little girl in a yellow raincoat and patterned rubber boots races her tricycle down the sidewalk in the drizzle. She squeals with delight when her dad plucks her from the seat, and she drifts away past the treetops. Her mama puts her hands on her hips. "Teresa Dawn Ryan, you get down here right now." Wearing an expensive diamond necklace around her neck, she runs towards her daughter with outstretched arms, but gets no closer.

His eyes black and sparking, Tyler rides in mounted on a majestic, snorting black stallion with thick gray smoke rising around them.

Cloaked in a black robe and hood, the grim reaper flashes beside him in a burst of lightning, emerging from the darkness holding a noose and a scythe. Suspended in the air, the reaper pulls his hood down. It's Aamon – laughing maniacally!

Tyler's black stallion bolts off into the eerie haze.

R adiant golden sunlight beamed through the open bedroom window, the glorious rays dancing on the bohemian tapestry above the king-size bed. Trying to quell her dizziness and ignore the incessant coo of pigeons on the balcony, Tessa threw the covers off to sit up. A light breeze delivered the heavenly scent of roses from the rooftop garden as it caressed the skin on her face.

Instinctively reaching for her heroin, Tessa sat on the edge of the bed to inject, searching for a spot on her arm that wasn't bruised. When the narcotic entered her bloodstream, she closed her eyes to welcome the familiar relief that the opiate gods provided.

Memories of the previous evening surfaced as Tessa grabbed her neck with both hands... it was fine. She raced to the bathroom. The mirror wasn't cracked. Her hand wasn't bloodied. *Did it really happen? Did she imagine it? Was it a dream?*

Overcome with relief, she burst into tears. Deep down, she didn't want to die – she only wanted to stop the hurt.

Gasping when she caught her bruised, pallid reflection, Tessa held her emaciated forearm across her protruding ribs. Her smooth, olive skin was ashen and stretched over her skeletal bones. She winced at her tired face and dark circles under her bloodshot eyes, barely recognizing the girl who'd arrived in New York just the summer before. Her signature feature, her beautiful, long, mahogany-brown hair, was dry and dull. The witch was right – she was no longer beautiful.

In the hot shower, with silent tears streaming down Tessa's cheeks, the steamy water sprayed on her frail, track-marked body. As she lifted her bony hand to grab her shampoo, her heart skipped a beat. Oh no! Her boyfriend turned *pimp* was returning from Italy this morning; he'd go straight to the club, furious if she wasn't there.

Jumping out of the muggy shower wrapped in turmoil and the delicate scent of lavender, Tessa scrambled to get ready for work. Wearing black stilettos and one of her fire-engine-red leather mini dresses, she hustled to Club 23 and got there just before Aamon arrived.

Instinctively knowing that her life was spared for a reason, Tessa settled into a new routine at the club with renewed focus. Although high on heroin, she was crafty enough to calculate the odds while she watched the blackjack dealers and examined the colors of the roulette wheel. Every chance she got, she studied the poker faces and eye movements of the high rollers and card counters. She watched and learned... as if her life literally depended on it.

Chapter 14

One hot and sunny Saturday morning in early July, Aamon called shortly before his plane departed from Rome – he'd be home by early evening. His friend, Tony Sorrentino, was in New York from Sicily, and he needed her at his club – Blue Memories Lounge and Casino near Times Square.

Not quite twenty minutes later, Tessa was dropped off in the alley behind the club where Tony, known as Tito, was waiting for her. Once inside, she enjoyed the more down-to-earth clientele, and the brighter, modern atmosphere. Thankfully, celebrity sightings weren't a common thing.

After dinner, Tessa turned up the charm as she began to work the room, soon impressing Tito with her knowledge of cowboy culture. Discreetly pointing to a poker match of what was clearly a table of high rollers, she tilted her head toward one of the players – a rancher in his forties with a large rodeo belt buckle beneath his denim shirt. Tall and slender, his cowboy hat cast a shadow over his long face. Impressed by the young girl's worldly knowledge, Tito winked.

Tessa slowly worked her way across the crowded room, stopping to charm the customers on the way. The Top 40 music was too loud, forcing the patrons to shout and order more drinks. Scanning the room, she located Tito's other girls, sickened at the age of one of them. Fourteen maybe? They were *all* younger than her and at least two of them had been forced to get abortions when the clientele carelessly impregnated them.

Unconsciously clenching her teeth, Tessa turned in the direction of the poker game. That's when she saw him – the famous actor. She couldn't believe her eyes. All the women wanted to be with him, and all the men wanted to *be* him. A beloved, good-looking golden boy with a squeaky-clean image, he was the last person she thought she'd see in a place like this.

While Tessa had grown accustomed to observing the seedy underbelly of the lifestyles of the rich and famous, nothing could have prepared her for this. He was falling down drunk, high on God knows what, and he had his filthy hands all over the fourteen-year-old. He was ungroomed, his zipper was undone, and it looked like he had wet himself. When she passed by, she caught a strong whiff of piss and cigars.

Mourning the loss of any faith in humanity she'd had, Tessa gagged and kept going. That was one celebrity sighting she could have done without. It was an A-lister she'd admired since she was twelve – most of his movies were blockbusters. Of all the people on the planet, he was one that she'd thought would be above reproach. It taught her a lesson – *nobody* was. We all have our demons.

Just as Tessa arrived at the poker table, Tito was beside her, slipping his hand around her waist and pressing against her right hip. "Something came up." He dropped his gaze to her shapely bosom. "At my other club. I need to go there now," he whispered in his sexy Sicilian accent while seductively brushing his warm lips against her ear.

Pretending she was a character in The Godfather, Tessa flipped her hair back. Batting her long, natural eyelashes, she leaned toward Tito's ear to whisper back. "You want me to come?"

"No. Just business. I'll be back before you know it." Tito tickled the back of Tessa's neck and kissed her hand. At the door, he spoke briefly to the bouncer, Vincente. Then, he was gone.

Locating the cowboy, Tessa rolled her shoulder and twirled a strand of hair around her index finger. When they made eye contact, he gave her the once over and gestured for her to join him. She took the seat next to him, unaware that she had just begun her ascent to freedom.

Besides Tessa's 'date', an interesting cast of characters was assembled. Farthest away from her was a graying man in his late 50s. His black fedora and pinstriped suit spoke of the dying ambitions of a whiskey-guzzling gangster wannabe. Next to him, his nervous son-in-law was drowning in a department store business suit and sporting a brand-new wedding ring. His cheap cologne obnoxiously filled the air around the table. An older, bleached blond woman wearing too much makeup and showing off her wrinkled cleavage flirted with all the young guys. Drunk as a skunk, she might have forgotten she no longer had it.

Vincente wasn't paying any attention to them, so Tessa observed the other players while she counted the cards. The aged gangster wannabe was sharp at the start. As time wore on, he nervously slammed his whiskey glass down after each card. It was obvious the kid was no good at poker when his excessive finger tapping gave him away. He'd come to learn from his father-in-law, but instead watched in silent disgust while his wife's still-married father did shots and flirted with the old hussy. *She* was betrayed by her blinking. Tweaking his mustache, the cowboy narrowed his eyes to study his cards. *Too obvious.*

The poker game was beginning to draw a crowd as other patrons formed a circle around them. As the gangster wannabe got more drunk and more flirtatious, he raised the bets in a heroic display of false bravado. Everyone at the table followed suit. Confident of a win, Tessa placed her last bet. It was the highest... drawing the attention of the other players through their drunken stupor. One by one, the players laid their cards down.

When the crowd erupted, everyone in the room was staring at Tessa and the straight flush she revealed. She'd just won $88,000! Amid the noise, she scrambled to collect her winnings, making a beeline for the door with her long hair over her face and her head down.

There was a commotion at the poker table. The old man was yelling at the cowboy, accusing him of working with the young woman. A crowd gathered around to watch the fireworks.

A strong hand clamped down on Tessa's bony shoulder. "Ms. Ryan. Come with me." Vincente ordered, leading her to the alley by her elbow.

Back at the poker table, the agitated cowboy threw a punch. The fight was on!

Terrified at what was in store for her, Tessa dragged her heels until they were at the back door to the alley. The hair on the back of her neck stood at attention.

Once outside, Vincente...hailed a taxi?!

Tessa was sure she was dreaming while she scrambled into the back of the yellow cab.

Before closing the door, Vincente leaned in. "Travel safe and be well, little one." With a wink and a gleam in his hazel eye, he sent her on her way. "Never let them steal your light again."

In all the commotion, Vincente's unexpectedly kind words and actions barely registered. All Tessa could think about was getting away before Aamon got home – before Tito talked to him.

In the high-stakes game of chance called life, the golden sun was getting lower in the early evening sky.

Driven by a renewed sense of purpose, Tessa's quick steps closed the gap between the taxi and the brass double doors of their building in record time. Out of breath by the time she ducked under the burgundy canopy, she wondered if she had the poker face for the concierge like she did for poker.

The dapper doorman was in his usual spot, the long tails of his black tuxedo complementing the red stripes and gold buttons on his uniform. "Are you alright, Ms. Ryan?" The elderly gentleman spoke with a refined British accent worthy of the British monarchy.

"Why?" With a nervous giggle, Tessa placed her hand over her rapidly beating heart. "Do I not *look* okay?"

"You appear flushed, madam."

"Oh, just a long day. That's all, Charles." Tessa thought about the money in her purse. Flushed? Did he *know*?

"Have a good evening, madam." With a slight bow, Charles tipped his captain's hat with his typical classy charm.

As Tessa neared the elevator, the pleasant scent of vanilla and classical music stirred her senses. She pushed the button several times. "Hurry up. Hurry up. Hurry up!" she mumbled under her breath.

The seconds turned to minutes as Tessa looked over both shoulders. She took a final glance toward the space that had housed her studio, now full of the clientele enjoying the enticing aroma of an elegant bistro. Turning her attention back to the elevator, she watched the numbers as the left elevator began to descend, holding her breath when it lit up on the fourth floor.

Ding *Thank God!*

Finally exhaling, Tessa wasted no time rushing in when the brass doors opened. Startled at the last moment, she collided with a well-dressed businessman; *he* was focused on his phone. It was likely buried in the contract legalese – the tech no fault clause.

Inside the darkened apartment, Tessa kicked off her heels, running straight to her family heirloom hidden in her dresser. Thank *God* Aamon hadn't found it. It was the symbol of her family's history – the extravagant diamond necklace that her grandmother's sister hid from the Nazis. She stuffed it in the bottom of a huge shopping bag, covering it with a week's worth of casual clothes, her toothbrush, and a pair of sneakers. No stilettos!

Ding In the stillness of the apartment, the elevator signal in the hallway sliced into the silence.

With her stiff back pressed against the beach mural on the bedroom wall, Tessa froze. She counted the hurried, heavy-set footsteps as they got closer and... a set of keys hit the floor in front of the door. She could feel every beat of her heart as the seconds ticked by, holding her breath, waiting for the beating. Those were *his* footsteps. *It was him!*

Then a miracle happened – the steps kept going. Daring to breathe, Tessa grabbed the stuffed bag and her purse. "Sweet Jesus. Thank you," she sighed. Not a second to waste.

The apartment door creaked when Tessa opened it to peek into the well-lit, long and empty hallway. Her erratic pulse accelerated as she sprinted to the stairwell. She grasped her flip-flops in her free hand to race down the eight flights of stairs at the back of the building where she'd asked the driver to wait for her. If he'd left, her nightmare wouldn't be over. Barely noticing when her bare feet made contact with the scorching pavement, her adrenaline soaring, the harried young woman slipped out the back door, and into the waiting taxi. *Oh, Lordy!*

The driver turned the corner just as Aamon was racing toward the front door, disappearing into the building, and out of her life.

Free at last!

Chapter 15

On this scorching July day in Dormin, the sun was getting lower in the early evening sky, that cherished time before sundown when families come together for community cookouts and baseball games.

The pervasive putrid odor downwind from the city was a constant reminder of who and what fueled their community. Officially founded by the Fisher family in 1916, the meatpacking plant had been the lifeblood of the local economy for nearly a century. No stench – no Atluko Industries – no Dormin.

Below ground, an ambitious construction project had begun deep beneath the surface of the Earth, the blueprints drawn up within weeks of the suspicious disappearance of old man Fisher. Inheriting the reins of Atluko from his father, Max Fisher IV donned a hardhat and lamp to tour the massive construction site. Amazingly, everything was on budget and ahead of schedule.

Meanwhile, in an air-conditioned fifth floor office suite, the buzzing rooms were packed full of mingling guests, most of them already tipsy and overly flirtatious. Among the boisterous laughter and lively, upbeat dance music, the combined scents of sweet perfumes and savory shrimp cocktail tantalized the senses and teased the mind.

Full of energy and in the mood to celebrate, the fifty-two-year-old Max arrived in his office with a spring in his step. On budget *and* ahead of schedule? *Unheard of.* He reached up for his most expensive scotch, waiting for just the right occasion to crack it – this was it.

A skinny young man with a crooked smile and a nose to match approached Max from the right, the look in his dark-brown eyes a combination of delight and wickedness. It was a fitting look for Neil Olsen – Dormin's mad scientist in residence. The image was enhanced by a long ponytail and loose strands of frizzy, light-brown hair clinging to his glistening forehead. Though only in his early 30s, matching gray patches had started to appear near the temples, partially obstructed by grossly oversized glasses held together with black electrical tape. "I brought the champagne!"

"Excellent." Max gave him a knowing nod. "Then I take it you have reason to celebrate?"

Neil poured two glasses of chilled bubbly as the noise level grew increasingly louder. "I got him! I got Herod." He handed a glass to his host. "*We* have reason to celebrate."

"Good work, Olsen." Max raised his glass as approval. "To the King."

"To the King – the future main attraction of the soon to be opened Dormin Reptile Gardens." Neil tipped most of the champagne down his throat with a twinkle in his lively eyes. "He arrives early next week."

"But the facility isn't open yet." Max reminded him as if the guy in charge wasn't aware. "Where are you going to keep him?"

"He'll live with me for now." Neil shrugged, wondering if Max feared snakes.

Eavesdropping, Max's public relations consultant chuckled. "To each their own." Nothing got by Miles Malone. "Hope you have a good cage for that beast."

"Shut up, Malone," Max barked.

"That *beast* is preferable to humans, thanks." Neil chugged down the rest of his warming champagne. With a snide sideways glance toward Miles, he continued. "I'll see myself out."

With Neil gone, Max turned his attention to the three men in his inner circle. Once they all had their scotch in hand, he raised his glass. "Praise be to the angel of light."

Chapter 16

In the fading daylight, Tessa leaned her stomach against the cold white bars of the ferry as it sped through the ocean. The silhouette of the Statue of Liberty loomed on the horizon. The freezing mist of the Atlantic sprayed on her warm skin, giving her goosebumps and depositing the taste of sea salt on her cracked lips. Suddenly, her relief turned to panic. What if Aamon found her?!

Reminding herself she was safe now, Tessa closed her eyes just as the sun was setting on her golden day. Upon lifting her heavy eyelids, she was transfixed by the kaleidoscope daylight, fading and surrounding spooky shapes in the shadows. Stacked layers of crimson and pastel purples reflected off the air and sea, shimmering behind the dark-rimmed clouds.

When a shrill horn ended Tessa's awe, reality set back in. They were nearing Liberty Island. She stepped down onto the wide, T-shaped dock, suddenly overcome by a sense of desperation and helplessness. She was so alone. *So broken.* Her bottom lip trembled.

Finding an unoccupied bench away from the other visitors, Tessa wistfully gazed at the sea, zoning out until her thoughts began to torment her. Over the past ten months, her very *essence* had been stolen from her – the innocent western girl was gone, replaced by an unsightly, anorexic waif tending to the remnants of her fractured soul.

Over the sounds of the sea, a giggle interrupted Tessa's thoughts; a little girl with pigtails and light freckles skipped over a jump rope toward her. "The witch was right." The younger version of herself floated up… and… vanished.

Falling to her knees in despair, Tessa begged to be freed from her agony. Please. No more apparitions! "Help me!" A sob escaped. She squeezed her eyes shut to dispel the image of her expressionless mother in a dreary, cold hospital bed – unable to recognize her own daughter. "Make it *stop*!" With her thoughts tormenting her mind, hot tears spilled down her cheeks, the ocean breeze cooling them as she wept.

"Tessa?" someone whispered. Several feet away, a Native American woman in a long, angelic gown was levitating. "My girl, you are loved."

Moonlight shone right through the translucent form in front of Tessa, the familiar gentle voice echoing in her head.

Holding an eagle feather in her small hands, the full moon formed a halo around the woman's beautiful face. "You must save yourself. It is time." A beaded headband adorned her single, tawny-brown braid that ended at her slim hips.

The image faded. "Anna?!" Tessa cried out in the darkness. "Don't leave me!" She was gone.

Tessa rode back to New York City with love for Anna running through her veins – she'd been the only person in her life who'd shown her unconditional love. But Anna wasn't here, and real-life wolves were breaking down the door. *Was it too late to phone a friend or ask the audience?*

As the ferry approached the glaring shores of Manhattan, the whistle shrieked like an alarm clock waking Tessa from a deep sleep. Above her, a glowing eagle feather drifted down from the celestial sky. When she crouched to pick it up, Tessa knew exactly what it meant – it was time to save herself.

S avoring the earthy scent of Lake Luis on Saboro Mountain, 49-year-old Cherokee Anna Hale snapped her yellow life jacket in place. The scorching July heat in western Wyoming had abated enough for the canoe ride she'd been waiting for all day. After receiving devastating news earlier, she could think of no better place to heal than on the tranquil waters of the breathtaking glacial lake. Hers was one of a dozen properties along the shore, the owners enjoying their privacy more with each passing year.

In the twilight, Anna glided back to the dock, the gentle ripples washing against the weathered logs as she approached. With her small feet resting on the smoothed rocks at the bottom of the refreshing turquoise water, she was reluctant to get out of the lake. Sighing, she flipped the canoe upside down and dragged it into place on the beach.

"Help me!" a faint voice whispered.

The hair on Anna's neck stood up when she spun around. Nobody. The voice! "Tessa?" she whispered.

"Make it stop!" It *was* Tessa's voice – full of despair.

Anna closed her eyes to project her energy, hoping to lessen the suffering of the young girl in trouble. 'My girl, you are loved. You must save yourself. It is time.' She spoke the words softly in her head, keeping her eyes closed until the dark energy dissipated.

When Anna opened her heavy eyelids, the bright-pink sun was reflecting a mirage of the mountainous landscape off the glassy lake. She felt herself transported to a magical dimension where the dimming day intertwined with the impending darkness – pure divinity.

The resident bulldog was asleep in his new doghouse under the tall yard light. A flourishing greenhouse was on one side of him, a chicken coop on the other. A dozen hens had retreated to their nests as darkness settled in and the night cooled.

Plentiful linden trees curtained Anna's replica gingerbread house – the dream home that she and her late husband had built together. As she neared the side porch, the motion light turned on, casting a cone of white light beneath it. A melodious greeting awaited her, courtesy of the northern cardinals and mockingbirds perched in the maples.

Inside the house, clean dishes were precariously stacked in the brown drain tray in the L shaped kitchen. Worn down around the water-stained sink, the green and gold pattern linoleum matched the '70s era green paint. A radio was balanced on a small stack of newspapers on the aging yellow refrigerator. *Harvest gold, they called it.* An eclectic assortment of magnets covered it, one of them still holding a drawing from Tessa in place.

Trying to forget the morning's news, Anna scanned the books that surrounded her, comforted by the combined familiar smell of ginger cookies and sweet grass. Among the decades old collection on natural healing, gardening, history, and political philosophy, she chose a horror novel. *A gal needed a little light reading, after all. Ha.*

Returning to the kitchen to make tea, Anna poured some milk in a pot to warm it. The original harvest gold stove had been replaced with an avocado green one of the same vintage. A black landline rotary-dial phone hung on the wall above the kitchen table. Kitschy canisters and ornaments abounded, granting visitors a journey to a bygone era.

When she sat, Anna was careful not to disturb her fluffy black-and-white tuxedo kitten, curled up and purring on the handwoven rug in front of the cold fireplace. Baby Puffball showed no such consideration for the burgundy leather recliner, shredding it with his sharp claws wherever it wasn't covered with the colorful, granny-squares Afghan.

Though the day was still warm, Anna shivered while she set her steaming cup of homegrown mint tea down. Transfixed by the full moon reflecting on the gentle ripples on the lake, she thought about the eerie encounter with Tessa earlier. Where was she?

Emerging from her trance, Anna picked up the daily newspaper from the bamboo coffee table beside her. **'Wyoming Woman Missing in California'**, the headline screamed. Recalling the conversation with her twin sister that morning, she thought about her niece, Jennifer – the missing girl.

Similar in age, Jennifer and Tessa had become fast friends, bonding over their fashion obsessions and love of abstract art. The summer they were all together, the two young teenagers spent entire days on the white sand beach of Lake Luis beside Anna's dock, not even stopping for lunch. In the evenings, the girls drove Anna crazy with their giggle-filled popcorn and movie nights – or so she told them. She loved every minute of it.

Now, both girls and their giggles were gone. All she had left were wistful memories and a child's painting hanging on her harvest gold fridge.

Part II

Renaissance

"Lessons in life will be repeated until they are learned."
~Frank Sonnenberg

Chapter 17

Located on a beautiful section of semi-developed land in upstate New York, Golden Horizons Recovery Center was a top-rated program designed with follow up and long-term success in mind. By the time Tessa boarded the air-conditioned train, she had her mind made up. It was just the place she needed to be made whole again. Complete with stables, the rural setting was perfect. New York City was too... *peopley.*

Choosing a quiet booth facing away from the handful of other passengers, Tessa hoped she could start to come to grips with her recent past. Was it only yesterday she got away from Aamon!? It wasn't long before distressed thoughts turned, instead, to disturbing memories of Dormin.

At the tender age of 11, the confused young Tessa was flooded with hormones when puberty hit early. Soon, the freckles had been replaced by make-up as if smothering the innocence of childhood would somehow bring about an inner transformation or an escape from her working-class neighborhood.

Getting teased about her childish hairstyle and the holes in her cheap shoes, Tessa started babysitting and working odd jobs at the age of twelve, soon sporting a funky, shoulder-length bob and brand-new designer shoes. By tenth grade, with a part-time job at the Near and Far Café, she'd been drawn into the superficial world of glamorous fashion magazines and handsome young cowboys.

Just when everything seemed to be going right, the popular teen's life took a dark turn. On a calm evening in late July, with the sun already disappearing behind the mountains, black storm clouds gathered on the horizon.

For days, fourteen-year-old Tessa had been watching her withdrawn, despondent mama on a rapid, downward spiral – the kind that resulted in a big crash with pieces scattered everywhere. Surrounded by pill bottles and overflowing ashtrays, Cecilia rarely left her room, barely moving even when her daughter came in to check on her.

Feeling helpless, Tessa retreated to her upstairs bedroom across the hall from her mom. Presently, she was admiring her metallic-blue fingernails while she painted them, holding them up to the light on her vanity table to watch them sparkle. When the doorbell sounded, she sprinted down the thick-carpeted stairs, expecting a group of her friends.

Instead of a bunch of kids, a uniformed police officer and two paramedics were standing on the front steps. Behind them, the flashing lights of a police car and an ambulance reflected off the mature trees and the rows of older two-story houses on both sides of Maple Street.

The smile fell from Tessa's panicked face. "Did something happen to my dad?!"

The paramedics rushed past Tessa and up the stairs, leaving the Chief of Police on the front steps to deal with the distraught teenager.

When she was escorted down the stairs, Cecilia's hollow eyes faded into her blank expression. Walking right past her bewildered daughter, she left without saying good-bye.

Tessa watched in disbelief while they led her catatonic mother to the ambulance. "Mama?!"

Cecilia kept going.

Somewhere in the fog, Tessa heard the Chief telling her that her mom had been imagining things and that her father was too busy to care for her, working as hard as he was just to put food on the table.

Abandoned and alone, the vulnerable young girl fell into the Chief's arms, her body wracked with heart-wrenching sobs while he gently led her to his cruiser. With all the neighbors watching from their front yards, the lights stopped flashing. It was a scene that would stay with her for the rest of her life.

The next thing Tessa remembered was arriving at Anna's. As she curled up and wept on the bed in the guest room, hushed voices drifted down the hall in the quiet house. The Chief was explaining to Anna what had really happened. Sickened and reeling from shock, she filed the information away, hoping it never resurfaced.

Heavy rain began to pelt the thatched roof – the storm had started.

Chapter 18

Three Months later

The witch was wrong. Tessa had gained twenty-one pounds. It was several short of her goal, but the track marks had faded to almost nothing. Her signature feature was shiny again, falling in loose, natural curls to the middle of her back. Life was returning to her eyes, the color to her cheeks. Regaining her health was a slow process, but she felt stronger than ever: mentally, physically, and emotionally.

It was the fall of 2002, still several weeks away from Tessa's eighteenth birthday and three months since she'd left Manhattan. She'd be finished treatment soon, sad to say goodbye to her new friends and the other residents she'd met during their various activities and meals together. The center had honored her wish not to contact her parents – she didn't want to worry and upset them.

After the meeting with the discharge team, Tessa retreated to her room, more suburban home vibe than clinical institution. Cross-legged on her comfy twin bed, Tessa lit some incense, making sure she got a good whiff of it as she placed the back of her wrists on her knees. Slipping into a hypnotic state, she closed her eyes. Ohm.

Throughout Tessa's ten-month ordeal, thoughts of the Arem River Valley had been replaced with the struggle for survival in a cold, inhospitable concrete jungle. Could she go back to New York City and pick up where she left off? Paint and dream? Thoughts of Manhattan triggered nausea and sweating, even in Tessa's altered state of consciousness. Aamon would be looking for her. Too risky.

When her mind wandered to the wholesome small city of her youth, Tessa was reminded that she had once known better days, filled with hope and promise. *The sparkling lights of Dormin dotted the landscape at the end of the long road where two mountains met, enticing anyone in search of a dream. Frozen in time at the intersection of 1950s Middle America and the spirit of the Old West. It was the stereotypical ranching community where sprawling estates were scattered for miles, and western wear was practically a uniform...*

A knock at the door snapped Tessa out of her trance.

"Dinnertime!"

After dinner, Tessa continued to contemplate her future while she soaked in a bubble bath. In the time she'd been gone, she hadn't even called home. She couldn't call *now*, not as a disappointment out of rehab, and she certainly couldn't go back to small town America as a *failure*.

That night, Tessa had a nightmare – Aamon was chasing her, dangling a noose, his maniacal laughter filling her mind with pure dread. Waking up with her heart pounding, it took her a moment to realize it was just a dream. In that moment, as the angry tears welled up inside her – she knew. She was declaring war on the old boys' club. Her gallery dreams would wait.

Chapter 19

Meanwhile, the first three generations of Fisher patriarchs must have been rolling over in their graves. The town they built had begun its swift descent into a degenerate hell. Graham Maxwell Fisher I, original pioneer, had settled the fertile land where the family estate was located. Originally settling in the south, the family brought their considerable wealth with them to the northwest when the civil war ended, establishing the new locale in 1857. They tamed the harsh wilderness, erected their legacy, took up arms, and planted trees in whose shade they knew they would never sit in.

For three generations, the Fisher clan had been satisfied with the trappings of success, enjoying the spoils of hard work and a fine lineage. For three generations, the Fisher family motto had kindled investments in family and community: Men die. Money lives forever.

Max IV? Not so much. Graham Maxwell Fisher IV – Max to those who knew and (said they) loved him – was the new boss in town. Soon after old man Fisher went missing, Max had his hands all over the vast family fortune within days, spending like a drunken sailor in a brothel. Somewhat odd, but apparently insufficient for a police investigation.

During his mad spending spree, Max drew up plans for expansion of his assets – no longer content with old-school rules restraining his ability to increase his wealth. His trove boasted six mansions in four different countries. He was the jet setter who needed his own private jet. He had a yacht worth $20 million that he barely used. His main showpiece was a fleet of exotic sports cars that would make even Jay Leno blush.

The primary, palace-like residence was in the Arem River valley on the sprawling family estate. Called Mystic Manor, it wasn't hard to imagine that plantation owners could have lived there in days gone by. The residents, frankly, didn't give a damn. They enjoyed their copious luxuries, especially the opulent diamond chandelier from the Titanic that graced their grand ballroom. A modern, state-of-the-art observatory had been added in recent years – a welcome variation from the dreadful milieu of deeply-rooted oppression.

When Max took over the ranch, the valued, long-serving staff were all fired and flown out of Jackson to parts unknown, allegedly. New servants were brought in and moved into newly constructed, cold and cramped bunkhouses reminiscent of a concentration camp. Mostly illegal migrants with limited language skills and desperate for work, 'the help' was willing to accept their menial quarters, limited rations, and restricted freedom. It was no worse than shanty towns, and $30 a day was almost double what they could earn where they came from – a fortune for their families back home.

Straddling the border between Wyoming and Montana, Saboro and Diablo Mountains were now the site of a trillion-dollar road construction project that would connect the city of Dormin to the rest of civilization. Between the exploding dynamite and the ensuing population boom, Tessa's hometown was becoming unrecognizable.

When moral decay settled in at city hall, a rapidly growing and increasingly neglected city wasn't far behind. Traditional values were slowly being replaced by a new age doctrine that promised utopia but delivered something *much* different. Removing Creator God was only the beginning – a *lot* can change in a year.

Chapter 20

Although the road to full recovery had just begun, Tessa left the treatment center feeling like her soul had been somewhat restored... in a bluesy kind of way. Her seasoned social worker, Maria, knew exactly what strings to pull to set in motion the manifestation of her client's inner warrior.

One early Monday morning, moving day arrived with mixed emotions, cautiously optimistic dreams, and a late October nip in the air. Tessa's scant belongings were packed into the back of a gray hatchback waiting to be transported to her new home on the east coast.

Underville, Maine was located in the shelter of Bethany Cove, not far from where huge crested waves broke on the jagged coastal rock. Postcard-perfect, the quaint seaside town was the stuff of ancient folklore and 17th century ghost stories, the perfect locale for a riveting suspense movie. Rows of rainbow-colorful houses on slanted streets, the backdrop for the sailboats and yachts in the marina, were opposite a majestic blue and white lighthouse – the answer to prayers for weary sailors navigating the stormy sea. It was the idyllic New England setting that Tessa needed to feel safe while she attended law school at Bethany Heights Professional College.

It was dusk when Maria angle parked in front of a small drug store on Eagle Feather Boulevard – a central thoroughfare with minimal traffic noise even in the middle of the afternoon rush hour. "We're here, sleepy head."

"Already? We just left." Tessa took in her new surroundings while she stretched and rubbed her eyes. She'd fallen asleep shortly after they'd left the center. The building in front of them was an old-time rectangular storefront with **Reynolds's Pharmacy** painted in dark green lettering. The narrow wooden staircase leading up to the apartment was unlit and in need of repair. "Not exactly the Taj Mahal," she mumbled.

"Well, it's a great location!" Maria tried to sound enthusiastic.

The apartment itself was welcoming and bright – open concept with a breakfast bar and an east-facing living room window. Newly renovated, the scent of fresh paint was still prominent throughout. Tessa unpacked, setting her faded, low-rise jeans to the side to pair with her favorite powder-blue peasant top – both baggy but turn-of-the-century fashionable and striking when paired with her striking hair. Zipping into her black knee boots, she was ready to explore the town.

In the brisk evening wind blowing in off the ocean, Tessa and Maria covered the two blocks to their destination quickly. THE BEEHIVE TAVERN was a locally owned restaurant with an impressive view of the Atlantic from its upper floor. Dark brown tablecloths and votive candles were placed on every table beneath the cedar beams. The lack of natural light on the main level enhanced the effect of the glowing orange mood lighting.

While the elderly proprietors greeted Maria with smiles and bear hugs, Tessa took in their surroundings. The overwhelming aroma in the log structure was fresh Atlantic lobster – served any way you wanted. The deep velvety sound of Louis Armstrong added to the already impressive ambiance in the packed restaurant, the combined chatter from both levels nearly rising above the volume of the music. A group of boisterous patrons, likely college students, were gathered near the stone fireplace downing pitchers of frothy craft beer.

"Tessa…" Maria waved one hand in front of Tessa's face while tucking her shoulder-length blonde hair behind her ear with the other.

Trying to figure out who the bartender reminded her of, Tessa realized that Maria was trying to get her attention. "Sorry. What?" *Was it the same guy that worked the bar at Tito's club? Looked like him. Nah.*

Maria gestured to the owners. "I'd like you to meet Nettie and Stefan Constantin. My aunt and uncle." She tilted her head toward her companion. "This is Tessa Ryan. The girl I was telling you about."

Annoyed, Tessa shot a puzzled look at Maria while the elderly couple watched the exchange. "What did you say about me?"

Gray-haired and pear-shaped, Nettie Constantin had the matronly look of Mrs. Claus, her wide smiling eyes shining behind her round, wire-rim glasses. When she spoke, it was with a heavy Dutch accent. "Don't worry, dear. It wasn't much." Her heavy bosom jiggled when she laughed.

Maria's Uncle Stefan was tall and slender with a full head of salt and pepper hair and a goatee on his long, expressionless face. Tessa saw her father in him immediately.

"Hello, Tessa." Stefan bowed.

As soon as Stefan spoke, Tessa knew he was from Transylvania. Recognizing Romanian dialects was a bonus skill she'd learned from her Roma art teacher back in Dormin. "Pleased to meet you, Mr. and Mrs. Constantin."

Stefan picked up two leather-bound menus. "Right this way, ladies." He led them upstairs to a private corner booth. Their table overlooked the colorful lights shimmering on the ocean and illuminating the rows of boats in the marina. He bowed to make his exit.

When Stefan was out of earshot, Tessa glared at Maria. "What did you *sssay* about me?" she hissed. "I don't like people knowing about my past!"

Pushing her black rim glasses up the bridge of her nose with her index finger, Maria responded without looking at her companion. "That you'd be joining me for dinner." She scanned the menu. "Your personal life is confidential."

Setting the menu down, Tessa stared at her long, manicured nails to avoid eye contact. "Sorry," she mumbled.

Maria leaned in as she tried to assure her young client that everything was okay. "You're letting your paranoia get the better of you. We talked about this."

Tessa's heart skipped a beat while she banished the thought from her mind. There was *no way* she was going on medication like her mother. "Can we order? I'm starving." She couldn't change the subject fast enough.

While they waited for their meals, Maria related the story about her Romanian roots and recounted the horrific ordeal of the Constantin family during World War II. Romania had initially joined the Axis forces for the launching of Operation Barbarossa – the German invasion of the Soviet Union.

Most of Maria's family were killed in retaliatory air strikes in 1941; her father and Uncle Stefan were the only surviving members. Whatever higher power the people were praying to, it seemed to not hear the exploding synagogue or the sickening stench of burning human flesh. It ignored the thick smoke and the bloodcurdling screams of the children.

Maria's father, Stan, was only thirteen at the time. His brother Stefan, at the age of seventeen, was forced to grow up overnight. Between watchful neighbors and the underground resistance, the boys were smuggled through the Carpathian Mountains and out of the Godless chasm that Europe had become. Eventually, they reached a safe house in Barcelona, Spain before boarding a ship destined for America.

When their meals arrived, Tessa gobbled her fish and chips like a starving house cat that hadn't been fed for twenty minutes. With her returning appetite satiated, she broke the lull in the conversation. "Maria, I don't know if I can do this." She sucked at the whole stoic thing.

"Okay." Maria called the gambler's bluff. "Do you want me to drop you off at the bus station? I'll buy you a ticket to wherever you want to go."

"What?" Tessa raised her shoulders in defiance. "No. Of course not!" she scoffed like the whole thing wasn't her idea.

A moment later, the pair stepped into the dark street, the area lit only by a single cone-shaped beam from the old streetlight. It was a cool autumn night with the huge harvest moon reflecting off the shop windows.

The knot in Tessa's stomach tightened at the thought of losing the woman who had become her beacon in the storm for the last three months. "I'm scared, Maria," she whispered, her eyes rapidly filling with tears. The last time she'd felt this kind of fear was the day her mother was hospitalized.

"Relax, Tessa." Maria tried to comfort her, patting her back during their long good-bye hug. "If you need anything, ask my aunt and uncle. They'd be happy to help you. Okay?" Maria pulled her head back to catch Tessa's eyes. "It's going to be okay."

"Alright. I will," Tessa sniveled though the queasiness in her stomach wasn't subsiding.

"Catch your breath and get settled in. School doesn't start until January." Maria got into the driver's seat of her hatchback. "Keep fighting, warrior. You got this." She closed the car door and backed out.

After watching Maria drive away into the night, Tessa turned to enter the dark stairwell. It was going to be a long, lonely night in an unfamiliar place that stunk of fresh paint.

Chapter 21

As the sun began to set, Anna Hale finally had a chance to open the day's edition of the Dormin Times. Sitting at her old wooden kitchen table with a fresh cup of tea, she dove into the lead story about old man Fisher. It had already been more than a year since he went missing and Dorminians had given up hope for his much-awaited safe return. They missed his vivid stories about the Fisher family's stellar history and his jovial way of relating that they were the builders, the movers, and the shakers. *A braggart, essentially*, she mused.

Working with the feds, the eager new Police Chief, Elijah Wade, promised the devastated Mrs. Fisher that they would find her beloved husband. Sadly, it wasn't meant to be. One year to the day that Mayor Fisher went missing, she died in her sleep, leaving the entire, expanding estate to the sole beneficiary. When the elder Fisher's only son inherited both the estate and the mayoral reins at the age of 51, the citizens who he now reigned over knew next to nothing about him.

Anna's mind drifted back to when she'd first moved to Dormin with her late husband, and the stories that circulated about the elusive Max. Having grown up in his father's charismatic shadow, the younger Fisher rarely left the property except for rodeos and their gold-digging buckle bunnies. He wasn't one for the limelight, preferring instead to avoid the company of anyone who couldn't fatten his already bulging wallet.

Unlike his heavy set and clean-shaven father, Max had inherited his mother's thin frame and long face, a feature that he kept partially hidden behind a prominent handlebar mustache. Overpriced cowboy boots were often paired with his signature look – a tailored black suit jacket and blue jeans. Openly displaying a pistol on his hip, he perched his black ten-gallon hat over his rapidly graying thick hair, an addition that added height to his already imposing frame.

On Halloween, Max announced that he'd canceled the annual tradition in Old Town Square; he had other plans, he said. With no Spooky Tales story time, the kids went directly from school to go trick-or-treating, their movements oddly robotic as they went door to door in the cold streets.

That pitch-black night, blazing fires were set all throughout the quiet Arem River valley for the first time in Dormin's history. It was rumored that deep within the thick forest, shady, hooded figures draped in blood-red robes gathered in a circle. Halloween – known to them as the Feast of Satan – was the most sacred of all their holy days. On *this* Feast of Satan, amongst the ritualistic chanting, a bloodcurdling scream rang out in the darkness.

That night, rumor also had it that there had been a close encounter across the state near Devil's Tower.

The ancient gods had returned.

Chapter 22

During the winter of 2002, Americans were still coming to terms with their new identity. In New York City, the telecommunications mogul, Jack Weber, had just received some devastating news – his estranged father had passed away in his sleep. There was always tomorrow to make amends, he had told himself repeatedly. Now, he had run out of tomorrows and the guilt was gnawing at him. To cope with his grief, he became even more of a workaholic while his sister Ruth settled the estate.

At the end of one very long day, Jack's wife was asleep in the guest room due to Jack's penchant for watching television late into the night. Sitting up in bed, unable to sleep, Jack surfed the channels – all of them were still pulsing the same gut-wrenching 9/11 footage on a loop. It was March 2003, a full year and a half after the attack.

Jack had an intuitive feeling about the coverage. It seemed so... contrived. So orchestrated. Like a carefully crafted movie production. Yet, it was too disturbingly real – he *watched* the towers fall, not far from his penthouse. Could it have anything to do with a power-hungry vulture called the Homeland Security Act swooping in to pick pieces of flesh from the corpse of the Constitution?

When the rulers claimed the enemy had weapons that could make the entire world go **kaboom**, confused and frightened citizens *begged* the government to keep them from harm – effectively drowning out the Founding Father's wisdom about exchanging liberty for temporary safety. *This* was different, they said. When the most secure air space in the world can be penetrated, peace is nothing but a fragile illusion. War *can* come to the homeland.

It seemed to Jack that Americans were oblivious to the long history of empires lying their way into hot military conflicts. Thirteen years earlier, the Persian Gulf War had been started with a similar appeal to emotion: Foreign terrorists were guilty of horrendous war crimes, they said. Later the world would learn that no babies were taken out of incubators. The result of the conflict was immense human suffering and the destabilization of the Middle East. Yet, they had carried on like nothing happened, happy to surrender their power to brazen liars.

Instinctively knowing that humanity was heading down the same road again, Jack predicted something much worse was coming. Forced mass migration and an endless stream of refugees into the West would create the chaos the global leaders needed to put their final plan in place – a one world government.

Although the semester had barely begun, two of Tessa's fellow law students left to answer the call of duty on the other side of the world. Bolstered and motivated by the anger they felt, they prepared for the war on terror – the invisible enemy.

Logan was one such classmate, a 21-year-old charismatic black kid from Alabama. His exhausted single mother worked two minimum-wage jobs and relied on food stamps to feed him, and it *still* wasn't enough. She went to bed hungry most nights so her baby wouldn't have to – sacrifices that paid off when he got accepted into law school in Maine.

Still feeling the immense joy of his success, Logan's unshakably strong mamma was unprepared when her only child came home in a body bag, his coffin draped in the Stars and Stripes. He'd only been gone for five months. Later that day, she was found on his neatly made twin bed with a half-finished bottle of vodka and two empty pill bottles beside her. Logan's baby picture had fallen from her cold dead hands.

Evan, from Southern California, left America as a prototypical surfer boy and came back as a pirate – missing a leg and blind in one eye. To his dismay, veterans' benefits were shockingly low, and the healthcare was atrocious. When physical and mental pain became his constant companions and prescribed morphine took over his life, the hard streets of Los Angeles became his home. Before long, the State of California was charged with deciding his fate. His classmates were left to wonder how Congress could dish out foreign aid to corrupt countries while homeless veterans died in the streets.

The stories from the devastated Middle East deeply affected the frazzled Tessa. Having heard all about Vietnam from her father, the war nightmares had started when she was six years old: horrific, fleeting images of shell-shocked soldiers in fatigues, slaughtering entire jungle villages – *even the babies,* amid the rat-tat-tat of machine guns. Survivors tried to flee the liquid fire, euphemistically called napalm, as it dropped from helicopters in the sky. But there was no place to hide amid the spine-tingling screams. All the attack left behind was burning flesh, carbon monoxide and terror.

Military commanders soothed the troops with fairy tales authored by the fever dreams of an evil empire – stories of mythical brave warriors fighting for democracy, rather than cold-blooded murderers unable to look into the innocent eyes of the children as their haunting cries sowed the seeds of mutual trauma. 58,220 Americans dead or missing. 1.1 million North Vietnamese and Viet-Cong fighters perished. 1.2 million civilian causalities. Death by government – *just another ho-hum day at the office?*

A Veteran's daughter knew better than anyone that no *real* people wanted war. Yet, over and over, America brought back broken men and women from war zones, former shells of themselves with PTSD and rage building inside, the ugly truth boldly staring them in the face: Only poor kids die in a rich man's war.

Chapter 23

Tessa's hope for humanity was dwindling, much like her bank account. She needed a part-time job to see her through the rest of school; it would also serve as a distraction from the conflict happening 'over there'.

It had almost been two years since Tessa had arrived in Underville, though it seemed longer – at least at first. Scared and lonely, she'd taken Maria's advice and developed a close relationship with the warm and generous Constantins who were quick to take her under their wing. The Beehive Tavern soon became Tessa's favorite coffee spot. On Saturdays, they welcomed her to their modest bungalow for gourmet home-cooked meals and a visit with their two corgis.

One brisk, rainy, early autumn evening, Tessa walked into the Beehive Tavern with her soggy resume in hand. Stefan offered her a job on the spot – they needed a combination hostess/backup server. Could she start tomorrow?

Using transferable skills from Club 23 (minus the sex and stilettos), Tessa settled into her new role with ease, strengthening her bond with Nettie and Stefan from the very first shift. The aging couple were content to let their efficient manager run things so they could step back from the daily operation and spend more time with their popular new server. When the girl from Wyoming started the increasingly popular steak nights, they happily watched her take charge.

With her quick smile and warm demeanor, Tessa had no trouble making friends. She was always the first to help someone in need, especially if the someone had fur and 4 legs. The people of Underville were cool too, reminding her of the honest, down-to-earth folks back home where your handshake is your word.

Dating, on the other hand? Tessa's blood ran cold. After Aamon, *everyone* was put into the friend zone, much to the chagrin of certain male customers who frequented the tavern when she was working. Between work, volunteering at the art gallery, and a heavy class load, she had no time for dating anyhow. She excelled in her law classes but *fell in love* with the cornucopia of liberal arts electives – she'd found her passion.

The soft arts opened Tessa up to a whole new group of friends; together, they called themselves the Hippies of the New Millennium (The Hippies). Fully immersed in social justice dogma and media talking points, the former free-spirited western girl started to become unrecognizable.

By the time the final year of law school arrived, the Constantins had come to think of Tessa as a daughter, often teasing her about her boyfriend wannabes. *She had never stopped longing for normal, loving parents and secretly wished that Stefan and Nettie were her mom and dad.* They taught her more about the war than the history books ever did, and when people of that vintage talked about 'the war', they meant, you know, *the* war – World War II.

Despite Nettie being a successful businesswoman in her own right, her role as a good wife was to be seen and not heard; the couple had seldom been apart in their nearly 50-year traditional marriage. On a cloudless day in early spring, with the ice melting along the frigid Eastern Seaboard, Stefan was away until after dinner. It was a rare opportunity for Nettie to be herself, so she was extra cheerful when she invited Tessa for an early afternoon visit.

With several mugs of Irish coffee inviting a heart to heart, the chattering women stopped to take in the spectacular view of the ocean from the Constantins' recently replaced back deck. With the sun beaming down, Nettie began recounting stories about her life – ones that Tessa had never heard. "I was one of eight children. We were Roman Catholic, you know." Her Dutch accent was as pronounced as if she'd gotten off the ship yesterday.

"My dad was Catholic, and I'm an only child," Tessa giggled.

"One of you was all the world needed, dear." Nettie joined in the laughter.

"Agreed. I'm a handful." Tessa carefully placed a wide birch log on the fire. Nettie had started it before Tessa arrived, and it was down to coals.

The smile fell from Nettie's face as she continued. "My mother died when I was ten, then... when the bombing started, we went from peace to hell like *that*." Watching two red hot coals, like eyes, glowing in the fire, Nettie snapped her fingers.

Struggling to control her nausea and shut out images of war, Tessa closed her eyes. She was still standing near the firepit.

"The Nazis were obsessed with the occult, you know." Seldom having a chance to talk to about her feelings to anyone, Nettie spoke rapidly, like she knew her time was running out.

Shaking with anger, Tessa approached Nettie. In no rush, she patiently waited for her hostess to continue sharing her memories of Man's inhumanity to Man.

Nettie ignored the tears spilling down her own cheeks, her eyes vacant when she spoke. "Their tanks rolled down our street, blasting in German: 'surrender your radios' on the loudspeakers." Her bottom lip quivered. "I loved that little transistor radio – it gave me a break from the war."

"I'm so sorry, Nettie." Tessa crouched down, grabbing Nettie's hand. "Let it out," she whispered.

"They needed the metal for the war…" Gently sobbing, Nettie drifted off, taken back to a place she never wanted to visit.

"That's despicable."

"By the end of the war, we were starving, you know?"

"What did you do?" Tessa asked, squeezing Nettie's hand a little tighter.

"Well… sometimes, people threw potato peelings and other scraps away." Nettie placed one hand on her stomach. "We took them out of the garbage to eat."

Unable to fathom the depravity human beings were capable of, Tessa teared up.

"The war went on for six years. Six long, unending years. When we were liberated by the Canadians, it was hard to believe it was over." Nettie dug deep to keep going. "Before the war, we didn't think governments would ever do that to their own people – we trusted them."

Tessa returned to her chair, picking up her third mug of spiked coffee that was now cool enough to drink. "Do *what* to their own people, exactly?"

"Dear, the history you've been told is not real. You –"

Behind them, someone cleared their throat.

Both women turned their heads to look at Stefan, standing right behind them with his younger brother, Stan. "People moved here from the old country after the Soviets fell. You could ask them what governments do to their own people."

Nettie removed her glasses to wipe away the tears with her index fingers. "I didn't hear you come in, dear." She was embarrassed to be showing emotion in front of her husband.

Stefan ignored her tears. "And now communism is taking over America."

"Communism?" Tessa was incredulous. "Just because capitalism isn't working, you don't have to go overboard."

"Ignoring it will only make it worse!" Stefan scolded. "I know what I know! They're destroying the West, whether you believe it or not."

Flippantly laughing off what Stefan said about the communist takeover, Tessa continued her liberal arts classes with fervor. She loved him like a father, but he sounded crazy. Did he mean Soviet communism? Chinese? Canadian? *Real* communism had never been tried. *Honestly!*

Not only did she fail to heed Stefan's warning, Tessa and her friends took it one step further, convinced that the country was being overrun with racism, misogyny, and hypocritical so-called Christian values. They needed separation of church and state. They needed a communist revolution.

Meanwhile in New York, Aamon's entire network was gone by the end of 2006. On a cold snowy night in December 2005, he'd been gunned down in the dark alley behind Blue Memories Lounge and Casino by Tito's bouncer, Vincente.

Tessa had last seen Vince in that very same alley when he hailed a taxi to let her escape with her poker winnings. When she heard the news, it dawned on her that she owed her life to a stranger.

Chapter 24

By the following spring, Jack Weber was back on the California coast enjoying his home in stunning Malibu. Now settled into the routine of semi-retirement, another uneventful year passed by while his fortune kept growing. As he continued to monitor the volatile markets throughout the summer, he knew there was a major crash looming.

Then one day in September, it happened.

Jack's slightly graying hair was still damp as he relaxed on the deck of his kidney-shaped swimming pool. The nearby Pacific Ocean's roaring waves soothed his nerves under the mid-afternoon cloudless sky.

When his phone rang, Jack put it on the speaker phone when he answered, prepared to listen to his sister's monologue. He watched his wife, Abby, step out of the water and put a royal-blue mesh beach cover over her white string bikini. She was a tall, slim beauty with long, light-brown hair and eyes to match, as brilliant as she was beautiful, as graceful as she was elegant. She took her favorite lounge chair next to him.

Trying to process what he'd just heard, Jack stared off into the distance. Six years after the funeral, after all the legal matters were settled with the contested will, he'd inherited the family homestead from his late father. The guilt he initially felt increased a thousand-fold. There were so many things he wanted to say, and now he had to settle for telling anyone who would listen to go see their parents while they're still alive – no matter how much you think you hate them.

"Do you want to go back to see the homestead?" Abby asked softly, interrupting Jack's wandering thoughts. "Help you deal with some of those surfacing emotions?" Her quiet demeanor was sometimes mistaken for disinterest, a cunning illusion she used to her advantage.

Smiling at his wife from behind his high-end shades, thankful to have such a good woman by his side, Jack didn't reply for a moment. "At some point, yes. Right now, there are bigger fish swimming in a bloodbath of corruption to fry."

"You mean the housing crisis?"

"Among other things," Jack confirmed. "The housing crisis. Banksters and their greed. Predatory lending to unqualified homebuyers." He mindlessly formed fists with both hands. "But when *the banks* are at risk, they stop lending to each other."

"They knew long before it happened that the bubble was going to burst, leaving people with worthless assets." Abby accepted a glass of red wine from their housekeeper. "Thanks, Jenny. You're the best."

Jack poured some bright green liquid from a jar into a tall cylindrical glass. A thin slice of green citrus fruit floated on top of his drink that he called limenade. It was his own concoction of lime crystals, slices of lime, club soda, and a splash of mint... a weird virgin twist on a mojito, he joked. "And now they're talking about a bipartisan trade bill."

"The one that will sell out American jobs to other countries?"

"Yep." Jack sipped his elixir. "And when the word 'bipartisan' is in it, you know we're getting screwed twice as bad. They mean a bill for the corporate lobbyists – *that's* who Congress serves."

Abby held her phone in the air. "I was just reading about that. It's called corporate capture."

"Exactly." Jack stood up to gather their things. "When corporate lobbyists *own* your government, why wouldn't the auto sector want a factory in Mexico? *There* they can pay starvation wages to the poor and desperate."

On her feet now, Abby put the wet towels inside their mesh bag, her uncharacteristic angry movements catching both her and Jack off guard. "The total collapse of Detroit, meanwhile, is collateral damage." She met her husband's eyes. "No matter how much you think you despise these people, it's not enough."

When the stock market crashed in September 2008, the political class informed the American people that Wall Street was too big to fail. Unless the banks got rescued, all 401K assets would be wiped out and working people would lose their retirement income.

On the day Congress approved the bailout, an ecstatic young woman from Wyoming graduated law school and was ready to begin articling. Academically gifted and taking classes year-round, she'd completed her studies in just five years.

Pissed off that corporate greed held the citizens hostage and took priority over everything else, Tessa was determined to fight the patriarchy to the death. Alas, because fate loves mind games. headhunters for one of the offending banks found her on the east coast, happenstance that led to an offer too lucrative to refuse. She laughed at the paradox... then quickly deleted her social media history. It was just what she needed to teach them a lesson – *she could sabotage them from within.*

Tessa's two worlds collided into a kaleidoscope of confusion when she heedlessly became enamored with Wall Street culture and money. Corporate lawyer by day; anti-corporate activist by night: Defending the oppressors against the oppressed and shielding the oppressed from the oppressors. It was the ultimate in psychological disharmony.

To appease her conscience, Tessa started an NYC chapter of Hippies of the New Millennium using her own money. The group was the perfect fit for the limousine liberals who networked in chic bistros over overpriced cups of caramel macchiatos. They soon got busy planning, fundraising, photocopying, printing leaflets, participating in online forums... whatever needed to be done.

Every other Saturday, the Hippies split up into pairs and trios and plastered the city with social justice messages. During one such campaign, a homeless man approached Tessa asking for spare change. Dressed to the nines, as usual, she looked down her nose at him. "Get a job," she scoffed and rolled her eyes. "White men caused this." She walked on.

The online social justice echo chamber was where Tessa met dark-haired beauty Megan Tremblay. Through their shared passion for diversity, equity, and inclusion, they became fast friends. When critics claimed that they were provoking racial tensions, they shrugged it off. They weren't divisive and condescending... like the *other* guys.

In the spring of 2009, a glowing Tessa was Megan's maid of honor in a beautiful ceremony in Central Park. In early winter, she became godmother to the couple's firstborn. The Tremblays considered Tessa part of their family and they became inseparable.

Meanwhile, the country was still in the hopey-changey honeymoon phase of having the first gay and mixed-race President. Tessa rolled her eyes at the haters who were *still* blathering on about potential election fraud. *Same old, same old.* Voter suppression. Gerrymandering. Ballot harvesting. Foreign influence. Dead people voting using the mail-in ballots all over hell. A break in. More votes than voters. Lack of oversight. Faulty machines. *Blah. Blah. Blah. The good old hive mind of partisan politics – the other side always cheats.*

Chapter 25

About a year and a half after the financial crash, it dawned on the public that insatiable predatory corporate greed had plunged the economy into a recession. The financial cost to the American economy was a cool thirty trillion dollars; the human costs were incalculable. For a fleeting moment, the common people directed their rage at the ruling class – collective action that culminated in something called Occupy Wall Street.

Recognizing the historical significance of a long overdue class war, Tessa kept a daily journal.

> **September 2011**
> **Occupy Wall Street**
> Day 1: *We are the 99%! Everyone is united and so full of peace and love.*
> Day 24: *People are getting tired and irritated. The organizers are dividing us by race, gender, and sexual orientation.*
> Day 59: *The final day. We lost.*
> Final thoughts. *We said we needed a communist revolution, and we got it. We accepted the fracturing of the lower classes into smaller and smaller factions until we surrendered all our power. We failed as all populist uprisings do, except the time when cake-eating peasants beheaded the King and Queen.*
> *The militarized police in riot gear seemed like overkill to us, but what do we know? They raided us at dawn, used tear gas, killed an innocent protester, rounded us up, arrested us en masse, and ultimately evicted us. Brute force is why the established order wins. They always win. The game is rigged.*
> *Corporate media framing of the long-term influence? Occupy encouraged a generation of revolutionaries (us) to take to the streets and demand systemic*

reform. We also apparently shifted what is deemed politically acceptable discourse. I guess we'll see.

Lying out of both sides of her mouth, Tessa was convinced that the American dream was a scam, disgusted that the top 1% owned almost all the wealth. It barely registered that she helped the 1% process over three million foreclosures. The millions of homeless and unemployed people were just the cost of doing business. Now that she had *really* made it, she couldn't be bothered with details like collateral damage.

Tessa's journey to oblivion was complete: She'd gone from declaring war on the old boys' club to *being* the old boys' club. Oppression comes in many forms.

PART III

Roots

"It's a big club, and you ain't in it."
~ George Carlin

Chapter 26

Five years later

Fifteen years had passed since Tessa arrived in New York City as a wide-eyed teen fueled by little more than lofty dreams and junk food. As the memories from back home had faded, she'd found herself amid a strange new world where secrets were currency and decency went to die.

One wintry April morning, Tessa's long-forgotten past arrived wrapped in a scarlet bow. Some rich associate of her late father's – who'd made a grandiose gesture of treating her like a daughter when she was growing up – was hosting an event. She cringed and tucked the invitation away. "Just no."

Tessa thought back to the end of 2012 when she'd received word that her father passed away. Details were scant. She shrugged it off without so much as a second thought about her mother. By that time, she'd settled into her role as a corporate attorney and made it her life mission to yell at reality until she changed it.

Several more pages were ripped from the calendar before Dormin came calling again. Turning down a standing invitation to join her colleagues for drinks at the Artful Dodger after work, Tessa was the last to leave the office. *Again.*

Growing weary as she watched the pastel coral September sun disappear behind the crooked architecture of Wall Street, Tessa splashed cold water on her tired face. In the gold-trimmed mirror of the elegant restroom, her olive skin appeared ashen under the vanity lighting. Her black turtleneck and rust-colored slacks transformed into dark bluish and some indescribable shade of pink. She giggled at her silly reflection – probably not the best name for the lighting.

Lost in the thought of taking a soothing hot bubble bath when she got home, Tessa locked her bulging file cabinet.

Beep beep beep! The obnoxious alarm was a signal that an urgent message was waiting on the company laptop. Thankfully, it was rare. The only other time Tessa received one, she'd hoped her perpetually depraved client was ready to meet his maker – he deserved it. Unprepared for whatever fresh hell awaited her this time, she slipped the laptop into her floral satchel bag and headed toward the familiar rancid stench of the subway.

Wasting no time kicking off her heels when she got home, Tessa set the heavy case down on the dining room table and rubbed her aching lower back. Moments later, she emerged from the steamy, coconut-scented bathroom, her slim body covered by a white terry towel robe.

Making a beeline for the kitchen island in her bare feet, Tessa reached for the bottle of smooth Tennessee bourbon that was calling her name. In one continuous motion, she poured the spirit into a shot glass, gulped it, slammed the glass down on the breakfast nook, and wiped her mouth with her sleeve. She stopped just short of belching.

Sadly, the company computer hadn't self-destructed on the ride home so Tessa had no choice but to deal with it like an adult – the beeping was getting on her nerves. Trying to find the courage to open the message, she shook the towel from her damp hair and dropped it on the floor.

Reading the message from St. Theresa's Hospital in Dormin over and over until the words faded into a combination of nothingness and guilty regrets, Tessa dabbed at an exiled tear. She slammed the computer shut and buried her hot face in her trembling hands.

With a blissful glow soon emanating from the brick fireplace, Tessa stood at the wall of windows in her luxury condo to study the dazzling Manhattan skyline. Many floors below, the great Atlantic diverged and two rivers flowed. With Kenny G playing on Bluetooth, she awaited the magic alchemy of her double on the rocks.

As an ambitious Manhattan girl surrounded by money and luxury, the world's best fashions and art, exciting nightlife, and awesome friends, Tessa barely remembered who she was when she'd arrived in New York City all those years ago. The Middle of Nowhere, Wyoming had left her ill-prepared for the burlesque thrill of the big city lights. Had she run away to pursue her dreams or to escape her troubled past?

Like a radio station not quite tuned to the right station, Tessa's early time in the concrete jungle had left her with fuzzy memories. Club 23 with an elaborate network of tunnels connected to other bawdy secret clubs, and oddly expensive junk food. Kidnapped children. An elite resort. Pentagrams? How many times had she looked the other way when high society slithered into their dens for secret affairs and con games, shed virtue like dry, scaly skin, and collected their thirty pieces of silver?

Though she hadn't thought much about her hometown in years, Tessa's memories flooded back in a rush of mixed emotions. It was where she'd first fallen in love, and where she learned to paint. It was where she watched her mother spend months in a hospital bed, barely able to make a sound through her medicated fog and grandiose delusions.

As the images played out in her mind, Tessa felt like she was watching strangers in another lifetime – people she had nothing in common with. It was too late to go back home now, no way to reclaim distant memories of a forgotten life in the valley, foreign and so long ago. Dormin was a place where the backward hicks would go to their graves, clinging to their bibles, guns, and flags.

Tessa was startled back to the present by a sudden, brilliant flash of light paired with rolling thunder. Dark storm clouds were looming over the city, and they were ready to burst.

Meanwhile, on his estate near Dormin, Wyoming, Max Fisher was wide awake after 10 pm, his usual bedtime. Leaving his snoring wife, he slipped out of the master bedroom and down the wide, spiral staircase to the mezzanine level. He paused at the wrought-iron banister to peer at the ballroom below, all set up and waiting for tomorrow's festivities. The enormous, tiered diamond chandelier partially obstructed his view of the podium where tomorrow he would make an exciting announcement.

The high marble walls, decorated with white gargoyle pillars and suggestive photos of prepubescent children wearing crimson shoes, held secrets about unspeakable acts and rituals with hooded figures. A bronze statue of a naked, arched, headless male corpse was suspended next to the spiral staircase.

The door of Max's private study creaked when he entered. When the lock clicked behind him, he dimmed the ceiling lights. Igniting the musky-forest-scented black candle on the end table, he shuffled the stereo until he found a shamanic drum recording – keeping the volume low so as not to disturb the guests sleeping on the third floor above him. *If* they were sleeping through the storm, that is. Outside, the fierce skies raged, a clap of raucous thunder shaking the slumbering mansion as a ray of lightning struck nearby, illuminating the elaborate gardens of the estate.

Sitting on a cushion imprinted with the Leviathan Cross, Max finished his invocation but left the candle burning. Above his head, a painting of an angel falling from the skies hung on the wall. Another flash of white light filled the darkened room, temporarily blinding him.

With a tall scotch in his hand, Max lit a fat cigar, the bright red ember glowing in the darkened room. He coughed several times, clutching his chest until the pain passed. In the candlelight, among the acres of books accumulated for over a century, the Fisher patriarch stared at his haunting reflection in the black-framed mirror. A tired old man with thinning white hair and waxy skin seemed the perfect vessel for a predator without a soul. He turned toward the window to gaze at the expansive glittering lights in the valley below.

Knowing his time was short, that he would soon be called to his grave, Max sat motionless in the eerily silent room and lamented. Following in his father's footsteps, he'd gradually been accepted as a pillar of the community. He'd had no idea how to govern, but thankfully, his new team of advisors had been worth every nickel – all three were still with him some fifteen years later. The formula for political success was simple: Tell the voters what they want to hear until fear thy neighbor and hate thine enemy was all they knew.

Max smirked, knowing just what empty platitudes to use and recalling how blatantly he'd been able to flaunt that the rules were only for the ruled. Never the rulers. He couldn't dazzle them with brilliance, so he baffled them with bullshit – a trick he'd learned in prep school. He attended the Met Gala to make a social justice statement and drank to protest alcoholism. *They always bought it – so small-minded indeed.*

Lately, disturbing rumors had been circulating about Max's heinous sexual appetite for young girls. And boys. He always had a reasonable explanation. The demonic artwork was just art. His connection to human traffickers and drug cartels was just a coincidence. Hearsay, he said. Misinformation. Fake news. They believed him.

Chuckling at the gullibility, Max ducked into the half-bath in his study, and when he urinated, a look of pain contorted his face from the agonizing burning sensation. Returning to the windows, he peered out at the rolling skies, his tense arms clasped behind his back. He shook his head as he shuffled back to his armchair, clicking on the table lamp while an ear-splitting lightning rod struck nearby, bathing the room in momentary white light. Outside, in the eye of the storm, a brown snake scurried for cover.

Filled with a sense of dread, Max stoked the flickering fire, unable to shake the feeling that there was a tear in the fabric of his empire – that restless spirits undisturbed for centuries had risen from the dead.

Chapter 27

The only remaining light in Tessa's condo was the fire of the burning logs and the occasional flash of lightning. Now in her fuzzy slippers and pink-and-gray elephant print pajamas, she chose some smooth jazz for her melancholy mood. Picking up the family portrait from the display shelf, she brushed the dust off with her sleeve and sat cross legged on the white leather loveseat. Comforted by the heat and aroma of the snapping birch, she turned on the stained-glass torchiere lamp above her head to zero in on the image.

Cecilia Ryan's long, raven hair framed the circles under her sunken chestnut eyes, her hollow cheekbones, and pale, droopy lips trying to smile. A navy and turquoise patterned dress that screamed church rummage sale was draped over skin and bone, the result of a diet of black coffee and cigarettes. She wore no makeup or accessories.

The rain had started again, pelting against the thick patio doors like pro-abortion rioters storming the Supreme Court. Digging her tired feet into the white shag rug, Tessa yawned and stoked the fire. Picking up the photo again, her eyes were instantly drawn to her father's piercing baby blues, popping out from behind his Buddy Hollyesque glasses. She studied the handsome face and the sandy blond hair that surrounded it in every direction. With thick brows, trimmed sideburns and fashionable goatee, he was possibly the original hipster.

Patrick Ryan was a tall man, standing around 6'2", several inches taller than his petite wife. His fair skin was as Irish as they come, which complemented his wife's olive complexion. No dark circles sullied *his* cheekbones, but his mournful eyes were overcast, the source of the clouds a cross he chose to bear alone. There was no way of knowing how many skeletons were hiding in those shadows, or what secrets had gone with him to the grave.

Another bolt of lightning lit up the city, illuminating every corner of the dark streets that cowered under the brilliant flash. With the thunder raging and the spooky inside lights flickering, Tessa shivered as she pulled the plaid throw blanket tighter around her shoulders. Balancing the portrait on her knees, her eyes moved to the likeness of her younger self. She was perched on the edge of an ivory wing back chair in her sapphire blue cap and gown. Her long hair surrounded her frightened, wide eyes. She couldn't remember what she had feared in the moment. Whatever it was, it was silly compared to the real world. She shook her head.

While others her age had morphed into wives and soccer moms, Tessa had hardly changed at all. With a sigh, she returned the photo to its resting place, brushing the dust off the upper frame with her index finger. It was the last photo taken of the three of them.

Walking away from the fireplace, Tessa was overcome with a sense of dread that compelled her to turn around. Spinning on her heel, she was instantly drawn to the image of her mother, who seemed to have tears in her eyes. What?? It was just a picture!

In that instant, a switch flipped, and Tessa knew she had to go. She *needed* to go. She'd never had a stronger feeling in her life. The tears in her mother's eyes were gone, but they'd left an indelible mark on Tessa's psyche.

Annoyed by the forceful call from the past that penetrated her fortress, Tessa slammed her empty bourbon glass down on the kitchen counter with a decisive thud. She would go to that silly peacock party tomorrow, after all.

Without further ado, Teresa Dawn Ryan, Attorney-at-law tendered her immediate resignation to Dewey, Cheatum, and Howe Barristers and Solicitors, and booked a flight to Wyoming.

Now that the storm had passed, the light of the full moon shimmered across the wet gardens of the Fisher estate. Featuring a full spectrum of colors, elegant waterfalls spilled into an infinity shaped pond near the cobblestone path. Marble statues kept watch over the towering fountains and flowerbeds. Puddles had pooled on the tennis courts and in the orchard. On the other side of the sculpted caragana hedge, massive stables boasted quarter horses and appaloosas.

When the clock struck midnight, Max muttered to himself as he paced back and forth in his paisley robe, sweat pooling on his creased forehead. His cigar glowing in the dark shadows and his heart racing, he read the text message from Dmitri one more time.

Max moved back to the window to scan the dense woodlands. Four years earlier, a discovery in the forest had sent shock waves throughout the valley. Burned white crosses, swastikas, and a bloody human skull were found in a clearing. It appeared to investigators that a ritual had been interrupted, causing the participants to flee. The perpetrators had never been caught.

Tonight, the guests would arrive for the centennial celebration – and not just any guests. These were the people who built mansions on the coasts as they preached about the rising sea levels. They had helipads and boats on their gold-plated yachts and lectured the masses about their spending. They flew their private jets all over the world and feigned concern for the climate. And they thought nothing about spending stolen millions on flowers for a three-year old's birthday party while millions of children lived in poverty.

Back upstairs, Max tiptoed into the master suite and slipped into the warm bed beside his wife, who'd slept through the storm. Tossing and turning until well into the wee hours of the morning, he tried to take his mind off the celebration...something wasn't right. It was a night he'd waited for, a night where billions of dollars would change hands in a matter of hours. It was also a night the city would never forget.

Chapter 28

Butterflies in her stomach, Tessa made herself comfortable for the flight back west, which wasn't that difficult in first class. A strange calm began to settle in, even though she hadn't been able to find the diamond necklace – her family heirloom. *Did she misplace it? Was it stolen?* Agitated from overthinking, she put her headphones in place and closed her eyes, her mind soon drifting to the peaceful town that waited her arrival...

Maple and elm trees formed canopies over comfortable family homes with attractive front yards and luscious backyard gardens.

The aroma of pot roast and fresh baked apple pie drifted through open windows, prompting the famished children to go home and eat. The wide streets and parks were filled with bicycles and innocent faces, their laughter a source of pure joy for residents. Little Leaguers arguing balls and strikes spent entire summers in the sandlot, hoping to become the next Mickey Mantle or Willie Mays.

During the week, the children learned about the three R's and Sundays were reserved for prayer and devotion. Families of every race and creed strolled through the beautiful parks on their way to worship, smiling at each other as they passed. Community centers and churches had potluck suppers where food was natural, plentiful, and locally sourced.

Thanksgiving and Christmas were celebrated with loved ones, renewed hope borne of the strengthening of family bonds. And on Good Friday, the Catholics packed the churches praying that the other 364 days of the year would be forgiven.

Every Fourth of July, a boisterous parade ended in Old Town Square where an all-day celebration kicked off. The Stars and Stripes were everywhere. Private porches. Flagpoles. Hats. Everyone proudly held their hands over their hearts as they belted out the Star-Spangled Banner. The day ended with cookouts and fireworks on the riverbank.

Everyone in town owned guns and even kids knew how to shoot; except for hunting season, a gunshot was a foreign sound.

In the evenings, moms and dads tucked their kids in for the night and caught up on the day's news. Courageous reporters venture into deserts, jungles and war zones to bring the people the latest breaking stories. Objective truth meant something to them. They were dedicated enough to risk – and sometimes lose – their lives so that everyone shared one reality.... or so they thought.

Dormin was Americana personified. Baseball and apple pie. God bless the USA.

About to begin their descent to the runway, the smiling flight attendant waved her hand in front of Tessa's face – time to buckle up.

Mesmerized by the endless twinkling lights in the dusk below, Tessa was in shock. It was so much bigger than she'd imagined. A cluster of skyscrapers poked out from the center of the skyline that expanded several miles down the valley in both directions.

By the time Tessa exited the airport terminal, a scrawny bald man in a black tuxedo and matching bow tie was waiting. He rushed toward her, checking the photo on his clipboard. "Tessa Ryan?"

"Yeah. That's me," Tessa confirmed.

"Right this way." The man ushered her through the crowded airport to a nearby curb where an elegant chauffeur and stretch limousine were waiting.

Once at the mansion, the butler led Tessa into a ballroom that was lit with violet and hot pink lamps, lending it an air of passion and romance. Dinner entertainment was provided by an accomplished pianist in white tux and tails, his full head of white hair glowing in the spotlight behind a concert grand piano. Champagne, worth thousands of dollars a bottle, was in the center of every round table.

The lavish event had already kicked off with a grandiose banquet, the aroma from the kitchens wafting throughout the entire wing of the mansion. World-class chefs had been flown in from *who knows where* to prepare mouth-watering appetizers of escargot and caviar. *Snails and fish eggs.* Tessa gagged. At least the duck and array of fancy French desserts were edible.

After dinner, while the guests mingled, Tessa turned heads while she made her way across the ballroom, radiating an enticing natural star quality – the envy of glamorous, air-brushed models who graced the covers of fashion magazines. Craving the cool of the night, she moved toward the open terrace doors where white lace curtains fluttered in the breeze. Snippets of conversation blended in the buzz of the packed room. A business deal here. A financial transaction there. Whatever boring, old, rich, and powerful people in ten-gallon hats at a black-tie event discuss when they get together at exclusive parties. *Golf and grandchildren, probably.*

With her eyes averted, a flushed Tessa rushed towards the stone patio, stepping outside to find her way through the crowd. Once near the railing, it wasn't long before she felt a presence beside her. He was around her age, and he was watching her. His sky-blue eyes and wavy blonde elicited vivid images of sandy California beaches and calendars for the ladies.

Blondie raised his glass. "Evening." He glanced in Tessa's direction. The party noise continued around them.

Tessa pretended she hadn't heard him while she scrolled on her phone.

"I'm Cole. What's your name, pretty lady?"

"Muffin." She didn't look up.

"Pleased to meet you, Muffy." Cole's smile was dazzling. "Can I get you a drink?"

Tessa let her guard down – they were just talking, for Pete's sake. "I'm Tessa. She/her."

Cole's gaze dropped to the royal blue dress that hugged her slender figure like a politician clinging to a lobbyist. "She/her looks kind of obvious." Their eyes met. "And you have a beautiful smile."

The full tangerine moon rested on the horizon, seemingly large enough to reach out and touch. Moonlight reflected across the tranquil pools and glinted off the half-full champagne glasses on the long tables in the courtyard, abandoned by the inebriated guests when they moved back inside.

Cole slipped behind Tessa and placed his tuxedo jacket over her shivering shoulders. He wore suspenders and a cummerbund, both scarlet-red, and a cologne that made Tessa weak in the knees. "How's that for a romantic harvest?" Returning to his spot, he pointed to the twinkling sky.

"It's delightful," Tessa murmured, intoxicated by the superb sounds of the orchestra, the fragrance of a nearby rose bush, and the sparkling champagne that was going down way too fast. "I used to come here when I was a little girl." She pointed at one of the pools. "When I raced my dad across the pool, he always let me win."

Moving his disinterested gaze from the pool, Cole turned his undivided attention back to Tessa until their eyes met.

A loud shriek pierced the air. "Max would like to say a few words!" They were being summoned inside by the flamboyant Mrs. Max. Her sagging breasts were covered with two minuscule strips of neon pink cloth, and the emeralds she wore seemed out of place... like a copy of the Constitution in a politician's office. Gravity was not her friend.

Tessa turned around to face Cole; he was gone. Was it something she said? She followed Mrs. Max back to the mansion. Rosalind was her real name, but everyone called her Mrs. Max – and she liked it that way. Everyone, that is, except Max. She was his Rosie, trophy wife, shameless buckle bunny, and twenty-three years his junior. When an unexpected pregnancy elevated her status from impoverished teen to landing the most eligible bachelor in Dormin, she became Mrs. Max – a marriage that had lasted for almost thirty years.

The older woman had a spring in her step, reminding Tessa of a younger Mrs. Max – a devoted wife with a valley girl vibe who once wore multi-colored ribbons in her perfectly-styled, bleached hair. When at the estate, her silicone body had always been decked out in either a string bikini or a short mini dress with stiletto heels, gaudy jewelry, and heavy makeup – the ideal canvas for the drama that followed her everywhere.

By the time Tessa got back inside, corporate news crews from all over the country streamed into the crowded press area at the back of the dimly-lit ballroom. The Dormin Times, EYE on Dormin and New World Now (NWN) were the big three on the local scene.

Adam Logose, on assignment for the local affiliate of NWN, observed the DC insiders while the cameraman worked his magic to make the establishment look good. Narcissistic stuffed suits with empty endorsements and a softball press conference sounded like a fun way to spend his Friday night. *Not.* The burning question on everyone's mind would likely be which flavor of ice cream Max liked, or where his wife got her vast collection of shoes. *Modern political journalism was so stunning and brave.*

Max was at the podium, trying to clear his throat. His emphysema flared up, triggering a vigorous coughing fit. As he picked up a glass of cold water and guzzled it, the nervous guests stared, wondering how the old man kept going. He was nearing seventy, for Pete's sake, with chronic lung problems and a history of strokes.

When the music stopped, Max began reading from the teleprompter with an audible wheeze, his voice uncharacteristically shaky. "Distinguished guests, friends, comrades." He scanned the faces in the colored glow. "Thank you all for coming to honor one hundred years of Atluko Industries."

The guests shifted uncomfortably in their seats.

"A century ago, my grandfather stood on this very spot and made a promise to this community. He promised that for as long as future generations lived, the spirit of independence and democracy would live on, and he passed that down to us. Now we must carry the torch and hand it off to our children."

While the guests applauded, Tessa checked the room for familiar faces from her vantage point at the entrance way to the ballroom.

"His determination has survived the test of time, as tonight, we kick off a celebration to honor that commitment," Max continued his hollow speech with a sense of apprehension in the air.

Though they clapped politely, the crowd was growing restless while they not-so-patiently waited for Max's announcement and the line-up of speakers that were to follow. The big reveal was the worst kept secret in the county.

Not seeing anyone she knew, Tessa took her phone out. She couldn't concentrate on stupid, meaningless, hollow speeches. *Okay boomer.* Suppressing a yawn, she checked the time. 11:11! *Already. Where did the night go?*

Finally, Max stopped. "May I propose a toast?"

Relieved, the guests rose, champagne glasses in hand.

"To Dormin." Max raised his glass. "Past, present, and future."

The guests clinked their glasses of bubbly. "To Dormin," they repeated. Everyone in the room was drawn to a sudden commotion near the press area when one of the guests marched toward Max and reached for the microphone.

Before anyone could react, the older man stared directly into the NWN camera and blurted out, "Folks, wouldn't you say Max has gotten a little too powerful? The city has become a hellhole under his watch."

All eyes were on the stranger when he spoke again – the vibe in the room had gone from stick-up-the-butt snob to a tight–cheeked cringe in the blink of an eye.

"He's been –" The microphone was cut with a nails-on-a-chalkboard screech, and the impromptu speech was over. The dudes in black suits were most perturbed.

The guests gawked in disbelief, dumbfounded at the awkward exchange. Once the unruly intruder was gone, the massive chandelier turned on, flooding the room with bright light – it appeared the party was over.

A few minutes later, Mrs. Max approached the abandoned podium. "I'm so sorry, friends," she screeched, revealing the rust-colored lipstick on her fake teeth. "Sadly, even with a carefully vetted guest list, sometimes one slips through that shouldn't."

Waiting for an update on their host, nobody moved.

"Max is a little shaken up right now; I think it might be best if we conclude for the night. We will continue the centennial celebration tomorrow at the plant." Mrs. Max glared at the press – if they wanted access to her husband, they had to go through her. "Remember our tour begins tomorrow afternoon at 1 pm. Sharp."

The spooked guests made their way to the overflowing coat check as the annoyed press corps packed up their bulky equipment. What a dud.

Tessa wondered why they didn't just use their cell phones like normal people. She pulled the invitation out of her purse while waiting for the limousine. The event was going on all weekend long: A tour of the factory and ranch tomorrow, another party, then the annual, public cookout at the plant on Sunday. *Boooring!*

Shivering, Tessa returned the envelope to her purse, unable to shake the feeling that something was terribly wrong in Dormin.

Chapter 29

Returning home from the party at the mansion, Adam Logose parked his shiny, apple-red convertible on the sloped driveway beside his covered motorcycle. Exhausted, he breathed a sigh of relief as he climbed the steps to his suburban-soccer-mom, two-story brick house – the last one before the neglected city park. Tossing his keys in the wooden bowl on the hall table, he checked his look in the mirrored wall in the entrance – a young, virile man in his 30s, desperately in need of a holiday.

Adam opened the back door and flicked the light on. It was his signal to his best friend, Ralph, that he was home. It was much later than usual – Ralph would be overly-eager to see him.

Ralph came bounding out of his fancy doghouse, wagging his tail, floppy ears bouncing all the way. He tackled his master to the ground, covering his face in slobbery kisses. *Golden retrievers could be such drama queens.*

Closing his weary eyes, Adam basked in momentary gratitude. *Humans don't deserve dogs*, he reminded himself. Jumping up, he remained fixated on his precious boy, drastically in need of a tummy rub.

Ralph wiped his muddy paws on the fresh door mat, bounding up the three steps to the kitchen in record time. He wolfed down his chunks of beef in gravy, streams of slobber finding their way to the floor in the sparkling kitchen.

While Ralph ate, Adam polished the stainless-steel appliances and unloaded the dishwasher – his entire house was spotless, like usual.

Race upstairs time! Ralph won, again.

Still fully clothed, Adam dragged himself across the master bedroom, kicking off his shoes as he flopped onto the immaculate bed where his best friend was waiting. He was asleep before his head hit the pillow.

Chapter 30

Max Fisher was in his silk, paisley bathrobe with his arms and legs crossed, puffing on a fat cigar. He was seated at the head of the oval table in the windowless boardroom of the mansion with his hairy chest exposed. The room smelled strongly of freshly shampooed carpet, scotch, and cigar smoke.

One by one, the meeting participants entered, bleary-eyed and exhausted. Still dark out, the room was chillingly quiet, the nervous tempo set by the resounding ticking of the wall clock.

When the other four men were seated, Max dropped his elbows on the table. "How the hell could you let this happen?!" he exploded. Everyone was fixated on the table in front of them, not daring to move. "You all know that that worm should never have been at the party last night. You all know he hates everything I stand for!"

To Max's right, a fortyish man with a long, pointy nose and a clipboard in his right hand rose to speak. His shaved head and short stature seemed fitting for his role as a trained bootlicker. "Sir, your wife was in charge of the guest list." His Eastern European accent was as pronounced as the names of foreign dignitaries with extra cash.

Max was standing now, his trembling palms squarely on the table. "And who is in charge of my wife, Dmitri?" he shouted.

Displaying a prominent tattoo of a broken chain on his forearm, Dmitri checked his clipboard. "Sir, I –"

"You're my personal assistant." Max raised his voice while he banged his fists on the table. "I expect you to keep that hag in line. Now, get out." He pointed to the door.

The others began to rise. "Sir –"

"The rest of you sit down," Max growled while he took his chair.

The door slammed behind Dmitri, bursting the tension in the air.

Folding his arms, Max leaned his back against the heavily padded high-back chair to study the other three men in his inner circle. All men. All white. All rich. All powerful. "Gentlemen." He nodded.

Miles Malone, Max's public relations advisor, rose to speak. "I –"

"Sit down, Malone," Max barked and rose out of his seat, struggling to control his voice.

Miles shrugged in defiance. "Fine."

"Let's be perfectly clear." Max began pacing, his dark energy following him like a storm cloud. He stopped to stare at each of the men in turn. "Jack Weber *must*...be...shut...down. That goes double for any fool who supports him."

An eerie silence filled the room like a concrete balloon.

Max's eyes narrowed to slits as he placed his hands on the back of his chair. "Immediately, and by any means necessary."

"I'm out." Miles rose to leave.

"Sit down, Malone!" Max shouted. "We talked about this a year ago! What part of shutting it down back then didn't you idiots understand? If that idiot wins, our entire mission will be destroyed."

"We underestimated them." Miles returned to his chair with a scowl on his face, struggling to control his panicked mind. "How do we put the cat back in the bag now?!"

At least a minute passed before Max spoke again, anger flashing in his eyes when he leaned forward. "Thanks for bringing that to my attention, Malone. I expect you to report back to my private office at 9:00 am."

The men rose.

"And have a new plan," Max added before dismissing them with a wave. "That'll be all."

Adam Logose awoke to a smooth, slobbery tongue on his cheek. He opened one eye to Ralph, on his back, limbs sprawled, tail wagging, his head cocked to one side – irresistible cuteness personified. After the mutually satisfying tummy rub, Ralph closed his puppy-dog eyes and laid his head on Adam's chest. A tear leaked from Adam's eye while he embraced Ralph's head in the crook of his elbow. The moment was killed by the obnoxious buzz of the alarm. The pair jumped up in unison.

While Adam found his blue sweatpants and a plain white T-shirt, Ralph watched the scene across the street, a little girl and her harried mother rushing to the half-ton idling in the driveway. With his front paws on the windowsill and his tail flicking back and forth, he waited for his human for the race to the bottom...of the stairs. He won.

During Adam's breakfast of lean bacon and organic sliced tomatoes, the radio announcer was happy to predict sunny skies and unseasonably warm temperatures after the stormy weather. Widespread bullshit followed by gusts of fear. Darkness is only a heartbeat away.

Adam's hands were submerged in lemon-scented, soapy water when something dropped on the floor behind him. He dried his hands to pick up the brand new leash, courtesy of the adorable panting bundle of joy sitting on his haunches with irresistible puppy dog eyes and wagging tail.

On the hushed street, Adam inhaled the pure, mountain air, slowing his run down while Ralph gleefully waded through every puddle. One by one, the neighbor's lights turned on in the pre-dawn haze.

Ralph led the way to Bero Spring – a glacial pool in the heart of rundown Max Fisher Park. He jumped in for a bath, making sure he stood right beside his master when he shook off.

Adam wiped a drop of dirty dog water out of his eye. "Thanks, Ralphie."

On the run home, Ralph disappeared into some bushes, emerging with the perfect stick, reminding Adam of a puppy four years earlier. He'd lost track of how many pairs of shoes he had to replace, but with puppy dog eyes and his head cocked to one side, Ralph was always forgiven. He got his fetch time.

Back home, Ralph curled up on the plush cushion in his deluxe doghouse to await his best friend's return. Complete with separate dining and sleeping areas, the heated two-story abode was the talk of the neighborhood. In the beautifully manicured backyard, Ralph had his own area in the shade to play and use the facilities. The spoiled little prince wanted for nothing.

After a luxurious hot shower, Adam studied himself in the steamy mirror; he was as strapping as he had been in the military. Not bad for a 34-year-old who'd been through a bitter divorce, he concluded. After shaving, he plucked several gray strands from his short, curly chestnut brown hair. Turning his face from side to side, he admired the cleanshaven square jaw line and Mulatto skin glowing caramel under the bright lighting while he slapped on his favorite cologne.

Sporting a gray towel around his hips, he chose a long sleeve, black, button-up T-shirt and faded jeans from the section of his closet labeled 'casual'. He put on his immaculate black sneakers and hurried down the stairs, stopping to give his reflection one more appreciative glance in the entrance hall while cleaning a smudge off the mirror.

Adam had no time for a wife or family. And he wasn't interested in love triangles. Or quadrants. If he ever met someone, they'd have to compete with his ego. And Ralph. They were a package deal.

Chapter 31

The taxi stopped on Old Town Road – the canopied scenic drive that wound its way along the lush banks of the beautiful and familiar Arem River. Full of mixed emotions for the day that lay ahead, Tessa's stomach flip-flopped as she paid the fare.

Clay planters filled with half-dead flowers and thirsty ornamental grasses were evenly spaced among the rows of blue spruce. Feeling something gross and squishy beneath her boot, Tessa glanced down at the littered sidewalk – she had stepped right into human waste. *Eww.* Cursing, she knelt to take her boot off, wiping it on the lawn as best she could and hoping the early morning moisture would wash off the stench.

Still on her knees, Tessa raised her head to look through the spruce trees; her jaw dropped. On the dew-glistened grass, tents of every size, shape, color, and condition were spread out as far as the eye could see. Discarded syringes and used condoms were strewn across the entire riverbank. One homeless man, wearing only boxers and a half-drunk smile, was outside his threadbare tent relieving himself. A few rail-thin dogs scavenged through the garbage strewn between the empty trash cans. A group of disheveled people warmed themselves around a flickering burning barrel.

Gagging on the combined stench of rotting food, used condoms, and human waste, Tessa studied the third world scene. She'd never expected to encounter a homeless encampment in her hometown.

Even more excited now to relive memories, Tessa raced up the slight incline toward Old Town Square. Later in the day, the park would be filled with happy families and excited tourists, there to learn about the founders, toss coins into the fountain, and make a wish. Almost there...

Tessa froze. Gone! The statues. The inscriptions. The fountain. Gone. All of it! Gone. No memorial benches. No Stars and Stripes. Just dark, empty space, wilted perennials, a few homeless stragglers, and trash.

Spinning around on wobbly knees, Tessa took the few steps to a wooden bench, the brown paint peeling from years of harsh conditions and neglect. A vigilant elm tree formed an umbrella over the bench, dropping tears of ambient color into the sea of drab. A frenzied dog barking in the distance and the blare of a car horn interrupted her shock. The world spun.

A gust of wind dispersed the leaves and scattered trash around the park as Tessa gazed up at the spot where Old Glory was supposed to be. In its place was an unfamiliar black and white flag waving in the wind. The hair on the back of her neck stood up. "Oh my God," she whispered. "It's worse than I thought."

A masked white youth drew near; he was covered head to toe in black. "Get out!" he ordered. "You don't belong here."

Puffing her chest out like a pelican, Tessa jumped to her feet, shoving her index finger in the youth's face. "Who do you think you are? This is a public park!" She was taller than him.

The outraged thug snarled while he showed her the machete in his boot. He pointed at a sign behind her. **Black Fist Warriors Park. No Whites Allowed.** He was white!

"What the...what?" Tessa's head swooned. Her knees were weak. This had to be a dream – a nightmare. Or she was losing her mind.

Tessa crawled out of the park, walking the next six blocks in record time, the rhythm of her heels on the broken sidewalk echoing a tale of surrealism on the dark street. She passed her old elementary school without so much as a glance, slowing only when she reached the corner. She froze again.

The old corner store was gone, replaced by the **Early to Late Bakery**. A rush of shoppers exited with brown bags full of fresh-baked goodies. The pyramid-shaped cone of light above the door shone on their emotionless faces in the dark. The stench of exhaust fumes and the sweet aroma of cinnamon buns lingered in the air.

Inside the store, Tessa listened to the hum of the machines and pretended to browse the shelves until she was the only customer. She approached the cashier – a young man with dreads under his hairnet. "What happened to the old corner store that was here?"

The cashier continued to package the fresh bread. "I don't know nuthin' about no corner store, lady." He wore an apron over his muscle shirt, prominently displaying the tattoo of a cannabis plant on his biceps. "This bakery has been here for as long as I can remember."

Tessa was adamant. "No. There was a corner store and café. Mr. Hutchinson, the old ma... the owner, would give all us kids free ice cream every Sunday. We loved that place."

The cashier shrugged. "I can ask my boss if you want."

"Thanks. If you wouldn't mind." Tessa agreed. "And don't assume my gender."

A middle-aged man of average stature emerged from a back room with specks of pink icing clinging to his apron. The hairnet covering his bald head made as much sense as homeless people while millions of houses sat empty.

"This *lady*," the young helper said in an 'I don't give a damn about your gender identity or preferred pronouns crap' voice, "says there used to be a corner store here. Some old guy gave them ice cream or something."

Pointing straight down at the floor, the manager frowned. "You sure it was here?" He scratched his head with his gloved finger, leaving a trail of pink icing on his gray hair under the net.

"Of course, I'm sure." Tessa insisted. "I walked by it every day on my way to school and back!"

"Then, nope." The older man started to turn around, then stopped. "I've been working at this store since I was in high school. Worked my way up from night baker to manager. Sorry I can't help you." He disappeared through a thick plastic partition into the kitchen.

"But that's impossible." Tessa moved toward the exit in stunned silence. "W h... why are there bars on all the windows?"

"What do you think this is? 1972?" It was the young cashier.

Tessa spun around, wide-eyed. "Don't be a smart ass. Look, when I left this town, the police were hardly ever needed. Nobody even locked their doors."

"Times have changed, lady."

Tessa continued like she hadn't heard him. "Sure, some of the kids got in trouble, but there was hardly any crime."

The cashier whistled. "Wow, lady. I don't know where you're from, but it ain't from here. That's all I'm saying." He shook his head and busied himself stocking the shelves. More customers had entered – the conversation was over.

"No..." Tessa began to protest and ran outside instead. She dropped to her haunches on the sidewalk and took a few deep breaths in the early morning light.

This was too much. She *had* to find out what was going on – and she knew just the person to talk to. But first, she had a visit to make.

Fidgeting with her dangling earrings, Tessa hesitated before she shuffled through the automatic doors at the main entrance of St. Theresa's hospital. This cold, sterilized dungeon was exactly the way she remembered it, spine-chilling crucifixes and all. They gave her the creeps – probably not the world's best Catholic.

Exiting the elevator on the fifth floor, Tessa tried to concentrate on the click of her heels on the polished concrete – anything to avoid what was facing her at the end of the hall. In slow motion, she pushed through the double doors labeled **Palliative Care.**

Inside Room 517, a burly young nurse in green scrubs was applying white cream to his patient's lips. "Are you Cecilia's daughter?" he asked without looking up. Slobber landed on the front of his uniform while his tongue repeatedly flicked the ring that pierced his bottom lip.

"Yes. Tessa." *Gross.*

While the nurse continued to tend to her mother's needs, Tessa trained her eyes on the poster above the bed – the caduceus glowed as one of the coiled snakes began to unwind from the winged staff. As she watched in horror, the snake's eyes turned red. It hissed. Startled, she stepped back.

The nurse moved his gaze to make eye contact. "Is everything okay?"

"Yes." A cold chill moved through Tessa as she slowly met his icy stare. "Can I stay until she wakes up?"

"She's been asking for you." The nurse left the room.

Swallowing the lump in her throat, Tessa tried to shake off the nurse's steely glare. Nobody had to tell her that death was imminent; a heavy foreboding permeated the entire, silent wing.

Cecilia Ryan was sleeping amid a cluster of machines and tubes everywhere, the monitor next to her measuring the rhythm of her beating heart.

Tessa was crushed by the sight of the frail, timid, seventy-one-year-old woman, weighing under a hundred pounds, her long black hair now short and ash white. She was grateful she'd chosen to say goodbye. "I'm sorry, mama," she whispered through misty eyes as she took her mother's hand, a bit cool to her touch. Adjusting the covers, she rehearsed the questions in her head. What had happened to her dad?

While Tessa's mind drifted, there was a commotion in the hall. Within seconds, the room was full of frantic medical personnel – Cecilia had flat lined.

Tessa plopped into a chair to examine her surroundings. What a godawful place. What a dreadful way to spend the last days of your life. So cold. So clinical. The sickening scent of antiseptic. And bleach. And death. Why hadn't she come here instead of going to that stupid party last night?

"Ms. Ryan?" A woman in green scrubs and a white hijab was standing next to Tessa.

Feeling like she'd been waiting an eternity, Tessa checked her watch. It was seventeen minutes. "Yeah, that's me."

"I'm afraid..." Her soft voice trailed off.

Tessa watched the nurse pull the sheet over her mother's face. "She's gone, isn't she?" she wailed as she jumped out of her chair.

"I'm sorry. We did all we could."

Back at the hotel, Tessa turned the lights out, crawling under the thick covers while she wept. With her eyes closed, her mind drifted back to a childhood full of unfinished business – being erased piece by piece. "What is happening?" she whispered to the empty room.

An ominous silence echoed back, heavy with chills and premonition. There was something unearthly going on, and Tessa intended to find out what.

Chapter 32

In September 2001, forty-year-old Miles Malone had been offered a lucrative job in public relations for both the City of Dormin and Atluko Inc – one of the first to be recruited for Max's exclusive inner circle after old man Fisher disappeared. Now in his mid-fifties, retiring was not an option, courtesy of hefty alimony payments to two high-maintenance ex-wives and a gambling addiction. His familiarity with Edward Bernays and the dirty tricks he used to manipulate people was what landed him the job.

Waiting on Max for their nine o'clock meeting, Miles bounced his ankle on his knee while he checked his watch. Twitching in a plush velvet chair at the mansion, he leafed through some paperwork while the uniformed maids cleaned the mezzanine level around him. It appeared that sloppy party guests had enjoyed themselves on this level unconcerned about who cleaned up after them. He would know; he was one of them.

The arched, double brass doors of Max's office opened with seconds to spare. Perturbed that he was on a damage control assignment rather than portfolio business as usual, Miles approached the fancy antique desk carrying a piece of paper and a paperback book in his hand. Acknowledging Dmitri with a nod, he whipped the wooden chair around to sit spreadeagled facing his boss.

Max adjusted his cowboy hat as he turned away from his computer. "I don't have time for psychobabble," he barked, lighting a cigar. "Just give me the highlights."

Resting his elbows on the back of the chair, Miles pushed his wire-rim glasses up his stubby nose with his middle finger. His clean-shaven face was surrounded by an abundance of platinum blonde hair. He held up the book in his hand.

"What do you have there, Malone?"

"<u>The Art of War</u> by Sun Tzu." Miles loosened the belt around his blue jeans. "The greatest victory is that which requires no battle. The supreme art of war is to subdue the enemy without fighting."

"War?" Max gasped. "We can't start a war!"

As he got to his feet, Miles removed his suit jacket to reveal his stark white dress shirt and the bluish-gray tie that matched his eyes. "The war has already started," he sighed, pushing the book across the desk.

"Whatever." Blowing smoke rings toward Dmitri, Max put his feet on the desk to reveal his shiny new boots.

"Now that you'll face a little bit of scrutiny, you must understand how people think." Miles stopped pacing. "Now... in the information age, people have trouble knowing what is real." He sniffed.

"It's that freak Weber." Max flicked his ashes on the floor. He's never served a day in office. Why is he doing this to me?"

"You're pretty out of touch if you think being outside the system is a bad thing." Miles rolled his sleeves up. "That's why he has a populist following – he's a man of the people."

Frowning, Max lit one cigar with another and stubbed out the butt in the overflowing ashtray. "So, you're saying... the people... are our enemy?"

"Think about it." Miles stared out the window at the grounds below. "Do you want them to know their own power? Do you want them to think about the Bill of Rights? The Constitution?"

"Of course not!" Max stormed toward the liquor cabinet, his cowboy boots stomping on the vinyl flooring. With a shaky hand, he reached for the gold and diamond trimmed decanter to pour a double scotch. Or so. He downed it in one gulp.

Without looking at this boss, Dmitri emptied the ashtray.

"Then any challenge to your authority *must* be shut down – swiftly and punitively," Miles stressed. He shoved a sheet of paper under his boss's nose.

With a now steady hand, Max grabbed the paper Miles was holding under his nose. "What the hell is this?"

"If we control the message, we control their reality. Read it, Max."

<u>Mind control techniques</u>
- **Absolutes.** Black or white. Good or bad. Up or down. No nuance. Kills further discussion. (Reductionist)

- **Avoid abstracts.** Appeal to emotions and authority

- **Repetition.** Repeat a lie often enough, and people will believe it

- **Sensationalism.** If it bleeds, it leads

- **Language.** Control language through – among others – banning, censorship, changing definitions, compelled speech and the introduction of new words

- **Imprinting**. Brand people and issues with stereotypes

- **Scapegoating.** Pick an enemy for special vilification, and incessantly criticize them

- **Centralized.** One authority controls the flow of information while dissenters are mocked; multiple outlets use identical language.

- **Authoritative.** Slick presentation of the message increases credibility in the mind of the viewer as authority cannot be questioned

- **Framing.** Present only one side

"Meanwhile, with the advances in artificial intelligence, we're mining data." Miles paused to accept a glass of scotch. "Like crazy. The human ego is a goldmine."

"Like?"

"We have information on everyone. Biometrics, face recognition, fingerprints, even DNA through those phony tests we run."

"What phony tests?" Max was not nearly as excited as his fixer.

Ignoring the question, Miles slammed the scotch down in one gulp. "All you need to know is that we can track, trace, and database everyone by telling them it's for convenience. People must be tricked into things."

Max stared at Miles, picturing what he would look like if his head literally exploded. Nah. *Too messy.*

"Do you know how easy it is to manipulate people through their emotions?" With too much excess energy surging through him, Miles jumped up.

"Nope."

"The problem is that it's hard to control messaging when you have a loud-mouth like Weber around." Miles always spoke like he had thirty seconds to live, and he needed to tell his life story – 90 miles an hour with gusts up to 110.

White knuckled, Max grunted as the morning sun shone on his face through the window. He muttered something under his breath.

Miles tossed a tissue in the trash. "Thankfully, we have the power to mess with memories, remove archived records, change online encyclopedias, manipulate search engines, and even change definitions to suit our agenda. We run tech, the news media, the entertainment industry, corporations, academia... all of it."

"Seriously?"

"Max." Miles tapped his feet for emphasis. "We *own* reality."

Chapter 33

Halfway up Saboro mountain, Tessa arrived at an isolated gingerbread replica house in the woods, obscured from the main road by thick bluffs of birch and pine. White smoke rose from the wide stone chimney as Tessa stepped out of the rental SUV. With her eyes stinging, she crouched to greet a tail-wagging bulldog with a stick in its mouth. "Hi, pooch." She heaved the stick toward the metal shed where several clear bags of Autumn leaves had accumulated.

Birch firewood was neatly stacked along the side of the house, curtained under a row of half-naked shade trees. The gardens were still mostly in full bloom in the early fall and bursting with the promise of a bountiful harvest. A cobblestone path wound its way to the front door, the vibrant colors of wildflowers and animal calls filling Tessa with a sense of calm.

At the top of the concrete steps, Tessa knocked. Shading the natural light from her eyes, she squinted to peek into the picture window. In the shadows, a small figure arose from an armchair in front of the dying fire.

The arched, stained-glass door creaked open and a slight woman in her sixties peeked up at Tessa past the chain. "May I help you?"

"Anna, it's me. Tessa! Rememb –"

"Oh, for Heaven's sake." With a smile spreading across her radiant face, Anna pulled the door wide open. "You're all grown up, child."

"I'm not exactly a child anymore, Anna. I'll be thirty-two in December." Returning the smile, Tessa leaned down to hug the petite woman. "My pronouns are she/her."

"Nonsense. You're always a child to someone as old as me." Anna led her surprise visitor to the alcove beside the living area, chuckling while she stoked the red-hot coals to add another log to the fire. *She/her!?*

Still shivering from her earlier experiences, Tessa moved closer to the fireplace. Zoned out, she watched somber tears fall from the skies and skim across the lake. Though it was still overcast, the wind had died down.

"It's chilly this morning, isn't it?" Anna was also gazing out the window, mesmerized as she watched the spooky mist rise from the water. "I fell asleep in front of the fire."

Tessa took a whiff of the distinct aroma of Anna's homey sanctuary – it always smelled like ginger cookies and sweet-grass. A CD of tribal drums and flutes was on low volume in the living room. "That's quite the watchdog you have there. I could have taken all the silverware," she joked.

"I'll be back shortly." Anna smiled and disappeared into the cozy kitchen. She was stooped over a bit, one hip clearly giving her trouble. Her hair was pulled back into a thick, single braid – a hairstyle she hadn't changed in years, though gray had now overtaken brown. Her beautiful face was remarkably smooth. Not a wrinkle.

Tessa scanned the dated house that had become her home halfway through high school. One ugly appliance had been replaced with another of around the same '70s vintage. Time travel is real.

"What's going on, child?" Anna interrupted Tessa's trip down memory lane. A well-worn, bookmarked bible was stuffed into the inner arm pocket of her frayed chair.

"Okay." Tessa's eyes were drawn to an overripe apple falling to the ground in the orchard. "Everything is different. The riverbank, the corner store, the park. Everything!"

Anna nodded as she picked up her latest knitting project. "Yeah. *Everything* started to change when old man Fisher disappeared. After –"

"Then, I went to see my mother at the hospital." Tears began to glide down Tessa's flushed face. "And she died right when I got there."

"Oh, my dear God." Anna gasped, covering her gaping mouth with a trembling hand. The lights in the house flickered.

"You know my history, Anna," Tessa sobbed. "I feel like I'm losing my mind!"

"Tsk. You're not losing your mind, child," Anna sighed. "The devil is using humans as dark entities to carry out his work."

Rubbing her temples, Tessa wondered if she was wasting her time. "The devil, Anna? Entities. *Really*? How is *this* supposed to help?"

Focused on her knitting, Anna hesitated before answering. "It doesn't matter if you think the devil is real. The evilest among us do and they call on his power. The Bible talks about demons for a reason." Knit one. Pearl two.

"Demons!? Seriously? Come on, Anna." Tessa's heart sunk. She'd turned to the spiritual Cherokee woman for wisdom, not a Grimm's Fairytale. "Sorry, but I live in the real world. I believe in science."

Her eyes clouding over, Anna shook her head – a young believer had left Dormin, and a radicalized atheist came back. *How sad.* "The greatest trick the devil ever pulled was convincing the world he didn't exist."

"You've lost me," Tessa sighed.

"Child," Anna sighed and set her knitting on her lap. "Do you believe that God will always win over the devil?"

"There is no God or devil," Tessa made no attempt to hide the contempt in her voice.

"Okay, then...do you believe that good will always win over evil?"

"Obviously." Tessa cast her eyes downward to concede the point. "But spiritual warfare is a myth."

After what seemed like an eternity of deafening silence, Anna set her knitting project on the bamboo table. "You're not listening. The devil is devious in his ways – he's a trickster, and he can take the shape of anyone."

"Ha. As if."

Anna picked up her bible and flipped to Ephesians 6:12.

> *"For we wrestle not against flesh and blood, but against principalities, against powers, against the rulers of the darkness of this world, against spiritual wickedness in high places."* (KJV)

"O... okay?" Tessa stared past Anna's head at the reverse image of a breathtaking landscape reflecting off the glassy surface of the lake. The sun was peeking through the clouds. "Anna, when I was young, I believed in God and the tooth fairy. Now I only believe in the tooth fairy."

Anna's eyes grew misty. "Our culture began to collapse the day we kicked God out of our schools, our families, our communities, and even our churches."

Ready for a change of subject, Tessa was transported back in time. She and Anna's niece, Jennifer, spent one summer together at Anna's. Carefree youth and swimming in the lake all day. "Hey, whatever happened to Jennifer?"

"I don't know." A single tear rolled down Anna's cheek. "She's been missing for fourteen years now."

Tessa was speechless as she tried to figure out what was going on. Was she in a dream? Had she entered some kind of parallel universe, another dimension? Had her soul been possessed? Did she...

"Hi?"

"Anna!" Tessa jumped. "I forgot you were here."

"Thanks," Anna sniffled, still emotional about her missing niece.

Tessa looked at the older woman with admiration. Anna had been her rock. "I was so little when I met you," she said softly.

"10 years old." Anna nodded in agreement. "All by yourself at the Farmer's Market. Little pigtails in your hair, and cute little freckles." Her lower lip quivered. Drying her eyes with her bony index fingers, she left the room again.

As Tessa stood, her eyes were drawn to the pristine picture on the mantle – Anna and her husband on a fishing trip in Manitoba. The proverbial hippy couple. Norman had been killed in a hunting accident in northern Saskatchewan in the early '80s, dying in the place he loved – the Canadian wilderness.

Anna returned with a little scrap of paper in her hand. "Go see this man. I think he can help." She handed Tessa a handwritten note – a first name and a phone number.

"How do you live without texting?"

"Peacefully." Bowing her head, Anna put her hand on Tessa's tense shoulder. "Creator God, watch over this child in her journeys throughout Your sacred shared land. Protect her spirit from evil and the ancient dark forces all around us. We pray in Jesus' name."

"Amen," the women chorused. Tessa instinctively made the sign of the cross and crouched down to put her boots on, hoping she didn't pick up too much cat litter on her white socks.

"You have the divine energy inside you, my girl; the Creator resides within you." Anna handed Tessa her jean jacket. "You just need to have faith."

"What do you mean I have divine energy?" Tessa stood up with a frown on her face. "I'm just a normal person. A nobody."

"The animal spirit knows goodness." Anna pointed outside. "Spike didn't bark. I guess he wanted you to have the silverware," she laughed.

"You were an influencer before social media. Legendary."

After Tessa left, Anna stared out the kitchen window at her paradise on Earth. She washed and rinsed the teacups before mindlessly setting them on the dish rack. Circling golden and rust leaves drifted to the ground. A dark winter was coming. This was the calm before the storm.

Chapter 34

With the early-morning cloud cover dispersing, the glittering sun flooded the streets in warmth and ambient light. Slow-moving traffic crawled around the city as the residents geared up for a full day of Saturday shopping.

Jack Weber leaned over the carved oak table in his formal dining room, quickly scrolling the Dormin Times headlines over the top of his black-framed glasses. He stroked his neatly trimmed salt-and-pepper beard, sighing as he ran his hand through his thick graying hair. The caffeine in his morning coffee and limenade chaser wasn't doing much to calm his jitters. Knowing what was real and what was fake was getting harder every day.

Through the French doors, an agitated Jack spotted his wife, Abby, in the garden pruning her lush tomato plants, filling him with temporary calm. While he watched, a sudden gust of wind whipped through the forest behind the secluded luxury home. The blast forced ripples to form in the deserted swimming pool – a hot-day oasis in the middle of the meticulous gardens. The estate that he'd inherited from his father had both a stone-exterior main luxury house, and an A-frame log guest house.

Just as Jack was ready to leave for work, the doorbell rang, startling him as he was putting his shoes on. He wasn't expecting company. "I've got it!" he shouted, letting Jenny know that she didn't need to answer.

The visitor was a long-time associate, Chris Simon. "Good morning!" Chris sounded positively gleeful.

Jack grimaced. That tone sounded like trouble – *this morning was going to be anything other than good.*

Gripping a thin, golden envelope in his hand, Chris followed his host up the carpeted stairs until they arrived at Jack's study on the third floor of the house. He wasted no time placing an 8 x 10 inch photograph on the desk. "Look."

Unprepared for the gut punch, Jack winced.

"Her name was Angela Esperanza." Chris's voice cracked. Half the sheet was of a smiling, angelic, dark-haired little girl about three or four years old with big, innocent eyes; the other half – a completely nude, battered tiny body. There were black circles around her eyes, and she was very much dead.

We are at war, Chris." Jack swallowed the lump in his throat. "How dare they?"

"You know it. I know it." Chris nodded. "Our challenge is breaking through the mind control to let *the people* know it."

"Whoever did that is a sick, evil monster. They must be stopped!" As the rage built inside him, Jack clenched his teeth.

"It will get much worse before it gets better. Animals are the most dangerous when they're backed into a corner. And they'll keep lying until they're in handcuffs."

Jack grunted. The next two photos were collages of drugs and weapons stored in massive warehouses. Still standing, he quickly scanned them. "You mean..." he trailed off.

"Dulce periculum, sir." Chris said softly. "That's Latin for live dangerously."

Jack looked up with his mouth agape. "This is all coming from the southern border to Dormin? How? *Why*?!"

"All over the country. They need that border open to carry out their plans." Chris placed another photo down – a collage of security camera footage of prominent global personalities in horrific, compromising situations. One likeness was a still of a snuff video.

The last one was full of symbolism: a horned hand, an inverted pentagram, an upside-down cross. Disturbing imagery from a dark chapter in 1930s German history. The caption read, 'Do what thou wilt be the whole of the law.'

With shaking hands, Jack removed his glasses, taking care to set them on his bible. He buried his face in his hands.

Chris turned around, startled by his own reflection in the window. Short, curly black hair covered the top of his head and complemented the goatee on his square jawline. He'd moved from the Ivory Coast where his handsome countenance was plastered all over billboards during his modeling days.

Forming a steeple with his fingers, Jack placed them over his lips. "The rumors were true, then?" He took a long sip of limenade.

"Appears that way." Chris scratched his head. "It's a massive blackmail operation."

Jack studied the unsettling photos one by one. "What's our next move, Chris?"

The corporate media will be broadcasting your every move, trying to make you look evil, dangerous and unstable. You'll be guilty of treason in trail by media, then labeled a terrorist. They'll assassinate your character and try to erase you. The public will gobble it up." Chris smiled. "Your supporters will be their enemy."

Jack whistled. "What makes you think they won't assassinate me? Am I not important enough?" He laughed.

"Ha. No, it's not that," Chris appreciated the dark humor – it's how they kept sane. "They don't want to murder you and make you a martyr."

"Hmm."

Chris made his way to the door, then turned around. "Oh, there are a couple of people I'd like you to meet. Do you have a few minutes this evening? It won't take up much of your time."

"Eight?"

"Perfect. I'll arrange it."

Chapter 35

Back at the hotel, Tessa closed her eyes in the shower to savor the hot, soapy water washing the early morning stress down the drain. Maybe she should just go back to Manhattan and ignore whatever was calling her to stay in Dormin. The draw of high fashion and celebrity culture were stronger than any roots she'd ever laid down in western Wyoming.

Of course, celebrity culture was nothing new to Tessa when she first arrived in the Big Apple. In the 1950s, Hollywood had descended on their peaceful little town to film the blockbuster, <u>Bell Hound</u>, a thriller that dazzled both worldwide audiences and autograph-seeking locals alike. When filming finished, the cast and crew returned to Hollywood – leaving a mystery in their wake that intrigued the residents of Dormin for decades to come. Afterward, the Arem River valley had become a vacation destination for A-listers.

As much as she tried to convince herself that she needed to go back to the shallowness of New York, Tessa knew she was lying to herself. There was something sinister happening to her hometown that she needed to figure out.

With the forecast calling for a warm, sunny afternoon, Tessa slipped into a forest-green halter dress and Greek sandals. Her hair was styled in waves that fell to her shoulder blades. Designer shades, raffia hat, straw bag... she was ready.

Arriving at an address in the east industrial area, Tessa checked the address she had jotted down – 2112 Igans Avenue. *Right place.* She was parked in front of an aging, two-story, brick strip mall where a handful of **For Lease** signs were among the couple of dozen retail spaces. Small cyclones of warm wind picked up leaves and garbage and deposited them throughout the ample, half-empty parking lot.

Inside the building, the scent of new construction was interwoven with the residual odor of old building – a mysterious space where past and present were one. With her footsteps echoing in the vacuous, rough concrete stairwell, Tessa held her breath to avoid inhaling the musty odor.

The entrance chime sounded in **Room 222** when Tessa entered. The radio was tuned to the popular rock station, ZZZA, the announcer's warning of doom and gloom reverberating in the large hollow space. Darkness is only a heartbeat away.

Rows of florescent lights glared down on the otherwise vacant room, covered in purple industrial carpet and white wall paneling. Two closed doors were symmetrically placed at the back of the room, reminding Tessa of a set of eyeballs. Curved hallways branched off in either direction, like a mustache. *It's alive!*

An older, bearded man emerged from one of the offices.

"Oh, my God. It's you!" Tessa blurted, covering her mouth.

Jack Weber waved her into a sparsely decorated, modest office. Above his head, there were a few books stacked on a shelf next to a poster with scenes from Heaven and Hell. Lucifer in chains.

Tessa perched on the edge of the chair with her hands between her knees. "My name is Tessa Ryan," she began. "I called earlier."

"Ah, yes. Of course." Jack's face softened. "What can I help you with, Tessa?"

"Okay," Tessa began. "I grew up in Dormin. I left when I was sixteen."

"Sixteen?!"

"I was young and stupid. Okay?" Tessa flipped him a dirty look – he was getting on her nerves. *That escalated quickly.* "A few months back, I get this invitation in the mail from Max Fisher – a friend of my late father's."

"Ah, yes. Max." Jack smirked. "He and I go way back."

The noise level was picking up on the other side of the thin wall – hammering interspersed with laughter and stifled voices. The entrance chime had sounded several times.

"Wait...you're from here?!" Tessa searched her memory...the name didn't ring a bell.

"I was. I grew up here and left to pursue my dreams." Jack paused for a reaction. "I left before you were born."

"Ahhh... okay."

"I'm retired, and here I am. Back in Dormin."

Something was being dragged across the floor on the other side of the wall, followed by several loud bangs and the whir of a drill.

"I ignored the invitation from Max, then Thursday evening, I got notice that my mother was dying." Tessa teared up. "I hadn't seen or talked to her since I left," she whispered.

"Go on." Intrigued now, Jack placed his elbows on the desk to lean forward – the story of an estranged parent sounded disturbingly familiar.

"My intuition told me that I had to come home. To say goodbye. And to stay...almost like a... call...a calling or something..." Tessa stared off into space. "It's hard to explain."

"Tessa?"

"Sorry." Tessa returned to the present and shook her weary head. "Anyway, I left everything behind like that." She snapped her fingers. "The bourbon made a decision that I may end up regretting."

"That's why I don't drink." Jack leaned back to sip his limenade.

"Anyway, I go to Max's party last night, and you were there causing a ruckus."

"A ruckus?" Seated again, Jack couldn't hold back a belly laugh. "Well, I could have said we need a border wall. How's that for a ruckus?"

Tessa glared at him. *A racist misogynist. Lovely.*

"Tessa," Jack's condescending tone was accompanied by a brief tilt of the head. "I interrupted Max's exclusive little party – as an *invited* guest."

"Mrs. Max said as much, actually," Tessa conceded.

Leaning forward, Jack bit into his muffin, several brown crumbs landing on the growing piles of paperwork on the desk. "I guess he forgot that I'm both an investor and a stakeholder. Not to mention a taxpayer."

"Whatever." Tessa was running out of patience. "Sorry to hear about your troubles, but I need answers."

"Me too." Jack glanced at the window. "I owe my life to this place."

"What are you doing about it, then?" Tessa's tone was harsher than she intended. No need to take her own pain out on others.

Jack was unfazed. "Trying to get the public's attention." He shrugged. "National press helps."

"So that's why you..." Tessa trailed off as she started to put the pieces together. The laughter and chatter outside the room were growing increasingly louder. "And then this morning, I went to Old Town Square, and it was gone! Everything except the obelisk." To Tessa's right, the glorious golden sun beamed in through the small window. "It's just an empty, rundown space."

"I know."

"No whites!? What in the effing eff is that?" Tessa was wound up. "It's the weirdest thing. I mean segregation in the name of anti-racism. What kind of twisted logic is needed to justify racism as anti-racist!?" She paused for a breath. "Come on."

"Uh huh. It all seems backward, doesn't it?"

"It seems like another dimension, honestly." Tessa waited for a lull in the chaos outside the door while she checked the time on her phone. "A bad one," she added.

"That's because America fell, and we're now an empire run by a few over the many, rather than a republic where the many rule over the few."

"Ohhhh...you *crazy*."

Jack had an ear-to-ear grin. "And so, it begins."

"What?... Never mind..." *Who was this guy and why had Anna sent her here?* Tessa wore a mask of confusion. "Anyway, I get to the old corner store, and it was gone, too. A bakery with bars on the windows. Nobody remembered. Even a guy who said he's been there for decades."

"Wow."

"Right? Then I go to St. Theresa's...Hospital..." Tessa's bottom lip quivered. "I was about to see my mother, and she died when I got there," she wailed. "I didn't even have a chance to say goodbye or ask her about my dad." It was sinking in – her parents were both gone. She was now an orphan.

Grabbing the hand sanitizer, Jack passed Tessa a tissue and made a showy display of cleaning his hands. The small space filled with the stench of rubbing alcohol.

"It was cruel of me to run away, but I literally had no idea how to deal with her mental health," Tessa sobbed. Avoiding eye contact, she took a long sip from her water bottle.

"That's rough. I d –"

"Like, why am I telling you all this?" Tessa whispered.

"Because I can relate. But I was gone for fifty years, not fifteen! When I left, Dormin was half the size of what it was when you left."

Tessa stared at Jack, trying to figure out how old he was. *A thousand?*

"Let's just say I, like, have ties older than you." Jack winked.

"Whatever." Tessa was embarrassed that he'd read her mind again. "I should never have left Manhattan where everything was safe and normal. What was I even thinking?"

"Manhattan? I had some business dealings there a few years back. Enjoyed it. Met some great people. Made a lot of money." He pointed to the photo of the New York City skyline before the twin towers fell. "But not anymore."

"Why not? I love New York. It's so progressive." It was difficult for Tessa not to be taken back to Central Park and the day the towers fell. "No backward hicks to get under my skin."

Scratching his head, Jack jumped up to sit on the edge of the desk right in front of Tessa. "Progressive?" He raised an eyebrow. "Are you sure what that even entails?"

"No. Yes. I mean... well... like, I haven't ever really thought about it. I guess..." Missing Manhattan now, Tessa wiped a runaway tear. "I guess I just like what their platforms are. I mean –"

There was a knock at the door. Jack rubbed his eyes, amplifying his thick index fingers behind his dark frame glasses. "Come in," he sighed.

A good-looking black man around Tessa's age entered. "You need to take a look at this." Hot man glared at her as he set a file on the desk. "Soon." He closed the door.

Jack checked the time. "So, what are their platforms?"

"Equity. Social justice. Healthcare for everybody. Free college. Gay rights. Open borders. Climate crisis. Anti-racist. Anti-fascist. Equal distribution of wealth. No hate." Tessa stopped counting. "I've run out of fingers."

"So, divide people into tribes." Jack shrugged, clearly frustrated. *This again.* "Weren't you *just* talking about segregation in Dormin?"

Tessa frowned. "No. Well, yeah, but... I mean, who can argue with it? It's all about caring about people and the planet. Diversity and inclusion. Kindness. Empathy. It's social justice."

"Slow down there, warrior." Jack caught Tessa's eyes. "So-called social justice is a Trojan Horse for authoritarianism, for controlling every aspect of our lives."

"You're exaggerating. The vulnerable need protecting." Tessa's tone was dismissive and judgmental. "And deflecting won't stop us from doing that. Just sayin'."

"You want to be the white savior? You'll be ushering in an era of even worse discrimination. Alternate political opinions will not be tolerated. Tyranny is still tyranny even if it's called political correctness."

"Oh, come on. Nobody has that much power."

"They certainly seem to have power over you. You're calling rural people backward hicks at the same time you wonder what happened to the idyllic town of your youth."

"They *are* backward hicks!" Tessa was adamant. "I despise them and everything they stand for."

"The persecution of the Jews didn't start with death camps. It started with dehumanizing a group of people... just saying."

Tessa was taken aback at the suggestion... it hit her. She *was* looking down on them as second-class citizens! *But not like that! Right?*

"It's how you go from sexed-up brand-name lingerie models to blue-haired fat men who think they're women. And bald, fat women who think they're sexy."

"Rude much?"

"The proverbial slippery slope. You best rethink your strategy if you want to take on whatever killed our city."

"But –"

"New York seemed safe to you because you accepted the gradual changes," Jack continued. "Dormin went from a fond memory to a nightmare – seemingly all at once. A place where nothing makes sense."

"Yup," Tessa agreed, leaning back to avoid the sun. "Literally nothing."

"It's simple. Everything tyrants touch turns to crap."

"It's warm in here." Tessa was fanning herself with a piece of stray paper.

Jack opened the window. "What was happening in New York?"

Shrugging her shoulders, Tessa caught the mild breeze. The day was getting longer by the minute, and it wasn't even noon.

"I'll tell you what was happening, Tessa." Jack drew a long sip of his limenade. "The normalization of perversion, corruption, and lawlessness. The erosion of community, family values, faith, and constitutional rights." He didn't know how that wasn't bloody obvious to her! "How bad does it have to get?"

"I want to be kind and inclusive. I want to stop fascists." Tessa hadn't even heard Jack's words. Nothing had sunk in, almost like there was some force field around her that stopped the truth from penetrating.

"Fascists? Do you even know what a fascist is?" Jack hopped back onto the desk.

"Yeah. It's the evil, racist white supremacists. You know. The far right."

Jack smacked his forehead with his palm. "Tessa, Mussolini defined fascism as the merger of state and corporate power. There *are* no wings! Only corporations and the people."

"And what does *that* even mean?" It was lost on Tessa that she'd done legal work for corporations with too much power the whole time she was in New York.

"*That* means you don't know what you're talking about."

"You don't need to mansplain anything to me." *Such toxic masculinity.*

"You're free to leave." Jack was annoyed. "You came to see me. If you don't want to figure it out, don't waste my time."

Gazing down at the several disposal bins lined up in the alley, Tessa clenched her jaw. The berm behind them separated the highway from the building. "Is that why they're taking down the statues?" she asked softly, willing to concede a partial point.

"Tessa, they're trying to nuke an idea." Jack sighed. "They don't want a population of free-thinking individuals. People who can recognize the wisdom of the founders. People who know what true individual liberty is."

"What are you saying?"

"I'm saying that progressives call the founders fascists, and we need to get real here. When America is functioning as it was designed, it's the best system in the world. We can never right the wrongs of the past, but we can heal. Together." There was a crash right outside the door. Jack didn't flinch. "That won't happen as long as you keep talking about so-called *right or left wingers*." He made air quotes.

Tessa's face was devoid of emotion as she tried to process everything she was hearing.

"Hopefully, we can pick up the broken pieces of this country and build again."

Drained, Tessa stared into empty space.

"Politics is a den of venomous snakes, Tessa." Jack returned his glasses to his face. "Including Max."

Trying to shake off the nagging feeling that Jack could be right, Tessa avoided eye contact.

"Some of these sociopaths would kill their own mother to worship at the altar of ultimate power. Jack got down off the desk. "*That* is what's happening in Dormin."

"What? No." Tessa shook her head. "Max wouldn't do that."

"No. *You* wouldn't do that." Jack took his chair. "*You* don't think like a psychopath. Corporations now own the government. Like George Carlin said, 'You have owners'. That's *actual* fascism."

Unable to grasp what she was hearing, Tessa closed her eyes. Maybe Anna was right – the whole system *was* a lie.

"Not only *would* they do it, they *are* doing it, and they're getting off on it. Then they make the innocent guilty and the guilty innocent."

Swallowing the persistent lump in her throat, Tessa opened her eyes. "No. No, I don't think so. Max was like a father to me. He's not a bad man."

"If you say so."

"Are we done?" Annoyed, Tessa stood up to pick up her sweater.

"Yes." Jack turned his attention to the file marked *urgent*. The meeting was over.

Tessa raced down the stairs to the parking lot. *What was Anna even thinking? Why was she associated with this crude, bigoted blowhard? What a colossal waste of time.*

Chapter 36

Anna Hale parked in the narrow alley behind the aging strip mall; using her building key to enter from the back, she was in Jack's office in under a minute. "From my garden," she announced as she set a wicker basket on the cluttered desk. "I brought lunch."

Jack cringed while Anna divided up the watercress and tomato sandwiches on homemade oat bread and was even less thrilled with the fresh apples for dessert. "I'll have limeade, thanks." He held up his hand to refuse the cold green tea. "Don't you know how to turn those things into pie?"

"A little proper food won't hurt you now and then." Anna pointed to the extra roll around Jack's midsection while she opened a plastic container with carrot sticks and cucumber slices. "It's quiet. Where is everybody?"

"Lunch. We got a late start." Pushing his spare tire forward for emphasis, Jack clasped his hands behind his head while he leaned back. "So, did you get a smart phone yet?"

"I do just fine with my landline, thanks. I'll pass."

"Alright, luddite," Jack teased.

Anna shrugged it off. "Technology can be used for good, and it can be used for evil. The Unabomber was right about that."

"Yeah, and look where *that* got him."

"He's probably sitting in jail laughing his butt off, giving us all the middle finger right now." Anna bit into her sandwich.

"Don't I know it." Jack sighed. "But for some of us, it's a necessary evil." He reached across the desk for his plate. "Fight fire with fire. Beat them at their own game. You can't bring a knife to a –"

"Enough with the clichés, Jack. I get it." Anna smirked. "Thankfully, my Norman left me enough money that I can live without it."

Jack's eyes misted over as he approached the window. *Norm had been such a kind man and a good friend who had never fallen out of love with this devoted wife.* He begrudgingly nibbled on a carrot stick.

"How did the meeting with Tessa go?" Anna poured herself some more cold tea as a gust of wind blew past Jack, rattling the blinds in the process.

"Anna," Jack shook his head, his back still turned to his visitor. "...she thinks Fisher is an okay dude."

"She has no reason to think anything else." Anna grabbed a napkin to dab the corners of her mouth. "Yet."

Jack trained his eyes on the loose papers floating in the wind in the alley below. "She told me something alarming."

"Uh oh."

Turning around to face his visitor, Jack leaned his rear on the wide windowsill. "The manager at the Early to Late didn't remember the old corner store. Said he's been at the bakery for decades."

"That's impossible." Anna stood up to stretch, her tiny stature dwarfed by Jack's larger-than-life presence. "That store didn't close down until the recession hit in what...2008 or 2009?"

"2009, if I recall," Jack offered. "I was in California at the time."

Another blast of wind rushed in, sending the loose papers flying. Anna grabbed them in mid-air and covered them with an old-fashioned iron paperweight.

"Good catch!" Jack grinned. "What do you do for an encore?"

"Make you eat an apple." Anna's joyful laughter lightened the mood, temporarily shielding them from the reality they were facing.

"Good luck with that." With his stomach rumbling, Jack tossed an apple in the air, like a baseball.

Ignoring him, Anna poured herself another cup of tea. "When Tessa left in July of 2001, the population was right around 10,000 people or so."

"And?"

"It makes me wonder if those who never left somehow had their memories wiped; it's not a large population to experiment on."

"Like *you*? *You* never left."

"I don't live in the city, and even if I did, I'm immune to their propaganda." Anna paused. "Because I'm a luddite," she added with a grin.

"Which means that the only people who remember are those who left and came back." Jack held up his hand. "Like me and Tessa."

"Appears that way. There's a few of us, at least." Anna grabbed a napkin. "Dorminians have already been captured. It's up to the outsiders at this point."

"When did all this start, Anna?" Jack ran his fingers through his hair.

"You mean how did we end up in the Godless chasm that is this culture?" Anna paused to sip her tea. "It started by removing prayer in schools. Now, they're openly worshiping the devil."

"So, when we kicked Jesus to the curb."

"Yeah. Something like that. When they destroyed the family, it was only a matter of time."

"The way I see it, it was one thing after another…the sexual revolution and drug culture, abortion, mothers being forced to put their children into daycare due to a recession –"

"Exactly." Anna dabbed at her mouth and began cutting up an apple with the letter opener from Jack's desk. "Do you remember what happened with the war criminals after World War II ended? Right at the beginning of the Cold War?"

Jack gasped. "Anna, don't you care about germs?" He grimaced while he dumped hand sanitizer into his palms. "I thought you were into health. That's disgusting."

Anna popped a piece of apple in her mouth. "Alternative health focuses on prevention and natural healing, not a sterile environment." She made a face at him while she savored the fruit.

"Are you talking about the recruitment by the CIA?" Jack dropped his eyes to the grimy letter opener. "Eww."

"Yeah. Project Paperclip. When Nazi war criminals took over our entire government. NASA. The CIA." Anna's eyes were smiling when she handed Jack the letter opener so that he had to touch the blade. "The Gestapo became the FBI."

"Thanks." Jack dropped the letter opener into the trash. "And they were hidden and protected from prosecution by our so-called leaders. Ostensibly so they could get help in the Cold War."

"Don't forget that American corporations were using slave labor from their concentration camps during the war."

There was a knock on the door.

Chapter 37

Tessa hustled past the second electrified security gate to find a parking spot in the nearly full lot. *The old bat said 1:00 pm. Sharp.* The dashboard clock read **12:59**.

As Tessa pulled into one of the few remaining spaces, Adam Logose was nearby with his backside against his shiny red convertible. As he scrolled through his social media, he glanced up just long enough to spot a goddess in a sleeveless green dress exiting a white SUV with a sunroof. Bare, olive legs went on forever. Her long hair blew in the light breeze, framing the big shades and slight frown on her delicate face. On this perfectly sunny day, the scene was like an ad for a tropical vacation. He couldn't take his eyes off her.

Tired and irritable, Tessa most certainly didn't *feel* like an ad.

At exactly **1:00**, the main doors of Atluko Industries opened. From the outside, the plant appeared to have at least tripled in size. As the agitated white-haired security guard waved the crowd inside, the impatient horde pushed and shoved their way through the double doors. *As yes. The upper crust.* The guests cleared security again, this time surrendering their personal belongings. No cell phones. No bags.

Inside the sparkling, arena-size reception area, the opulence was surpassed only by the foul perpetual stench that reminded the party goers that they were in a meatpacking plant. Complete with a theater area and bar, exquisite sculptures throughout, and bronze busts of the previous three generations of Fisher patriarchs, one may have imagined they were in an art museum. The room had a showroom vibe with floor to ceiling windows on three sides where bright sunlight poured in, reflecting off the gold railings of the upper floor outer hallways.

Full of themselves and ridiculously expensive refreshments, hundreds of attendees mingled about in business suits worth tens of thousands of dollars and designer dresses from Zurich and Milan. Exchanging empty pretentious greetings, they turned their backs on the faux and nouveau rich – the class of wannabes about as inconspicuous as an NBA player at a midget's convention. *This* party was for billionaires.

With the aroma of assorted imported cheeses and peppermint catching Tessa's attention, she spotted a table laden with fine foods. *This crowd really knew how to flex.*

"Tessa, is that you?" Max made his way past the gleaming statue of the golden calf towards her, hustling and wheezing. "I didn't see you last night. What a beautiful young woman you've grown up to be."

"Hi Max." Tessa curtsied.

Cole was a few feet away, staring at her with a sardonic smile. He gave her a thumbs up and a wink as if he hadn't disappeared into thin air last night. Her pulse raced.

The chatter stopped when a hefty employee emerged from behind a double steel door in a wrinkled beige guard's uniform. *You didn't mess with Olga*, a serious woman with a rifle on her hip. With her unkempt mousy brown hair, it looked like she had just woken up from a nap.

An echo reverberated throughout the quieted room when the doors slammed together and locked, prompting a coifed middle-aged woman to approach the riser. Tessa couldn't place the decade, but it looked like the woman's clothes were vintage '70s – every fashionista cell in her body was offended.

The woman at the podium lowered the microphone to begin her presentation. "Good afternoon, everyone. Please take a seat." Her melodic voice had a slight accent...*Dutch?* The guests shuffled into the several long rows of chairs set up beneath the skylight. "Honored guests. Welcome. My name is Sheila Van Slyke, and I'll be the MC for this event..." *Yep. Dutch.*

Tessa scanned the crowd. *The 1%. The degenerate scent of old money dripping with exploitation and corruption.* She tried to mentally calculate their total net worth, giving up when she got to over a trillion dollars.

"...So, without further ado, I will waste no time getting to our first speaker. He's a man who needs no introduction. You know him. You love him. Please welcome our beloved Mayor, Graham Maxwell Fisher IV: businessman, philanthropist, mentor."

Through the hollow applause, Max approached the podium. When the Vice President of the United States is among the attendees, what was coming was no surprise: Max was being recruited for a top job in DC – *the* top job. He gave a canned speech and thanked the crowd for their support before retreating to his office.

With Max gone, the jumbo screen behind Sheila turned on. Everyone was mesmerized by the gigantic face of the dolled-up blond in the center of the screen – an effect enhanced by the permanent flashing *Breaking News* banner at the bottom: ***Darkness is only a heartbeat away.***

Jack Weber's face was prominently displayed in the upper right corner. Underneath it, the photo was labeled, *Guilty*. The anchor began her report in the highly recognizable and widely used language of journalists: Fakerish. "Jack Weber, the racist failed telecommunications contractor and perennial fraud, *appears* to be on the campaign trail. In an unprecedented attack on our beloved mayor and exalted humanitarian, Max Fisher IV, he crashed the special centennial celebration held at the mayor's private residence – as an uninvited guest."

Tessa blinked to snap out of her trance. "Uninvited? No. No." She pointed at the screen. "Mrs. Max herself said he had been invited."

Everyone ignored her.

Tessa returned her attention to the newscaster. "...assaulted Mr. Fisher, knocking him down. The unprovoked attack took place yesterday evening."

Standing up this time, Tessa thought she broke the spell. "That's not true. He's lying. I don't care what they are showing on the screen."

No reaction. It was like she was invisible.

"That's not what happened. I saw it with my own eyes." Tessa pleaded. "You were all there. Didn't you see for yourself?"

The news anchor looked directly into the camera with her spiraling eyes. "Jack Weber is a liar and a thief."

"Oh my God. You believe them. But it's not true." Tessa's eyes darted back and forth. Her heart was racing; she was drenched in sweat. *How could that be? Was she having a psychotic breakdown? Was she going to end up like her mother?*

With the screen now off, Sheila resumed her presentation like there hadn't been any disruption. Within seconds, an aggressive pasty-white guard with a military haircut grabbed Tessa by the elbow and pulled her toward the elevators.

"Do you mind?" Tessa snapped, noticing the Double S symbol on his lapel. *Literal gestapo? Whoa.*

When they were around the corner, away from prying eyes, the guard answered her. "I don't mind at all." His rifle was visible. "I'm just following orders."

Feeling a strong push of the rifle against her back, Tessa fell to the smooth concrete floor on her bare knees. *This guy wasn't playing.* She slowly got to her feet and followed him to the elevator.

The doors opened on the fifth floor to a magnificent wooden hallway with round, stained glass windows, and a high, molded arched ceiling. Numerous velvet-padded, deep mauve benches placed on either side of the oriental rug ran the entire length of the hall. Sunlight was pouring in from the huge, curved windows every several feet. After what seemed like a half mile, they arrived at a corner office labeled **Max Fisher IV, CEO.** Without taking his darkened eyes off Tessa, the guard knocked on the door with the butt of his rifle and disappeared back down the hallway.

"Come in!" a voice from inside shouted.

The view from the office was pure western Wyoming – wide open spaces surrounded by a rugged mountain range in the background. The secluded corner room was the perfect vantage point for Max to look down on the community.

Tessa barely heard the click of the lock over the sound of her beating heart. *What had she done?*

Max's lanky frame was formidable even hidden behind his massive custom-made desk. "Tessa." He motioned to a plush armchair across from him. The office was approximately the size of Houston and smelled like stale smoke and commercial cleaners.

"Hi again, Max." Tessa smiled sheepishly.

The bald man from the airport sprung out of his seat, clipboard in hand.

"Sit down, Dmitri!" Max snapped. His black ten-gallon hat was slightly forward on his balding head, creating shade across the top half of his face. A gaudy red corduroy blazer was paired with jeans. Dmitri slumped into his chair like an obedient little poodle.

Seated now, Tessa scanned the room. A recessed meeting area was filled with an oval, smoked glass table and fourteen high-back leather chairs – one of which was occupied by Dmitri. The walls were a metallic pattern that reflected the changing colors of the string of ambient lights.

Max lit a cigar, twirling it in his fingers before taking several puffs.

Tessa waved the repulsive spicy scent away from her face. "This place smells a lot more like bullshit than it does beef, Max." She fake coughed. "And smoking is disgusting."

With a quivering hand, Max twirled his handlebar mustache. Removing his aviator shades, he stroked his clean-shaven chin, blowing smoke directly in Tessa's face while he set the sunglasses on the desk. "Ah, Tessa." Smoke rings floated in her direction. "Little Tessa."

"Big Max," Tessa mimicked.

"An awkward tomboy always skinning your knees. An ugly duckling. And here you are, you return as a beautiful swan." His gaze dropped to her shapely bosom.

"My eyes are up here." Tessa pointed. "And they're stinging." A shiver went up her spine when they locked eyes – it was like he was possessed.

Max shook his head as he broke eye contact. "Where were we?"

Repulsed by Max's lustful stare, Tessa grimaced. "God's country."

"Tessa, you may not know this, but Jack Weber is a liar and a thief."

"I don't really know the first thing about him, Max," Tessa lied, pretending she didn't notice the several lines of white powder on the bar counter behind Max. She couldn't ignore what was across the room from it – a small stage with a pole. Anxiety welled up in her stomach when memories of **Club 23** surfaced. She blocked it out.

"He's a criminal and a fraud. Satan incarnate. Both an evil genius hatching a master plan to blow up the world, and a bumbling idiot buffoon. As bad as Hitler. Literally Hitler. No. Worse than Hitler. Jack Weber is a liar and a thief."

"Wow. That's impressive."

"I'm sorry you had to witness him pushing me down last night."

"That's not what happened, Max, and you know it." Tessa's eyes narrowed as she glanced toward Dmitri for backup.

Dmitri studied his trusty clipboard as if it contained the secret for escaping the zombie apocalypse.

"He might be a creep and a bigot, but you're telling lies about him. All he did was approach you and talk," Tessa snapped, wondering if maybe Jack Weber could be right about him.

"Dmitri, pour me a scotch, then go check on the guests." Max gazed past Tessa's head towards his assistant. "And bring me back some appetizers. This is going to be a long meeting."

Chapter 38

At Jack Weber's campaign headquarters, the pace had picked up. The resulting atmosphere one of both concern and urgency. The rapid knock on the door startled both Jack and his visitor.

"Come in if you have lunch." Jack answered, teasing Anna with a smirk.

The handsome visitor with a dark complexion was dynamite in an untucked, pale-blue, short-sleeve dress shirt and black jeans – high end brands from Paris left over from his modeling career in the Ivory Coast.

"Chris Simon, I'd like you to meet Anna." With his feet on the desk, Jack gestured toward Anna.

"Jack, you need to take a look at this." Chris put a thin orange file on the desk and turned his attention to Anna. "I've heard a lot about you."

"So, this is the whiz kid you hired?" Anna jerked her thumb to her left, her eyes lighting up when she smiled.

"Best detective in the country." Jack nodded. "If anyone can get to the bottom of it, it's him."

"Hot *and* smart? Irresistible combo." Anna winked at the visitor.

Chris smiled at Anna; he liked her energy. "Good time to give you two an update?"

"Perfect time, actually." Jack glanced at Anna with a gleam in his eye.

"They're planning something major in retaliation." Chris's eyes darted back and forth between Anna and his boss.

Dropping his feet to the floor, Jack set the top of his hands on the desk. "Like?" He didn't like the sound of this.

"I don't know yet. All I can tell you is that it's going to get much, much worse before it gets better." Chris turned to leave.

"So you told me," Jack's tone was flat.

"That's quite the introduction." Anna winked.

"I could tell you everything is rosy... but I'd be lying." Chris closed the door behind him when he exited.

Jack drew a long sip of his limenade. "What do you think that was all about?"

"You familiar with MK Ultra?"

"MK Ultra." Jack watched a rat scurry from under one of the disposal bins before turning his attention back to Anna. "Was that the LSD experiments?" he guessed.

"Partially. But there was a lot more to it than that. They were given massive amounts of a bunch of different drugs – including devil's breath. Plus, electroshock therapy and other horrible treatments that are too upsetting to talk about."

"What is devil's breath?"

"It's the drug scopolamine. Anyone under the influence will do whatever they are instructed to and have no memory of it afterwards."

"They could do *anything* with that!" Jack's mouth was agape as it sunk in. "They could program anyone they wanted."

"Not to sound like a conspiracy theorist here, but.... yeah, think of the possibilities...." Anna rubbed her blurry left eye, making a mental note to make an appointment with the optometrist.

"A conspiracy out in the open, you mean." Jack shook his head, still trying to wrap his head around how easy it would be to use devil's breath in false flag events.

"Trauma-based mind control. They're *still* using it."

"Which means?"

"It means they torture and traumatize people until they break their spirit. That's how they get them to do things against their will." The tears in Anna's eyes suggested she knew more about the subject than she was letting on.

"Are you okay?" Jack handed her a glass of cold water.

"Thanks, Jack." Anna smiled. "Yeah. I'm fine. I've been studying this stuff for years. Nothing shocks me anymore."

"It goes so deep."

"Let's not forget about Project Mockingbird – CIA infiltration of the media and culture." Anna downed her water. "They said it ended in the '70s after they got caught. It didn't."

"How can you be sure?"

"In the '70s, they prepared the stories they wanted aired and someone else read them. Now they're panelists on the six o'clock news."

"What do you mean *'panelists'*?"

"They're paid contributors. They use their position of authority to smear anyone who won't parrot the media. In any war, truth is the first casualty."

"How do you know this if you don't have a TV?" Jack muttered.

Anna couldn't suppress a laugh. "I know how to read... you know... what they call the rabbit hole?"

"And they've been planning all this since the beginning of the Cold War?"

"Likely sooner. The Third Reich learned something from their failures – namely, that they need total control of the mind."

His sleeves now rolled up, Jack put his feet back on the desk. "Anna, what are you implying?"

Not sure she understood the question, Anna blinked several times beneath her frown. "I'm not *implying* anything. I'm telling you that we need to learn from history – governments *do* turn against their people." She paused. "Did I ever tell you about Wounded Knee?"

"Touché." Jack graciously conceded.

Picking up her picnic basket, Anna turned toward the door. "We are going to take this country back from this criminal cartel if it's the last thing I do."

Jack's feet hit the floor with a thud. "So, you're saying this isn't just a constitutional crisis, but rather an existential one?"

"Precisely. We are in a spiritual war, my friend."

After watching Anna drive out of the alley from his second-floor window, Jack dropped the rest of his lunch in the trash. It was a hamburger and large fries kind of day. And two scoops of ice cream with sprinkles to top it off.

Chapter 39

While the speakers droned on about quarterly and annual earnings, profit margins, and investment opportunities, Adam Logose wondered what happened to the beautiful mystery woman. They'd already been here for over an hour and all he heard was *blah blah blah*. With hidden hands and shushed lips, nobody cared what happened in the building *if they got their big, fat payday for their 'charitable' foundations*. The entire weekend turned out to be an extravagant sales pitch.

From behind the press area, someone tapped Adam on the shoulder. He turned to face a small man who appeared to be in his 40s, though his round frames made him look younger. His prominent mustache and the goatee on his bottom lip were surrounded by a ridiculously full head of curly brown hair.

"I am Boris." The man whispered – he had a thick Russian accent.

"A pleasure to meet you, Boris." Adam timed his hushed reply with a nod while he reached for the outstretched hand.

Pleading with his eyes, Boris pressed something into the palm of Adam's hand before he disappeared into the crowd.

Sweeping his eyes around the room, Adam discreetly put the tiny wadded-up paper into his pocket. He got a sudden tingle up his spine. *What the hell was this place? Bleach and bullshit. Something was off. Way off.* He intended to find out what.

"Tessa. My dear girl." Max leaned forward to loosen his black tie. "You seem to be having some trouble understanding me."

"Uh huh." Tessa continued to stare out the windows of Max's office.

Without taking his eyes off her, Max rolled up his sleeves, simultaneously pulling a dark-blue, hard-cover book out of his desk drawer.

Tessa watched as he scrolled with his finger.

"*Blessed are the destroyers of false hope, for they are the true Messiahs.*"[1] Avoiding eye contact, Max slid the book back into the drawer.

"What are you saying, Max?" Tessa caught the image of a pentagram out of the corner of her eye.

"There's a natural order of things, Tessa." Max approached the table where Dmitri had laid out the food. "And that natural order must never be upended." He piled his plate high with shrimp cocktail and caviar, oblivious when a big drop of hot sauce splattered on his cowboy boots.

Watching the sauce fall in slow motion, Tessa was mesmerized. The dark circle on his boot looked so much like blood, the source of more than a few bad memories.

"Thank you for accepting my invitation for this weekend. Would you like something to eat? A drink perhaps?"

Dmitri appeared at Tessa's side.

"I would never miss such a monumental event," Tessa gushed. Turning, she flashed her genuine dazzling smile at Dmitri. "And I'm good, thanks."

"Sit." Dmitri wagged his tailbone and returned to his chair. The programming was strong in this one.

Max bit into the zesty shrimp sauce. "Tessa, you know as well as I do that I have given my heart and soul to this place, this plant, this city, the ranch, the county." Another blob of sauce fell to the napkin beneath his chin.

"Uh huh." Tessa suppressed a yawn. *This again – the Fisher family legacy.*

"My family were the founders and the builders of Dormin, and we've always fought for the people." Max licked his fingers.

Behind Dmitri, something caught Tessa's eye – partially obscured by a black velvet curtain that had shifted out of place. She wasn't certain, but the exposed part looked like an inverted cross.

Dmitri glared at her while he pulled the curtain back into position.

Tessa refocused on Max. He was going on and on. *Blah. Blah. Blah.*

---

1. LaVey, The Satanic Bible,1969.

"...I will do everything in my power to ensure that a man like Jack Weber doesn't ruin everything we've worked so hard for. He's very deceptive. Lies all the time. He's a danger to our democracy. Jack Weber is a liar and a thief."

"Okay, Max. I'll admit. I hadn't slept in almost two days. And I *was* standing at the back of the room. Maybe he did push you and I missed it."

Max smiled and nodded. "Exactly. Things aren't always as they appear." He dipped another shrimp in the sauce and shook it off. "So, when are you returning to New York?"

With her gaze on the sunny valley bellow, Tessa twirled a strand of hair around her finger. "I'm actually going to stay in Dormin."

"Stay?" Shaking his head, Max raised his eyebrows. "Why? I don't understand. Why would you come back? There's nothing here for you. Your parents are both dead and –"

"Wait, how did you know about my mother? That just happened, like, a few hours ago."

"I've got friends everywhere." Max shrugged, unmoved by the impact her mother's death might have on Tessa.

"Thanks for the condolences," Tessa shot back, irritated. "Let's just say I have my own reasons for being here. And I'm staying."

"Okay. Okay. I'm just trying to look out for your best interests," Max sighed. "And I'm sorry about your mother. I never really got to know her too well. She wasn't out to the estate very much. Just you and your father."

"I know." Tessa replied sarcastically. "I was there."

Max stood with his back to Tessa, choosing to ignore her cheekiness while he browsed the overflowing bookshelf. "And are you planning on practicing law while you're here?"

"Well, yeah. At some point. I'll worry about that after the funeral." Tessa was unable to suppress a yawn. "You know what it's like – so much red tape."

Having retrieved what he was looking for, Max turned around. "You've always been a voracious reader." He handed the book to Tessa. "Maybe this will get you started."

Tessa slipped it into her purse without looking at it.

"Welcome home." Max smiled. "You are free to come and enjoy the estate anytime, darling."

"Thank you." *Not feeling it.*

"Do you need money?"

"No. I'm good." She wasn't making *that* mistake again.

"Before you leave today, let's get one thing straight, Tessa."

"Yeah?" The energy shifted from bad to ugly.

"Jack Weber is a liar and a thief." Max returned the shades to his face for emphasis.

"Yeah, you've made your point, Max." Tessa sighed. "Although I'm not sure he's literally Hitler since that would take another dimension to pull off." She gestured that her lips were zipped. "Are we done?"

Max scowled over his shades. "If you forget what I said today, you'll regret it."

Tessa leaned her tense back on the door after she closed it, trying to catch her breath and slow her heart rate. *Shit just got real in there. Was that a warning or a threat?*

Gestapo guard appeared within seconds, slamming Tessa's bag against her chest. By the time he released his grip on her arm in the parking lot, white marks were visible – she'd clearly worn out her welcome.

Chapter 40

Full of racing thoughts about her telling conversation with Jack, Anna returned home from her trip to the valley. The tires on the van crunched on the graveled driveway when she pulled up to the house, prompting Spike to dash toward his beloved owner, groveling for a tummy rub when he reached her feet. With no wind, the surface of Lake Luis was like glass – a perfect day for a canoe ride.

Once inside, Anna retrieved the stepladder from the tidy storage room. Standing on her tiptoes, she reached into the corner of the hall closet with both hands, using her elbows to push the haphazard pile of seasonal gear out of the way.

"Tessa will need that." Anna set a small safe next to her overflowing basket of wool and a disinterested Puffball. He'd lost interest in everything but food and sleep in his senior years. She joked it was getting harder to differentiate him from the lifers in Congress.

In response to Anna's announcement, Puffball rolled onto his back to expose his round tummy. "Meow." Before long, he was sleeping again.

When Anna unlocked the safe, long-dead spirits roared back to life. And they were most unhappy.

At the plant, the huge parking lot was enclosed in a ridiculously high chain-link fence topped with barbed wire. Another enclosure, just outside the lot, housed several agitated, mouthy German Shepherds. *Where were they before the event?*

"Tessa!" Cole ran toward her as she got behind the wheel. "What happened in there?" He was out of breath.

"They er...requested I leave. After I told everyone that guy was lying, I was marched to Max's office." Tessa pressed the ignition key.

"Imagine that." Cole chuckled.

"It's not funny. That place is like a freaking prison." Tessa attempted to slam the door shut.

Cole grabbed it and leaned in. "Tessa, can I take you out for dinner? I'd like to continue where we left off last night." He pushed himself against her hip.

With her hormones out of whack, Tessa played with her watch. Since Aamon... it was dinner out, not a relationship... "Sure. Why not?" *At least he didn't assume her gender.*

Cole programmed Tessa's number into his phone. "I'll pick you up at seven." He pecked her cheek.

It was early afternoon, the perfect time for Tessa to grab a few hours of sleep. By the time 7:00 arrived, she turned sideways to study her trim figure in the long mirror. She spritzed on her favorite perfume. Grinning at her reflection, she silently thanked the fashion capital of the world. *Like a boss!*

While she waited for Cole, Tessa pulled out the book that Max had given her. **Fishers of Men** – the history of Max's family since they settled the Arem River Valley. *God complex much?* Rolling her eyes, she returned the book to her bag and forgot all about it.

Chapter 41

Neil Olsen, the herpetologist at the Dormin reptile facility, made his rounds to check on his residents. Scrawny Ronny, the thirteen-and-a-half-foot alligator, was motionless in his pen, basking under the heat lamps. Visitors to the Gardens were amused by his character: He was vicious, loved attention, and never shut his mouth – making him indistinguishable from most celebrities.

Neil saved the best for last – feeding a live rabbit to the king cobra, aptly named King Herod. When the ravenous snake needed his monthly meal, the thrill of watching the hooded twelve-foot snake devour the suffering animal was the perfect way to end the day. The sacrifice of innocents into the belly of the beast.

At this time of night, the only remaining employee in the dark, deathly quiet building was the custodian. In his lab across the hall from King Herod, Neil placed two vials of a clear fluid in his canvas briefcase and searched for the exit sign. He was late for a very important meeting.

In his meticulous office at **New World Now** (NWN), Adam Logose was enchanted by the images of the stunning woman on the computer screen. He'd taken photos of her with his contraband tablet (disguised as a paper notebook) from every possible angle without getting noticed. He sat back with his sock feet on the desk, fantasizing.

Sighing, Adam dropped his feet to the floor; it was time to get to work. Inserting the thumb drive from Boris, he forced himself to read the computer screen.

Having trouble concentrating, he read it again. One more time... it looked like a code... but something was missing.

Adam retrieved the crumpled-up note from the trash and smoothed it out to reveal the clearly visible imprint of the drive. He held it up to the light and spotted something faint. It came into focus when he squinted. The symbol sent a shiver down his spine.

Trying to downplay the information Boris had given him as either contrived or overblown, Adam focused on the expose he was working on for NWN. Deadlines always came too soon. He scanned the images from the party the night before and... There she was! *S*tanding at the back of the room near the grand entrance to the ballroom. He cursed for not having seen her at the party, blowing his chance to meet her. He couldn't focus *now*!

When Adam arrived home, Ralph was waiting for him on the back step. "Woof! Woof!" He bounded into the house and went straight to his food dish.

"Oh boy. A two-bark day. Must have been interesting."

Waiting for his dinner, Ralph used his secret weapon to speed it up – big puppy dog eyes and fluffy tail at high speed.

Adam unloaded the dishwasher and polished the appliances while Ralph ate.

"Woof!"

"Bedtime?"

As per their ritual, Ralph beat Adam up the stairs.

Chapter 42

The Bonjour ~ Au Revoir French Bistro was perched high above the sparkling city lights with a spectacular view of the winding Arem River. The upscale restaurant was packed, the wealthy patrons savoring the polished classical sound of a tuxedo-laden string quartet, and arguably the finest dining experience in the county. The delectable aroma reminded Tessa that she hadn't eaten since early morning.

Cole's burgundy turtleneck sweater fashionably framed his muscular physique, the bold color softly enhancing his surfer boy complexion. Faded jeans and a black, high-end blazer were complemented by a thick gold chain and an inverted cross through his left earlobe. He signaled for the waiter.

"Oui, monsieur?" The young waiter's black vest and bow tie made his white shirt appear luminescent under the mood lighting.

"Bring us a bottle of your best champagne," Cole ordered.

"Oui. Of course, monsieur." The waiter bowed and was gone.

Surprised by her date's lack of politeness, Tessa glared at him, wasting no time getting to her point. "What happened to the park, Cole?" Her voice was full of urgency.

"Park?" Cole's face was obscured by the elegant menu. "I'll need a... bit more information."

"Old Town Square," Tessa stressed. She hadn't even picked up her menu yet. "A prominent, central gathering place at city hall! Now it's no whites?!"

"In Black Fist Warrior's Park, *No Whites* is what we call diversity." In the uncomfortable silence that followed, they both intensely studied the menu like it contained instructions on how to escape from Alcatraz. After they placed their order, Cole patted the top of Tessa's hand. "Sweetheart, sometimes things are false memories. They only exist in our minds."

"Get lost with your microaggressions!" Tessa yanked her hand away. "Old Town Square was real."

"Of course, it is," Cole agreed. "In *your* world."

"Stop it!" Tessa hissed.

Cole ignored her. "Maybe things we *think* we remember are better left in the past."

"Like what?" Tessa snapped.

"Like relationships. We don't want to drudge them up, do we? If so, I'd have to tell you about my ex-wife."

Not liking the sound of the impending misogyny, Tessa narrowed her eyes. "What about her?"

"Well...she imagined things too." Cole broke eye contact. "Believed conspiracy theories she heard online, thought the media was lying."

"About what?"

"It doesn't matter about what. The point is that she didn't trust authority as a source of information."

"So... she was –"

"That's when she ended up in the sanitarium."

"What?" Tessa's heart raced while she thought about her catatonic mother in a hospital bed.

"Paranoid schizophrenia. She was hallucinating – a total nut job." Cole's gaze moved to the dazzling lights in the valley. He dropped his voice. "She's finally on the medication she so desperately needs."

The room spun around Tessa. "Oh my God," she whispered.

"I couldn't handle it anymore. Imagine having to listen to her drivel on and on about a powerful cabal of reptiles who drink the blood of children and something about adrenaline or adrenochrome or some other wild shit." Cole waved his arms around to emphasize his frustration. "Secret societies, a plot to kill everyone, CIA black ops. All kinds of stupid crap on and on and on."

"Cole, I..." Tessa grasped her stomach.

"What?"

Memories from New York crashed through Tessa's mind like a tsunami. *Those tunnels. Kids.* "Never mind..." She pushed the disturbing thoughts away.

"Maybe they have a big area in the Swiss Alps where they control the world or something." Cole winked at her with a half-smile.

"You never know." Tessa tossed her head back in genuine laughter.

Taking in the beauty of Tessa's dimpled face, Cole chuckled. "Never mind Switzerland. I'd rather talk about you. You smell delicious." He smiled as he grabbed her hand.

After the laughter, Tessa let her guard down. "So do you." He wore a cologne that reminded her of Tyler. Contemporary French music played on the sound system during the quartet's break, enhancing the soft flirtation between them.

"I've never heard of any Ryans in Dormin. No...wait. I've heard of Liam. Are you related?" His eyes dropped to her exposed cleavage.

"Hey! Up here, buddy." Tessa snapped her fingers.

"Sorry." Slightly blushing, Cole met Tessa's gaze.

Looking away, Tessa continued recounting her family's history. "My father was Patrick Ryan. He died four years ago."

Cole shook his head. "Not ringing a bell. Sorry." He wasn't about to tell her he knew exactly who her father was. "What about your mother?"

"Dad met her when he was stationed at Fort William in El Futuro County. My mom was adopted by a family from Colorado Springs after my grandmother died –" Tessa stopped in mid-sentence. "Why am I telling you all this?"

"My superior interviewing skills?" Cole's flirty smile made his eyes sparkle in the candlelight.

"I suppose I don't get the chance to talk about my family much. They're all gone." Tessa's hushed voice was full of guilt and regret.

"Is something wrong?"

"I'm okay." Tessa smiled. "Dad was in Vietnam. Painful memories. That's all."

"A Veteran. God bless him."

The lights in the restaurant flickered, then a bulb shattered a couple of tables over from them. The entire restaurant fell into silence while the harried staff attended to the scattered mess.

When normal conversation resumed, Cole continued coaxing Tessa to talk about her family. "What branch did he serve in?"

"Cole, I'd rather not."

Ignoring Tessa's plea, Cole continued to bombard her with questions. "Did he work after his service?"

"He was a mechanic." Tessa drifted off, turning her attention to the twinkling urban scene below.

"Did you have any brothers or sisters?"

"No. My mother was almost forty when she had me. It's probably for the best. One of me was enough." Tessa's eyes clouded when she recalled what a handful she was. "I guess that's why my dad doted on me."

Cole's eyes softened when he smiled. "So, what happened in the Ryan clan before your father?"

Tessa sighed. "My grandfather's name was Sean. His father was the first of our clan to settle in the area. His name was Liam. He –"

"I'm not following, Tessa. Are you talking about Liam *Ryan*?" Cole raised his eyebrows in shock.

"Yeah." Tessa nodded. "My great-grandfather."

Cole gasped. "You mean you don't know?"

"Know... what?"

"Who your great-grandfather *really* was."

"What are you talking about?" Tessa had her back up now.

"Oh, Tessa. Please don't tell me you don't know about his history? Come on, man." Cole's expression was a mixture of surprise and disgust. "He was a Klansman!"

"That's not true!" Tessa protested, her eyes instantly filling with tears. "I know a bit about my family history, Cole." She grasped her napkin until her knuckles turned white.

"Obviously, not enough."

"Whatever." With her usually soft blue eyes darkened in hurt, Tessa tore them away. "I traced my father's side back for generations in Ireland. He fought *against* racism – hardly the lineage of the Klan," she seethed.

"You can't believe anything you read on the internet." The waiter appeared with warm artichoke dip and pita chips.

Tessa scratched the inner corner of her eye with her middle finger. "Bless your heart," she murmured.

"Everyone knows the white settlers and founders were racist. They had backwards ideas that seemed acceptable at the time, but the country was built on hate."

"Actually, Cole, I don't think it was." Tessa banged her fist on the table, an action that drew the attention of the other patrons. "I think it was built on individual liberty."

"That's bullshit and you know it. It was built by slaves." Cole dipped a pita chip and took a long sip of his champagne. "Max's lineage was an exception – they were just a humble family, doing their best to help humanity."

"Seems sus." Tessa muttered under her breath.

"Didn't Max give you a copy of his book? He hands them out like candy."

"I know the story of my family. My grandmother was a Polish Jew during the second world war. Not exactly a *racist*," Tessa sneered.

"But you obviously don't know the real history of your ancestors."

"Cole," Tessa sighed. "it's been one long-ass, miserable day. I'd rather not talk about this right now."

"Of course." Cole downed the rest of his champagne. "Hey, what about that Jack Weber, huh?" He poured them each another glass of red wine.

"What about him?" Tessa was unsure about Jack Weber. He didn't seem to have many fans, and she wasn't that interested in politics except to be outraged at whomever the media hated.

"Well, it's just..." Cole hesitated. "It's just that I've heard some bad things about him, like how he hates women." When Tessa didn't reply, he continued. "He surrounds himself with criminals of all kinds – Italians, Russians, Arabs." He dipped another pita in the sauce. "And then last night, he punched and shoved Max at the party."

Sipping her champagne, Tessa locked eyes with Cole. "Cole, I was there. I didn't see you." Her memory seemed to be the opposite of what everyone else remembered – *was it, like, the opposite of the Mandela Effect or was she psychotic?*

"Well, I do have friends," Cole reminded her.

"Speaking of friends, how do you know Max, anyway?" Tessa's stomach growled while she nibbled on a tasty pita chip, freshly made from corn.

"I do some work for him from time to time. And I've seen Weber's ugly side. If that man gets any power in this city, he'll destroy it. He's not only a liar and a thief. He's dangerous."

"What a jerk!" With the alcohol beginning to take effect, Tessa mocked him. "Literally Hitler. Worse than Hitler."

Biting down on yet another chip, Cole ignored the trolling. "So, you're a lawyer, what kind of work do you do?" He reached for her hand, and their meals arrived.

Saved by the food. Tessa enjoyed the cultivated sound of the gifted quartet as she bit into the fragrant, delectable quiche.

Launching into tangential stories about San Diego and the deadly drug war in the Mexican border city of Tijuana, Cole sliced into his perfectly prepared rare steak brimming with seared portabella mushrooms. Something about busy ports where somebody was always up to no good.

Tessa watched his lips move until his voice faded into the background. She was getting a nagging feeling about this guy, certain by now that he was holding something back. She wasn't interested in any creepy skeletons in anybody's hidden closets. *Not again.*

The remainder of the meal passed without incident, the buzz of the champagne lightening their pleasant chatter.

Right outside the lavish glass building, a group of intoxicated teenagers had gathered to play on their phones and look for trouble. *So much for Dormin of old.*

Cole shoulder checked as he backed his black luxury out of the parking spot. "Do you want to come to my place for a night cap?"

"Thanks, but no. I'm exhausted. Could you please just take me back to the hotel?"

"Of course. I hope you enjoyed dinner." That was bro code for 'I'll be ghosting you'.

"It was lovely. Thank-you." That was finishing school for 'Go to hell'. "I want to get some rest."

"Of course, you do. I forgot what you've been through today. Good night." Cole squeezed her tense shoulder as she stepped out of the car.

Making her way through the familiar gold-trimmed lobby, Tessa glanced back at the silhouette of the car as it pulled away. That whole thing was just bizarre.

Chapter 43

In Jack Weber's luxurious study, a dim chandelier cast flickering yellow shadows onto the scene below. The grandfather clock was the only sound in the hushed room. Tick tock.

From the corner, a decorated military man sat motionless in the rocking chair, his facial expression a mixed bag of amusement and irritation.

The baroque energy of the ruby walls magically blended with the modern windows, arched and open. A hint of rain was interwoven with the nostalgic scent of the aging books.

Chris and the woman on the sofa fed their mobile habits, neither of them taking their eyes off the screens for even a second until…

"So, Chris, what did you come up with?" Jack broke the tension hanging in the air.

Clearing his throat, Chris put his phone on the coffee table. He rose to his feet, his nervous energy palpable in the quiet room as he paced back and forth in front of the windows. "We have a crisis on our hands. And it's urgent!"

"Oh…kay?" Jack scratched his creased forehead.

"This afternoon, we got information from an informant that they are going to destroy this town. *Before* the election." Chris stopped pacing.

Jack jumped out of his chair in shock. "That doesn't give us much time!"

"I know," Chris agreed. "We must find a way to combat the mind control, *now*. They'd rather burn it all down than relinquish power."

The prim and proper woman on the sofa, in her forties, gazed up at her host. "Hello, Jack. Call me Emma. I'm a clinical psychologist." She had a quick smile and spoke with a British accent, refined and sensuous to the ear.

"Good. I'm going to need one." Jack quipped, now nervously pacing behind his chair.

Emma crouched down at the coffee table to pour herself a glass of white wine. Her dark hair was in a bob cut, framing her round face and white cat eyeglasses. "Chris is right, Mr. Weber."

"Jack."

Emma's warm presence put the others at ease, despite the seriousness of her words. "When ruthless criminals control information, people are enslaved to a narrative that doesn't even exist."

"What do you mean, *doesn't exist*?" Jack asked.

"Well...what happens when you turn on your nightly TV news?" Emma remained standing. "Is it real?"

"You mean Operation Mockingbird?"

"All forms of media, actually." Chris leaned one elbow on a nearby bookshelf. In the large recess, a black-and-white Persian rug covered the center – the ideal canvas for the elegant Victorian furniture, patterned, and trimmed with gold.

Jack's eyes darted back and forth as he scanned his memory. "It's in war movies, too." He took his chair.

"*All* movies," Chris stressed again. "Whatever they are planning, Dormin is the test lab for the world. Have you ever seen the Truman Show? It's just like that – but for real."

"That movie is a metaphor for the imprisonment and torture of the mind." Emma tucked one dainty foot underneath her when she sat down. "As long as people *think* they're free, why would they want to stir the pot?"

"Subdue them with technology, and the ancient game of divide and conquer is easy." Chris tipped his red wine back to finish it. "Isn't that right, General?"

General Fowler, a man of few words sitting quietly in the rocking chair in the corner, replied with a half-smile.

Jack thought about all the hot-button issues people constantly fought over. "Hmm."

"That's why they only want to create problems. Problem – reaction – solution. It's another ancient game." Emma gazed off into the still, dense forest.

"Oh, come on. They're not *that* bad." Jack didn't sound convinced even as he spoke the words.

An unlit marble fireplace covered one wall, white layered drapes the other. The drapery was adorned with golden tassels that blended perfectly with the rest of the room.

"Problem – reaction – solution: It's called the Hegelian Dialectic." General Fowler leaned forward. "Think of 9/11."

Chris sat down across from Emma. "So, how do we reason with them?" He stroked his goatee. "Convince them that their fellow citizens are not their enemies?"

"We're competing against thirty-second soundbites and manipulated headlines that shape the people's worldview." Emma paused to sip her wine. "They keep us so distracted just trying to earn –"

`Ping! Ping! Ping!` The three mobile phones on the coffee table interrupted Emma with news alerts.

Jack automatically picked up his smart phone to check the headlines, sitting down in the process.

Emma and the General exchanged a knowing look.

"Yeah." Sweeping her eyes around the room, Emma nodded. "At some point, they need to decide they've seen or heard enough."

Embarrassed, Jack set his phone down.

Chris scanned the headlines. Stocks. Hollywood awards. Still troops in Afghanistan. He read the last article.

Waiting for his chance to address the room amid the distractions, General Fowler grunted.

In her attempt to lighten the mood, Emma drew Chris's attention away from his phone. "Here's this then. You know how many wizards it takes to change a light bulb?"

"Don't know." Chris shrugged as if he'd never heard the joke.

"Depends on what you want it to change into. Didn't you read Harry Potter?"

"No triggers, please," Chris laughed. "How many flies does it take to screw in a light bulb?" He grinned.

Nobody answered.

"Just two, but don't ask me how they got in there. *Badum tish*." Chris used his imaginary drumsticks to smack the imaginary hi-hat cymbal.

Emma blushed while the three men laughed at the off-color joke. "Well, I can see this team isn't going to be boring." Returning to more serious thoughts, her smile faded. "Anyway, it's all done to keep people stupid and dependent."

"It's working." Jack bowed his head. "Thanks, Emma."

"My pleasure." Dr. Langford exuded an elegance not unlike royalty in princess hats.

Jack turned his attention to the quiet, older gentleman rocking in the corner chair. "Thank you for your service, General." He nodded, respectfully. "What do *you* have?"

General Fowler cleared his throat. In his early 70s, he was a healthy, vibrant man who still maintained a strong military presence with his deep, commanding voice. "Manfred Fowler. US Special Operations."

"Thank you for your service, General." Chris and Emma exchanged smiles when they spoke in unison.

General Fowler acknowledged them with a nod. "We've been trying to warn people about this fuckery for decades."

"Is that the military term, General?" Chris teased.

"Okay. We tried to warn people about this *SNAFU* for decades." The General made air quotes with his index fingers. "Better?"

"Language more befitting of a refined lady, is all." Chris bowed.

"We tried to warn you that there was a massive military operation being waged against the American citizens. Everyone laughed and dismissed it as a conspiracy theory." General Fowler's voice was gruff, making it easy to imagine how the lower ranks responded to his commands.

"It *does* sound absurd and unbelievable to the average citizen, General." Chris acknowledged.

Jack and Emma exchanged quick glances.

"The corporate cartel has their own set of rules. They don't think like us. They don't feel like us. They don't act like us." General Fowler cleared his throat. "They're psychopaths." Silence. "You don't understand how critical this is. It goes way beyond a damned election." With his eyes darting around the room, General Fowler was leaving no room for misinterpretation. "It's apocalyptic!"

Emma was hesitant about the fear mongering. "But, General –"

"But nothing. That's so typical," General Fowler scoffed. "Your parents were all promised the white picket fence. And they fell for it."

"However –" Jack tried to speak.

"Sitting on your phones like that, you've fallen right into the trap," General Fowler snapped.

"How can we get around the use of tech in the modern world, General? Especially when they are using it against us?" Jack rubbed his sweating palms on his pant legs.

"They're using Artificial Intelligence against you." General Fowler stopped to scoff at the blank faces. "Think about it. They can develop the world in their own so-called *woke* image. That's a bloody nightmare."

A stunned silence filled the room when the rest of the team realized what they were up against.

"This country will look like China unless we stop the '*Woke*'." General Fowler meant business when he made air quotes again. "It needs to be taken down. Now!"

"But how?!" The panic in Chris's voice rose as the evening wore on.

"We need a parallel society with our own *everything* – tech, communications, finance, businesses…the whole nine yards." The General leaned back to survey the room. "They can scream into the abyss while we create our own reality – *actual* reality."

Rubbing his beard, Jack moved to the window to gaze at the dark forest behind his house, keeping his back to the room. "General, how do we create a parallel society? I assume it's more complicated than changing a light bulb." He turned to wink at Emma.

"Information is the new weapon of war." General Fowler stressed. "Independent media will create culture; combat their lies and thus, influences politics."

Jack appeared confused. "We don't have any institutional power, General," he sighed.

"We *are* the power," General Fowler scolded. "It *must* be done. Unless you want to live with the government controlling every aspect of your life."

"Not in this lifetime," Jack's mumble was barely audible.

"You think all these tech companies are organic, or privately owned?" General Fowler was incredulous. "You believe the stories that these start-ups were created by college dropouts without money?"

"Well…yeah." Jack was now even *more* confused.

"Absolute nonsense. The Pentagon runs social media, online dictionaries and encyclopedias *and* the search engines." General Fowler had run out of patience for doubters – what did they think *they* knew that the Military didn't? "They've got us by the balls."

"The General is correct," Emma confirmed.

"But now, it's going to backfire on them." General Fowler predicted.

"I hope so. The whole purpose of this operation is to launch a counterattack," Chris reminded them. "I just didn't know how bad it was."

"You ain't seen nothing yet, son." General Fowler stood up to stretch his legs, his commanding presence filling the room.

Jack leaned forward, clasping his hands together as a symbolic gesture that he'd connected the dots. "Sounds like a war, alright."

"And so, it is." Chris nodded. "But this war wasn't of our choosing. We just want to raise our families and be left alone. These lunatics have other ideas."

Jack pondered for a moment. "Chris, set up a war room – a command center."

"Where?" Chris wasn't aware they had any real estate outside a chunk of an old strip mall.

"Guess what." Jack's statement was a declaration, not a question. "I am the proud new owner of the abandoned Moreno Theater. It's yours. Do whatever you need. Money is no object."

"You're kidding??" Chris beamed, unable to suppress a grin. "I'll get on it tomorrow morning." He could hardly wait.

"I've taken up enough of your Saturday night." Pointing to Emma and Manfred, Jack stood up. "Are you aware that I'm running for mayor in the upcoming election?" They both nodded. "All eyes will be on this county – particularly the continuously expanding city of Dormin and their top recruit." He led the group down the stairs.

"Are we going to have enough time?" Emma slipped her shoes over her stocking feet in the entrance hall.

General Fowler turned to her while he slipped his leather jacket over his decorated chest. "Do we have a choice?"

Chris opened the door, allowing the cool, humid night air in. "We'll do a press release on Monday morning. Fresh news cycle. This should make their heads explode."

Jack enjoyed the visual as he locked the front door behind his guests. He wished his opponents' heads *would* literally explode – *that* would be awesome.

He clicked off the light.

Chapter 44

Checking himself out in the steamy bathroom mirror as he toweled off, Adam smiled at his reflection. With his athletic physique rippling under black boxers and a light blue t-shirt, he sat down to work. Although he wasn't looking forward to working into the wee hours of the morning, he knew it couldn't wait – what he was learning was spine-chilling.

Just before daybreak, Adam finally clicked off the lamp in his basement office to join a sleeping Ralph on the bed. The pair slept late on Sunday, another warm day with a golden sun and the nip of early autumn in the air.

Adam arrived at the busy plant for the cook-out around noon. The huge grounds were full of cheerful laughter and happy citizens – young and old, rich and poor, black and white. Bouncy castles were lined up next to the thick forest. A happy clown milled about, entertaining the kids. Young girls offered face painting.

While the growing city had become dangerous and divided, the citizens felt safe and united within the locked confines of the Atluko compound. Hustling local, state, and federal government politicians mingled among the undesirables, reminding them that citizens are too small-minded to govern themselves.

The citizens downed sweet tea by the pitcher. Loaded hamburgers, potato salad, and corn on the cob were on the menu. For dessert, everyone got a slice of centennial cake topped with ice cream and a special, unknown ingredient.

The public cook-out, an annual event, was special this year in honor of the festive occasion. It was the one day of the year the citizens gave thanks for Max's unselfish giving. Everyone in attendance received a special gift for attending – a glossy movie poster of the Miles Malone production: **Fishers of Men**. It displayed four generations of the Fisher family with Max IV shining, front and center.

After lunch, the expertly edited documentary – a convincing, tear-jerking tale of sacrifice and philanthropy – aired on the jumbo screen, the music carefully chosen to move the audience to tears. The impressionable children, their skin painted with instant tattoos of the company logo, stared directly into the news caster's spiraling, hypnotic eyes.

By nightfall, Dormin Reptile Gardens was shut down for the day. The custodian whistled as he made his rounds, cleaning around the enclosures of the residents. He turned the corner to... his heart skipped a beat. King Herod wasn't basking under the heat lamp. *Odd.*

Under the glare of the hall light, the custodian cautiously entered the enclosure, whipping his flashlight from side to side, almost anticipating a snake bite to the back of the neck.

The room was empty!

Chapter 45

Before sunup on Monday morning, most of the tables at the iconic Near and Far Café were already full. Just down the street from city hall, it had remained one of the few constants in the declining city center. Originally a '50s diner that had retained its retro charm, the café was rundown, but had a reputation for the best home-style meals and cinnamon rolls in the county.

In their regular booth, Jack Weber and his sidekick, Chris Simon, were holding an impromptu breakfast meeting to discuss the next step in their plan.

"What was the good General going on about on Saturday night?" Jack sipped his sweet coffee.

"You heard him." Chris spread raspberry jam on his toast. "We need to develop a parallel society, parallel media, parallel culture, parallel finance, parallel economy... the people's law enforcement... everything."

"This again?" Jack sighed while he salted his pan fries. "Chris, I get a headache just thinking about it."

Dropping his eyes to Jack's chest, Chris downed a full glass of ice water. "Aren't you supposed to cut back on salt?"

The noise level fluctuated as customers picked up their fresh-baked cinnamon rolls. Jack picked up the saltshaker and sprinkled all his food liberally.

As Jack massaged his stiff neck, the reflection of the overhead light drew out the defeat in his eyes. "How are we going to go up against that kind of power? When they literally decide what reality is?"

"Considering the Pentagon has taken over the little freaks in Silicon Valley, it's going to be a challenge. Especially when their Alma Mater consists of Stanford, the Harvard University drop-out list, and communist rallies." A grin spread across Chris's face. "I'm not sure if that's connected to the blue hair, or if it's wokeness itself that causes brain damage."

The men's raucous laughter drew the attention of other patrons.

"Gentlemen," Jack looked around while he summoned his inner New Yorker. "Thanks for the moment, but my buddy and I are trying to have a little meeting, here. Ya dig?"

"Ya dig?" Chris couldn't suppress his man giggle. "I'm down with that."

Unamused, Jack picked up his last piece of bacon. Burnt – just the way he liked it.

Chris tossed his napkin on the empty plate. "The politicians –"

"Don't get me going on politicians." Jack snorted. "I mean, have you seen some of those fossils? Most of them live to be about 800 years old if Congress and...like the Canadian Privy Council are any indication."

"Ha. You aren't kidding." Chris excused himself. When he returned from the restroom, the table was cleared of their empty plates and a fresh, steaming cup of coffee awaited him. He leaned over the steam, closing his eyes while he inhaled the aroma. "Money talks. Bullshit walks."

Overhearing what the two men were talking about, several other patrons turned their heads toward them. Chris gave them all the thumbs up – then it was the most interesting meal they'd ever eaten, and they were Gordon Ramsey.

Chris dropped his voice. "Society is split in two – two distinct factions with irreconcilable differences have emerged."

"Isn't that why we're at war?" Jack whispered.

"Indeed. Our side believes in a unified constitutional republic with decentralized power structures. We believe the Constitution governs our representatives."

"As it should," Jack acknowledged with a nod.

"Exactly. Well, *their* side believes in a multicultural democracy governed by mob rule. They think the Constitution is an archaic document, and their intention is to take over the country through violent revolt."

"Exactly what they accuse our side of doing. So, again. How do we fight back against that kind of extremism?

Chapter 46

When the sun rose, Dorminians awoke to the persistent call of a bald eagle perched high above the tranquil city. The mighty Arem River wound its way down Diablo Mountain like a belly dancer, the thundering rapids a reminder of the Creator's awesome power. On another unseasonably warm day, sunlight beamed down from the cloudless sky, the mild breeze scattering the mysterious ambiance of the celebratory mood.

In a massive facility deep beneath the surface of the Earth, teams of energetic researchers in goggles and white lab coats worked around the clock with a growing sense of urgency. It was early Monday morning, and production was in full gear in the hidden laboratories at Atluko Industries. Among the beakers and vials, the noxious odor of chemicals was overpowering.

Several floors above them, Max Fisher and his inner circle prepared to take part in two days of video discussions for the Global Dormin Group. They were a collection of thirteen sociopaths from around the globe, a group about as diverse as a bag of white marshmallows. Comprised of all the usual suspects, the worst parts of humanity were well represented. Among others, the Bermuda Triangle of virtue met in London for the conference – London, Paris, and New York. The empire's Public Relations team was in DC with Hollywood and the corporate media. Of course, *nothing* happened without the Vatican.

Today's meeting was with a branch of the group called *Lectumi Incolui Edaxacis Secutoris* (LIES). The **League of LIES** had been started by Dr. Wolfgang Benedict Hertzig in 1984. A German microbiologist, he had since been rewarded by the pharmaceutical industry with numerous prestigious awards and hefty research grants. He would be chairing the event from Switzerland.

Sporting a white lab coat and a holier-than-thou mindset, the 89-year-old Wolfgang occupied a seat underneath an eye-shaped shadow on the wall – a Bond villain, if ever there was one. His receding hairline framed the wire-rim bifocals that rested on the end of his nose, thin lips punctuating his excessively drooping jowls. Everyone was now on the call, ready for the meeting to begin.

"Gentlemen." Wolfgang leaned forward when he spoke, commanding the attention of the entire group with the edge in his voice. "Ze time has arrived."

Chapter 47

Exhausted, Tessa barely got out of bed on Sunday, trying to recover from the wild whirlwind that was dismantling her life; she needed just one day to indulge her self-pity. By Monday around noon, she found herself at the **Diablo Mountain Mall**, scanning the infinite area in the noisy food court for an empty seat.

"Teresa Ryan?"

Tessa turned around at the sound of her official name being uttered by a soft, feminine voice. "It's Tessa," she corrected the speaker. Two women around her age were seated; she recognized them instantly. "Hey guys!"

"Looking for a place to sit down, darling?" Amy Thompson was a former classmate who hadn't aged a day in 15 years.

The other woman, Kaitlin Sinclair, was as opposite her companion as you could get. Covered in tattoos and piercings, she gave off a definitive 'don't mess with me' vibe. Cursed with stunted growth, she'd barely made it past five feet, a matter made worse by her considerable width. Political correctness aside, she was short and fat.

Tessa plunked her tray down to take what seemed like the last seat on Earth. "Teresa is what my mother called me when she was angry," she reminded them.

"Hi, Tess." Kaitlin's smile was overshadowed by the harshness in her eyes – this gal had been around the block.

"Imagine this. Haven't seen you two since we graduated." When Tessa smiled, her pronounced dimples sunk into her cheeks.

"We're married!" Amy gushed, barely able to contain the news.

Tessa inspected their rings. "Nice." She wasn't impressed with diamonds, those so-called precious rocks. *Sure, they were rare, but had no useful purpose. Marketing.* "Congratulations."

"Thanks." Tessa's companions chorused, apparently not noticing that her comment on the rings was less than enthusiastic.

"What happened to the old class? Where is everyone?" Tessa sipped a spoonful of hot and sour soup, ready for a change of subject. "What happened to Old Town Square?"

Patrons were circulating through the area, the noise level picking up as the day wore on. The blended scents of several ethnic foods were tantalizing and pervasive – curry and cinnamon the most noticeable.

Kaitlin and Amy exchanged puzzled glances.

"The park! At city hall." She searched their faces for any sign of a memory.

"At city hall? You mean... Black Fist Warriors Park?" Amy's eyes lit up. "Where they had those God-awful *racist* statues?" After scrolling for a minute, she handed her phone to Tessa.

Swiping through the photos of an angry crowd defacing and tearing down the statues in Old Town Square, Tessa felt sick to her stomach. She set her spoon down as she handed the phone back to Amy. "Well, that's one way of looking at it. I guess."

Now, Amy was confused. "What do you mean by that?"

"Well...to me..." Tessa stopped, trying to decide if she should even continue. "Well, it looks like history being erased."

Kaitlin broke the uncomfortable silence that followed. "Tessa, I'm not sure what happened to you. You never used to be racist?"

"Racist?!" With an exasperated sigh, Tessa dropped her shoulders. "What are you talking about? I've always believed that those who forget history are doomed to repeat it."

The exchange had drawn the attention of several other patrons – they were looking at Tessa like she had horns on two of her three heads. She swept her eyes around the room like a magic wand, instantly making the spectators disappear back to their substandard food.

"Well –" Amy began.

"For sure the founding fathers had faults, but they understood human nature, and humanity's necessity to protect their liberty from power-hungry tyrants." Tessa searched their blank faces for some sign of understanding.

"We can't be held back by outdated thinking, Tessa." Amy was adamant. "The founders owned slaves."

"I know." Annoyed at the suggestion she didn't know history, Tessa nodded. "The guy who wrote the Declaration of Independence wanted an anti-slavery clause, but too many in Congress had a vested interest – so it was removed."

Amy's frowning face said it all.

"Sadly, not a lot has changed about Congress – they're *still* in power for themselves. But slavery didn't start in America. It ended in America. It's been abolished." Tessa downed another spoonful of soup. "Too bad black Americans are *still* slaves."

"Huh?" Kaitlin belched again. "Are you a crazy lady?"

"The destruction of black people happened right before our eyes – long after the Civil War was over." Several tables away, a baby began to cry. "Social policy in the middle of the last century intentionally *destroyed* black communities."

"How were they destroyed?" After making air quotes, Kaitlin leaned back with her arms crossed. "Jim Crow ended in the middle of last century. Are you in favor of segregation?"

"They were destroyed when fathers were removed from the homes and government became the provider." Tessa picked up her coffee cup.

Amy raised her eyebrows. "If they get everything they need, I don't see the problem with that."

"They had room and board on plantations, too," Tessa reminded them.

The look of shock on Kaitlin and Amy's faces was priceless.

"That's not the same, Tessa." Amy was irritated. "They need us to help them. They don't know where the DMV is or how to use a computer."

"That's why we can't have voter ID," Kaitlin added.

Tessa's jaw dropped. "You think black people are so stupid and useless that they need white saviors? The soft bigotry of low expectations is about as racist as it gets."

"But –"

"Everything good about this town has been decimated. All I've seen here is pain. Broken families. High crime. Poverty. Homelessness. Drug epidemic. A crumbling city." Tessa stopped to scan the audience they'd amassed. "How is that better than when we grew up?"

"Abortion is legal." Amy crumpled up her sandwich wrapper.

"Look. I'm not going to get into debating such a complex issue, but just know that the woman who started the most prolific abortion clinics in the country – and best-known lobbyist, I might add, was a known white supremacist. *Margaret Sanger.*"

"More conspiracy theories." Amy sighed. "I can't believe this happened to you."

"She literally wanted to kill black babies and ssssaid as much!" Tessa unintentionally hissed.

Kaitlin paused. "By the way, weed is legal in Dormin. And we can get married now."

Seeing exactly where it was heading, Tessa got to her feet. These gals were overlooking dystopia for the cult doctrine. "I'm in the process of moving back here, and I got stuff I gotta get done." Though they'd exchanged phone numbers, she hoped she never talked to them again. She had a gut feeling about this crazy tag team, and it wasn't good.

With a final glance around at the people who had gathered, Tessa walked away.

Chapter 48

With Max and his inner circle once again gathered in his fifth-floor office at Atluko Industries, the League of LIES group kicked off their afternoon global video discussions. The session began when the chair, Wolfgang Hertzig, held up a thick report to the camera entitled **Project 8-ball** – a psychological operation (PSYOP) that Wolfgang's protégé and sadistic advisor had been working on for years.

Though Wolfgang's advisor wasn't taking part in the event, his chilling philosophy permeated the entire event: *There is no God. There are no choices. Humans are controllable animals.*

Chapter 49

As she left the mall, Tessa scrolled her phone with her right hand while she balanced several large bags in her left. Something cold, hard, and metal smacked her in the forehead, forcing her bony rear to hit the concrete floor with momentum. Dazed, she looked up from her rather unusual vantage point – she had been trying to go Out through the In door.

The man on the other side of that door was there in an instant. "I'm so sorry. Are you okay?" It was *her*! Adam's heart skipped a beat.

"Yeah, just my ego is bruised. Well, that and my as...tailbone. I should've been paying attention." It was dark outside, the mall traffic slowing down – was it that late already? She glanced at her watch while she and the stranger crouched to gather the contents of her shopping spree.

"You seem pressed for time. I won't keep you." The stranger extended his hand. "I'm Adam, by the way."

"Tessa. Pleased to meet you."

"The pleasure is all mine, Tessa." Adam waited for her to get steady on her feet. "Not to sound creepy, but I couldn't help but notice you at the plant on Saturday. I was there with **New World Now**."

Tessa's pulse raced at the sound of her name on his lips. With her in heels, they were the same height. "Oh no. Cringe," she giggled, enjoying the accidental meeting.

"Don't worry. Nobody else did." Eyeing Tessa with a mixture of enchantment and amusement, Adam winked.

Tessa studied the impeccably groomed, attractive man. "I thought you looked familiar." He appeared to be mixed race, but she couldn't tell exactly what ethnicity, not that it mattered – he was hot as hell.

"The way you stood up to that crowd at the plant on Saturday, most of them probably wished they had your balls," Adam chuckled. "Metaphorically speaking, of course."

"My metaphorical gonads are made of only the best silicone," Tessa laughed. "Like most bodies these days."

Adam decided to take a chance, his mind and body both alive with excitement. "Hey, Tessa, if you're not busy, do you want to go to the Over Under Irish pub in the mall for dinner?" He gestured with his head.

"No thanks, I've gotta...." Tessa began.

'*What? I've gotta what? Go back to an empty hotel room?*' "Yeah. I would like that. I'm starving," Tessa accepted the invitation. "I'll put my things in the vehicle and meet you inside."

Inside the pub, haunting Celtic music was playing – a rhythm that the busty young servers in short highland dresses and double braids kept time with. Steaming plates full of lamb stew and shepherd's pie were presented on big trays, their scents tantalizing the imagination. The bartender kept busy serving shots of Irish whiskey and beer on tap to the increasingly intoxicated patrons. Myriad silk plants and mirrored walls surrounded them, creating the illusion of dining in a jungle.

With her head full of stories about her Irish roots and the memories of the trip she took in 2010, Tessa ducked into the high back booth across from Adam. Scanning the busy restaurant in the soft light, she was almost...giddy. The burly blond bartender with a cupid tattoo on his forearm set a glass of chilled white wine and a mug full of dark stout on the polished wooden table.

Aware of the instant chemistry between them, the dinner companions studied the menu like it revealed the location of the crown jewels. Without looking at each other, they placed their orders...then their eyes met. Tessa's stomach did a somersault like a hesitant acrobat on a dangerous trampoline. "So, Adam...here we are." She batted her long, natural eyelashes to break the ice.

"Here we are... pretty lady." Adam's voice was low and sensuous.

Tempted by his charm, Tessa put her guard up. "So, you work with New World Now, huh? What do you do there?"

"I'm an investigative reporter." Adam made a face like he knew exactly what society thought about reporters these days. "I'm working on an expose for them."

"Ohhh... sounds adventurous! What's *that* like?"

"I haven't been there long enough to know. Let's just say the honeymoon is over."

"What are you working on?"

"I'm not at liberty to say. It's a special assignment contract."

"And that is?"

"A big pain in the ass." Adam finished.

Tessa grinned. A sense of humor; she liked that. "When do we get to hear the story?"

"When it's finished. At the rate I'm going, that will be in the year 2099."

"Then stop asking random women to dinner and get to work," Tessa suggested with a provocative smile.

"Not on your life, beautiful. I want to get to know you better."

Tessa's pulse raced while she twirled a strand of hair around her index finger. "What did you do before New World Now?"

"I worked for EYE On Dormin."

"You consider NWN a step up?" Skeptical, Tessa raised an eyebrow.

"It's complicated." Adam winked. "I'd tell you, but then I'd have to kill you."

"Ha ha..." Tessa eyed her companion suspiciously. "I think."

"So, Tessa... what happened to you yesterday after you... um..."

Once again, Tessa relished the way he said her name. "I was escorted out after an impromptu meeting with Max. I feel like I'm in Crazytown. I can't believe what I see with my own eyesss now," she hissed, her speech barely keeping up with the rushing thoughts.

With Tessa's tone catching Adam off guard, he lowered his head. "Well, I wouldn't go –"

"What happened after I left, Adam?" Tessa whispered as she looked around, not even trusting the booth to keep its mouth shut.

Adam also dropped his voice to a whisper. "An elaborate sales pitch for investors." He leaned in like he was going to drop a bombshell report on a comic book villain's tax returns. "The tour was a lie."

Although they were using hushed tones, Tessa looked around again, hoping nobody was eavesdropping. "Were you invited to anything else?" She wondered if this was what it was like to star in a spy thriller as the exotic leading lady.

"Got an invitation to the whole event, and an all-inclusive vacation package. For two." Adam grinned as he scanned her breasts.

Feeling a sudden rush of excitement, Tessa didn't feel the urge to redirect his gaze to her eyes. "If I didn't know better, I'd say that is a bribe for favorable coverage." She lifted her head to reveal more of her alluring neckline.

"Tessa...I –" Adam caught Tessa's eye while his smile faded.
"Did anything else happen besides, well...what Jack and I did?"
"Jack?"
"The guy who interrupted Max's big event?"
"Oh... him." Adam shook his head. "No. After *you* were shown the door, the rest of it was a snoozefest." He pretended to yawn. "A few of us were wishing you'd stuck around. Especially this few." He focused on Tessa's naked ring finger before taking her dainty fingers in his strong hands.

To Tessa's chagrin, a strange, shocking sensation went through her. In the fortress she'd erected around herself after Aamon, she thought she could extinguish any spark. Yet here she was.

Chapter 50

Opaque, seemingly impenetrable fog rose from the icy cold water of the Arem River like a fat, puffy white snake slithering its way down the valley and devouring everything in its path. Regular Tuesday morning commuters navigated their way through the thick clouds at a snail's pace, completely unaware that at Atluko Industries, something sinister was taking place in Max Fisher's office.

By the time the morning traffic had started, the thirteen men of the global League of LIES group were well into their last day of video meetings. Presentations on the use of the internet in psychological operations and how to deal with dissenters were scheduled for the morning.

The group learned that before there was the internet, there was ARPAnet, its grandfather. It had been developed by the US Department of Defense in conjunction with CERN – the entire *premise* of the internet was a lie. In fact, even television had started using a similar deceptive technique – if they could find a way to broadcast into every living room, they could control the narrative. All the world's a stage, they said. Sold as entertainment, it was mind control on steroids. For the actors, it's a job in the performing arts. For the spectators, it's reality.

As new technology threatened the official narrative, the empire gobbled up every new startup as soon as they began. Once they'd taken over every nook and cranny of cyberspace, the entire industry was crawling with feds. Their job was to avoid nuance by keeping discussions black and white – a well-known technique for controlling the population through shaming and ridicule. They openly admitted they had six ways from Sunday to shut down anyone going against the security state, and they weren't afraid to use them.

A discussion about the very real threat of independent journalism ensued as they collectively lamented a new breed of resistant influencers. The empire was prepared to go thermonuclear on dissidents with the implementation of **Operation 5D:** Destroy. Discard. Deny. Deflect. Diffuse.

The bag of tricks was varied. A distortion or misrepresentation of the opponent's actual points or exploitation of a weakness (strawman fallacy) was one such method. Attacking the messenger instead of the message (ad hominem) was another technique they used to take the focus off themselves. They could financially cripple their opponents until they didn't have the means to fight back. Targeting advertisers and the use of lawsuits to drive them into bankruptcy. They have no choice but to surrender.

A favorite of the empire was the wrap up smear in which they leaked falsehoods to the press and then used the press to back up their accusations. Another was employing euphemisms such as 'trust and safety', a polite term for censorship – hate speech was their golden goose. If they could get regular people to believe absurdities, those very same people would commit atrocities.

Above all, the empire knew that lies only work if they're dispersed among the truth.

Chapter 51

Driving past her old school, Tessa squinted to see the crumbling building through the thick fog. Both the State and American flags were gone, replaced by a rainbow and a black fist. *Wow*! America was being replaced. It didn't seem like a big deal back in New York, but *this* was different. *Now*, it was personal.

A row of iconic school buses spewed noxious fumes into the air while they idled, and through the sea of yellow, Tessa spotted murals of Max on either side of the main double doors. Above them, the school's name was prominent: Max Fisher IV Elementary School. His condescending presence was everywhere. A rush of bundled up, robotic, demoralized kids made their way inside while the bell rang.

Turning the volume down on the radio, Tessa continued up a gradual incline, a short distance up the mountain. Just past the bakery, she entered a residential area where a few dried brown leaves dangled from the mostly barren branches of the maples on Broken Arrow boulevard. A patchwork quilt of vibrant Autumn foliage covered the weedy lawn and flowerbeds below.

A light mist accumulated on the windshield, creating fog on the inside of the windows. Setting the wipers to intermittent, Tessa turned the heat up in the SUV. She turned right onto Maple Street into an older neighborhood with rows of matching houses, verandas, century old vegetation, and narrow sidewalks in need of repair.

The knot in Tessa's stomach tightened as she approached....

Her childhood home was gone! In its place was an overgrown lot with a bent and weathered **For Sale** sign, swaying and creaking in the brisk wind. The elms remained. The lilac bushes and caragana that had once surrounded her family's house were still there. It was like the house disintegrated.

Despite the rain, Tessa left the SUV door open when she exited, dragging the heels of her boots across the damp soil on the front yard. Several feet onto the lot, she crouched down to look for the foundation in the thickets.

"Good morning."

Struggling to regain her balance when she jumped to her feet, Tessa spun around on her heel. "Hi?"

The greeting had come from an apprehensive, young woman with bright-pink, messy hair and a sleeping toddler in an enclosed stroller. Barely out of her teens, she was holding a black umbrella to shield her pajamas and exposed midriff. "Can I help you?" She pointed to a prairie-style blue house with a white picket fence across the street. "We live across the street."

A wind gust whipped at Tessa's face, cooling the rain on her cheeks and reminding her of Maine. "There used to be a white house with dark green shutters here."

The young woman's eyes clouded over as she recalled the horrible scene. "That place burned down a few years back."

"It... what?" Tessa turned back toward where her house should have been; there was no sign it had ever existed – a metaphor for her entire childhood.

"It... burned down..." The young mother repeated. Her sleeping toddler was awake now, eyeing Tessa with suspicion. "Apparently some messed-up guy died in there. I heard it was gruesome."

With the world spinning around her, Tessa covered her gaping mouth with a shaky hand. "Oh my God."

"I know. Right?" The stranger pointed to the empty lot. "Horrid."

Chilled to the bone from more than the wind and rain, Tessa jumped into her rental vehicle. With her mind racing, she sped away, leaving the puzzled woman and her baby standing there. She couldn't get away fast enough.

Chapter 52

Tuesday afternoon arrived with a heavy sense of foreboding – everyone in town sensed it and nobody knew why. Meanwhile at Atluko Industries, the League of LIES group had resumed their video discussions. No one was prepared for the disturbing nature of the final segment.

In Southeast Asia, a subcommittee of the League of LIES group had been studying therapeutics for a deadly disease called Tetracimia. Though it was a blood disease found only in reptiles, the scientists had been infecting humans with it for over twenty years. The purpose of the study was to test the effectiveness of the antidote they had developed: LIFE-0666-cur. The scientific community called it Li-cur.

The team tested thirty thousand subjects and the results were shocking. Not only could the pathogen jump species, it was even *more* deadly in humans. Sterilization of both sexes was conclusive with approximately 30% of females and 50% of males. A quarter of the test subjects died within six months. Pleased with the results, Xenco Pharmaceuticals was ready.

After the presentation concluded, Chair Wolfgang Hertzig took over the session to conclude their video discussions. From Switzerland, he looked directly into the camera as he spoke to the other participants. "Gentlemen, as you are aware, we cannot sustain current population levels for the Earth's resources."

"Abortion and gangsta rap aren't sufficient for reducing people of color, or what?" Miles Malone asked with a gleam in his eye.

"Shut up, Malone." Max glared at him.

Unfazed, Wolfgang continued. "If we had a *smart* dictatorship, we could manage eight... or maybe nine billion on the planet. But dictatorships are always stupid, and it's too difficult to limit consumption."

"Give us some hard numbers." Miles ordered. "How many?"

Wolfgang glared at Max. "Shut your attack dog up." He glanced at Miles then refocused his attention on the task at hand. "We can have a billion... maybe two for the available resources, so we need to liquidate six billion within the next five years."

The collective gasp was loud enough to be picked up by the microphones.

"Civilly. Peacefully." Wolfgang urged them, trying his best to convince them that genocide was the virtuous thing to do. "If we can willingly lead most of the population to their deaths while convincing them it's for their health, that's our golden ticket. See, it matters not what *is* real. It matters only what they *think* is real." For his tone, he could have been talking about the steak he had for dinner. "It's much less costly and messy than crematoriums and gas chambers. They will just fade away quietly."

The dead silence that followed unnerved even this group of coldhearted men. The seconds ticked by slowly.

"It's the final solution to the overpopulation question."

Chapter 53

Meanwhile, in Jack Weber's study, Chris Simon lowered both his head and his voice when he delivered the devastating news to his boss. "I got word that once they put their plan in motion, Dormin will make the Warsaw Ghetto look like a country club." As usual, he was back resting his back on the wall between two tall bookshelves like he was shielding himself.

Having trouble processing what he'd just heard, Jack didn't reply right away. He knew Chris wasn't one to exaggerate. "Did I hear what I just heard?"

"You think things are bad *now*?" Chris flexed his biceps, reminding himself he needed to get to the gym soon. "Even if we find a way around the censorship and propaganda, nobody is going to believe that people can be that evil."

"It *is* inconceivable." Jack loosened his tie to quell the anxiety welling up in his throat.

Alerted by Jack's abrupt reaction, Chris paused. Without taking his eyes off his boss, he left his spot on the wall to sit on the edge of the love seat.

"How can they convince intelligent, civilized people to participate in this?" Jack searched his own soul for an answer.

"How did the Holocaust happen?" Chris raised his eyebrows over the rim of this coffee cup as he savored the aroma.

Struck by the similarity, Jack was quick to respond. "By convincing intelligent, civilized people to participate in crimes against humanity?"

A rapid knock on the door startled the men back to the 3D world.

Jack acknowledged Jenny when she entered. Always at the top of her game, she set a tray down on the coffee table and left the room. He continued the conversation. "It can't happen again...can it? Mass extermination, I mean?"

"We humans haven't somehow evolved beyond our dark side." Chris assured him while he selected a warm peanut butter cookie.

"Wow," Jack mumbled. He was just starting to grasp how deep it went. "We foolishly thought it could never get that bad again – then it went global. *All* the powerful people have ties to the Third Reich."

"True. Humans don't have any natural predators. The enemy of man is man."

"I'm beginning to think slavery was outwardly abolished because they figured out how they could control people through the financial system and get rich beyond their wildest dreams in the process." Jack's bones creaked when he stood up to stretch. "Didn't Henry Ford allude to such a thing?"

Snapping his fingers with one hand, Chris reached into his pocket to pull out a paperback book. "I keep forgetting to give this to you."

"What do you have for me there?" The skepticism on Jack's face signaled his disdain for the idea. "Like I have time to read."

Chris was undeterred. "You ever heard of Saul Alinsky?"

"Saul Alinsky. Alinsky," Jack repeated. "I don't think so...at my age, you know so much, you run out of space on your hard drive." He grinned, happily noting how easy it was to turn memory loss into a positive.

"Ha. Nice save." Chris handed a well-worn paperback to Jack. "He wrote this book called Rules for Radicals in 1971." *Jack had an excuse for everything.*

Leafing through the book, Jack stopped to read the odd sentence to get the gist: The threat is more powerful than the thing itself. Ridicule is the strongest weapon. "Interesting." He frowned. "Who was he?"

"A community organizer from Chicago. He was well versed in Machiavellian tactics, especially the construction of symbols tied to grassroots organizing."

"Symbols?"

"We're surrounded by symbols for brand recognition *all the time*. The power of marketing an idea using a single image can't be understated."

Jack's eyes darted around the room as he tried to think of examples.

"Tie that image to an emotion, and you've done your job."

"Like the swastika? Or the rainbow flag?" Jack' snapped his finger. "That's their playbook!"

"It is, indeed." Chris agreed. "The old Nazis corrupted the swastika, and the new ones corrupted the rainbow."

"It makes more sense now."

"It's a playbook of dirty tactics, a step-by-step guide to implement tyranny, if you will. It's been used by dirty politicians and organizations for ages."

"So, can we –"

"I told you. Symbolism will be their downfall. Oh, by the way, he dedicated it to Lucifer – said he was the first radical known to man." Chris pointed to the book with his chin.

"Lucifer? Seriously?!" The sun went behind a cloud while Jack removed his tie. He was ready to get into something more casual.

"Yeah. They also worship Aleister Crowley for much the same reason. Combined with Goebbels's style propaganda, it completely messes with the mind."

"I can see that." Jack nodded, still only half sure he *could* see it.

"The public has trouble remembering that actors and their characters are separate people. When the lines are blurry, fantasy merges with reality." Chris made a weird circular gesture with both hands. "Way too many people think that what they're seeing on their TV screens is real life."

Having dabbled in some reality television production, Jack nodded in agreement. He knew exactly how that was. *Reality* TV was as fake as the day is long – including the so-called news.

"We need to remind the people that they're the real people, that the power belongs to them...not the people on their television sets. It's like the movie 'Network', but in real life."

"I'm as mad as hell and I'm not going to take it anymore!" Jack had seen the movie back in the '70s, especially enjoying the infamous scene where they threw their TVs out their windows. Then, he got addicted to watching the news.

"That's the one." Chris paused – *boomer probably saw it back in the '70s*. "The media industrial complex is a big incestuous inbred snake pit. They all have a coordinated message that they 'pulse' through the public consciousness."

"How bad *is* it?"

"They have a thing called The Covenant. It's basically been the plan of an ancient order. It was dormant until about the 1950s. It came roaring back to life by the '80s."

"So, I'm aware – we've seen the results."

"Well, when he was mayor, Max III was successfully challenging the established order. He was on the verge of handing the government back to the people."

"Hmm."

"Then he disappeared." Chris put his jacket on. "And that's what I'm going to do. No need to see me out."

After Chris left, Jack pondered his current life. Now that he was back in his childhood home, he was having more guilty regrets about his father than he cared to admit. He picked up the family photo from the antique carved desk just as the door opened.

"Sorry." Jenny was back to get the tray.

"Dear Jenny." Jack looked up with tears visible in his eyes. "What would we do without you?"

"You seem upset." Jenny set the tray back down and sat down on the loveseat. "Anything you want to talk about?"

"Nah." Jack's eyes were distant while memories of his strict father surfaced, and he recalled the feeling of never being good enough.

"It's your dad, isn't it?" Jenny prompted.

"I don't know." Setting the photo back down, Jack shrugged. "Maybe it's me."

"Wait here, Jack." Jenny picked up the tray and made her way to the door. "I'll be right back." True to her word, she was back in under two minutes. She carried a bulging leather bag, as black as the midnight sky.

"What do you have there?" Jack hadn't moved from his standing position near the desk.

"Have a seat." Jenny moved to the coffee table. "I'll show you." She lifted a Ouija board from the leather bag and removed several black candles. After she lit them, she returned the board to the bag.

The apprehension in Jack's voice didn't appear to concern Jenny as she continued what she was doing. "I don't know about this, Jenny. Are you sure?"

"We're having a séance to see if we can summon your father from the other side." Jenny waited for a reaction. There was none. "Are you ready?" She began to chant.

Chapter 54

By Wednesday morning, the temperature had dropped, and Dormin was once again blanketed by dense fog. Commuters made their way to work in rush hour through the heavy clouds, surrounded by blaring horns and nervous pedestrians.

Inside Atluko Industries, Max's inner circle mingled in his luxurious office. With the Dormin Group conference over, he was back in charge – just the way he liked it. Being subordinate to Wolfgang Hertzig was torture for a man like Max.

Jack Weber had announced he was running for mayor on Monday morning, and for the first time since he'd taken office, Max would have to campaign. There had never been a mayor who wasn't a Fisher. It was practically a rite of passage for fine political stock like the Fisher clan.

Everyone in the room hushed when Max slammed his laptop shut and the lights dimmed. Miles pointed to the far wall as it morphed into a jumbo screen.

With his hypnotic eyes, the charismatic New World Now newscaster began his story in the language known as Fakerish – confident, trustworthy, full of dark energy, and understood universally through nonverbals: body language, facial expressions, and gestures that sold the news with authority. The anchor knew, as they all did, that his job wasn't journalism – it was marketing. It's why they paid him $33,000 an episode – advertising costs for 24/7 coverage of the corporation's agenda didn't come cheap.

Using just the right pace and inflections to elicit the desired emotional reaction, the skilled, plastic broadcaster blabbed on about foreign influence, trafficking, and questionable sources. His expression changed to an unmistakable hybrid of confusion and concern – like the prime-time anchors who were all owned by the same billionaires.

Miles studied the blank faces, one indistinguishable from the next, lulled by the mesmerizing voice and the words scrolling at the bottom of the screen: **BREAKING: Darkness is only a heartbeat away.**

"We now go live to Samantha Isaac for more on this story. Watch."

The dolled-up blond was posing at the US-Mexico border, smiling seductively into the camera. After a brief delay, she began her report. "Thanks, Josh. Good morning. We just spoke to anonymous sources connected to ICE. They have confirmed that mayoral candidate, Jack Weber, may have been involved with trafficking as early as 1982. Additional sources with the FBI have suggested that Weber is the leader of a murderous cult that holds victims against their will, not unlike the conditions present at Jonestown."

As the reporter droned on, Dmitri fiddled with the top of his clipboard, earning him a stern look from Max.

"It's alleged that the candidate is involved in a worldwide human trafficking ring and may be hiding hundreds of millions or even *billions* of dollars from the IRS. Experts have gone on record to confirm that Weber is guilty of treason. It's likely he was selling open borders and national security secrets to the highest bidders to destabilize the country."

Max leaned back and rearranged his crotch while he watched the attractive young reporter conjure up her voice of caring and concern.

"Weber has denied these claims, without evidence. A criminal investigation has been launched into his actions. Shocking, if true. Jack Weber is a liar and a thief." Samantha looked directly into the eye of the camera. "We will continue to bring you updates on this breaking story. Back to you, Josh." It didn't have to be true. It just had to be plausible. In this case, it was neither and nobody batted an eye.

"Thanks, Samantha." The words, 'King Herod Escapes His Enclosure' were flashing across the bottom of the screen. The newscaster appeared sincerely alarmed. "Just in! Dormin's most well-known resident, and local celebrity – our king cobra, King Herod – has escaped his enclosure at the reptile facility."

The screen cut to a live shot: A mid-forties man with a crooked smile and a thirty-foot snake was standing in front of the reptile facility in a white lab coat. It was the mad scientist, herpetologist Dr. Neil Olsen. He'd been working with King Herod since he'd arrived in Dormin in 2002. Neil's work was called BP Research – Boosted Power Labs.

"Can you hear me, Neil?"

After a slight delay, Neil nodded. "Loud and clear, Josh."

"Good morning. Can you tell us what's happening?"

"Yes. Good morning. We are asking the public to be on the alert for our king cobra, Herod, who escaped his enclosure on Sunday night. It is believed that he is no longer in the facility."

"So, he could be anywhere in the city?"

"That's correct, Josh. Residents can go about their daily activities but should exercise caution and be aware of their surroundings."

"It's so stunning and brave of you to work with a dangerous snake to save humanity. Are there any other precautions the public should be taking?"

"None currently. If anyone spots him, we ask that you not approach the snake, but to call the facility or the city police."

"Thanks, Neil." Josh looked into the camera to conclude the story: "If you have any information, please call one of the numbers at the bottom of the screen. We will continue to bring you information on this important, developing story as it happens. Back to you, Samantha."

The screen faded to black.

"Good work, Malone." Max leaned back, waving as he lit a cigar. "That'll be all, gentlemen."

Chapter 55

At the hotel, Tessa Ryan tossed and turned before she finally drifted back to sleep...

An aging two-story house with peeling white paint and dark green shutters came into focus through the fog. Drying blood was splattered across the greasy kitchen ceiling, the pungent scent of gunpowder hanging in the air. A lifeless body was slumped on the old wooden kitchen table.

The focus zoomed out. Maple Street. Neighbors gathered under the eerie silver moonlight while dark shadows danced, and haunting sirens howled through the night. Curious onlookers gathered on the cold street where the roaring orange flames reflected off the snow. Firefighters raced into the blaze, the potent odor of thick smoke choking their senses.

In the surreal glow of the fire, a small, shadowy figure was led away in handcuffs to the flashing red and blue lights...

Tessa's eyes shot open. She didn't know what time or day it was, only that her hotel room was dark, her mouth was dry, and she'd just had another nightmare. Dragging herself out of the warm bed, she pulled back the thick drapes to another foggy and gloomy day – it matched her mood.

While her coffee brewed, Tessa sat on the bed with her knees pulled up to her chest and her back against the wall. How did she get here?? Never mind that. What better place to figure it out than in the woods beside a picturesque glacial lake? With her travel mug filled with breakfast blend, she grabbed her *I Love New York* jean jacket.

The weather hadn't changed much since the day before. The inside of the SUV was toasty warm. The radio was off; the wipers were on. On the way to Anna's,

Tessa passed the huge digital billboard just before the steep incline on Saboro Mountain. It was a news bulletin: King Herod had escaped. Be alert. Darkness is only a heartbeat away.

Tessa continued up the interstate, now completed between Saboro and Diablo Mountains – the reason for the massive explosion in physical size and population since she'd left. With the strategic passage through the mountains and its proximity to Yellowstone, Dormin was not only a major tourist attraction, but also a Northwest hub.

By the time she pulled up to Anna's Tessa was hysterical. "What's happening!?" she wailed when Anna opened the door, leaning toward the slight woman for comfort. "Now my house is gone!"

Anna patted Tessa's back. "Go have a seat in front of the fire, my girl. I'll bring you some nice tea." Other than the snapping birch in the fireplace, the house was quiet, with even the hum of the refrigerator suspended – like time itself, it seemed.

Once the steaming cups were on the coffee table, the knitting needles began to fly at a dizzying rate. Anna remained silent, waiting for Tessa to begin.

With her head still spinning, Tessa struggled to find her voice – she'd been trying to cope with too much information, too fast. "I had a nightmare about the house burning down. Just last night," she croaked.

"Do you remember it?"

"Clear as day. It wasn't like a normal dream. It was so *real* – like I was there."

Anna's soft voice landed in the quiet room like an explosion. "We're in a spiritual war, child." Yarn over.

As Tessa moved from the chair to the floor, silent tears rolled down her hot cheeks. She wiped the salt off her upper lip with the sleeve of her jacket.

"The people we've been taught to trust are possessed by the dark side."

Tessa's head was throbbing. Something was *very* wrong. "You mean...like the paranormal?

"I mean.... like demonic possession."

"Oh my God, *this* again!? I don't have time for this!" Tessa scrambled to her feet. She'd heard enough. "I need answers, not some stupid, made-up crap! There's no sky wizard."

Anna remained seated, casually bending over to find a ball of dark-green wool. It was time to teach the snarky little New Yorker a lesson – the world didn't revolve around her.

With no response to her outburst, Tessa stopped, staying frozen in place, the adrenaline rushing through her. Fight or flight?

Anna couldn't suppress a smile. Her little girl was about to grow up a little bit.

Tessa would fight. *Like an adult.* No more participation trophies for being offended. The energy in the room shifted.

Gazing at the lake with a distant look in her eyes, Anna set the ball of wool on her lap. Mission complete. "Your father was in the house when it happened." She swallowed the lump in her throat, her voice soft and loving.

"I saw him," Tessa whispered, slowly returning to her chair. Silently pleading for some reprieve from the visions, the defeat in her voice was palpable. "I saw him... dead at the kitchen table. Blood and gore were everywhere."

"Nobody knows *for sure* how the fire started... they have some unproven theories." Anna paused to check on her guest. "I'm so sorry, child." Her tired eyes filled with sympathetic tears as she turned her head away.

Remembering her mother needed rest after completing the simplest of tasks, Tessa knew Cecilia would never have been able to cope with that.

"That's when your mother was hospitalized for good. It was too much. She became catatonic."

The wall phone in the kitchen rang, piercing the tender moment.

With Anna on the phone, Tessa caught the headline on the top copy of the Dormin Times: **King Herod Escapes Enclosure.**

"Sorry about that." Anna picked up a beading project for a change of pace. "I'm expecting a delivery today. I've been waiting for that call."

Tessa held up the paper. "What's this?"

"Call me crazy, but I think they're planning something with that snake."

"Stop it. They wouldn't do that!" Tessa was unable to suppress an eyeroll. "It's always doomsday to you," she sighed.

"No. *You* wouldn't do that." Anna kept her head down. "You don't think like a psychopath."

It was the second time Tessa had heard those words, and deep down, she knew it was true. She was quickly learning that some people are capable of *anything*, humanity be damned.

Chapter 56

Jack Weber's crowded campaign headquarters buzzed with a cautiously optimistic energy. The combined aroma of percolating coffee and fresh baking wafted from a narrow table pushed up against one makeshift wall.

On another wall, multiple televisions were tuned to different stations, the plastic newscasters reminding citizens that snakes are cold-blooded; they rely on their environment to regulate their body temperature. As a result, King Herod could go into shock quickly if he wasn't located. They again urged the public to report any sightings; public health and safety was their top priority.

With the Fakerish broadcasts over, Jack retreated to his small office with his sidekick. The noise level was still audible but muffled. Soon, he was peering across the desk over the frame of his glasses. "What kind of battle are we engaged in here..." He trailed off.

"We're not taking on earthly enemies, Jack." Chris perched on the edge of the leather chair.

"What are you talking about, Chris?" Jack reached for his hand sanitizer as if it would ward off the evil they were discussing. "They seem pretty real to me." He recalled Jenny's failed attempt to contact his dad from beyond the grave.

"Oh, they're real." Chris massaged his tense neck muscles. "They're real psychopaths, yeah. With ultimate earthly power, and they're waging psychological warfare using technology that thinks it's human."

"Are you saying we need to bring in a priest?"

"No." Chris tipped his chair back. "Well...maybe. But not yet." The chair wheels slammed back on the floor. He stood up.

"For something a little bit more tangible, what's happening with the election?"

"Other than you emerging as a phenomenon, we're monitoring their every move." Chris was now on his phone, near the window.

"So what?"

"I don't really know. I thought it was a good idea to have a Plan D. Just in case." The back of Chris's Hawaiian shirt had a welcoming sunset on the beach with an active volcano in the background. "Great view of the alley."

"It's not like the city wanted me to rent prime real estate," Jack snapped. The irritating road noise from the interstate was constant in the small space, aggravating his daily headache. "What else do you have?"

A pensive expression on his face, Chris turned around to sit on the windowsill. "Jack, they've infiltrated the people's army. They're purging everyone loyal to the Constitution at all levels of government."

"Holy mother of –"

"But rest assured that they're diverse and inclusive – the pacification of men. Plus, they've trained an army of people who hate America, supply weapons to the cartels from the south, and train terrorists in the Middle East – where they guard the poppy fields, incidentally." Chris swallowed the lump in his throat. "The borders are wide open. We're being invaded from all directions."

"Enough!" Jack stood up, his presence filling the room with agitation. "There are millions of people in this country ready, able, and willing to defend the Constitution!"

"Against their own government," Chris agreed. "Who, incidentally, told the people that if they wanted to take on the government, they'd need F-15s. And possibly nuclear weapons."

"Wow. So, they've declared material war against the American people."

"Indeed," Chris confirmed. "Shit just got real."

Chapter 57

On Saturday, Cecilia Ryan was laid to rest in the shady cemetery next to century-old St. Theresa's Catholic Church, the oldest parish in the county. With only a handful of people there to pay their respects, the social worker from long-term stay gave the eulogy – glossy poetic prose to hide a troubled life. The obituary erased the human condition as if there was nothing more to humans than superficial skin. No flaws. No feelings. No meaning.

Seeing her mother's bony, lifeless body in the cheap casket elicited a range of emotions in Tessa, but no closure. Too many unanswered questions. Too much guilt. The service and burial lasted thirty-seven minutes. There was no lunch.

Tessa returned to the hotel with a heavy heart, moving through the lobby on autopilot. As she passed the gift shop, the front page of the Dormin Times again caught her eye. There was a photo of a frail and gravely ill Cecilia Ryan next to a headline: **Mayoral Candidate Takes Advantage of Sick Woman on Death Bed.**

"What the actual what?!" Tessa paid for the paper and opened it right in the shop.

According to the story, an unidentified philanthropist was paying all her mother's expenses in long term stay. It was alleged that Jack Weber had deceitfully endeared himself to her mother to steal her money, according to an anonymous source. Shocking, if true. Weber denied the claims – without evidence. He'd have to prove his innocence in court.

Half an hour later, still in the clothes she'd worn to the funeral, Tessa stomped up the cobblestone path to Anna's door clutching the newspaper in one hand. She pounded loud enough to wake Spike who'd been asleep in his doghouse.

Spike charged at her, barking and growling.

The door opened. "Spike!" Anna yelled.

"We need to talk." Tessa shoved the newspaper in Anna's face. "You told me if I wanted help, go see this guy – this Jack Weber guy. How *could* you?!"

Saddened by the predictable dark energy, Anna swallowed the lump in her throat as she closed the door to a growling Spike. She knew where this was going. Her unexpected visitor was about to parrot the cable news channels like a programmed cyborg.

"Did you know that he was stealing from my mother, that he assaulted Max, that he is racist, a criminal, sexist pig, a fascist, a dictator and a misogynist? Worse than Hitler."

Anna had already read the story. Not only was it fabricated, but it was also the inverse of reality. Adding to her aggravation, the reporter apparently didn't understand the most fundamental human right – the presumption of innocence. Nobody must *prove* their innocence. The onus is on the prosecution to prove *guilt*.

"And he's running a human trafficking ring! All the intelligence agencies said so. Jack Weber is a liar and a thief."

Without saying a word, Anna left Tessa standing in the entrance to return to the kitchen. *Programmed cyborg, indeed.* She turned up the volume on the radio – her uninvited and unwelcome guest had interrupted her favorite syndicated talk show.

Tessa stomped after her. "How could you?" she repeated.

Turning the heat down on the stove, Anna stopped for a moment to enjoy the tantalizing aroma of freshly harvested fruit. Grabbing the wooden spoon on the stove, she stirred the thick red liquid bubbling in a big pot. Sterilized raspberry jam jars were labeled and ready for the finished product. Fresh baking powder biscuits cooled on the racks beside the homemade butter. "Are you hungry?"

"I'm not hungry," Tessa lied. "I'm upset! Why won't you answer me?"

"My child, there's a lot you don't know about what happened in Dormin after you left." Anna changed into a clean apron. "I told you; the devil uses deception." As if the entire world were a simulation, the guest on the radio program was also speaking about Satan being the great deceiver.

Hesitant to say anything about it to Anna, Tessa remembered the story about Jack at the centennial celebration.

"What's really on your mind?"

Staring at the blue sky reflecting off the glassy lake, Tessa's voice was barely a whisper. "I saw it with my own eyes, Anna. The story about Jack shoving Max at the centennial was a lie."

"I know." Anna ladled jam into the prepared jars. "I've known Jack Weber for years."

"But the news.... it's on the news!" Tessa protested. "The news doesn't lie!"

"My God." Anna avoided eye contact to conceal her mixed emotions. "You have so much to learn, child. One day, you will know the truth."

"The truth?" Tessa glanced at the ceiling where the light seemed to suddenly get a lot brighter. *Hopefully not an old house electrical problem.* "What do you mean, *the truth*?" she shouted.

"The truth is objective, my girl," Anna sighed as she began sealing the warm jars. "Postmodernism and critical theory and all that stuff they told you in New York is trash."

Had Anna just insulted her? "I don't believe this! Maybe it's you who needs a reality check." Tessa stomped out. The media did exaggerate and stretch the truth a bit, but there was no way that they would tell lies *that* big.

Chapter 58

Screeeeech! Screeeeech! Screeeeech! Hummmm. Hummmm. Screech. Screech. Screech. Screeeeech! Screeeeech! Screeeeech!

The obnoxious emergency alert system screeched and hummed on computers, mobiles, watches, radios and televisions from one end of Dormin to the other. Herod had been spotted in the vicinity of Redemption Boulevard and Church Street in Rosemont, one of the new subdivisions.

Addicted to the incessant news coverage by now, Dorminians tuned in to learn that their celebrity king cobra had a disease called Tetracimia – blood poisoning caused by infected venom glands. If not promptly treated, the pathogen could cause multiple pus-filled lesions on his skin shortly before death. Alarmingly, researchers were trying to determine if the disease could possibly transfer from snakes to humans.

Reminiscent of the coverage after 9/11, there was only one story in the news cycle that the people of Dormin cared about, but this time it was about a local celebrity and the fate of the residents.

They hung on every word.

Chapter 59

On the drive back to the valley, Tessa's mind wouldn't slow down. *How much more? Could it all have been a lie? Why was she so rude to Anna? It wasn't **her** fault everything was so weird.*

In the aching silence of the dark hotel room, Tessa checked her phone for the alert – the snake had been spotted. Yawning, she fluffed up the pillows in her hotel room to rest her throbbing head. The lingering remains of harsh chemical cleaners made her sick to her stomach and she was getting a migraine. Not that it would help, but she popped some painkillers.

Not quite an hour later, Tessa was startled awake by a text alert.

> Adam: Do you want to go for a drive?

> Tessa: More than anything. Please get me out of here ;)

The roof was down on Adam's sports car to enjoy the spectacular, sunny late September day. Within ten minutes, the pair were on the interstate heading west out of town.

"Where are we going?" Tessa's loose hair blew in the wind. Her headache was gone.

"It's a surprise." Adam's new military haircut and government issued shades made him look like a fed.

"I don't like surprises." Tessa was suddenly on edge. *What was she getting herself into?* "Maybe you're a psychotic serial killer," she half-joked, trying to lighten the mood. "And/or a fed."

"Maybe you'll like this one." Adam grinned. "And I don't like puffy rice, but I'm not going to shoot it." He stroked Tessa's wrist. "Good lawyer lingo, by the way."

With her heart racing, Tessa scolded herself when she giggled. *She couldn't fall for this guy. No way. No how.* She was playing with fire.

The pair continued up Saboro Mountain, the newly refinished blacktop on the interstate guiding them through the thick, bountiful forest. The colors of the changing leaves and abundant wildflowers were splashed across the mostly clear horizon, like God had painted a masterpiece on His canvas.

"Did you see the stories about Jack Weber!? He was stealing from my mother, Adam!" Tessa still believed it, even though she knew deep down it was *probably* a lie – the path of least resistance is to go along with the narrative and forget that you *could* be living in a world of deception. *At least people would still like her.*

"I know. It's unreal." Adam's musky cologne made Tessa weak in the knees. "Are his supporters stupid or just bigoted like he is?"

As they ascended, Tessa was struck by the beauty of the fall foliage interspersed among several species of evergreens. "Wow." They were on a plateau at the tree line.

"You ain't seen nothing yet, sweetheart." Adam slowed to turn right onto a winding, gravel road through the forest. They continued for about another ten minutes or so before Adam slowed down to park his convertible. Good day to leave the top down – not a cloud.

Stunned by their rocky surroundings, Tessa stepped out of the car like she was in another world – the type of adventure that makes you forget about places like New York City.

"Let's go." Adam grabbed her hand, tugging her towards a set of wide metal stairs and a sign: **SABORO RECREATION AREA**

A heavily wooded section of the plateau had been developed into a campground with hiking trails. Another set of steps, narrow and newly constructed with treated lumber, was next to the steamy hot springs. In the raised flower bed, a rainbow of late-blooming marigolds and petunias were surrounded by daisies, a stunning backdrop for the shady picnic area.

"Nice!"

Adam mentally patted himself on the back, secretly wishing it was that easy to impress all beautiful women. "We're not there yet." He pulled Tessa toward the final set of old wooden steps. *She was checking all his boxes.*

When they reached Saboro Ridge Lookout, Tessa gasped, the view of the valley in all its Autumn splendor taking her breath away. They were standing high above the city of Dormin, the tallest of its peaks dwarfed by their unobstructed vantage point, sunlight filling the valley and reflecting off the sparse low-lying clouds. She knew instantly what a special, spiritual place it was, bemoaning the fact that she didn't bring her art supplies.

With their hearts filled with peace, the pair parked on a metal bench overlooking the distant city and talked until sundown.

Chapter 60

October 1 was moving day. An ultramodern suite housed in a beautiful heritage building didn't exactly bring back *positive* memories, but Tessa was determined to adapt with the wind at her back. Sooner or later, she had to leave Aamon in her past. He'd been dead for almost ten years!

Colorful shrubs, shady maples, and blue spruce surrounded the cluster of aging buildings on Old Town Road, shielding the residents' view from the undesirables who aimlessly wandered the downtown core. The view from the 21st floor was spectacular, the perfect place to bask in the sunsets along the lush riverbank.

Thanks to Megan, Tessa's best friend back in Manhattan, her belongings arrived neatly packed and catalogued. On time. *Plus*, she'd taken care of all the loose ends with her condo and job in New York. She was *so incredibly blessed* to have a friend like Megan.

Finding her precious artwork, Tessa held the still-wrapped package to her chest and closed her eyes. "Thank you." Presently, the chronological abstract reminders of the changing seasons of her complex life were tastefully displayed on her new apartment walls.

With her packing finished, Tessa walked the several blocks to city hall to attend to *bureaucratic claptrap*. Distracted passersby kept their eyes on their phones, somehow avoiding lampposts, other people, litter and pots of dying flowers on the cracked sidewalks. *Not to mention the snake. Impressive.*

With the late morning sun on her face and the cool Autumn wind in her hair, Tessa arrived at city hall, adjacent to Old Town Square – it would always be Old Town Square to her. A mosaic of fall colors crunched under her black ankle boots as she passed the neglected, mostly empty fountain covered in rain-soaked yellow and rust-colored leaves. Just outside the main double doors of city hall, she paused briefly between the imposing ivory columns at the top of the crumbling steps.

The huge bulletin board inside the main entrance displayed the names and photos of the council wards, which were...identical to the board at the plant? Yep. Every single one of them. Corporate to boot – like a major parasitic bank selected them or something. How did they get away with it?!

Another bulletin board was filled with accolades for a newly opened franchise, Delicacy, a chain of high-end restaurants that was taking the country by storm. City council was lauded as magicians for attracting them to Dormin because they missed the population threshold by a few hundred thousand people. *Interesting.* Its opening had put Dormin on the map again as people came from far and wide to taste the fabulously best bacon anyone had ever tasted, served in every dish – including appetizers, drinks, and desserts. *Because bacon.*

Back home, Tessa opened all the windows to combat the abrasive stench of commercial cleaning solutions still permeating everything in her new home. *Ugh. Why didn't hicks use natural products?* Soft jazz on the Bluetooth, a cold beer, a vanilla-scented candle, and the love seat in the sunroom – either a perfect date, or...she had a phone call to make. She dialed the number.

"Max here." He was out of breath.

Tessa tried to sound enthused. "Hi Max." She failed.

"Tessa! How are you, darling?" To Tessa's surprise, Max sounded genuinely happy to hear from her. "Are you getting settled in?"

"I'm alright." Was there a nice way to say the next sentence? "But-the-city-isn't."

"You're talking too fast. Say that again."

"Max, the city is falling apart," Tessa sighed.

"Why do you say *that*?!" Max gasped. "It's a *beautiful* city. It's a tourist attraction. People come here from all over the world! And now we have a Delicacy. How can *that* be bad?"

"First of all, no it's *not* a beautiful city. Secondly, it's not just *a* city, Max. It's *our* city." Tessa paused for a sip of beer. "At least it used to be. I stepped in literal crap my first day here!"

Barely listening, Max dismissed her concern. "Well, you know ... kids will be kids."

Tessa wondered if it was possible to be that much of a liar, that stupid, that indifferent, or just that misinformed. She'd run out of patience. "You threw a nice party the other night, didn't you, Max? A nice, succulent dinner."

"Thank-you. I'm glad you –"

"Meanwhile, there are homeless people everywhere, the infrastructure is crumbling, there's a race war with *actual* segregation, people are eating bugs and dying in a drug epidemic, crime is skyrocketing, there's staggering poverty, children are hungry, and –"

"Minor things that will pass." Max's gruff, impatient tone cut Tessa off.

"Holy f –" Tessa caught herself. "Holy frick. If those are minor, what in the *hell* is major?!"

"Our most pressing issue right now is white supremacy." Max paused. "We award contracts to organizations to address those other pesky issues so we can focus on diversity, equity, and inclusion."

Other issues? Holy. Diversity, equity, and inclusion? The foundation of the Hippies – the organization that Tessa had started in Maine. "It's good to hear you're trying, Max, but it won't work." Her tone had softened.

"Why do you say that?" Max asked.

"What contractor is going to fix problems and work themselves out of a job?" *How dumb was he, anyway?*

"Are you questioning my judgment?" Max was incredulous.

"All I'm saying is that this was not the way things were done when I was a kid. Real people built this town, and we cared about our community."

"Tessa," Max snapped, clearly irritated. "Leave the governing to me, okay? We've taken care of the important things."

"Like?"

"Aren't you listening? We have the best civic Environmental Social Governance score in the country. ESG for short." Max said the words like he was proud of dividing people. "Gays can get married. Weed is legal. There are no restrictions on abortions. We have inclusive bathrooms, and misgendering is hate speech. Nobody is forced to work. We have racial and social justice. Everyone will be equal. What more do you want?"

Tessa had just moved from a place like that. It hit her! The Utopia she thought she wanted was Hell!

Max continued. "Soon, we'll be giving away free crack pipes."

"Huh?"

"We want inclusion for *all*. We take good care of the oppressed. So, what are you talking about?"

"You know what, Max? You're right," Tessa conceded. "*Your* city is great." It certainly wasn't *her* city anymore. "Sorry for bringing it up."

"No trouble, darling." Max had resumed his fatherly role with ease, like it would erase what a dick he was. "Take care."

Swiping to end the call, Tessa's gaze turned toward the corporate tourist boats gliding along the river, lit up by the fire-red twilight sun. *Jack Weber was right! The progressive agenda is dystopia – a Trojan Horse to divide the population and trick people into accepting their own slavery.*

Dark forces were present in the valley, indeed – just like Anna had said.

B zzzzzzzt....!!

The door alarm on Tessa's phone startled her out of her slumber. She had fallen asleep on the love seat, awakening to a dark and hauntingly quiet apartment. The music had stopped, the sun had disappeared behind the horizon, and the beer was warm and flat.

Tessa didn't recognize the man standing at the door with Anna, though she had a feeling she'd seen this hottie somewhere before. She swiped to let them in, relieved that Anna wasn't mad about their latest encounter. She still had an elevator ride to the 21st floor to think about it.

"Huh?" Tessa could think of nothing more intelligent to say when she opened the door to her guests, flustered when she realized her other visitor was the hot guy she'd seen in Jack Weber's office. *How had Anna gotten her new address already?*

"Sorry, child." Aware of the trust issues, Anna looked upon Tessa with sympathy. "I'd like to introduce you to Chris Simon."

Remembering how Chris had dismissed her without a word in Jack's office, Tessa was annoyed at the abrupt intrusion into her new fortress.

"Pleasure to meet you, Ms. Ryan." Chris had both a dazzling smile, and a heavenly masculine scent. His smooth voice instantly put Tessa at ease. *Easy on the all the senses... quite the specimen... wearing a wedding ring. Damn.*

"Hi Chris." Tessa stepped aside to let them in. "It's Tessa." She turned her attention to Anna. "Well, *this* is a surprise."

Grinning, Chris removed his vinyl windbreaker. "Don't tell me...you don't like surprises?" He draped the jacket over his forearm.

"Depends." Tessa thought about her time with Adam at Saboro Point...not all surprises were bad. She showed her guests to the living room where the patio doors to the sunroom were still open, allowing the cool evening breeze to come in.

"I'll go find some tea." Anna disappeared into the kitchen.

Tessa couldn't resist the urge to be sassy. "Make yourself at home, Anna." Sarcasm was her second language, and she was fluent in it.

Seated across from Tessa, Chris leaned in like he had a bombshell news report about a breaking scandal. He had a sense of urgency about him, wasting no time making small talk. "Tessa, are you aware of what's *actually* going on with your city?"

"Well, kind of. I guess. Too many gradual societal changes...or at least that's what I heard."

"From who?" Chris raised an eyebrow.

"Jack Weber. You should know. That's where I saw you." Tessa's tone was flippant and dismissive. "You didn't seem to have much use for me taking up his time. I've heard everything about him, you know."

Chris hesitated. "If you'd listen more than you talk, you'll be less likely to play the victim." He could dish it out as well as he could take it, and he could handle an entitled New York brat.

"*Victim?*" Tessa's scowl decimated any goodwill she previously had for her unwelcome guest. "I can't help it that some people are evil."

Burying his strained face in his hands, Chris slowly exhaled. "I really don't want to waste my time," he mumbled. "I haven't slept in over thirty-six hours."

"Sorry." Tessa tucked her hair behind her ear. "But...why are you here to see *me* about what's happening in the city?"

"Well... we have a network... sort of an alliance." Chris stood up to stretch his legs. "Anna is part of it too."

Her dry mouth agape, the blood drained from Tessa's face. "I have questions."

"I'm sure you do. Save them for another time." As Chris paced, the energy surrounding him had 'race against time' vibes. "We have a plan to get around the globalists' stranglehold on information."

"Great." Tessa tossed her hand in the air. "And?"

"And, well, it kind of involves...you?" Chris was groveling and he didn't care. *Image be damned.*

"Batting her eyelashes, Tessa placed her hand on her shapely cleavage. "Little ol' me?"

Keeping his eyes trained on Tessa's face, Chris leaned his back against the wall. "Yes."

Maybe he was one of those gay frogs she'd heard about. Alien maybe? Or he's just professional. Tessa silently admonished herself for her bigotry. *Poor frogs. She didn't have it anymore.*

"Hellooo?" Chris waved his hand in front of Tessa's face. "Anyone home?"

"Why?" Tessa sighed. "I'm a nobody."

"You're relatable and authentic. That can go a long way to having influence."

Tessa made a scrunched-up face while she mulled it over. "Hmm."

"You're also beautiful and smart, and I'd be a fool to discount the impact of the outer package." Chris paused for a reaction. "Should I keep going?"

With a satisfied smirk, Tessa nodded in agreement. "No. I get it." *Maybe she did still have it.*

"Nobody knows what '*It*' is, but whatever *It* is, you have it."

"Time is of the essence, as they say." Anna set a tray with three mugs of a steaming liquid on the glass coffee table, choosing to sit in the reclining rocking chair with her feet up – it wasn't every day she got to sit in a comfy chair that wasn't a scratching post. "We need someone like you to tell the tale of two Dormins, my girl."

Taking the seat across from Tessa again, Chris grabbed his cup. "That's *exactly* the perspective we need."

While the trio enjoyed their peppermint tea, a discussion about Tessa's potential law practice ensued, followed by more details of Chris's proposal.

Before long, her handsome visitor was on his feet, handing her his card. "How about you take some time to think about it?"

"Thanks." Tessa glanced at the name on the card. Her jaw dropped.

By the time Chris left Tessa's apartment, the tangerine glow of the low-hanging full moon and cones of yellow light cast spooky shadows across Old Town Road. The half-naked maples and elms shivered as they formed a canopy, partially obstructing the English-style streetlamps on the quiet street. The late evening was cool with the spell of fall in the air.

Arriving at the security gates of Jack's estate, Chris noticed that only ten minutes had passed...about half the time it usually took. The moon was now partially hidden behind luminescent puffy clouds and the temperature was dropping like the calendar figured out it had flipped to October.

The meticulous tall hedges on either side of the ornate, bell-shaped front gates were decorated with a string of visible, white security cameras. In addition to the surveillance, 24/7 security patrolled the well-lit property. The sports car that had been tailing him took off like a demon fleeing heaven.

Wearing a blue terry-towel robe and plaid grandpa slippers, Jack yanked the door open. "That was fast!"

"After I texted you, I had to shake a spook." Chris winked. "Just another day at the office."

Jack moved aside, waving his guest toward the stairs.

The entrance hall, as always, was immaculate and smelled like pine cleaner. The aroma of fresh-baked pecan pie drifted from the kitchen. Fresh-cut flowers adorned the marble entrance table. Wow. Jenny really *was* the perfect housekeeper – amazing what happens when you pay your staff and treat them well.

At the top of the stairs, Jack followed his guest into the study. "What's up?"

"Almost all the trafficking is controlled by a global crime syndicate. Pretty much the same people who start wars, crash economies, and manufacture famines."

"Oh, yeah?" Jack found his favorite chair.

"There's a massive open market for unpaid or underpaid labor of both adults and minors. And of course, the sex trafficking. Kids earn a ton of money for these monsters." Remaining on his feet, Chris paced nervously.

Jack tightened his grip around the yellow pencil in his hands.

"And unlike oil, drugs, and weapons, they can be sold many times over." Chris slowed both his speech and his pacing. "I told you. We have open borders for a reason."

"So, that's why they're accusing me!" The yellow pencil in Jack's hands snapped in half.

"It's all about managing their reputations... as in blackmail."

"Of course, that's it!" Jack snapped his fingers as he opened his eyes. He *knew* they all hung out in the French Riviera together – he'd met the infamous predator in Malibu. Supposed executive of a Fortune 500 company in Los Angelos or something.

"That's why the people have lost hope." Chris took a seat on the loveseat. "But I still hold out hope that with the right candidates, voters can still have a say."

"Ha! The rulers *own* the courts, the police force. Face it, they own and control everything." Jack knew how impenetrable the wall was. "Everything is recorded, I hope," he added as an afterthought.

"Of course. What do you take me for? A boomer?" Chris squeezed his eyes shut. "Sorry about that, boss."

Jack couldn't suppress a belly laugh. *These days, that was the nicest thing he was called.*

"We can only hope we'll reach the voters who feel powerless."

"*That's* the brand they're going to make toxic – your supporters. Subhuman, if you will." Chris rubbed his bloodshot eyes while he yawned. He needed to sleep so badly.

Jack threw his hands in the air in defeat. "How did we let it get so out of control, Chris? My God, what has happened to this country? This world?"

"Ideological subversion happened. Did you read Rules for Radicals?"

"Just get to the point. We're in the middle of being superheroes, here." Jack winked.

"Alinsky spoke about eight levels of control you need to achieve in order to create a nanny state."

"Who wants that?"

Chris crossed the room to grab the book. Leaning his backside against the desk, he flipped through the book to recite the main points. "Let's see. Healthcare. Poverty. Debt. Gun control. Welfare. Education. Religion. Class warfare."

"Great bunch of words. How do they create, as you say, a 'nanny' state?"

"Good question. That's why I gave you the book. *All* of those are systems of control that restrict our humanity." Chris knew Jack was annoyed, and he didn't care – his boss had some conspiracy theories to catch up on.

Chapter 61

With the candidates' slogans and colors splashed across banners, lawn signs, t-shirts, and ball caps, and campaigners knocking on every door, election season was in full gear. As Dorminians were glued to their preferred news sources around the clock, the contentious race heated up. Public interest was at an all-time high with the mayoral debate drawing the most viewers in the city's history.

King Herod, meanwhile, continued to be elusive. Neil Olsen was begging for the public's assistance in locating him, reminding them that they still didn't know if Tetracimia could transfer to the human population. *Darkness is only a heartbeat away.*

The bacon chain, Delicacy, had their one-year anniversary, going all out with a big fair for the kids. A parade that ended with a pancake and bacon breakfast in the facility's parking lot. Colorful, scary clowns roamed among the lucky citizens as they savored their breakfast. There were games and a dunk tank and rides. That two kids went missing from the event never even made the news.

Part IV

Awakening

"A lie that is half-truth is the darkest of all lies."
~ Alfred Tennyson

Chapter 62

While Tessa sipped her Irish coffee in her sunroom, she knew that whatever path she chose, she *would* be exposed. Her rabid thirst for the Utopia she *thought* she wanted had blinded her to the necessity of traditional values and rational minds – concepts she'd considered oppressive by modern standards. The road to Hell is paved with good intentions, and *nobody* escaped scrutiny in the age of the internet.

Knowing that Dormin was a justice-in-name-only, two-tiered hellhole, Tessa knew she had to do *something*. One group was a special class of citizens who'd elevated themselves to never face justice. The other included minorities, the poor, the vulnerable, and those with the wrong political opinions – customers for the prison industrial complex and the government gulags. *No* branch of the judicial system had escaped the corruption, she bemoaned, even extending to the military where men were men and so were the women.

To practice law, Tessa would either once again cater to the rich and powerful or... defend the oppressed, that would be the... wait...? *What!? Had the world flipped upside down?*

What the media branded as "right wing extremism" was the modern counterculture – the anti-establishment 'right'. *They* were the Hippies of the New Millennium. *They* were the exploited working classes. *They* embodied the American spirit of individual liberty and responsibility, equal justice under the law, and respect for the Constitution. *They* were **We, The People**. *Make it make sense!*

Mortified that she'd been on the wrong side of history, Tessa realized Malcolm X was right: The media had her hating the oppressed! Right was left and left was right. Right and left and blue and red were bullshit.

Tessa had made her decision — she'd become the media darling for the working class, try once again to unite the 99% like back in the day. It was the only way.

Halfway through the month of October, King Herod still had not been located. A string of 'experts' appeared on the cable news programs to inform the public that the longer he was at large, the more danger the community was in.

Daily news coverage was aired from Dormin Reptile Gardens where researchers were examining the disease that King Herod was carrying. Studies showed that once an infected cobra contacted the ground, the pathogen could seep into the soil where it would remain deadly for an unspecified amount of time. They were advising the public to exercise caution in the event it could spread to the human population.

The citizens of Dormin were grateful for the news coverage. How else would they know how to keep themselves safe?

Chapter 63

Tessa began her journey into independent journalism by clicking off the media-censorship industrial complex. It seemed to her that some people will believe *anything* if it's sold with authority. Those same people would also laugh at those who got their news from 'the internet', where the only thing available was conspiracy theory stuff, allegedly.

According to the corporate media, the 'rabbit hole' – a term that had at one time been called 'reading' or 'the library' was now considered 'debunked' – no matter what the story was. Alternative news sources were spreading disinformation, they said. They made it clear that critical thinking was harmful, doing your own research was stupid, and anyone going against the empire's narrative would be viewed as a villain in the annals of history.

In the rabbit hole, Tessa stumbled upon a treasure trove of independent truth tellers who were talking about things that were never 'on the news'. Inspired by the magic of authentic citizen journalism, she watched real people motivated by serving real people. *What a concept!* Two notable independent news channels were a mixed-race, milquetoast fence-sitter and some jag-off pothead comedian in his garage.

To Tessa's shock, Jack Weber was footing the bill for launching the parallel infrastructure that made AltMedia Group possible – life was full of interesting twists and turns. Her show, TDR (Tessa Dawn Ryan) Report, was the newest member. Broadcasting on local cable and streamed online, citizen journalism was the way of the future.

The group's guiding principle was TRUTH: timely, rational, unedited, truthful, and heartfelt.

On Monday evening, the third week of October, the barren trees shivered in the moonlight, leaves curling up like brown cocoons and stragglers clinging to the branches. If the forecast was right, the valley could be covered in a light layer of frost by morning.

Ready for her first TDR Report broadcast, Tessa looked into the camera, the studio lighting flattering her natural look. To introduce herself, she had no script, but rather wanted to speak from the heart – a formula she would continue for all her future shows. She was going to wing it.

To her own surprise, she opened with scripture.

File Notes: TDR Report (transcribed)
October 17, 2016

"The coming of the lawless one is according to the working of Satan, with all power, signs, and lying wonders, and with all unrighteous deception among those who perish, because they did not receive the love of the truth, that they might be saved. And for this reason, God will send them strong delusion, that they should believe the lie, that they all may be condemned who did not believe the truth but had pleasure in unrighteousness." (Thessalonians 2:9-12)

Hi there! Welcome to my brand-new channel, TDR Report, and my very first broadcast. I'm Tessa Ryan and I hardly know where to start.

First, a little bit about me. I grew up in Dormin, I only recently returned from Manhattan where I was a practicing Wall Street attorney. I've seen the light. Please don't hate me. You'll soon see why I'm doing this.

To put it bluntly, Dormin has been turned on its head from when I was a kid, from fond memories to a scene out of a horror movie. The history is gone. The ideas are gone. The traditions are gone. The values are gone. The sense of community is gone.

People walk around like zombies, afraid to speak up or challenge our so-called elected leaders? Or do we just not know how to take on such powerful entities?

Friends, we are already at war, embroiled in a biblical battle between good and evil, humans and machines, the rising up of the human spirit against those who would see it perish. We know there's meaning beyond ourselves and deep down, we yearn for the return of God in a defeated, materialistic, superficial world.

*Fear not, friends. Have hope. Everything hidden will be brought to light. They **will** be exposed.*

This is Tessa Ryan, signing out.

Chapter 64

The next day broke with a fall nip in the air, but no frost. The entire city was on edge, waiting for updates on the infected snake and the risk of Tetracimia to the human population.

In his favorite chrome-trimmed vinyl booth at the Near and Far Café, Jack Weber was already hard at work, meeting with his sidekick/keen investigator.

Chris waited while the frumpy server poured more coffee, popping a piece of bacon in his mouth as she walked away. "I've got an inside source that's going to help us break this wide open." With every other table in the coffee shop occupied, his voice was barely audible over the din.

Jack finished his poached eggs, carefully setting his fork on the empty plate. "And that is?" Reaching for his hand sanitizer, he dabbed at his mouth with a crumpled napkin.

"It's a guy..." Sensing someone nearby, Chris glanced over his shoulder while the server removed their empty plates. When she was well out of earshot, he continued. "It's a guy named Adam Logose. He's on contract with New World Now – an investigative journalist," he whispered.

"NWN." Jack shook his head. "They're liars."

"I know that! That's the whole purpose of our operation. But if he gets us good information?" Chris implored. "As a whistle-blower?"

Jack looked at the ice cubes in his glass while he jiggled them. "Yeah. I'll believe it when I see it."

"Hear me out, Jack." Chris seemed to have something critical to say.

Jack resigned with a single nod. "Fine," he sighed.

"Well," Chris glanced over both shoulders. "Adam was invited to the centennial celebration and noticed something seemed off at the plant. While the big club was busy schmoozing, someone slipped him a note. Introduced himself as Boris."

"And how do *you* know Adam?"

"Let's just say walls have ears." Chris winked. "He thinks he knows what happened to old man Fisher."

"Really?" Jack was stunned; he thought that case would never be solved. "So, if Adam has information, why isn't *he* doing a story about it?"

Chris added a packet of sugar to his fresh cup of steaming coffee, whacking it to get the last several grains. "Because they discredit real journalists and use the full force of the law against them. Malicious prosecution."

"So, targeting journalists *and* political opponents." Jack guzzled the rest of his coffee. "How Hitleresque of them."

"Uh huh," Chris agreed. "Then they pay millions of dollars a year to *their* puppets who will say exactly what's in the script. I believe that's called propaganda."

"I believe you are right." Jack flipped the bill over. "People want a source they can trust, and it's too easy to discredit internet sources. Their 'fact checkers' are considered the authority on truth." He banged his plastic water glass on the table. *Cardboard straw. Plastic glass. That mega-wealthy Mars guy had it right... they were only interested in looking good, not doing good. Also known as virtue signaling.* He chuckled to himself.

"The first casualty of war is the truth – that's why we need to build culture."

"Come on, Chris. We're struggling to be heard over their lies. I'm doing all I can to launch AltMedia Group just to get the truth out. But how can we begin to make a dent in *their culture*?"

Chris leaned back and cracked his knuckles. "I have a few ideas."

Chapter 65

Earth to Sky Gallery was a former linen factory housed in an old, faded two-story brick building. The upper floor had been converted to an exclusive, modern social space for the affluent of the art community, while the main floor retained its warehouse charm and the nostalgic scent of oily wood floors. The gallery was a community-owned co-op, staffed by volunteers, and managed by the handsome, happily married, 48-year-old Rajesh Kumar.

On Tessa's first visit, it didn't take long for her to discover the Jackson Pollock corner – the Wyoming artist who'd inspired her to first pick up a paintbrush! While she inspected the display, she wiped away a tear to mourn the life that might have been. *Maybe these backward hicks did have the taste for fine art, after all.*

With Hindustani music playing softly in the background, Rajesh noticed Tessa's tears, offering her comfort until he knew her whole sordid life story. At the end of the impromptu counseling session, he asked if she'd like to volunteer for a special project, leading her to the back of the building near the alley.

Panicked, Tessa froze halfway down the narrow wooden steps. She didn't know anything about the guy!

Sensing Tessa's apprehension, Rajesh continued across the dusty, concrete basement lit only by a dangling, single light bulb. Basements like this always had a certain musty smell, and it was especially strong in this space. She watched every move he made, ready to bolt if he turned around.

When he reached the corner between the storage and maintenance rooms, Rajesh pulled the heavy drop cloth off three medium-sized cardboard boxes full of random abstracts.

With her fine-art eagle eye recognizing one of the pieces instantly, Tessa closed the gap in no time, crouching down to inspect the treasure at her feet, having forgotten all about her fear.

"You're the perfect person to catalog these." Rajesh waved his hand over the boxes. "You interested?"

"Yes!" Tessa beamed, a look of pure delight spreading across her face. "When can I start?!"

"How about now?" Rajesh's fatherly smile warmed Tessa's judgmental little heart – *maybe there were still some good people in the world*. He helped her set up a sorting table, then disappeared up the creaky stairs.

In the dust and eerie silence, Tessa rolled up the sleeves of her fuzzy pink cardigan and got on her knees to go to work. She selected four pieces to start with, setting them beside the supplies on the table.

With her self-proclaimed bony butt on the concrete floor, inspecting one of the paintings with a magnifying glass, Tessa spotted something across the room. She adjusted the magnifying glass and squinted. Above a shelf, covered with a drop cloth to keep the dust off, was a painting that was visible on one corner where the covering had slipped. From her unusual vantage point, it looked like a piece she might recognize. She scrambled to her feet.

It was in a dark area of the basement, off-limits behind a rope, so naturally Tessa had to check it out. As she got closer, her heart skipped a beat. *It was...what? A...a Kandinsky? An original!?* If so, it was worth millions!

Tessa quickly removed the painting to inspect it, and....the shelf moved in two different directions until it revealed an eerie, strangely lit brick tunnel. The rough concrete wall and the shelf itself were a flimsy façade! Alarmed, she returned the painting to its place, prompting the shelves to close.

Footsteps! And they were coming down the stairs! Tessa's heart thumped. *How was she going to get out of this one?*

T he moment the gallery manager came around the corner, the emergency alert system screamed across the city. Screeeeech! Screeeeech! Screeeeech! Hummm. Hummm. Screech. Screech! Screech!

Saved by the screech. After bidding a hasty goodbye to Rajesh, Tessa rushed home to catch the updates on corporate media. It was five days before the election, and the snake had finally been captured.

New World Now (NWN) immediately cut to live footage, captured on a home security camera: It's early morning. A man is entering his shed. With his back to the camera, a hooded king cobra comes into view and strikes the man in the back of his neck.

From the NWN studios, the broadcaster reported that "experts from the facility confirmed that King Herod survived the cold by taking shelter in a man's storage shed near a baseboard heater. When the owner of the property entered the dark shed, he was struck in the back of the neck by the threatened cobra." At Dormin Reptile Gardens, the cameras zoomed in on the diseased celebrity snake, who'd been returned to his enclosure. He had no visible signs of illness.

"And now we go to St. Theresa's Hospital for this developing story." The anchor waited while the reporter came into focus. "What can you tell us about what's going on, Miranda?"

"Hi Josh... the man in question is a recent Asian immigrant, Dr. Kai Li. After he was struck, he went into shock immediately and was rushed to emergency here at St. Theresa's." Miranda paused while the camera panned the full ICU. "He was successfully treated for the snakebite, but doctors *have* confirmed that Dr. Li is the first human case of Tetracimia and is in critical condition. Aside from the prognostic full body rash, he is running a high fever and is currently breathing with the help of a ventilator. The medical staff continues to fight to save his life." The camera's eye was again on the reporter. "Miranda Black. New World Now. St. Ther–"

With a major story to prepare, Tessa turned the TV off.

Meanwhile, at Dormin Reptile Gardens, a young man was winding down his research on King Herod. International graduate student, Gabriel Sorenson, had the looks of a soap opera star and the drive of an athlete. Of all the places he wanted to complete his doctoral studies in ophiology, it was here, at the world-famous facility – not everyone gets a chance to work with a celebrity snake.

Partway through his research, Gabriel had become aware of a discrepancy between the official Tetracimia story and reality – a *glaring* discrepancy. He _had to get_ the information out to the public. It was a risk, but too important to keep hidden. It was the right thing to do.

The next day, Dr. Li slipped into a coma and died of Tetracimia, unable to hear his hysterical wife begging the medical staff to let her see him. While health authorities ascertained transmissibility in human populations, it was best to keep him in isolation until an autopsy could be performed, they told her. The pathogen *could* be airborne, and carriers *could* be asymptomatic.

Chapter 66

That brisk November evening, Jack Weber's supporters lined up by the thousands for the finale of his legendary campaign events. There was something much bigger to worry about than getting sick – recapturing their power from the global elites.

Alt Media's star anchor and reporter, Tessa Ryan, was in attendance to cover the story, a natural for her first time reporting live on location. A growing number of curious viewers were counting on her to make sense of the senseless and convey that there was *no* stopping the momentum of their movement – even if they *all* got arrested and killed. The people were slowly waking up.

"*The atmosphere at the Moreno Theater is electric tonight, making it near impossible to hear above the roar of the crowd. It's the joyful sound of passionate patriots refusing to bow down to powers trying to crush the will of the people. They can't kill an idea, despite their lack of trying.*" Tessa was nearly shouting.

On that fabled November night, Jack's campaign message was loud and clear: "**The power belongs to the people,** not an elite group of unrestrained, corporate-owned, unaccountable bureaucrats."

The crowd booed in a show of support.

Cutting away from Jack's speech, Tessa continued to update her followers. "*In the crowd tonight are people of all ages, both sexes, and every class, race and creed. We even have people who like pineapple on pizza, and the weirdos who don't,*" she laughed. "*United by principles, this is **actual** diversity, equity, and inclusion in action.*"

By now, Jack was winding down his speech. "Tomorrow, we say *enough*! The spirit of the founders lives on through us. Never give up. We will never surrender! God! Bless! America!"

Beyond the sound of the music, the cheering crowd could be heard for miles as the anticipation built and echoed throughout the valley.

In the din, Tessa continued her story. "*Despite the branding as racist backward hicks and white trash, Weber supporters continue to cling to their traditional values. They will never surrender the idea of true individual liberty or family.*" She panned the huge, cheering crowd with her cellphone. "*It's interesting to note that despite what I'm seeing, the rally will be twisted into a Klan event by the press, predictably. They'll say that the campaign slogan, "Power to the people" is a racist dog whistle that's both disruptive and dangerous.*"

With gigantic Stars and Stripes waving on the jumbo screen, the emotional crowd lifted their voice to sing as if calling on the Heavens to save their country.

O say can you see by the dawn's early light
What we proudly so hailed at the twilight's last gleaming[1]

When the anthem finished, Tessa wiped away a tear and zipped her bag closed. She'd managed to capture footage of the media deception. Their clever camera angles captured only white people, and none of the hundreds of people of color. Tricks were used to reduce the size of the crowd in the mind of the viewer. Selective editing took Jack's words out of context, until 'white supremacist' was code for people who valued the content of one's character rather than the color of one's skin.

While it appeared that Jack Weber was the most popular, *by far*, the newscasters reported that voters rejected him. What the citizens were being told, and what they were seeing didn't match – the 24/7 rage fests about his supporters were outlandish yarns in which a diverse and passionate group of people was reduced to a wildly inaccurate caricature.

Conversely, Max Fisher barely campaigned, kissed a lot of fussing babies, and read from a teleprompter to his tens of supporters from the upper crust.

---

1. <u>The Star Spangled Banner</u>, Francis Scott Key

Max ended his campaign the same way he started it – with an ostentatious display of his wealth and connections. His grand ballroom, with the majestic mountains and the estate's grand gardens as the backdrop, was the setting for the exclusive fundraiser that lasted until the wee hours of the morning. Tickets were a not-so-subtle $66,666 per person.

Though the lackluster soiree wasn't televised, secretly recorded footage was released to the public on social media by an anonymous account that went by the moniker Mr. X. Because of Tetracimia, Dormin was now based on a caste system in which the slave class could be identified by the white armbands they wore. The elite wore black armbands, and there were only two classes at *this* event.

With the biggest and wealthiest celebrities in the world at the black-tie affair, an offering was made to Lucifer: Covered from head to toe in blood red, they flashed devil horns while dancing in a circle. A pentagram was enclosed within it. A ring of fire blazed.

Chapter 67

The morning after the election, daybreak was gloomy and surreal, much like the mood of the city.

As much as she just wanted to go back to sleep – metaphorically and literally, Tessa tuned into the corporate news coverage for updates. The consensus was that no winner could be declared; there were still thousands of uncounted ballots. EYE on Dormin covered the story by interviewing elections officials at several polling locations.

New World Now, meanwhile, didn't touch it. The coverage was exclusively Tetracimia.

NWN: *Although little is known about the mysterious illness, a state of emergency has been declared. They're now certain it is highly contagious and as much as one tenth of the population of Dormin could die if it isn't contained. They're predicting that if it gets beyond the boundaries of the city, it could spell doom for human populations globally. Darkness is only a heartbeat away.*

Shocked at how quickly it escalated, Tessa wondered where they were going with it. She flipped back to EYE on Dormin and didn't have to wait long.

EYE: *Symptoms of Tetracimia poisoning are red, inflamed skin, often accompanied by small, fluid-filled blisters that can appear anywhere on the body and in severe cases, all over the body. Other warning signs include numbness, confusion and fatigue.*

If not treated promptly, the pathogen can cause a lowered immune response, difficulty breathing, brain swelling and death. Alarmingly, carriers could be asymptomatic – they could be spreading the disease without knowing they have it. The only way to know for certain is to get tested.

As she gulped the last of her third now-cold coffee, Tessa turned off the TV to begin her report. The show must go on.

File notes: TDR Report (transcribed)
November 9, 2016

With election day over, we don't have a winner, the media is back to the Tetracimia story on a loop, and collective sanity has taken a good old smack right upside the head.

Do y'all have your armbands? And what do those colors mean, anyway? We didn't pick those colors; they were picked for us. Why? The official story is that it's to do with different levels of immunity or something. Like, what? [Laughter] Well, maybe, but not like they mean.

Black is the ruling class. White is the slave class. We are red – we won't comply. Yellow is the group that goes along to get along. Green are the ruling class boot lickers and useful idiots.

How do they know so much about all of us? We tell them every time we go online or use a credit card. They know what we buy and what we eat and who we love and what our political opinions are. Not only do we have a digital footprint, we've reached Orwellian level surveillance.

The health authorities are now saying that the pathogen is highly contagious but is not airborne as they'd originally theorized. It can, however, live on surfaces for days, weeks, or even months. If it gets on the skin, it's likely to cause the telltale rash.

The authorities also claim that it clings to cash like leeches on fresh blood. Cash will be outlawed – just watch. In the name of public health, of course. Do you see where this is going? Digital everything until humans are reduced by machines. What does a social credit score look like? Obedience, conditioned responses, rewards, and punishments – like a dog.

Consider that under a state of emergency, unelected bureaucrats make all the rules. They'll decide what businesses are considered essential and which ones aren't. They will control when you can leave your house and who you can hang around with. They'll use the climate crisis as an excuse to put limits on what we can buy. Have you noticed that everything that is supposedly good for the planet is bad for humanity?

Also consider that digital shipping, big box stores and giant corporations have been given the green light to stay in operation because? Reasons. They've ordered mom and pop shops and churches to close. Sports teams will continue to play, but there will be no real fans. We'll be replaced by CGI, cardboard cutouts, and fake crowd noise. Playgrounds are roped off, skate parks filled with sand, and the riverbank monitored. Everyone is under house arrest.

This is bad, folks.

If I get more information, you'll be the first to know. Stay free.

Hold the line, patriots. We got this.

This is Tessa Ryan, signing out.

Chapter 68

In Jack's electronics room, he and Chris watched Tessa's broadcast with renewed interest.

"Don't you find it odd that the corporate media isn't touching the election story?"

"Nope," Chris disagreed. "Cockroaches scurry away when you turn the light on. We've been going about this all wrong."

"What do you mean?"

Chris rose from the end of the sofa to stretch. "It's not who votes. It's who counts the votes."

Jack hesitated. "So, we have to take over the count?"

"Something like that."

Chapter 69

Several days had passed since Tessa last spoke to a key source – Gabriel Sorenson from the reptile facility. He was *still* ignoring her repeated texts. She'd been trying to reach him by phone all day, to no avail. It went straight to voice mail. *Again.*

Beep

"Hi Gabe," Tessa sighed. "It's Tessa Ryan with TDR Report following up on our last discussion." She checked her watch. "There's urgency in getting this story out, so if you could *please* give me a call, I'd appreciate it. Thanks."

Lemon-scented essential oils burst forth from the diffuser on the round table beside Tessa's feet, the aroma drifting throughout the sunroom – her preferred spot for enjoying the twilight and cool evenings. Mesmerized by the slow gliding lights of a tourist boat on the river, her mind wandered. *Had Gabriel changed his mind? Gotten cold feet? Had he been threatened? Was he okay?*

A loud, obnoxious ringtone jerked a pensive Tessa out of her reverie... a voice call. *Gabe! Oh.* "Hi Adam." She failed to hide the disappointment in her voice.

"Hello, beautiful. What're you up to?" Adam sounded upbeat and full of energy.

"Waiting to hear from a source. He promised he'd get me some information about the origins of the Tetracimia outbreak." Tessa stood up to stretch. "That was a week ago."

"It's all anyone is talking about these days, it seems." Adam chuckled. "That, and how they're going to get their precious vastly overpriced avocado toast."

"Perceived media-induced scarcity," Tessa giggled.

"I know," Adam sighed, picturing Tessa's beautiful baby-blue eyes. "People aren't rational anymore. Why would they support restricting healthy populations rather than quarantining the sick?"

"Could it be because of those scrolling case and death counts at the bottom of their TV screens when they have your channel on? Like they're hypnotized? Or maybe the screens are scrying mirrors?"

"Could be, I guess." Adam's tone was a mixture of acceptance and remorse. Journalism wasn't what it once was.

"All I hear is blah blah blah." Tessa filed the nail on her index finger. "I don't even know what's real anymore." Her dreamy mind wandered to Saboro Point, where she and Adam had enjoyed each other's company such a short time ago. *That* was real. "What are *you* up to?"

"Because it's such a beautiful evening, me and my good boy are lounging in the back yard."

"Woof!"

"Ralph! Hi Ralph!" Tessa gushed. "Woof!"

"He's wagging his tail. I think he likes you." The delight in Adam's voice was unmistakable. This trio had a mutual admiration society going that got him right in the feelers.

"I think I like him too," Tessa laughed. "He melts my heart."

"Do you want to know what you do to my heart?" Adam's tone was low and sensuous.

"Adam, I...we...I mean... never mind," Tessa stammered, instantly changing gears. "Um, have I told you it's getting more difficult to get the word out using their infrastructure?"

The heavy sigh on the other end of the call was audible. "Really?"

"MainStreet is working on new terms of service, which can only mean one thing – they're going to crank up the content moderation and deplatforming. AKA censorship."

"Trust a corporation," Adam rolled his eyes, unable to hide the disinterest in his voice.

"Why does it feel like the government is running it? A corporation has only one goal – to maximize profits for shareholders." Tessa filed her thumb nail. "Government, on the other hand, tries to censor people. It will come down to two choices: Toe the empire's line or be banned."

"Do you think it will really get that bad?" Adam had reengaged. As a *real* journalist, he *did* care about censorship.

"I do have to go, though," Tessa sighed. "I'm working on a high-priority story. I'll call soon. Bye, Ad –"

"Babe, don't hang up on me!" Tessa was caught off guard by the drama in his voice. "Why won't you talk to me? What's *really* going on?"

"Nothing's *going on*, Adam. I'm only working on the biggest story of our lifetime." Her tone was impatient and abrupt, leaving little doubt that she was stressed to the max.

"I get that, sweetheart," Adam closed his eyes. "I know you're stressed, but not even a text?"

A moment passed before Tessa found the courage to say it. "I'm sorry, Adam!" She stifled a sob. "I can't explain."

"What?!" On his feet now, his eyes fully open, Adam felt like he'd been kicked in the stomach. "Are you telling me it's over? Just like that?"

Tessa swiped to end the call and flopped onto her unmade bed without another word. She couldn't tell Adam that she was falling in love with him, that Aamon had ruined any chance of happiness she had, or that she could never fully trust again. She needed to put the whole thing behind her.

Chapter 70

Dormin Times

November 30, 2016

**MAJOR UPSET!
LYING WEBER DECLARED WINNER IN CLOSE MAYORAL RACE!
FRAUD SUSPECTED IN ELECTION RESULTS**

In the shadow of majestic Saboro Mountain, an emergency meeting convened on the same snowy day the election results were announced. Light flakes, each different from the last, fell gently from the dark sky like tiny fluffy pillows clinging to the bed of thick branches of the evergreens.

Worried about the tone of Jack's ominous text message, three guests were present in his study, helping themselves to the refreshments on the coffee table.

Chris Simon had his back to the other guests, mesmerized by the expertly groomed and well-lit grounds on Jack's property, just as beautiful in the winter as they were in summer, especially with the Christmas display all lit up. He took a sip of red wine as he turned around. "What's so urgent that it couldn't wait? Asking for an entire team."

Jack leaned back in his wing-back chair to study the troubled faces around him, all doing their best to avoid eye contact. With his ankle resting on his knee, he formed a steeple with his fingertips, slowly raising it to his mouth. Tension hung in the air like a black storm cloud ready to burst.

"Jack?" The soft coaxing had come from Emma Langford, the British psychologist with the sweet, sensuous voice.

"I'm starting to question whether this task is a losing battle." Jack's voice betrayed his usual bravado.

"I thought you knew what you were getting into," Chris reminded him, not sure how he forgot about the blackmail operation.

"I thought I did. But I wasn't expecting my term to be MINO – mayor in name only."

For several seconds, the steady ticking of the grandfather clock was the only sound in the strained room, vigilant as it stood watch over the nervous guests. Next to the distinguished family heirloom, a trimmed and fragrant spruce tree was blinking hypnotic red, white, and blue in the soft light.

General Manfred Fowler had claimed his spot in the corner. Exhausted and slumped against the back of the rocking chair, he cleared his throat. "In the military, we swear an oath to the Constitution. We don't surrender to enemies – foreign or domestic."

"We've been so zeroed in on countering the propaganda, I forgot about transferring power back to the people." Jack was visibly agitated, having to admit to himself and others that he didn't have all the answers.

"Well, if it helps, Fisher just released a statement saying that his administration had been scandal free." Chris smirked while the group enjoyed a good laugh. "Then he warned us about deep fakes. You know what that means."

"It means there's a war on for your mind." All heads turned toward Emma. Her dark hair was in a low bun and accessorized by her signature white cat-eyeglasses; the look lent the air of a stern elderly librarian.

"Okay." Chris paced, rubbing his hands together. "So, where do we go with our media alliance? I thought that was our plan."

"Take a cue from our enemy. The information doesn't matter." Emma raised her dainty shoulders. "Have you heard of Edward Bernays?"

"Bernays..." Chris stopped pacing. "Freud's nephew? The marketing guy?"

"That's the one." Emma confirmed. "The proverbial evil genius."

"How does that relate to what we're doing, Emma?" Jack sighed while she checked the time.

"Through his manipulation of human psychology, he fundamentally changed society in some disturbing ways." Emma scanned the room to make sure she had their attention. "He knew you don't market products or even ideas, you market emotions."

"Emma's right. The information is irrelevant. It's how it's sold." General Fowler reminded the group that the military had extensive experience with psychological operations.

"What do you mean?" Jack asked, frowning.

"Well, I'm making a prediction that one day, the empire will jail the leaders of so-called rogue nations and convince the people it's to save democracy." General Fowler broke character to smirk.

The room erupted in laughter.

"They'll bully and weaponize law enforcement against innocent citizens." General Fowler stood up to stretch, his larger-than-life presence filling the room.

Several seconds passed before Emma spoke. "The average person trusts the government more than they trust their family and friends."

Staring at the wall above General Fowler's head, Jack whistled. "That's a hell of a place to be – the people have been trained to trust authority all their lives."

"Precisely. They think the government cares about them, so they conclude that their friends and family are crazy." Emma was clearly sympathetic to those experiencing such cognitive dissonance – confirmation of their bias was all it took.

"That explains why so many people claim to have crazy relatives," Jack mused.

"So, what's the plan?" Jack dropped his trembling palms on the arms of his chair. "Where do we go from here?"

"They will do everything they can to stop the flow of information. And I mean *everything*." Everyone turned to look at General Fowler. "There's a whole division of the military *dedicated* to it."

"That's the idea of this project, isn't it? Find a way that *we* can set the narrative – tell the *real* stories that serve the people, not the empire. *We* can unite under one working-class banner and take on their League of LIES." Chris thought it funny that they were called the League – like a group of professional sports team owners with the balls of neutered insects.

Leaning back, Jack picked at the arms of his chair with both hands. The room fell silent while everyone waited for his reply. "Okay." He stood up. "I'm more convinced than ever of two things: one, the war might be in vain." He held up one finger. "And two, it's worth fighting. The alternative leaves us no choice." He held up the second finger.

General Fowler was back on his feet. "Like our founding fathers who fought for independence – either you do it, or you live under the thumb of a self-declared emperor. This is the second American Revolution."

"*This* is also a spiritual war – the proverbial biblical battle between good and evil." Chris placed his hands on the back of Jack's empty chair. "Are we in the end times?"

Chapter 71

Sickened at the thought of not having Adam in her life, Tessa forced herself to focus on her work. It was already the beginning of December and they had so much work to do.

File notes: TDR Report (transcribed)
December 3, 2016
"Thou shalt not kill." (Exodus 20:13, KJV)
Breaking! Twenty-two days after the ballots were cast, the November 8 Mayoral election finally has a winner. In a shocking upset, Jack Weber toppled a giant. There's a whole lot more to this story than I know right now. All I can say is that there will be hell to pay. I will inform you of any breaking news.
That was a nice reprieve; now, let's back to Tetracimia.
I can now name my facility insider and report that he's gone missing. I repeat, my primary source has gone missing! His name is Gabriel Sorenson. He's an international ophiology doctorate student completing his research on king cobras. That's his photo on the screen.
When I called the lead scientist on the Tetracimia task force, Dr. Neil Olsen, he informed me that Gabriel had returned to Sweden due to the illness. Well, we did a little sleuthing, and I'll tell ya what. We could find no evidence to support that claim – no digital footprint, no flight records, no sightings. Strangely, the police don't seem at all interested. If you know Gabriel, or if you see him, please contact any one of us with the AltMedia Group. Something really stinks about this.
Tonight, I am releasing the raw intelligence on the origin of Tetracimia and was going to give me more concrete proof. The story goes that King Herod

was imported as a baby snake from Indonesia back in 2001. Dormin Reptile Gardens was a still a few months away from opening, so he went to live with the man in charge – one Dr. Neil Olsen. Yes, the same one I spoke to. During that time, Herod's venom glands were removed to reduce the danger to his handler.

The official story was that infected venom glands had poisoned his blood. If there are no infected venom glands, what's the illness we're seeing?

I will bring you any updates as they break. Gabriel's bravery will not be in vain.

Hold the line, Patriots, we got this.

This is Tessa Ryan, signing out.

Chapter 72

The glaring white exit light and the glow of a lit cigar were the only things visible in the dark movie theater at the Fisher mansion. The double door behind Max squeaked open. A cone of white light shone across the rows of seats and onto the blank screen.

"Who's there?" Max was seated in the front row with his paisley silk robe open, exposing several white chest hairs. He opened the nearly empty bottle of scotch from the brown bag beside him to throw back a couple of stiff ounces.

"I'm worried about you, Max." The visitor cleared her throat as she started down the side aisle. "Do you even know what day it is?"

Max remained perfectly still. "Rosie, where did I go wrong? How did it get so off the rails?"

In her sky-blue cotton robe, Rosie was barefoot, without makeup, and wearing her long, bleached hair loose. "Max, you lost touch with the people, and they knew it." She sat next to Max to comfort him.

"It was working perfectly, Rosie. We were so close to having full control of them. Full control of their minds." He pinched his fingers together and held them in the air.

"Well, Max –"

"Having them revel in their servitude, charging a fee to live on their own planet and a tax on their own labor. Working long and hard just to survive. Being able to track their every move, flattering them and praising their obedience."

"Maybe that was the wrong approach." Rosie's gentle voice was barely a whisper.

"That's how we filled our coffers with their blood, sweat, and tears. They financed their own demise." Max was shaking.

"That's harsh, Max."

"Harsh? No, Rosie. You haven't seen harsh yet." Max slurped his scotch as he shifted in his seat. "Maybe it was easier to keep them in line when they *knew* they were slaves."

Rosie's voice was thick with emotion when she stood up. "Max, it's Christmas Eve. Sober up get some sleep." She gently massaged his tense shoulders. "Maybe you'd feel better if you paid more attention to the ranch."

Max's face turned red, the liquid splashing out of his glass and onto the sleeve of his robe. "The ranch won't give me what I want, you stupid woman!" He tried to get up. "I swear Rosie, it's payback time!" The glass shattered on the floor.

Chapter 73

Three days after Christmas, morning broke with a tinge of pastel pink reflecting off the hoarfrost, the sense of time all but suspended until the arrival of the new year. Contrasting with the diverse Moreno Forest along the vibrant north bank, the whitewater of the mighty Arem was frozen in place, brimming tributaries snaking their way through the Arctic floe. Ice crystals sparkled like diamonds in the snowbanks where the suspended mist had settled.

Exactly one week after she turned thirty-two, Tessa woke up with the same thought she always had – where was Adam, and what was he doing? Was he seeing someone else? Squeezing her eyes shut, she cursed herself for not having the courage to continue their friendship. Her head *knew* he wasn't Aamon, but her heart didn't get the memo.

After a good cry and a long, refreshing shower, full of energy and covered in fashionable layers, Tessa braved the elements for her daily walk along the river. A hooded fleece and matching blue winter accessories *mostly* sheltered her from the biting wind, despite clouds of her breath forming in front of her rosy-red cheeks.

Carefully navigating her way down the snow-packed, deteriorating wood steps to the crumbling pavement, Tessa paused on the narrow path to appreciate the sun dogs lighting up the clear sky across the river. It was almost as if the surreal and intricately designed Earth was one of superior intelligence. *Almost.*

Tessa's sense of serenity was shattered when she tripped over her own feet on the sidewalk, spun around, and landed on the snow-covered concrete. From her vantage point of a sore butt, Dormin's new, shocking reality came into focus. The entire city had been shut off from the outside world!? The roads were barricaded, the riverbank patrolled by menacing robotic dogs.

Judging from the World War II stories Tessa had heard, *this* was bad. *Really bad!* Little did she know it was going to get a whole lot worse.

By the time the calendar flipped to the new year, Tessa regretted her decision to leave New York City. Manhattan, for all its faults, wasn't dealing with mass stupidity. *They were shallow, not stupid.* There were bad cops there, like everywhere, but at least they didn't have robot dogs – that she knew about. She missed her best friend, Megan, who was still in the Big Apple raising a family and running the Hippies group. Regardless, she couldn't go back. Not yet.

In Dormin, January came in like a raging lion – blizzard conditions with gale-force winds and wet, heavy snow. Outside Tessa's studio window, thick clouds rendered the sun but a dim spot in the rose-tinged gray noise. The wind whipped at the windowpane as it howled.

Inside her AltMedia Group studio, Tessa hunched over her laptop, ready to broadcast an unscheduled news alert. Swallowing the rest of her cold coffee, she turned off the smooth jazz music. The show must go on.

File Notes: TDR Report (transcribed)
January 1, 2017

"And be not conformed to this world; but be ye transformed by the renewing of your mind, that ye may prove what is that good, and acceptable, and perfect, will of God." (Romans 12:2 KJV)

Happy New Year from TDR Report! I wasn't going to do a show today, but I have a breaking news bulletin. I'll be quick.

*EYE on Dormin's most popular host got fired today! On New Years, no less. Tiffany Lynn Kyle was the **only** voice of truth and reason in the entirety of the corporate media. I think it's because she was talking about an international fraud ring that fixes global elections. Nobody else will risk their livelihood.*

*According to Tiffany's reporting, it's the **Pentagon** running elections, which doesn't surprise me. It's **how** they're doing it that surprised me.*

Think about the shape of the Pentagon for a minute – a five-pointed star... like a... you know... a pentagram. Imagine a government that works in the shadows, that is closely connected to the dark path...the dark arts, if you will. Imagine that spells and rituals take place around elections to convince the unsuspecting public that they don't have sinister intentions.

Are you starting to connect the dots? A handful of major corporations own Congress. That means they own the military. **That's** *who the corporate media work for, so they can't do the right thing even if they wanted to. They know they're a dying breed, so they lash out in anger like cornered animals while they try to silence us. Independent journalism is the way of the future.*

It looks like we've ignited the wrath of an ancient empire.

Hold the line, patriots. We got this.

This is Tessa Ryan, signing out.

Chapter 74

On a bitterly cold January morning, the hallowed halls of the city administration offices were eerily silent but for the nervous man behind the closed door of the mayor's office. The otherwise generic bureaucratic room was flooded with gleaming rays of sunlight, somewhat lessening the sense of frustration and pessimism that permeated the entire building.

It was the second week of the year; Jack had only been in power for a few days and already he was to blame for the extinction of the dinosaurs and the founding of the KKK. *Probably.* He shook his head and chuckled. *Nutcases.*

Peering down at the empty streets five floors below city hall, Jack's mind drifted. It was all so sinister, so insidious. Half the city believed that he was Satan Incarnate, and the other half knew that the empire would have done the same thing to *anyone* who challenged their power.

Upon the arrival of his visitor, Jack turned off the muted 'news' coverage; the screen mounted on the wall across from the weathered desk faded to black.

Chris's face was still beet-red from exposure to the elements when he set two take-out cups of steaming hot liquid on the desk. With the scent of coffee and chocolate in the air, he removed his gloves and heavy coat to reveal a light pink golf shirt that somehow made him look even more masculine and sexy.

"Mocha?" Jack swung his legs off the desk to pick up the hot liquid, closing his eyes as he inhaled the aroma. "Thanks."

"Of course." Leaning back in one of the duct-taped dark-green chairs with the hot coffee warming his hands, Chris pondered their current situation: the people had inherited a segregated, run-down, disease-and-crime-ridden hell hole with a mysterious illness and tons of fentanyl circulating in the streets – an infernal purgatory where hope went to die.

"What's on your mind?" Jack asked the question he already knew the answer to.

"Is there some way we can convince Dorminians that what's causing their misery isn't incompetence, or poor planning, or neglect? It's the *goal* – healthy communities don't have daddy issues."

"I know. We're woefully short of resources for our most vulnerable citizens." Jack slapped a thick file with his palm – the file was labeled, simply '**2016-2017 Budget**'. "All the money is spent but nothing ever gets done. If the government wants to be daddy, they should be a better provider."

"A good start would be decriminalizing intoxicants."

"Is that wise?"

"Well, think about it. Addiction is hard enough without being thrown in jail; nobody benefits from that."

"Definitely." Jack was on his feet again. "Trafficking is a different matter."

"*They're* the criminals," Chris agreed.

"Speaking of criminals, how do they have so much money to investigate *me* for trafficking so they can take the heat off themselves?"

"True. But counter surveillance works both ways. We're gathering quite an evidence folder on their *actual* trafficking operation." Chris detected the faint odor of disinfectant, as if sterilizing the ivory tower would somehow cleanse the city of its social problems. "Did you have any idea the corruption was so far reaching?"

"Not even close. With their ownership of the legal system, and I use that term loosely, will it make a difference?" Jack sighed. He'd had no intention of governing like a traditional politician in the lost city, but his determination was short-lived, courtesy of unwittingly surrounding himself with backstabbers – the permanent power sometimes referred to as the deep state. "So, what do you have for me, there?"

"Election stuff. Prepare to be shocked." Chris put the report on the desk in front of Jack.

"Shocked?" Jack ignored the thick file.

"What we were looking for wasn't there. We found something way bigger."

"No kidding?"

"Okay. You know how people have been talking about cheating on ballots and voting machines and that?"

"Yeah. For many years now."

"Correct." Chris nodded. "Well, turns out it's all irrelevant. The US military runs elections." He searched the cluttered desk for a tissue. "And... in a spiritual battle, they call on the power of Satan."

"You mean... literally?"

"Very much so." Chris nodded emphatically. "According to our sources, they have *rituals* to influence the outcome."

"Get out of here! Their rituals don't have that much power. God can squash Satan like a bug."

"Exactly. And that's what happened. That's why you won."

"I'm not following."

"Unbeknownst to us at the time, a group of citizens had formed a prayer group, and every night at 10 pm, they had a national video conference to pray a certain prayer."

"Wow. What was the prayer?"

Grabbing his phone, Chris scrolled for a minute then cleared his throat while he made the sign of the cross.

> *Creator God, the devil fights hard against us because we're making a difference for Your Kingdom. Today we remember that the battle is Yours, Lord, and You can take them down in one fell swoop. Fill us with the Holy Spirit as we strive to do your good works. We ask this in Jesus' name.*

"Amen," the two men said in unison while they made eye contact. An instant understanding took place in that gaze, that winning the election was only a symbolic gesture.

"We're a long way from winning against these evil bastards. What's the purpose of these damned elections?"

"Considering we haven't really won anything *yet*, I'm inclined to agree." Chris smiled. "Elections are like everything else – all theater. Until we count the votes, all we can do is attempt to restore trust in the system."

"Yeah. Good luck with that."

"Right? The city is bursting with the resentful decay of the voiceless and oppressed – what the empire calls vermin."

"What the hell kind of evil are we really us against, here?" Jack buried his face in his hands.

"They do whatever they want." Chris shrugged. "Because we let them." He closed his eyes and tipped his cup back to get a mouthful of Colombian blend. Ahh.

Clenching his jaw tighter, Jack poured himself some more limeade. "We can't have clean elections until we fix the legal system, and we can't fix the legal system because we can't have clean elections!"

"I believe that's what we call a quandary, a constitutional crisis, perhaps? When the lawmakers are lawless?" Running his fingertips across his goatee, Chris cleared his throat.

"Uh huh."

"Well, guess what?" Chris dug deep for his characteristic intestinal fortitude, AKA guts. "They can either bring our elections into this century, or they can step aside and let us do it." He sat up straight. "*Especially* tech."

"Absolutely. Not only are the big tech companies fronts for the CIA, the Pentagon *designed* them with psychological warfare in mind." Jack dumped hand sanitizer into his palm.

"And the voting machines. They tell us that they might glitch, but there's nothing they can do about it. That's total BS." Chris sat on the edge of the seat with his spine perfectly aligned. "If we can see life on a planet millions of miles away, perform laser surgery, and use AI to manipulate the world, we can have voting machines that work... and everybody knows they don't."

"What do you suggest?"

"My generation is all about technology. If we can wrestle control away from the oligarchs, we can vote online using blockchain. One social security number, one vote." Rolling his head around his tensed shoulders, Chris massaged his neck. "People want more convenience and less interaction with other people these days."

"And for those who don't feel safe voting online?"

"They can still choose to vote in person. On hand-counted ballots. Not those garbage machines." Chris moved his head from side to side.

"Without the political will, that's *not* going to happen. They'll come up with excuses of why it won't work – like they call voter ID racist."

"You and I both know that." Chris reminded Jack who he was dealing with – as a black man, there was nothing more offensive than the soft bigotry of low expectations. *Enough already.* "Let's remind them who their boss is. That's *our* political will."

"The joys of modern warfare."

"The enemy's power isn't only what they have, it's what the people *think* they have." Trying to suppress a yawn, Chris stood up to stretch, "You'd know that if you read Rules for Radicals."

"Yeah. Yeah." Jack sucked his limenade through a straw. "Whatever. What's next?"

"What's next?" Chris was now perfectly erect, ready for combat. He narrowed his eyes to gaze out the window at the hauntingly empty Sunday streets, slowly turning to face Jack. "Since they've lost the moral authority to govern, we no longer recognize their authority," he said softly. "It's time for the mind militia – they *are* the tyrants our founders warned us about."

Chapter 96

As the dark winter dragged on, record snowfall and bone-chilling cold took turns delivering the January doldrums to a city in distress. The unnerving silence in the abandoned streets bore the deep scars of daily suffering and a testament to civic failure.

Inside Tessa's comfortable high-rise apartment, she was on the unmade bed blow drying her hair and trying to stuff down intrusive thoughts about Adam. *Where was he? What was he doing? Was he seeing anyone?*

Tessa was falling so hard for him – frightening territory for anyone who had ever known the shocking sting of betrayal. Sleepless nights. Endless tears. Hollow inside. She'd tried to fill the void with work, but her mind wandered, and her head ached.

Watching the enormous snowflakes fall from the overcast skies like shimmering kaleidoscopes, Tessa tried to assure herself that she could weather whatever storm was coming. As if to kick the meddling blues to the curb, she was in the mood for bright colors. Her favorite patterned dress, light makeup and a messy bun would do the trick. Another cup of coffee.

The show must go on.

File notes: TDR Report (transcribed)
January 15, 2017
[Intro music]

"For nothing is secret, that shall not be made manifest, neither anything hid, that shall not be known and come abroad." (Luke 8:17, KJV)

Have faith, my friends. We **will** get to the truth.

Okay. First, the good news! Dormin's fight has become a global fight; we have support and donations pouring in from all over the world. Wow! It's very humbling and super inspiring! Thanks so much.

So, yesterday, I got a message from someone well known in independent journalism circles – as a nemesis, not an ally. They tried to silence me by offering $20 million to read their script. Not in this lifetime, pal.

That's how they do it. Pay truth tellers to work for their side. I'm at a place in my life where I can refuse, but not everyone is, and it explains why some people do a 180. It's frightening how much control money has over both corporate and alternative news coverage.

In somewhat related news, since EYE on Dormin fired their most popular newscaster, more journalists are leaving corporate media to become independent or join legitimate news organizations. That's an exciting and promising shift in momentum as we wrestle for control of the narrative to serve the people.

In case you were wondering how we ended up as characters in a dystopian novel, this is it. Mind games. Maybe it's time to bring God back into the world. Just maybe.

Hold the line, patriots. We got this.

This is Tessa Ryan, signing out.

Chapter 75

During a welcome chinook in late January, the empire boldly announced their true, sinister intentions: The peoples' freedoms were never coming back. What the masses had accepted in the name of Tetracimia would henceforth be used to save the climate.

Not one to panic, but on high alert now, Chris Simon summoned a small group to Anna Hale's isolated house on the shore of frozen Lake Luis. Sheltered from prying eyes by the dense forest, Saboro Mountain was the perfect meeting place. Arriving together in Tessa's SUV with the tinted windows open and the loud crunch of the tires on the snow packed driveway, it seemed more like March than January.

The stained-glass front door swung open as the three visitors walked up the pathway. "Welcome," Anna greeted them with a wide smile while she dried her hands on a tea towel. "Hang your jackets in the closet and come join me in the kitchen. I have ginger cookies."

Jack removed his slushy boots. "Smells good in here."

The '70s vertical sliding window over the water-stained kitchen sink was open and covered in steam, the old radio on top of the humming fridge tuned to a talk station – the dial hadn't moved in years. Anna lowered the volume and busied herself at the stove.

After several minutes of small talk Chris got the meeting started. "There's no need to rehash what's going on…we all know. But, if we play our cards right, this *could* be a turning point for independent media."

"Yeah. All we need is a miracle," Jack joked.

Waiting for inspiration, the four of them exchanged inquisitive glances.

Her back leaning against the kitchen counter, Anna was the first to speak. "Maybe the best way to reach them is to get as many people as possible out to Old Town Square."

Jack stood up, his imposing presence filling the small kitchen with confident energy. "We could have an old-fashioned Speaker's Corner," he suggested.

"Great idea, but we can't use the park, remember?" Tessa still couldn't believe Old Town Square was occupied. "It belongs to the empire."

"Wrong. It's on city land, and I'm the mayor. It belongs to the people." Jack reminded them. "If we're taking our country back, Old Town Square is a good place to start."

"Alright!" Suddenly, Tessa had hope again. If nothing else, it would be a symbolic victory. "Will you be there?"

"No. The public is too triggered by the media coverage. I'd be too much of a distraction." Jack took a warm cookie.

"Can your staff not handle them?" Tessa asked innocently.

"Tessa." Chris scolded her. "Read the room."

"What?" Tessa had no idea what he was talking about.

"Anna, find an organizer and stop by city hall for a permit." Still on his feet, Jack leaned against the wall with one hand. "It's a great way to tell the people they're being ruled by assholes. Plan it for Valentine's Day with free food."

"You got it," Anna agreed.

"I'll arrange the broadcast – it'll be killer." *Ping!* Chris picked up his phone to check the incoming text message.

When Anna's guests left half an hour later, she mulled over the discussion that had just taken place. Now that the veil had been pulled back, more and more people wanted a return to the old world, a truly representative government – of, for, and by the people. But first, they'd need to learn the difficult truth.

Chapter 76

In Tessa's state-of-the-art broadcasting studio, a pastel pink and purple prism spiraled across the gray vinyl floor and the tidy bookshelf behind the desk. Across from the bushy fern on the top shelf, a custom-made dreamcatcher, a gift from Anna, hung in front of the new old-fashioned casement window. Tidy and functional, the entire room was a lesson in minimalism.

In the early morning, Tessa was already at her desk, dressed to the nines, as usual, and hard at work on her daily show. While she sipped her mint-flavored strong coffee with cream, she paused to appreciate the view of the icy river from her breathtaking vantage point on the 21st floor. The combination of warmer temperatures *and* sunshine was holding, for now – a rare treat for Dorminians this winter.

Ping! Tessa picked up her phone to check the text; her heart skipped a beat. It was Adam! Setting her device face down on the desk, she picked up a piece of paper to study as if it had cheat notes for the big test.

"*All Hits! All the time! Triple Z99 –*".

Click. With the radio off, the room was instantly filled with an unnerving stillness. The show must go on. Cue video in 5...4...3...

File Notes: TDR Report (transcribed)
   February 2, 2017
      [Intro music]

"For, behold, I will send serpents, cockatrices, among you, which will not be charmed, and they shall bite you, saith the LORD." (Jeremiah 8:17 KJV)

Good morning, friends. So, I have a quick update for you.

*The empire is up to their old tricks, trying to implement what the corporate media has dubbed 'the mighty shift'. In true epidemic fashion, **every** cause of death is now Tetracimia, apparently. They inflate the numbers. They bring in their experts who present opinions as fact. They play with our perception, shaking it down for lunch money to feed the imaginary fear. That's how health officials are using Tetracimia as an excuse – despite the sketchy official story.*

Missed medical screenings, isolation and being hospitalized are what is leading to excess deaths – according to my inside source. She tells me that the predatory medical industry profits from dead Tetracimia patients.

*Why do we always fall for it? What a disgusting way to divide people. Are we at the place where we see half the population as soulless government bootlickers, and the other half as cold and heartless science-deniers? Is that who we **really are** as a society?*

Have we sold our souls to the devil? Have we lost our ever-loving collective minds? What if none of those things are true? What if turning against our neighbors is considered noble?

Hypnotic corporate media trickery establishes rapport with the viewer, leading us to think they're our friends. They're not. They're slimy, soulless, bottom-feeding ghouls. If the corporate media were a jellybean flavor, they'd be vomit and exhaust.

*It is **these** soulless ghouls who want us fighting. They want us dehumanized. They thrive on inciting violence against anyone who doesn't share their cult doctrine. The police, who **should** be on the side of the people, mutter 'just doing my job' as innocent citizens are hauled away, their assets seized, never to be seen or heard from again. Shades of 1930s Germany?*

Let's see what New World Now has to say about our current situation. [Feed cut to NWN anchor]. Watch:

NWN: Due to the now drastically restricted supermarket hours, city health officials will start going door to door with weekly rations this morning. Citizens are warned that those who publicly oppose the Tetracimia measures **will be unable** to enter any public establishment and **will** receive fewer supplies.

If you answer the door without your armband, you will not get your rations.

We won't get out of this if everyone doesn't comply. No one is safe until everyone is safe. Obedience is liberty. Darkness is only a heartbeat away.

Good news, though, if you live in the homeless encampments or in the Saboro Mountain subdivision, officials will distribute to you as well. You can check –

Tessa: *What they're **not** telling you is that they're forbidding people from getting supplies to their neighbors or that rations are purchased from the major corporations at 3x the markup in the name of wealth transfer. They know that starving people don't give two hoots where their food comes from. The predator class rides in like white knights on mounted steeds at just the right time to feed them.*

And about those homeless encampments? How are they surviving the outbreak? [cough] Makes you wonder.

One of my sources has informed me that the generic drug, Pharmavillin, has shown potential for treating the illness. The drug has been safely and successfully used to treat nerve damage going back to the 1920s. Apparently, some unelected bureaucrats disagree. Watch this clip from EYE on Dormin:

EYE: The Pharmavillin that some doctors are prescribing hasn't been approved for treatment of Tetracimia in humans. While vets **do** use it to treat a similar disease in cobras, the public misuse of this dangerous drug is clogging up the emergency rooms due to overdose. You're not a snake, y'all.

Tessa: *And that's a flat out lie. So, there you have it. Manipulation of data. Hypnosis. Half-truth. Omissions. Lies.*

*This is a master class in how to implement social credit scores, by the way. Tie your very **survival** to compliance – if you refuse, you die.*

[Inaudible]

A reminder about Valentine's Day: AltMedia Group is hosting an event on February 14 in Old Town Square. I'm so excited! We're having an old-fashioned hot dog and marshmallow roast. When's the last time Dormin had one…? The year that old man Fisher died, from what I've been told. Maybe it's time. Bring your date and make it a romantic hot dog for two. [laughter]

Please folks, stay peaceful. The weapons of this war aren't physical. The empire will try and provoke us, but violence is never the answer.

Bring your flags – any kind you want. Everyone is welcome. Bring your voice – all political opinions are welcome. Anyone can talk – it's how we give a voice to the voiceless and find community leaders. We also have a great line up of citizens from across the political spectrum to share in the open exchange of ideas. Dress for the America you want, not the America you have. And, as a bonus, we'll be introducing an emerging local recording artist that I'm sure we will all enjoy. It's how we bring community together.

*We need to start **living** again. The children had been cooped up since the state of emergency was declared, with many of them now showing signs of aggression, despondency, or delay. Suicides, addictions and domestic violence are up. Business incomes and job numbers are down. People are dying alone and having virtual funerals. So, come out and have some fun with the family, forget about our woes for a while. We hope to meet many of you there.*

I want to end today's show on a positive note. For the first time since our launch, we are reaching more people than the corporate media! There are several channels, including mine, that get more views than all their primetime shows – combined.

In similar news, we have people starting to contribute from across the globe. It seems that the people of the world are joining together to create a better world for future generations. We've received so many submissions from people anxious to share their creations – movies, books, tv shows, games, songs, videos, and the like. Please continue to do so. Let's create healthy culture to shape our society. It's so incredibly exciting and gives me hope!

The tide is turning!

Hold the line, patriots. We got this.

This is Tessa Ryan, signing out.

Chapter 77

When the cold front finally moved in, most of Dormin was still under house arrest, watching TV, and not so patiently awaiting their next instructions.

Driven by an unseen force, workaholic Tessa Ryan pulled into her designated spot in the underground parking lot and exited her SUV with the robotic gait of a woman on a mission. She never thought she'd witness collective insanity take over as an ideology, yet here they were. The elevator to the 21st floor seemed to take forever, another irritant in the race against time.

Having just returned from an infrastructure meeting at the mayor's office with Jack Weber and the team, Tessa was eager to go. Developing infrastructure was the *only* way to take on the sophistication of the empire's operation. AltMedia Group now had their own servers – developed and donated to independent media by Jack. No wonder the empire wanted everyone to hate the man.

Most exciting of all, the AltMedia Group was 100% *of the people, by the people, for the people*. Due to the censorship, ad revenue had long since ceased, so crowd-funding, donations and subscriptions kept them going while citizen journalists covered the stories that mattered to *them*. They'd gained the trust of the public – no easy feat in a world of lies.

Incredibly, they were going international! They'd have boots on the ground in war zones and during natural disasters, they'd entertain and educate, they'd create a world that worked. A massive fundraiser was underway to launch. Tessa could hardly wait.

Grateful that she'd finally have a lighter workload, Tessa poured a fresh, steaming cup of Brazilian roast coffee to sip while she worked. On the way to her sound studio, she doublechecked her look in the hall mirror. Her skin was looking better, but she needed to put on a few pounds. Her long hair had a few split ends, but overall, not bad. She was clean, and the bold red, white and blue colors conjured a continuous tale of fierce determination in the face of impossible odds.

While Tessa awaited the video call from her show's weekly guest, she checked her social media feed, translating the headlines into the people's language in her head as she scanned.

TECH SECTOR VOWS USER SAFETY *(Government agents are posing as big tech and corporate media to silence and intimidate independent voices.)*

GOVERNMENT TO CRACK DOWN ON MISINFORMATION *(Expect more censorship, algorithms, shadow banning and hit pieces. Anything that goes against the approved narrative will be cancelled.)*

By this time, a few channels in the AltMedia Group had already been purged. For some reason, Tessa's survived. *Maybe they thought they could control her? Let them try.* The empire was making it almost impossible to get the truth out, but *people* were hungry for this type of journalism, and the people *would* find a way to set the narrative.

A new thing, #Metoo, was trending. Tessa scanned her TownSquare account to read the townies. Some Hollywood bigwig was using his power and influence to pressure fame-seeking, doe-eyed starlets into sex. She rolled her eyes. *The casting couch is news? Not likely. World's oldest profession.*

In trial by corporate media, the accused was always guilty, and every woman was a victim. Tessa wondered if they cared at all about the pain and suffering the lies caused. It was almost as if they were backed by big bucks, had teams of lawyers on retainer, and hired spy chiefs as panelists.

As Tessa continued to scan, she burst out laughing. The corporate media had 'proof' that Jack Weber was guilty of human trafficking and his arrest was imminent. What should have been cause for societal upheaval and a moral reckoning had simply become another political weapon, not unlike reducing 'racist', 'hate', and 'fascist' to meaningless words. Alas, *evidence was no longer required in a world gone mad*, only accusations and anyone who got too close to the truth would be accused.

"This won't end well," Tessa murmured. As a former empire bot, she would know. Mindlessly staring at the ceiling, she thought about her own history, the grooming, the gang rape. Despite what she'd been through, she *still* believed that everyone had a fundamental right to a fair trial – innocent until proven guilty. Rational thought rather than emotional reaction. The public being whipped into a witch-hunting frenzy served only to further divide and destroy society...

Ping! Dr. Thakur was calling, interrupting her contemplation. The show must go on.

File Notes: TDR Report (transcribed)
February 11, 2017

[Intro music]

"When the righteous are in authority, the people rejoice; but when the wicked beareth rule, the people mourn." (Proverbs 29:2, KJV)

Tessa: *Good morning, everyone. I have a cool show for you today. We have a special guest, a former wildlife biologist who at one time specialized in venomous snake habitats and diseases. He's now a medical doctor with a family practice here in Dormin. He joined us to explain some of the things he's seeing. Please welcome Dr. Kabir Thakur. Thanks for coming on today's show, Dr. Thakur.*

Dr. Thakur: *Thanks for having me, Tessa.*

Tessa: *Of course. You stated that you are seeing some unusual patterns emerging in your practice.*

Dr. Thakur: *That's correct. The most troubling is the demographics. We are seeing young people being admitted to hospital who test positive but are displaying no symptoms. They are usually dead within hours.*

Tessa: *Omigosh. How young?*

Dr. Thakur: *I've seen as young as seventeen. Most are in their twenties and thirties.*

Tessa: *My age and younger. Wow!*

Dr. Thakur: *We're still trying to figure out how a disease previously only seen in snakes has transferred to humans. With no venom glands to examine, researchers are trying to isolate the pathogen. As it's a blood disease – blood poisoning, if you will, it's highly unusual for a carrier to be asymptomatic. Similar diseases seem to have fallen off the charts.*

Tessa: *Taking a year off, vacationing on a tropical island somewhere. Probably. Ha!*

Dr. Thakur: *If it's psychological warfare, people only need to **think** they're sick, and that only works if they're scared and suffering. I never thought I would see this in America, but something very sinister is going on.*

Tessa: *It's looking that way.*

Dr. Thakur: *This is also very concerning – the doctors who are prescribing Pharmavillin off-label are being stripped of their medical licenses. Physicians talking about natural defenses and prevention are vilified as quacks and censored. You'll notice there's no emphasis on getting enough sunlight or exercise,* *proper nutrition, or adequate rest. They're all needed in the fight against illness.*

Tessa: *Independent media is being majorly suppressed right now as well. We have citizen journalists on the ground whose channels are disappearing. In fact, some of **them** are disappearing. It's an extremely disturbing trend, perpetrated for the sole purpose of shutting us all up.*

Dr. Thakur: *We're in a race against time, Tessa.*

Tessa: *I know. It's scary. To get back to your earlier point, are you suggesting that doctors are forbidden to successfully treat their patients?!*

Dr. Thakur: *That's right. If there's a cheap, effective treatment available, Xenco Pharmaceuticals can't get emergency approval for their antidote. It's almost as if those making the drugs and those approving them are the same people.*

Tessa: *Things that make you go 'hmm'. Dr. Thakur, thanks so much for joining us today, but we're out of time. I hope you come back soon to give us updates.*

Dr. Thakur: *Of course. Anytime.*

[Inaudible]

Tessa: *There you have it. Amid all this chaos, we find ourselves on the precipice of something major. As societal tensions keep mounting, two distinct factions are emerging from the ashes of this dead city, and we both believe we're on the right side of history. We are indeed in a cold war.*

We'll see you at American Pride Day in the Park.

Hold the line, patriots. We got this.

This is Tessa Ryan, signing out.

Chapter 78

Three days later, the morning broke with billowing gray clouds chasing away the clear skies. Even without sunshine, the forsaken city was in a festive, patriotic mood for the First Annual American Pride Day in the Park.

On behalf of the AltMedia Group, a smiling Tessa Ryan arrived by midmorning, ready to witness the community come together under one banner – the precursor for better things to come. Livestreaming from her mobile with the corporate media on location would allow viewers to compare the storylines in real time. New World Now (NWN) and EYE on Dormin (EYE) were there with their broadcast teams, and the Dormin Times sent a hipster with an arrogant attitude and a cellphone.

By noon, when hordes of cautiously optimistic citizens began arriving at Old Town Square for the 2 pm start, Dorminians began to let their guard down. *Could it be?* Though they were still under house arrest, the police had agreed to a twenty-four-hour suspension.

Shortly before showtime, Tessa glanced up from scrolling her TownSquare account, through the crowd, and at the NWN team set up near the edge of the park underneath a barren elm tree. Her pulse raced. Adam was watching her. She tore her eyes away.

The show must go on.

TDR Report
File Notes: American Pride Day in the Park (transcribed)
February 14, 2017

Tessa: *Good afternoon, everyone! It's Tessa Ryan, streaming live from Old Town Square. This American Pride Day in the Park is the first of its kind, and as you* can see behind me, citizens are showing up by the **thousands** to reclaim their public space. [Crowd noise] There are people here of all ages, both sexes, all classes, and an eclectic group of races, creeds and professions. Here, nobody cares about social divisions – we are all united by the spirit of American liberty as our message of hope and unity continues to spread. You can clearly see that we are the majority, though the corporate media tries to convince you otherwise.

Although there's a heavy police presence, we have private security spread throughout the park as law enforcement has been given orders to stand down. Our request for additional security was denied even as special interest groups call for the force to be abolished and partial truths about police brutality continue to fester amid mounting racial tensions. This rumbling threatens to disrupt the peaceful intent of our gathering as it's now up to the citizens to defend ourselves and the city from government sponsored and empowered rioters.

EYE

Julia: Good afternoon, everyone. My name is Julia Blume. We're at Black Fist Warriors Park, reporting live on today's bigoted event, the so-called American Pride Day in the Park. Despite the name, it's an illegal occupation of land belonging to the descendants of slaves, a move that's sure to further fan the flames of racial division. They've also appropriated the word 'Pride' from the gay community in another shameful affront to human decency.

I'm joined today by three members of the Unified Rainbow Coalition, local 1102. Please welcome union president Bud Jenkins and members Daryl Cobb and Richard Darrel Perez. They're also known as Bud, his brother Daryl and his other brother Darrel. [Laughter]

The union members are here today to counter protest the organizer's radical ideology who are trying to force familial rights and traditional Western values on society. We *all* know those are rightwing dog whistles for homophobia and hate.

Julia: Bud, can you give me your opinion on what you're seeing here today?

Bud: What I'm seeing is disgusting, Julia. Not only is this group of Christian nationalists free to spread racial and gender hatred, but they're also making a mockery out of unions.

Julia: What do you mean?

Bud: Organized labor has collective bargaining power so we're able to influence public opinion. These AltMedia guys are a ragtag bunch of basement-dwelling thugs whose only language is violence.

Julia: Indeed, Bud. And with police brutality against minorities at an all-time high, they brought their own mob. More to come. Back to you, Josh.

TDR Report

Tessa: *As a form of peaceful protest, participants have torn off their armbands and thrown them on the icy ground. The crowd walking all over them is a symbolic gesture of disobedience. They'll be picked up at the end of the day because we're not slobs. There is an agreement in place via the permit that attendees will not be fined for armband violations if they stay in the designated area.*

Christian, Muslim, and Jewish families have joined together today to send a message. **'Let kids be kids'** *and* **'Leave the kids alone'** *are two of the signs with the prevailing sentiment that people have had enough of the government overreach, the radical trans agenda and the sexualization of children.*

The common motif, **'We will not comply'**, *is visible pm signs as far as the eye can see. This crowd isn't playing ball with unelected bureaucrats and their unilateral decrees. This is decentralized people power at its best.*

The people, united, will never be defeated!

Dormin Times

Hey guys, it's Jared here, hanging out at Black Fist Warriors Park.

The host group are here in force, cheering, as if having a massive crowd of transphobic racists is a good thing. Their lack of respect for a contagious illness and the environment is here on full display today as they've carelessly tossed their armbands on the cold ground. If you pay attention to the real news, you know that those immunity armbands save lives. Lots more to come.

TDR Report

Tessa: *I'm back with more live coverage. Everyone appears to be in a good mood, thanks to the cookout and toboggan rides that just concluded. The kids are buzzing, giggling, and releasing weeks of pent-up energy after being cooped up for the last three months. Currently, families are enjoying roasting marshmallows on the dying fire while they try to avoid the smoke getting in their eyes. [Children's laughter]*

EYE

Julia: With no armbands or communal separation, the organizers have little regard for public health or concern for the immunocompromised. The parents bringing their children are clearly unfit, begging the question of whether the state should take the children into care, or if such reckless behavior should be rewarded with food and healthcare. Bud, what's going on with the gay community's right to be recognized as people by the education system?

Bud: Well, Julia. Since I identify as gender-fluid on weekends and non-binary during the week, I support *all* human rights. Hate groups are popping up, trying to erase gay people from society. It's literally genocide that they're forcing kids to come out to their parents.

Julia: Despite what the host group is telling you, don't be fooled about the true purpose of this event. It's a homophobic, transphobic hate rally for fascists. An anonymous source has told me that their goal is to eliminate both racial minorities and gays.

TDR Report

Tessa: *As the day is dimming, the organizers will be opening the microphone for citizens to have their say. Our message to the empire is clear: We will now be returning to a foundation of traditional family values, objective morality, and truth. We are reclaiming our power!*

As the earthy aroma of sweetgrass overtakes the last remnants of smoke in the air, the crowd is loud, and the stage is set to open the evening with a prayer.

[The silhouette of a tiny woman draped in a star blanket crosses the dark stage to take the microphone. The spotlight turns on and shines on her long greying braid. Crowd noise diminishes; a voice rings out in the silence.]

Anna: *Grandfather Great Spirit. Let us walk softly on the Earth as relatives to all living beings, great and small...*

Tessa: *[Whispering] While Anna is praying, an incredibly moving scene is taking place right now...*

Anna: *Give us the strength to understand and the eyes to see. Look upon us that we may face the winds...*

Tessa: *[Whispering] Some in the crowd are on their knees in the snow with their faces turned to the sky, their palms raised in worship...*

Anna: *Amen.*

Crowd: *Amen!! [Loud cheering]*

Tessa: *It appears that for the first time in years, the faithful dare to believe that the Creator has heard their anguished pleas.*

Signing off.

NWN

(Miranda). What we are witnessing here today is people completely out of touch with reality. As we zoom in, you can see them on their knees with their palms raised to the sky. In today's world of rational thought, there is no excuse for this type of brazen disregard for science. It's as if the event is being hosted by the Flat Earth Society. They say they're not in a cult. You decide.

TDR Report

Random voices from the crowd: *Leave the kids alone! Let kids be kids! We will not comply!*

Tessa: *Indeed. A good rule of thumb is to never trust an adult that tells you to keep a secret from your parents.*

Watch as I scan the crowd. Thousands upon thousands of American flags of every size are waving in the light winter breeze, a magical, transformative moment enhanced by the multitude of cellphone lights sprinkled throughout the twilight.
[Spontaneous crowd rendition of the Star-Spangled Banner]
O say can you see
By the dawn's early light...

Dormin Times

[Shouting over the sound of the national anthem] Despite the word 'Pride' in their event name, there are no Pride flags present here today. Instead, this extremist hate group has removed both the rainbow and the Black Fist Warrior flags and replaced them with one of their own.

Watch while I zoom in – *this* flag, with the stars and stripes, is a symbol of oppression and hate, and a reminder of the country's racist roots; a symbol that strives to keep the gay and trans communities oppressed, and one that represents the roots of slavery to so many.

TDR Report

Tessa: *Temperatures are dropping, and the wind has picked up. It will have to get super cold to disrupt the spirit of this crowd – they're not going anywhere, even as our breaths are suspended in the air.*

Speaker: *Welcome, my fellow proud Americans! [In the style of UFC announcer, Bruce Buffer]*

Crowd: *USA! USA! USA!*

Speaker: *Are you ready to make some noise? [Echoing throughout the park]*
[Raucous crowd noise]

Speaker: *My name is Guy, one of the producers with the AltMedia Group, and the main organizer. I'm pleased to announce that this is* **YOUR** *media! You make our work possible. Thus, we work for you, and we are accountable to you!*
[Crowd cheering]

Guy: *Citizen journalism is how we share the stories that matter to us, and not a group of unelected billionaires.*
[Sustained crowd noise]

Guy: *The day will end with the music of a newly discovered local talent, so make sure you stick around for that.*
[Boisterous applause]

Guy: *Remember folks, it is not only your right, but your* **duty**, *to disobey unjust laws.*
[Thunderous applause]

Crowd: *Do not comply! Do not comply! Do not comply!*

Tessa: *Hasta luego. I'll be back.*

EYE

Julia: Conspiracy theories are rampant here today, folks. In addition to spreading boldfaced lies about press freedom, they are blatantly advising people that they don't have to follow the Tetracimia rules. Both anti-science and censorship are on full display.

After the open mic, tonight's hillbilly entertainer will take the stage. His name is Jimmy-Ray 'pitchfork' McCoy – I don't want to know how he got his nickname. He's a controversial and outspoken critic of government intervention even though they are doing their best to control the spread of the illness. To find out more, listen to the lyrics of his songs where he pretends to be a victim.

TDR Report

Tessa: *The corporate press is all here now, pushing and shoving their way through the crowd to the stage. Interesting to note that the reporters are in armbands, but the camera operators aren't.*

More people have arrived to take part in something truly historic. At the open mic, individual voices continue to take turns calling for freedom, peace and unity as the excitement for this organic movement continues to build.

[Inaudible]

You can feel the sense of community tonight, folks. Listen to them! It's bringing a tear to my eye. What a time to be alive.

[Crowd roaring]

Crowd: *USA! USA! USA! –*

[Inaudible]

NWN

As the crowd noise picks up, there appears to be a group of Neo-Nazis near the stage who're carrying swastikas and chanting 'Heil Hitler'. The hate isn't even hidden anymore.

TDR Report

Tessa: *Sorry for cutting out folks. My phone was knocked to the ground during a scuffle and now all hell has broken loose down here!*

The day's messages have grown increasingly violent; one guy with a knife was tackled by security. Right after, a punk couple rushed the mic, draped in swastikas, suggesting that armed revolt may be necessary.

I will reiterate, ***again****. We are 100% nonviolent! Violence is what the enemy wants. I don't know who those people are, but they don't share our philosophy. This war is a battle of the mind and spirit, and our side knows it.*

EYE

Julia: As expected, the gathering has erupted into violence. For the last half hour, calls for armed revolt continue to grow.

TDR Report

Tessa: *I'm back. So, there are agent provocateurs here tonight, also known as feds. The military-issue boots and high-end sunglasses give them away every time. Thanks to these infiltrators, our message of peace and freedom will be conflated with hatred and violence, and they'll have an excuse to bring in the military.*

Dormin Times

The AltMedia Group is claiming, without evidence, that this is a false flag, that it was staged by the feds and the Black Fist Warriors. It's typical for them to shift blame when they're the ones inciting violence.

I've also been told, off the record, that they're calling for kidnappings and assassinations of people in high places.

TDR Report

Tessa: *About half an hour ago, the park was invaded by hundreds of rioters. Here they are, covered head to toe in satanic black with bandana masks to hide their identity. They are the Black Fist Warriors extremist group, and they're armed with rifles, baseball bats, and knives.*

As you can see, pandemonium has ensued. When the unarmed crowd panicked, screaming and running in multiple directions, escape routes were blocked, and the police wouldn't intervene. We were forced onto Old Town Road. I've moved across the street, where I'm currently filming near the vacated homeless encampment.

The Black Fist Warriors continue their chants as they guard the perimeter of the park.

Black Fist Warriors: *"Black Fist Warriors!" "Bigots beware." "No whites welcome!"*

Tessa: *I'll be back.*

NWN

Finally, I have some good news to share tonight. Our heroes on the ground, the peaceful counter protesters, have reclaimed their land from the haters. This is the kind of direct action we need to take against racial and police brutality. It's the language of the oppressed and the voice of the voiceless.

TDR Report

Tessa: *Good evening, everyone. What started out as a day of promise, a day of peace and of hope, has ended in violence and bloodshed. At least two people are dead: among them a teenage girl.*

During the frenzied attack, Molotov cocktails and concrete balloons were heaved into the thick crowd. The perpetrators, so far, remain unidentified. Immediately after, an unknown assailant fired two shots.

[Inaudible]

EYE

A few minutes ago, a member of the AltMedia Group fired two shots into the crowd. This came immediately after they heaved Molotov cocktails and bricks at innocent protesters.

It's good to see the people finally revolt against this group; they represent the worst people on the planet and were rightfully evicted from land belonging to the Black Fist Warriors. It's a bittersweet victory over what will go down as one of the darkest days in our city's history.

TDR Report

Tessa*: I'm hearing now that three churches and a synagogue were burned down tonight, and several cop cars set on fire. After the violent mob torched city hall, they poured onto the streets, actively hunting political opponents.*

Calls for violence are growing louder as the rioters continue to spread their terror, actively seeking to kill or injure political opponents whom they call fascist – a now meaningless word. It appears that their blood lust is just beginning as self-proclaimed vigilantes are still going from street-to-street basking in the glowing flames of their destruction.

NWN

You may be concerned about the local heroes on the ground here tonight. Experts have assured us that there is no risk of spreading the pathogen because they are protesting for a social justice cause. Studies show that the pathogen is a sentient being, and experts tell us it's much more highly contagious around people with traditional family values.

The District Attorney's office is telling us that the AltMedia Group *will* be brought to justice to deal with the white supremacy that has grown to become the country's most pressing problem. If you have any information about anyone involved in this horrific, violent attack on the Black Fist Warriors, please contact the police.

TDR Report

Tessa*: Desperate small business owners – most of them minorities – are watching their dreams and lifetime of hard work go up in smoke tonight, including the shops displaying Black Fist Warriors signs in their windows. After an elderly downtown business owner was dragged out of his shop and beaten, rioters looted and torched his store.*

They're now stopping motorists, dragging them from their vehicles, and terrorizing them.

Dormin Times

I'm still here at the flaming, but largely tranquil protests. The AltMedia Group has caused a tremendous amount of damage tonight, not only in terms of vandalism and arson, but also in terms of social costs, racial division, and the loss of a local hero.

This is Jared Brown with the Dormin Times, reporting live. Good night on this sad day from Black Fist Warriors Park.

TDR Report

Tessa: *On behalf of the AltMedia Group, our hearts go out to the victims and their families tonight. Our condolences on this tragic day – a day that will go down as one of the darkest chapters in Dormin's history. As you can see, the downtown area has been devastated by vandalism, assault, murder, and arson. Behind me, one lone American flag is still standing – damaged but standing – vigilant and proud. Maybe that's a sign of things to come.*

Good night from city hall. This is Tessa Ryan, signing out.

Chapter 79

After Bloody Valentine's, Tessa lost track of time, unsure of how she ended up seated in a burgundy chaise lounge in a counsellor's office with silent tears trickling from her bloodshot eyes. When the salt reached her lips, she wiped her clammy face with the sleeve of her penguin-print shirt. Perspiration had pooled on her stringy, unwashed hair.

The cluttered desk was strangely coated with a layer of thick dust, the wall behind it covered in beautifully framed credentials for Lucas Belzac – accolades awarded decades earlier in France. Right above his head hung a glowing crucifix.

Lucas was a highly intelligent man of slight stature with a few wisps of gray hair combed over his bald spot. In his sixties now, the suit he wore looked dated. He stroked his thin white mustache and pushed his wire rim glasses into place.

"You were afraid to come to me because of your mother's history. Is that correct?" Lucas set his fancy pen down, recalling the long-ago days of seeing little Tessa and her devoted mother at mass every Sunday, rain or shine.

Fragrant hanging baskets and potted plants filled the room with an earthy sense of calm, the lights soft and dim. Tessa swung her thin legs onto the edge of the chaise lounge. "I know. I'm going to follow in her footsteps." She buried her hands in her face and groaned. The lasting images of those flashing emergency lights were as vivid in her memory as the night it happened.

Lucas slowly removed his glasses, gently setting them on the desk before responding. "Well, not exactly."

Picking her fuzzy head up, Tessa looked Lucas in the eye. "What do you mean?"

"In my opinion, you're having a *breakthrough*. Not a breakdown."

Tessa realized she was looking right through Lucas at the ivory wall, not sure if she heard him right. "What?" Her heart was pounding.

"You're waking up to the reality of a society in chaos. You know that truth without the courage to speak it is a place of torment, a blessing and a curse, an albatross and an eagle."

"Probably explains why people hide from it." Tessa paused to massage her stiff neck muscles. Her bottom lip quivered as she watched snowflakes melting and snaking their way down the windowpane.

"You see the lies online every day."

"Right," Tessa acknowledged.

"Social media has fundamentally changed society in ways that are irredeemably harmful. It's not real life, as people *think*. It's more like a huge social experiment where they engage in voyeurism of what they think are perfect lives."

"Nobody's life is as perfect as they pretend."

"Correct. But it doesn't matter what is real. That's why it's the devil's playground – deceptive and designed to be addictive because we have a social need to be liked and accepted. Most are afraid to speak the truth for that reason."

Tessa fixed her gaze on the busy street to avoid eye contact. "Wait. So, we're all driven by ego?" A floor below, the headlights of the bumper-to-bumper traffic gleamed through the moisture. *Bumper-to-bumper? What happened to all the restrictions that were in place?!*

"Nothing is ever that simple." Lucas interrupted Tessa's confusion. "It's an addiction."

"Like, a real addiction? Like heroin?"

"Yes, we *literally* get addicted to online attention. Like any other addiction, it causes disruption, chaos, and can even have deadly consequences."

"True."

"See, every time we get a like or a follower on social media, someone that confirms our world view, we feel validated and get a little dose of dopamine." Lucas indicated with his thumb and forefinger the size of the dose. "As lovers of ourselves rather than a higher power, we begin to crave it."

"So, why me? How am *I* any different?" Tessa was sure Lucas was a bit grayish in his pallor. Was he feeling alright?

"Tessa, it depends where one is on their spiritual journey. *You* have emerged from the hellfire, and the Holy Spirit is guiding you on your journey." Now Lucas' voice was fading in and out. "It's leading you straight to the truth."

"Meaning?"

"Most people aren't able to exorcise their demons because they won't do the inner work." As if lost in thought, Lucas stared mindlessly out the window.

"My demons need exercise." Tessa had finally stopped sniffling. "They're fat."

Lucas smiled at Tessa's joke, instantly putting her more at ease. Suddenly, she was looking at a younger Lucas, conjuring memories of the purple lollipop he always had for her. He delivered it himself while she waited for her mom all those decades ago, her little feet not yet touching the gleaming tile floor.

"I don't understand what you mean." More at ease now, Tessa reclined on the chaise lounge, rapidly blinking her eyes. *Was the wall calendar on August 2010?!* Tessa blinked again...it was on February 2017. *She needed to get her eyes checked.*

Lucas was suddenly standing by the water cooler. "Tessa, I'm ready to get off this crazy merry-go-round. I'm at the end of my career, and I'm not worried about being cancelled or what people think of me. If that makes me a truth warrior, I welcome the freedom it brings my soul."

"You know what they're doing to us, right?" Tessa warned.

"Uh huh. I also know that disobedience is the foundation of liberty."

"Okay. But how?" Tessa was suddenly flushed, the tears on her cheeks feeling cool. "How will what I'm doing make any difference?"

"You'll see, but you must first let go of your ego. Get in touch with your true essence – your spirit."

"How?"

"Listen to the Creator, or the universe, or the collective consciousness, or God – whatever resonates with your soul. If you're open to listening, you will guide yourself to your own inner wisdom." Lucas handed Tessa a purple lollipop. "Seek and ye shall find – the truth will set you free.

Waking up in her perspiration-soaked bed with no memory of how she got there, a disoriented Tessa sat up to check the date and time – five days had passed since Bloody Valentine's. It was as if cosmos had chewed her up and spit her out somewhere along the space-time continuum.

The radiant, mid-morning sun poured through the open sky-blue blinds, the ambient light filling the black-and-white themed bedroom with inspiration. The counsellor's words had given Tessa renewed hope to stay on the right path. Another cold/sunny combo day called for extra coffee.

Sipping her third cup of dark roast, Tessa supported her head in her palms to gaze upon the spectacular scene outside her dining room window. There was something strangely romantic about glittering snow under a cloudless sky and puffs of white smoke rising from every chimney.

Sighing as she turned her devices on, Tessa wasn't looking forward to learning what had happened during her dissociative absence.

First story: They had the antidote. By this time, the population was so miserable, so demoralized, and oh-so-hungry for a return to whatever normal they could get, they just gave in, hardly able to make sense of the world anymore. *The government response was akin to dropping a nuclear bomb to kill one Christian. Come to think of it, these sickos probably had.*

Second story: Jack Weber had *tried* to intervene and was told in no uncertain terms that his authority (as top boss of the city) was neither needed nor wanted. Instead, the unelected, unaccountable bureaucrats ridiculed and sidelined him, accused him of heinous crimes, doxed, harassed, and threatened his family, bankrupted him with lawfare, and tried to destroy him.

Third story: Chris had learned that a Fisher megadonor had offered Jack $3 billion not to run. He turned it down – there was way too much at stake. Also, he had no intention of obeying or enforcing any of their ridiculous unconstitutional orders. They weren't fit to govern.

When tyranny becomes law, resistance becomes duty.

Independent media *tried* to tell the public that they were up against was an elaborate lie, that hospitals were killing fields, and that patients were abandoned to die alone while the corrupt medical officials collected a pretty sum. All it took was manipulating the cause of death. Exasperated, Tessa got ready to start her day.

The show must go on.

File Notes: TDR Report (transcribed)
February 21, 2017
[Intro music]
"And he said unto them in His doctrine, beware of the scribes, which love to go in long clothing, and love salutations in the marketplace."
(Mark 12:38, KJV)
I'm back, and holy cow, we've got a lot to catch up on, so I'll get right to the point.

Bloody Valentine's was a dismal failure. The Speaker's Corner was a dud, and we are now being labelled as violent extremists thanks to Agent Provocateurs. Law enforcement has been weaponized against the people, so we are under martial law. The rulers got exactly what they wanted.

[cough]

Breaking: The empire has the antidote. Starting tomorrow morning, health authorities will be going door to door to distribute the liquid that you take orally, its street name is Li-cur. Yes...really.

It hasn't been through the usual trials, so consider that it's experimental and developed by known eugenicists with formal ties to Nazi scientists. **Actual** Nazis scientists.

Lack of informed consent is pretty much the reason the Nuremberg Code was written. Nevertheless, they're saying to trust the experts and the scientific method, that for our convenience, all information will come from one source, and disagreeing with the authorities is not an option.

Of course, we **do** have the right to refuse. We'll be subject to browbeating, dogpiling, cajoling, threats, bribes, violence, despotism, scare tactics, assault, coercion, estrangement from family, ridicule, contempt, disdain, name-calling, mockery, jeering, public shaming, bullying, intimidation, pouncing, relentless pressure, destroyed friendships, banishment from public places, restriction of rations, loss of income, and jail time. But hey, we have a choice, right? Watch when they use that in the future to say they didn't force anyone. These people really are pure evil.

If you decide to take the magic potion, you'll have some of your so-called freedoms restored – their words, not mine. Movements will still be restricted, you'll still need armbands, you'll still have to follow all the public protocols, and you'll still be isolated, but at least they were nice enough to give us permission to enjoy some freedom in our own homes. [Several second pause]. You still won't be able to hold your loved one's hand when they take their last breath.

[Inaudible]

About that... based on information obtained by the AltMedia Group, we have reason to believe that some people are getting sick from the antidote. That doesn't mean I put my tinfoil hat on. There are side effects to medication all the time. Also, the health authorities are currently beginning the second dose distribution, with another three planned over the next several weeks.

The fascists, commies, dictators... whatever they are... I have never seen anything like the current throttling of independent voices! They're trying to stop **all** communications outside their control.

If I disappear, you'll know why. More likely, **when** I disappear. You'll find me on Buzz and Thunder – platforms dedicated to free speech, both of whom have come under relentless attack.

If we citizen reporters don't follow their strict guidelines, our videos get demonetized and no longer recommended. We are constantly worried about losing our channels while they boost corporate media – their so-called authoritative sources. We get shadow banned and down ranked, given strikes, and removed. They come after our advertisers, our family and friends, our livelihoods, our reputations, our sanity. We can't allow this to go on.

Staying strong in the face of impossible odds is what the American spirit is. On meagre rations, diseased, exposed to the harsh elements, and with inadequate supplies, the founders refused to back down from the most powerful empire in the world. They were the rebels, not career politicians. We should consider ourselves fortunate.

To my freedom warriors: We must fight for the restoration of the Constitution. Like they've manipulated so much of the language already, now they're trying to turn freedom into a dirty word. Stay safe. Stay free. Stay strong.

Hold the line, patriots. We got this.

This is Tessa Ryan, signing off.

The very second Tessa wrapped up her broadcast, her cellphone beeped – *she was a bad, bad girl.*

"Tessa! What are you doing?!" It was Chris, and he was pissed. "We can't afford to lose your voice in this fight!"

"What do you mean, what am I doing? These guys are sociopaths! You don't want me to warn people, or what?"

"Well, I –"

"Why aren't we using the alternative platforms?" Tessa interrupted. "Buzz's terms of service? The Constitution."

"You're too stubborn to do it any other way, aren't you?" Chris sighed, annoyed.

"Good call, Chris." Tessa stood up to stretch, the view out the window catching her attention again. "We can't let their characterization of us stop us from doing the right thing!"

`Click`. Chris had hung up. *Was it something she did? Haha*

Tessa shuffled toward the kitchen for a coffee refill wondering how it would all end.

Chapter 80

File notes: TDR Report (transcribed)
March 5, 2017
[New Intro music – first five seconds of Beethoven's 5th Symphony in C Minor]

"Woe unto them that call evil good, and good evil; that put darkness for light, and light for darkness; that put bitter for sweet, and sweet for bitter." (Isiah 5:20 KJV)

Well, folks. We knew it was coming. These sociopaths have thrown down the gauntlet.

In upside down world, the ruling class has labelled ordinary Americans who love America – enemies of the state. The mass arrests have begun. GPS tracking, digital financial records, cell phone data, search engines, facial recognition software and other biometrics. They don't seem so convenient now, huh?

We're being hunted down and jailed without charges or due process. Imagine you're asleep in the dead of night and the anti-terrorism task force comes with multiple cars, their sirens blaring. They raid you, shine a blinding flashlight in your face, train their guns on your babies, kill your pets, and haul you into the cold while angry German Shepherds growl and snap at your heels. You have no criminal history. Your only crime is that you love your country.

As a lawyer, I know we will get no justice. The judges are in the back pocket of the corporations and the District Attorney is installed by a non-US citizen billionaire. Any lawyer defending us will be disbarred. Police brutality is the norm, and any officer attempting to protect us will get arrested alongside the civilians.

How much more are we going to take? How much longer are we willing to be persecuted by our own government? How much longer will we watch while they encourage our loved ones to report us as anti-government collaborators?

Changing gears here.

How about them Black Fist Warriors, huh? Who are they, really?

Well, thanks to one of my viewers, Robbie S, we have footage from one of their recent rallies in which they make their true intentions known. Watch:

[Founder of Black Fist Warriors (Jamal) interview following their rally at Old Town Square]

Interviewer (Robbie): What would you say your main goal is? Equality?

Jamal: We're not interested in equality. We are trained Marxists! Our goal is equity!

Tessa: *So, there you have it. Black Fist Warriors is a front for a criminal syndicate masquerading as a worthy cause. Where do all those donations go? Extremist candidates? Luxury homes? Lavish parties? While* **we** *rot in jail, they are free to terrorize lawmakers, burn down entire cities, loot stores at will, and murder innocent, law abiding business owners trying to defend themselves and their property. It's grifting with a sadistic twist.*

On Bloody Valentine's, they had help, The courts released child rapists, murderers, and other violent criminals onto the unpatrolled streets. They could have their sentence suspended if they took part in the bloodthirsty frenzy. As a bonus, drugs flowed freely. We witnessed the quick escalation of mob mentality – things people would never do on their own seem acceptable when done in a group. To encourage them, elected officials posted their bail and set up fundraisers. While the empire bends the knee, law enforcement is publishing our photos on their website.

Ironically, black fists are mostly 'defended' in the streets by young, white people whose mugshots later reveal blank eyes, open sores and missing teeth, high on meth. The use of these lost, empty souls as terrorists is no different than the training of extremists in other parts of the world.

Our cell phone footage from Bloody Valentine's is being called fake news, and it's not. The empire literally brought in a producer from New World Now to frame the footage. On TV, we saw the studio version – we saw what they wanted us to see. Now, we must sit by while they tear down the artifacts of western culture and just accept it.

Now, the purge begins – a massive, coordinated erasing of opposing voices across all tech and all media. Now, more than ever, independent journalism is at great risk for censorship and targeted propaganda. **Now**, more than ever, the attacks will escalate.

What I want you to take away from today's show is that the predator class spends a lot of time, money, and effort to convince the public that they're the good guys. What do you think?

Well, they may have won the battle, but they will **never** win the war.

Hold the line, patriots. We got this.

This is Tessa Ryan, signing out.

Chapter 81

In aromatic heaven as she inhaled the clean smell from a basket of fresh laundry, Tessa pushed her heavy steel apartment door open with her back. When the overflowing basket hit the floor, folded clothing and loose laundry pucks flew in three different directions. Her belongings were strewn everywhere, drawers emptied, the patio door wide open, and the vertical blinds rattling in the wind. In shock, she fled to the building lobby to call the police.

After the police left and the apartment was secure, Tessa tried to cope with her latest source of stress by parking herself on the paint-splotched, turquoise stool in her art studio with paintbrush in hand, alert to every little noise. Maybe the surrealist-style emotions flowing onto the canvas would help her make sense of this crazy, backwards, *dangerous* world. She dabbed at the...

Footsteps were approaching in the hall! Tessa froze, trying to slow her rapidly beating heart as the stomps got closer. Grabbing the string mop from the broom closet, she peeked through the hole...and sighed before yanking the door open.

"Surprise!" Adam had an ear-to-ear grin and something behind his back.

"You scared the crap out of me, Adam!"

"Good to see you, too." Adam handed Tessa the bouquet of velvety red roses he'd hidden from her view. "What's going on? That mop looked so menacing," he teased.

Tessa couldn't suppress a smile; she missed Adam's sense of humor. Her face right against the flowers, the delicate petals tickled her nose with their scent. "My apartment was broken in to!"

"What?!"

"The cops just left. What an experience *that* was."

"Why? What happened?" With his back to Tessa at the kitchen sink, Adam filled the crystal vase with water.

"*I* get broken into, have several electronic devices stolen, and the cops act like *I'm* the criminal."

"What did they do?" Adam turned around.

"First, they made me wear a useless armband, then told me to back off. When they were done with.... whatever they do after a break-in, they started grilling me about my politics!" Arranging the freshly cut flowers to her liking, Tessa placed the sparkling vase in the middle of the lace-covered bar table.

After a heavy pause, Adam gestured to the balcony with his head. "Can we talk?" he asked softly.

"Um," Tessa hesitated. "Care for a drink?"

"No. I'm good." Adam slid the thick balcony door open.

"It's cold," Tessa whined, dropping her shoulders.

"It's a beautiful evening." Adam stepped outside. "Come get some air. You'll feel better."

Taking one more look at Adam, Tessa grew weak. She followed him to the balcony.

With his elbows bent on the railing, Adam casually pointed to the triad of cobalt blue, golden yellow, and fire orange gracing the landscape in the distance. In the remaining daylight, the puffs of cloud appeared black, casting shadows on the sinking sun as it rippled across the river.

"Adam, what is going on?" Tessa massaged her temples. "One minute I..."

Lost in her captivating beauty, Tessa's unexpected visitor watched her speak but the words faded into the white noise in the background, his tone softening to a near whisper. "Ever since that afternoon at Saboro Point together, I've wanted to get to know you better." He slipped his hand around her thin waist.

So starved was she for physical human contact, Adam's warm touch sent a melodramatic jolt through Tessa's entire body. Blushing, she pulled her light sweater around her tighter.

"Yeah, it's a little nippy once the sun disappears at this time of year." Overcome by desire, Adam slid behind Tessa and enclosed her in his strong arms. "Maybe this will help warm you up." He inhaled the fresh scent of her hair – he liked that.

Tessa's body involuntarily tensed up, his musky cologne making her weak in the knees. *God, give me strength.*

"What's up?" Adam murmured as his eager lips pressed against the back of her head.

"I'm scared," Tessa whispered as uneasiness gripped both her body and her mind.

"I know." Adam's soft hand spread out across Tessa's abdomen as he stroked her hair. "You told me the story." He pressed his hard body against her.

When a shiver of unexpected pleasure ran up Tessa's spine, she dropped her heavy eyelids and leaned back against Adam.

"What if we just take it slow?" Adam's voice was low and sensuous. He turned Tessa around to find her voluptuous lips, his intense passion awakening something long forgotten inside her. It was their first erotic kiss – lingering and unforgettable.

Delirious with excitement, Tessa laid her weary head on Adam's muscular chest, basking in his masculine aura and the cologne she loved. For one blissful moment, everything was perfect with the world. She would just take it slow, she promised herself. *But she wouldn't fall in love.*

Chapter 82

Around sunrise the next morning, Chris rushed to answer his front doorbell, tripping over the fat orange tabby in the hallway. "Dammit, Garfield!" He tied his dark green robe as he got back to his feet.

Rather uninterested in the plight of bothersome humans, Garfield yawned and rolled over to take up even more space. Chris felt a temporary surge of gratitude, thanking God that he got to experience the aloof little jerk every day. Now that Maria and their two sons had returned to Hawaii for their safety, little pudge was the only family he had left in Wyoming. They'd rescued grandpa cat from the shelter right before he was scheduled to be executed, and he was getting up in age.

By the time Chris reached the front door, his thoughts had shifted to Jack and how much danger the man was in, checking the monitor above the door while he pulled it open. "Think of the devil."

"Got a minute?" Jack was clearly not impressed by something.

Suspecting it was unrelated to being compared to the Prince of Darkness, Chris moved aside. "Come on in." He did a quick scan around the property at the strategically located dudes in black – Jack's security detail, and deadbolted the door. "Coffee?"

Jack grunted while he followed Chris down the hall to the dining room, taking a seat at the head of the table. He ignored his growling stomach even when tempted by the aroma of the world's best bacon – he didn't have food on his mind.

"Hungry?" Chris placed a steaming mug of Colombian coffee with three sugars, two creams down in front of his visitor, and a big plate of steaming bacon and eggs in front of himself.

"No." Jack picked up the Santa mug. *Nice touch, but Christmas was a while ago.*

"Are you sure? It's Delicacy bacon – the best there is."

"What in the world is going on, Chris?" Not one to be ignored, Garfield rubbed up against Jack's black dress pants.

Unable to suppress a chuckle, Chris retrieved the lint roller from the drawer. "Could you be a bit more specific?"

"What is happening to the people who're disappearing? Where are they going?" As an opportunistic distraction, Jack was fixated on a sunspot on the floor – he had no control over the law in the wretched city, and it gnawed at him.

Liberally sprinkling black pepper on his eggs, Chris sat down to his waiting meal. "They're likely under the control of two global corporations: X-Forefront and Y-Whitestone."

"The ones buying up all the housing?"

"The same. Only now, they're seizing damaged and abandoned property, looting the owners, and emptying bank accounts. Excuse me a minute." Chris trotted down the hall.

"Alright." Jack mumbled, rolling the brush across his left pant leg while Garfield eyed him suspiciously from the sunspot. The stained-glass windows in the skylight cast rainbow-like prisms across the white tablecloth turned canvas – art created by the rising sun.

Chris was back. "We have footage of innocent people being raided and hauled away – where to is anyone's guess." He set a file down on the table beside the fruit bowl brimming with fresh peaches and shiny purple grapes. "Jack, do you think that what Max runs is a meatpacking plant?"

The file was labelled with a code, one that Jack wasn't privy to, apparently. "What are you talking about, Chris? What else would it be?" The color drained from Jack's face.

"It's all a front, Jack. Nothing more than a facade. An illusion." Pointing to the folder, Chris slid a piece of ketchup-smothered cold egg in his mouth.

"So, you're telling me that that place is something other than a meat packing plant?? How could we know?" Jack stared at the file as if it were about to jump up and devour him. "It *smells* like a meat packing plant. It *looks* like a meat packing plant. There are financial reports. A board of directors. The whole nine yards! We've all been in the building."

Chris tied his robe again as he pointed at the file, now in Jack's hands. "I can't tell you yet what exactly it *is*, but I can say with certainty what it's *not*. The place is locked down tighter than Fort Knox, by the way. It's going to be tough."

"Why does this assignment mean so much to you, Chris?" Jack asked softly while he downed the rest of his coffee.

"Jack, you're American by birth." Chris swallowed the lump in his throat. "I am American by choice."

"And?"

"And this isn't Canada – a country without an identity. We aren't passive, obedient slaves who do what the authorities tell us."

"Right?" Jack nodded his agreement. "What does that have to do with this assignment?"

"Everything. America will never be a country without an identity."

"How can you be so sure?" Jack's voice was shaky.

"Because our foundation was borne of revolution," Chris reminded his visitor. "We fight back."

"Yeah. About that...how, exactly?" Jack sighed.

"Trying to erase our culture through mass migration will not work here."

Waiting for more, Jack gestured with his hand.

"First, they create the refugees through war, then they flood countries unable to cope with the rapid changes."

"Right."

"Turns out diversity is *not* our strength."

By nightfall, something sinister was brewing at Atluko Industries. Outside the grounds, an impenetrable hedge of enclosed two electrified fences, both of them topped with rolls of barbed wire. Inside the perimeter, guard towers were erected on every side of the massive building and aggressive German Shepherds roamed the extensive grounds at night. Public visitors to Atluko were privy to no such imagery, nor were they privy to the private runway and system of roads built in the remotest part of the forest.

Buried in the details of the several trillion-dollar construction project years earlier, a chimera emerged: a backward world where CGI and deep fakes became real life, where green screens lied, and where clones and holograms replaced people. Magical scepters conjured white rabbits to appear in top hats as the illusion of normalcy replaced reality. Every person. Any narrative. Anytime. Crowded Tetracimia hospitals. King cobras. Politicians. Wars. Natural disasters. In a central news factory, *anything* could be real.

The visiting public was also unaware that the underground mega city housed beneath the plant kept secrets so dark, it was rumored that demons squealed with delight at the doors of the locked rooms. Nearby, the bunkers waited.

Among the unending rows of costumes inside the wardrobe room, Miles Malone was hunched over his laptop at a sewing table. A thick, brown envelope landed on his keyboard with a resounding thud. He didn't flinch.

"Dude, it's after midnight. What are you still doing here?"

"I was about to ask you the same thing." Miles looked up. "I thought you were security. Only people around this part of the plant at night."

"You want to head to main control with me?" Standing next to him was Tessa's dinner date the day after she'd arrived back – Cole Adams.

Moving through the dark halls, the two nervous men passed auditions and central casting on the way to Studio 17, a massive section that seemed to go on forever. If one continued further down, they'd encounter doors labelled 'elections', 'pandemics', 'climate change', 'social division', 'war' and more. One was ominously called 'independent media' printed on a bullseye.

Pushing through a heavy set of double doors, the pair watched a team of weary technicians, the last to work on a project before it aired. Presently, they were polishing a bombshell news story about Tessa Ryan and her crazy mother, the veracity of which was irrelevant. Their job was to elicit emotion through narrative – it had worked since before television news was a thing, and there was nothing she could do about it. The purpose was to assassinate her character, not make her a martyr. That the story was based on vague intelligence from a sketchy confidential-human-source with a low probability rating on accuracy was not their concern.

"I want to crush that ungrateful wench." a voice behind them growled.

"Max! You startled me. What the hell?" Miles tapped his feet, trying to keep rhythm with his rapidly beating heart. "You haven't been here in ages. Since, well...you know..."

Not wanting to deal with the old man's wrath, Cole was outta there without so much as a glance.

"I couldn't sleep. I want to see my herd." Max looked rough. They were still in control of the empire, but he needed the *title*, too.

The pair exited the elevator at Level B3: three levels underground. Miles entered the electronic combination on the thick vault door of the wing, then unlocked the room labelled 'Kill Room # 7'. Cramped stalls lined the walls on either side, the mixed aroma of blood and straw assaulting one's nostrils upon entry.

Slowly inspecting the stalls, Max avoided getting anything dirty on his new cowboy boots. The cold, arrogant expression on his face was befitting a serial killer collecting his trophy. Slight moans escaped from some of the prisoners. He looked down his nose at the tormented faces with indifference. Talking, furless animals deserve no compassion – maybe this would teach them to follow orders and keep their mouths shut.

Back on the fifth floor, Dmitri opened the door to Max's office, stoic as always, clipboard in hand. The lights were dimmed, and the scotch on the rocks was poured.

With the three men seated at the smoky round table beside the desk, Max threw the scotch down his throat, wiping his mouth with the sleeve of his golf shirt. "Miles, we have lost control!" He lit a cigar. "I don't understand. We've thrown everything we have at them."

"You wouldn't." Miles mumbled under his breath. "The people are starting to realize it's all political, they're maybe smarter than we thought. The more we persecute Jack, the more support he gains."

"I hate that slimy rat bastard!" The ringtone on Max's phone startled all three of them.

Once Wolfgang Hertzig appeared on the wall screen, he wasted no time. "You are failing in your mission." He made eye contact with Miles. "Explain yourself!" In his rage, spittle flew from his mouth.

"It's like a dam that's springing leaks," Miles explained, not in the mood to antagonize the old man. "Eventually you run out of fingers to plug the holes."

"And what are you doing to fix it?" Wolfgang seethed.

In the unnerving silence, Miles picked up his scotch glass, carrying it with him when he stumbled to the windows. He watched the flickering city lights in the distance, the twinkling merely a shiny distraction from the nightmare happening on the ground.

"Agreed. What are you doing to fix it, Malone?" Max's impatient sneer yielded to a violent cough. The haunting silence that followed screamed a premonition into the nervous room. like an alarm.

Miles slowly turned around with the barrel of a loaded pistol pressed against his temple. "We fucked around. Now we're finding out." He cocked the trigger.

Chapter 83

Come morning, the Moreno Theater was alive with an intense sense of urgency and without rules on armbands or antidotes or communal separation. *Communal separation?* Jack's team often laughed at whatever the hell kind of Orwellian oxymoron *that* was.

With the AltMedia team now meeting in shifts around the clock, even germaphobe Jack Weber had no intention of either complying or paying overreaching fines – the gestapo wasn't welcome there. The corporate media narrative was dead to them; their medical scientists had discovered that there was no pathogen – something else was making people sick. They had tested the antidote and detected no issues.

Using all his knowledge and experience in security detail, Chris had converted the basement of the theater into a modern, state-of-the-art war room with a high security epicenter. Surrounded by the standard office rooms, the cubed fishbowl was observable from all sides. Inside the heavily guarded cube, all sizes of screens and monitors covered the walls, each dedicated to a different task. Neat rows of computer stations were obscured but visible through the thick, tempered glass exterior that could be hermetically sealed in case of a chemical attack.

With the team hard at work in the war room, the hectic pace was set by a group of ambitious young scientists and tech experts on a special assignment. Among them were brilliant quantum physicists and mathematicians, engineers and clergy. Their goal was to break through the opponent's Roswell-level technological and spiritual defenses. If they could crack the elusive code to the airwaves and frequencies, locate the master switch and dismantle the empire's system, they could broadcast their critical message to the world using a higher frequency.

One section of monitors was dedicated to corporate news coverage. Programmed cyborgs: *Harmless and powerful. Darkness is only a heartbeat away. Independent media is dangerous misinformation.* Headlines and 15-second soundbites. Rinse. Repeat.

Another section of the wall was dedicated to monitoring the AltMedia coverage, where presently TDR Report was on the screen.

File notes: TDR Report (transcribed)
March 12, 2017

[Intro music]

"And that no man might buy or sell, save he that had the mark, or the name of the beast, or the number of his name." (Revelation 13:17, KJV)

*I'm starting today's show with a clip from EYE on Dormin in which they interview **thee** authoritative source, Dr. Aril, also known as he who shall not be questioned. He's balding and bespeckled which must make him trustworthy or something. Watch this:*

EYE:

Becky (Interviewer): Dr. Aril, I'm sure you're aware that a wayward group of scientists from Dormin U have released a questionable report to the public entitled The Grand Dormin Revelation. The report alleges that there are enormous economic, psychological, and social costs of the Tetracimia measures. The disgraced authors have argued that authoritarian overreach will do more harm than good in the long run.

Dr. Aril: I'm familiar with it, Becky. As expected, this is not a report grounded in science. The idea of quarantining the sick to contain this illness is a fringe notion that belongs in the annals of quackery.

Becky: Experts say they're also suggesting getting enough sun and other crackpot cures, and something called 'antibodies'.

Dr. Aril: That's correct. That kind of dangerous misinformation is the reason for these extreme transmission events that make it difficult for us to monitor the illness. We continue to implement policies to make it as easy as possible. When you get your harmless and powerful antidote, the practitioner will stamp your right palm for easy identification. My team is working on the rollout now.

Becky: As you indicated, studies show the antidote is harmless and powerful. What's your message for those who continue to refuse it?

Dr. Aril: My message to these people is that we've lost patience with them. Their behavior is selfish and abhorrent and puts everyone at risk. Why they won't take the antidote is something only they can answer.

Becky: What can we, as the collective, do to ensure that public health remains our top priority because some people refuse to comply?

Dr. Aril: Actions have consequences. No entitlement to health care. No job. No food. Jailtime. Camps. Perhaps we should let natural selection take its course, and they'll be nominated for a Darwin Award.

Becky: Other experts agree. They deserve to die.

Tessa: *So, yeah. And **they** still want you to believe that they're the good guys. What do the experts say about that?*

Anyway, I have an update on Tetracimia. A former nurse, who wishes to remain anonymous, is coming forward to blow the lid off the whole story. This is nothing we didn't already know, but now we have an insider to confirm that hospitals are killing fields. Nobody is dying of Tetracimia. Armbands are useless. The antidote doesn't work. Hospitals are handsomely rewarded for murdering patients at the behest of the government. It's called democide.

We've also had a former executive come forward from Xenco Pharmaceuticals, and his message is chilling: Resist digital ID at all costs. Whoever has control of the algorithms in the global digital age can completely control you. Limited mobility, cold unless in a warm country, hungry unless you eat the bugs. Is it digital ID they're putting on the right palm when you take antidote?

And don't forget the first whistleblower – Gabriel Sorenson. Thanks to him, we know the origin story is a lie. We are, however, starting to see a lot of people die of some mysterious illness. It could be related to climate change. I dunno.

[Five second delay]

So, wow. That's a lot of whistles. With compliance tied to our livelihoods, people are folding like cheap accordions. No antidote – no job, no participation in polite society, no government benefits. No antidote – monthly fines and a knock at the door. But we have a choice! [Redacted]

*This whole thing has **got** to be a psychological operation. Political convenience is now known as science, so anti-government protests, family gatherings, and worship services are considered extreme transmission events. Acceptable political views are exempt because the pathogen is aware of social justice issues, allegedly. No work. No church. No school. No fun. Just big government, big corporations, and technology.*

Facts withheld on purpose, no perspective, no proportion – just emotional manipulation. They use carefully crafted, uniform language and selected images to convince the viewer how dangerous their political opponents are.

Notice also how the corporate media continues to talk about left and right, often characterizing anything that opposes them as extremists. They won't tell you that the political spectrum is a circle – like a color wheel. Not a line. Not a seesaw. A circle. And where it joins – that's when the so-called left and right merge to become the same thing: Authoritarian fascists.

The answer to this, of course, is what we're trying to do – crowd funded independent journalism – the voice of the people, where citizens are allowed to have opinions. Don't let anyone filter the information for you. Be intellectually honest and eager to learn.

Hold the line, patriots. We got this.

This is Tessa Ryan, signing out.

As the stream ended, the small group gathered around the screens exchanged glances. Anna, Jack, and Chris were in jeans with their sleeves rolled up. Nearby, Emma's fuchsia dress suit and the General's military uniform contrasted with the otherwise sterile environment.

The ominous five second delay occurred when a translucent, ghostly white bear appeared at Tessa's side. When she spoke of Gabriel, two golden symbols, the size of the most gigantic snowflakes, floated down behind her.

"Amen," Anna concluded.

"She's a light warrior," Chris added, wiping a tear from his eye.

Nearby, on the sound monitors, a low drumming started, slowly growing louder, the beat instantly alerting Anna. "It's the Cree war cry." With her eyes darting around the room, she paused to listen. "The ancestors have arrived."

Part V

Premonition

"When it is dark enough, you can see the stars."
~ **Ralph Walso Emerson**

Chapter 84

An intruder was at the foot of Tessa's bed.

In a cold sweat, her heart racing, unable to move, Tessa... opened her eyes. "Bah." *Another nightmare*, just the latest in a running commentary of feeling violated, alert to every little noise, and sleeping with a baseball bat beside her. She'd moved on from the string mop.

Tossing the heavy covers to the side, Tessa rolled out of bed, her bare feet landing with a thud in the dead silence of the night. It was the darkest time of the day, just before dawn, and the streets were deserted. She moved to the three-season sunroom with her full coffee mug, raising one cold bare foot after the other to the tufted green footstool to warm them with the space heater.

Curled up underneath a fuzzy checkered blanket on her favorite yellow armchair, Tessa searched the twinkling stars in the bluish-black predawn sky. Presently, white clouds, like cotton balls, were lit by a combination of moonlight and break of day, the scene filling her with a sense of peace.

The rising golden sun was rimmed with crimson red – a bad omen. Alarmed, Tessa sat up, trying to quell her chaotic thoughts. Something terrible was going to happen!

As she moved back inside, she pondered the possibility of it being related to the federal raid – disguised as a burglary. The Dormin Police had been close-lipped about the investigation, knowing far more than they let on. The feds had seized two cell phones, a laptop, and several USB drives, along with some handwritten notes and a painting. *Hmmm. She wasn't getting her stuff back. Out of gang loyalty, nobody would cross the thin blue line.*

In the quiet sound studio next to her bedroom, Tessa clicked the radio on, already tuned to her favorite station: *ZZZA – Triple Z Rock 99.9. All hits! All the time!* A subtle vanilla scent puffed forth from the air diffuser as she found her chair.

AltMedia Group's back channel was abuzz even this early in the day. As the corporate media wouldn't touch the stories that mattered to the people, the underground press never ran out of things to talk about.

The big news was that with the antidote roll out, the barrier around the city had been removed. The authorities felt that the illness had been contained sufficiently to allow traffic to flow again, even loosening the restrictions a little bit. Visitors would receive blue armbands at the perimeter checkpoints. The Black Fist Warriors' rage seemed to have burnt itself out temporarily, allowing the residents more freedom. The timing couldn't have been better – Adam's parents were expected to arrive from Canada for a long-awaited visit.

The big chain supermarkets had reopened at full capacity, so the citizens were no longer receiving rations. Schooling was now done online. The health authorities had announced that small and medium-sized businesses could increase capacity – 40% for most. Liquor stores, strip clubs, weed stores and places where the elite gathered were exempt from the restrictions. Synagogues and mosques were open while churches remained closed.

As Tessa read the next article, anger welled up inside her. *How much was enough?* The authorities assured the people that a crashed local economy was a small price to pay for defeating the pathogen. They were doing it because they cared about saving lives. *Like an abusive man tells his wife he beats her because he loves her? Sickos.*

Needing to get away from her studio for a while, Tessa stopped at the supermarket to pick up some thick Wyoming ribeye for dinner and some smooth Tennessee bourbon for a soak in the hot tub later. The store was busy even though it was still early; she was not wearing her armband and her expression said it all – back off.

The price of alcohol hadn't increased, but beef had tripled. Near the beef products, neat packages of crickets and cicadas were arranged in white Styrofoam and plastic wrap – both very cheap.

At the counter, Tessa used her bank card to pay. Instead of the transaction going through, she received a message: You have exceeded your allowable beef consumption for March. Access denied.

Unable to believe what had just happened, Tessa double checked what card she had used. They couldn't track everything. *Could they?* "Can I pay cash?"

"You can try another card," the disinterested cashier informed her. "We don't take cash."

"What?!" *Could this really be happening?*

Tessa's head was throbbing by the time she arrived home. Exhausted, she fell asleep on the loveseat in the sunroom. Sometime later, a text alert jolted her out of her zone.

Kelly (Channel Investigator)*: Check your payment systems.*

Tessa's heart thumped. *Now what?*

Every stream of income was gone! All online payments. Bank accounts – access denied. Credit cards – access denied! Everything was canceled.

In a panic, Tessa checked her MainStreet channel. It was still there...but she'd received another strike, no reason given. If she disagreed, she could appeal. Weird how Searchify, MainStreet's parent company, was run like a government agency.

The sense of dread was real – independent media was being punished for thought crimes, just like George Orwell warned about in his epic novel, <u>1984.</u> Did she still have TownSquare?! *Yes! And she was trending?*

Corporate media had done more hit pieces about the evil ways of telling the truth. Day after day after day. *One of the stories was so stupid, it was laughable.* Tessa had an American flag on her balcony and experts had concluded she was a white supremacist because of it. *Hahaha. Nobody's going to believe that. It's Old Glory! La vida loca!*

`Ping! Ping! Beep! Ping! Beep!` Messages and cancellations started coming in almost immediately. Advertisers and subscribers were bailing. Staff were quitting.

Come on, people, just do an internet search! In trying to find her bookmarked genealogy page, Tessa got a 404-error code! The page had been removed. With her stomach now in knots, she typed her family name into the Searchify – every entry tied her to the Klan. Someone had even done a completely fabricated online encyclopedia story about her.

With her head still throbbing, Tessa leaned back in her chair and covered her hot face in her trembling hands. It was going to be a long day.

By noon, the morning's clear blue skies had turned into a gloomy gray to match Tessa's mood. Dodging the piles of snow in the parking lot with her white SUV, she parked beside Adam's metallic blue sports car in front of PJ Bar

& Grill. Wedged between a proctologist and a divorce attorney in an older strip mall, the drab restaurant was nondescript except for the sign in the front window: ARMBAND REQUIRED.

Molly Jacobs, the owner and neighborhood drunk, was known more for her addiction to plastic surgery than her business acumen. After she bought it, she discovered she had little interest in running it, so it continued to decline after she put it up for sale.

Upon walking through the porch to the second door, Tessa's senses were assaulted by grease and dust. Linoleum by the cash register had worn down to the wood. The booths were torn and faded. Not exactly prime real estate.

With the repugnant smell choking her, Tessa spotted Adam and his parents at the first booth.

A young server greeted Tessa at the door. No older than sixteen, her brown doe eyes were dull and lifeless, her hair greasy and pulled back into a sloppy ponytail. "You need an armband to get in." The girl's look matched the disinterested monotone of her voice.

Tessa smiled warmly and kept going.

Confused, the server followed Tessa to the table.

"Hi, babe." Adam winked, knowing that the use of that endearment melted her heart.

While sitting down, Tessa caught the young lady's eye. "Honey, they're stringing you along. You shouldn't have to enforce such stupid rules."

"But –"

"I'm no doctor, but I have a brain, and I'm sure the armband isn't doing what people think it is. It's useless, except to identify dissidents."

Adam snickered while the couple with him had the deer-in-the-headlights look. Laughing out loud, he captured their expression on his cell phone.

The young girl walked away with her jaw dropped – few people know how to react to the denial of authority.

Fred Logose, Adam's dad, was Ugandan-Canadian, a successful accountant with an international firm. His flaxen-haired Swedish mother, Lauren, was a chattery, soft-spoken nurse who was looking forward to retirement. She was a warm woman with a quick smile and sparkling blue eyes.

"Adam's photos don't do you justice," Lauren observed. "You're more beautiful than your picture." She had nothing to add to Tessa's medical assessment about armbands.

"Why, thank you," Tessa gushed. She scanned through the photos of Adam's Mulato siblings on Lauren's phone – a fraternal twin brother, Aaron, and a younger sister, Ashley. All had their mother's blue eyes. "Beautiful family." She glanced at Adam. "You three could be triplets."

"We've heard that before." Leaning back to snap a selfie of the group, Adam smiled to reveal his perfect teeth as his parents laughed.

"I hear you're a lawyer." Seated across from Tessa, Fred Logose put his reading glasses on to scan the choice of dishes on the greasy paper menu.

"Yes. But I'm not practicing." With her stomach growling, Tessa eyed the soup and sandwich special. "I'm doing something else currently." Theirs was the only occupied table.

"So, I've heard," Fred replied. He was an older, darker version of Adam.

The group gathered their menus to set on the edge of the table, making small talk while they waited. And waited. And waited. The server was leaning against the counter, on her phone.

Adam waved to catch the young girl's attention. "It's been twenty minutes. Can we order, please?"

The young server didn't budge. Several seconds later, a pale man in his forties emerged from the kitchen, his spiked black hair making him impossible to overlook. He closed the gap to the table in several strides. "Sorry folks. We can't serve you." The goatee and ring through his nose completed his punk look, even with the hairnet and white apron.

"You can't *serve* us?" Adam was shocked. "What do you mean you can't **serve** us?! I eat here all the time! I'm probably the only person brave enough to order your salad."

"I *know*, Mr. Logose." The cook was calm and controlled. "Orders from Molly, herself."

"Molly?" *Adam's friend had betrayed him!?*

"We don't want to be associated with terrorists. It's bad for business." He tilted his head toward Tessa. "Have you seen the news coverage?"

"The *news* coverage? You believe that crap?" Adam was incredulous. "Two of us are black, if you hadn't noticed!"

Tessa was chuckling inside. *News coverage is crap. Ha. Adam works in the media industry. Ha ha ha.*

The cook's steely glare warned Adam that he wasn't playing. "You're welcome to eat here." He pointed at Tessa. "*She* isn't."

Adam stood up ready for a fight. A handful of people from the kitchen had gathered in the narrow hall to observe the impending fireworks. A young couple who'd just entered watched with widened eyes from the nearby entrance.

"Adam, it's okay. We'll go somewhere else. Let's go." Tessa grabbed his elbow.

Outside, Fred Logose fished his truck keys out of his coat pocket. "What the h e double hockey sticks was that all about?"

Tessa couldn't suppress a giggle. "Only a Canadian would find a way to make it about hockey."

"Not *just* a Canadian. A Saskatchewanian! From Saskatoon – home of Gordie Howe," Fred beamed. "Sort of."

"Quite the flex." Tessa giggled more.

Adam put his arm across Tessa's slumped shoulders. "It's a long story, dad. Tessa has been speaking out against the powers that be. Her face has been all over the news as a white supremacist terrorist, or something." He wanted so badly to tell Tessa what he was hiding from her, but he couldn't. Not yet.

Tessa pecked Adam on the cheek. "I've lost my appetite. Enjoy your lunch. I'm going home." She couldn't bring herself to tell him about her morning.

Chapter 85

Since Miles Malone blew his brains out in front of him in his Atluko office, a despondent Max Fisher slid further into a deep depression. Malone was irreplaceable, and Max knew he would never make it without him. His alcohol consumption exploded, and he soon became even more of an incoherent, bumbling, secluded fool.

Elsewhere in the cursed city, Jack Weber had developed a rash unlike the ones they showed on TV – the fake Tetracimia rash. He had suddenly developed hives, and doctors had no idea why.

Chapter 86

Like fluffy marshmallows, snowflakes floated past Tessa's studio window on the 21st floor. Inside, she was inundated with messages from angry people until her entire body ached.

Amanda (Producer): *Before he killed himself, Miles Malone contacted me to ask if I wanted to be associated with you. Said that information would follow me for the rest of my career. His death has me more scared than before – they take care of their own. I can't allow my reputation to be ruined. I'm a single mother with two kids to support. Sorry.*

Matt (Researcher): *Did Miles Malone really kill himself or did he know too much? I can't take chances; if I continue to work for you, they will kill my family and I have every reason to believe they are capable of it. This is not a reflection on you or the TDR Report.*

Kane (Supporter): *I am sickened at what you've become. You started off speaking truth to power, and now you're opening admitting your allegiance to the KKK. My financial support ends today.*

Phil (In-video Sponsor): Our business relationship is over.

The day had turned cold, with every chimney spewing acrid, white smoke into the air. A few feather-like snowflakes floated to the icy ground where several inches had accumulated...now the cold was back. With her identity concealed by a disguise, Tessa left her apartment to get to the library. Black shades completed the mysterious witch ensemble when accessorizing a long black wig and matching wide brim hat.

Pulling into the mostly empty parking lot of the downtown public library, Tessa discovered the library was open with no limited capacity. *Odd.* Armband was still required, though. The huge banner advertising Drag Queen Story Hour in the entrance couldn't be missed. *Now it made sense.* Diversity, equity and inclusion. Environmental social governance. She could see the social media comments in her head: 'Relax, bigots. They just want to read to the kids'. *Get bent, wackos.*

Searching the archived materials for records of her family, Tessa found nothing. It was all gone. She tried to find something, *anything,* about the old corner store, Old Town Square. *Nada.* Like they never existed. The real history of Dormin was purged and in its place was a story that America was founded on slavery, hate, and injustice – it had become a cliche.

Okay. Deep breath. Get home, pour some red wine, soak in the hot tub, and think. In that order. Stepping out of the elevator, Tessa dug in her purse for her key card when she spotted a notice taped to the door. Her heart pounded as she ran toward it, her legs heavy and rubbery.

Evicted!? Despite the notice, Tessa tried her card; it didn't work. With her back against the door, her entire body slumped to the floor. After several minutes of inner turmoil, she found her inner warrior. They had won *this* battle, but they would *never* win the war.

At Atluko Industries, a beefy woman with mousy brown hair and vacuous gaps for eyes slowly rose from the long table in the guard's lunchroom. The aging Olga brushed piecrust crumbs from her mouth and watched them land on the table; aside from the vending machines, the room was dark and silent. Checking for her semi-automatic, she straightened out the bulky beige uniform covering her mid spare tire.

Three levels below ground, Olga yawned as she emerged from the private elevator and into a well-lit, wide corridor. At the end of this institutional hall was the prison wing reserved for the hardest to handle inmates. At the room labeled 'Kill room #1', she again checked for her rifle before opening the door.

Once inside, Olga shone her blinding flashlight into the darkened cages to complete the twelve-hour 'death' check. The metric was the baton – if the prisoner didn't respond to a crack on the head, they were dead. The sadistic guard stopped at three cages to make notes on her phone, then continued her rounds. There was a noise behind her!

Rifle in hand, her pulse racing, the startled Olga whipped around coming face to face with...nothing. She was *certain* she heard something and saw a shadow in the bales. Her heart was still thumping when the beam of her flashlight swept up and down the bale stack. "Who's there!" Her uncertain words bounced off the cold concrete walls.

Nobody was there. With a heavy sigh, Olga rubbed her tired eyes. When she started imagining things, it was time for a break – she clocked out and went home.

Chapter 87

At dusk, a deflated Tessa arrived at Anna's cozy house in the secluded Saboro Mountain subdivision. With her warm breath clouding in the frigid air, the cold wind cut to the bone. Before she reached the concrete steps, the heavy decorative door creaked open.

"Anna!" Tessa wailed, the delectable aromas emanating from the kitchen providing her with some temporary comfort.

"Shhhh, child," Anna scolded as she gently pulled Tessa inside by the hand. "You're letting the cold in. Go sit in front of the fire. I'll bring you a blanket." With a blast of freezing cold air remaining inside, she secured the door.

The stack of newspapers occupying Tessa's old armchair existed in perpetuity; as she moved them, an angry sob escaped – it was so unfair! She rocked back and forth with her eyes closed until a clay pottery mug filled with steaming peppermint tea was in her hand – just what one needed to soothe their nerves. She was tired. And annoyed. Her phone was dead. Her ear was ringing, and no one would answer it.

With a fuzzy blanket now covering her visitor, Anna took her place in front of the roaring fire. The snapping of the birch logs broke the silence.

"Anna," Tessa pulled her feet to the edge of the chair. "I don't know how much more I can take. We got kicked out of PJ Bar and Grill because of me." To stifle her cries, she buried her flushed face in her elbows and knees.

"You didn't have lunch? I made traditional bean bread."

Bean bread? Tessa *loved* bean bread, and Anna knew it. Regardless, she held up her hand to refuse. "Thanks, but no. Feeling sick."

"I'll save you some, my girl." Anna picked up her latest beading project – a pair of beautiful earrings.

"I went to talk to Lucas Belzac, he gave me some advice."

"Sorry, dear." Anna looked up from her beading, the full moon shining in the bay window forming a halo around her head. "Who?"

"You *know*, Anna! My mom's psychologist. Lucas."

With her hands resting on her lap and her gaze fixed on the dark lake, Anna didn't respond for several seconds. "Excuse me for a bit." She was gone for over five minutes, returning with a newspaper from August 2010 opened to the obituaries.

In Tessa's dissociative state, it took her a minute to realize that she was looking at Lucas's obituary in the Dormin Times – almost seven years earlier? "No! That's impossible. Look!"

"Impossible?"

Tessa dug in the pocket of her plaid coat draped over the back of the chair. "He gave me a purple lollipop...just like when I was little." She checked both pockets. No lollipop!

"Maybe you ate it," Anna teased.

"But I talked to him!"

"Maybe everything you *thought* he said was already inside you. Perhaps you needed the Great Spirit to lead you to truth you always knew in your heart."

"It's déjà vu. That's exactly what he said!" Tessa gasped, remembering how weird everything was in his office. The old suit. The musty smell. Seeing right through him. All the traffic. She had no idea how she got there, or how she got home... "Omigod, Anna. It was a dream! I took advice from a dream?"

With a knowing smile, Anna brought the flowery teapot to the alcove for refills. "What else is going on?"

"Well...I..." Tessa was starting to nod off.

"You know what you need right now, my girl? Some rest and a good cry, let all those healing tears flow. You'll feel better." Anna stood up. "Come with me. I have your room ready."

"Anna," Tessa hesitated while she yawned. "How'd you know I'd be here today?"

"A little birdie told me," Anna's motherly smile suggested the conversation was over.

In the guest room, where Tessa had stayed all those years ago when it was *her* room, a blue towel and a floral housecoat were neatly laid on the striped bedspread, one of her own framed paintings hanging on the wall above it. "My art!" She raised her hands over her mouth.

"Did you forget you hung it on my fridge?"

Preparing to lie down, Tessa stopped sniffling while she pulled a long-forgotten book from Max out of a zipped pocket on the side of her purse.

On her tiptoes, Anna reached into the closet for an extra pillow. "What book do you have?"

"It's a book that Max gave me a long time ago. When I got turfed from the plant. The history of the Fisher clan."

The blood drained from Anna's face. "Wait here." She returned with another book, trying to wipe the dust off with the sleeve of her sweatshirt. "This is the *actual* history of Max's family. It might be a good night for you to read it."

By now, Tessa knew there was so much more to Dormin than they'd ever been told. The book was called Rocky Road: Slaves of Wyoming.

Grabbing Fishers of Men from Tessa's hand, Anna left and closed the door, mumbling to herself. "I'm going to burn this other trash in the fireplace."

Like props in a western, the rectangular straw bales piled in the corner doubled as an opportunistic place to hide. Beside them, Will Garcia's weak heart raced when the beam of Olga's bright flashlight stopped inches from where he was hidden, trying to remain perfectly still. Holding his breath until the thick steel door shut, he exhaled with relief and crawled out from under a heap of musty, prickly hay.

Using a dim flashlight, the senior janitor peered into the cold concrete enclosures, stacked like kennels, leaving no room to stand up and barely enough to turn around. No good existed here, only a macabre form of evil: Stall after stall of captive prey, beaten, barely alive, skin stretched over bone, covered in sores and fleas, broken spirits calling out through sunken eyes. It was a concentration camp!

Still crouched, Will rested his spinning head against the cold cement wall, trying to control the nausea. ***This** is what Hell looks like!* His bottom lip quivered.

Faint stomps!? Growing louder. Military! And they were right outside the room. Dogs barking. Muffled voices.

Diving back under the hay, Will waited, shaking and trying to stifle the sniveling while hiding his stocky frame in the shadows. Pieces of straw clung to his brown hair. Based on his research, he wasn't expecting anyone. *Who could this be?*

The footsteps slowed...and stopped. The slit of light in the door disappeared, temporarily converting the room into a pitch-black cavern. The stomps marched on...the footsteps faded.

Finally taking the opportunity to exhale, Will moved quickly along the rows in the semi-dark, his cell phone repeatedly flashing until he reached the glaring exit sign.

On the other side of the emergency exit was an elaborate maze of tunnels that ran all under the city. *Certain* restaurants, bars, churches, schools, daycare centers, libraries, hotels, casinos, **galleries**, so much more...all connected. And if you had a tunnel, you were one of *them*.

Most intriguing of all, a huge tunnel ran right through Diablo Mountain, both entrances somehow hidden from public view. A possible human trafficking operation was what was flying around the gossip circuit, though many thought it impossible. After all, the Fishers were a standup family whose very existence was integral to the survival of the city. *Just ask them.*

If the alarm switch had been reactivated, Will was a dead man. Otherwise, one of the routes would lead him to the other side of the outer perimeter fence and a waiting vehicle.

"Mister. Help..." A faint, female voice croaked behind him and trailed off. The woman was lying in a fetal position, completely naked. Her long blond hair was matted and dirty, and her skin was caked with a leaky rash.

Will crouched down to grab her cold, skeletal hand. "What's going on in here?" His voice was full of desperation.

"They're here..." The woman's body went limp.

Will shook her bony shoulder through the metal bars. "Lady. Lady! Who's here?" He needed to get out of there! He felt for a pulse. *Damn. She's gone. What did she mean, they're here?*

With his eyes closed, Will said a silent prayer for the woman and got to his feet. The next few seconds would determine if he lived or died. He reached for the horizontal bar...

The dead woman grabbed Will's ankle with... claws? He crouched down again and came face-to-face with a shapeshifter – her skin was now covered in rough scales, her forked tongue moving in and out of her mouth. Shit just got real. He was so outta there.

No alarm!

On pure adrenaline now, Will raced through the tunnels, the map he'd studied for months vivid in his mind's eye. Once on the other side of the thick hedge, he scrambled into the extremely cold night and the back door of a black rental car with tinted rear windows.

"Stay down!" Adam hissed as Will pulled a thick folded blanket over his entire body. "The city is crawling with gestapo!" Using his press credentials, he had more freedom of movement than other people, and he couldn't take a chance. He pulled onto the main road, heading east. On the way to his house, he drove past Tessa's darkened apartment, wondering why he hadn't heard from her – especially after such an unsettling lunch.

Avoiding all the checkpoints, Adam pulled onto his driveway with the garage door already half up. His sports car was at the rental agency, and his motorcycle took up the other half of his two-car garage. Sports car and motorcycle. He was at that magic age – had he not outgrown his youth or was he *already* having a midlife crisis?

"We made it?" Will didn't wait for an answer.

"My parents are upstairs. Go on downstairs, and I'll join you in a minute."

With muffled voices above him, Will scrolled the grainy photos on his phone while he waited, once again struggling to control his nausea. Ralph came bounding down the stairs. "Hey, Ralph!" Will shook a paw. "Bad news today."

Whimpering, Ralph found his favorite basement dog bed, big puppy-dog eyes watching his best friend carry a can of cold Canadian beer in each hand. Adam turned his attention to the human in his midst while he rubbed his pooch's ears. "So, what did you get?"

"Sorry about the digital noise." Will handed his phone over. "Bad lighting in there."

Adam remained standing while he sipped his cold, delicious, Canadian beer. As if he were watching a train wreck, he was both transfixed and horrified, but couldn't look away, unable to comprehend the nature of the demon they were dealing with. Photo after photo was like a kick in the gut. His hand shook.

"Sorry, man."

Then Adam saw it! He was barely recognizable in the photo, but with the crescent-shaped scar above his eye, there was no doubt it was him. It was Gabriel Sorenson! No *wonder* he hadn't contacted Tessa! "So that's where they're taking everyone. That's the *real* quarantine camp? Here's another one that went missing – Maria, Tessa's producer." He showed Will the photo. It looked like she had just arrived and was heavily drugged.

"I never would have believed it if I hadn't seen it with my own eyes." Will's voice was shaking. He dabbed at the corners of his eyes with a soggy tissue. "Keep going."

The sheer size of the underground city was mind-boggling, layer upon layer of people for live test subjects. Slave labor. A massive jail. A hybrid zoo. An altar. Slaughter and kill rooms.

"Slaughter and kill rooms! What the hell is going on in there!? They look like death camp victims!" Adam was vibrating. Will's phone had fallen to the floor in slow motion. "And children? Is there no bottom to this depravity?!"

"Adam, even I didn't know how bad it was, and I work there. You're lucky I didn't capture the shape shifter!"

"Oh, come on!"

Will got to his feet, putting his hands to the sides to steady himself. "I'm just the token fat maintenance guy, but I hear things when I go to the boiler room."

"What *did* you hear?"

"A scream I'll never forget." Will cast his eyes downward. "Goosebumps. And not the good kind."

"This explains it!" Adam picked up Will's phone. "Probably known only to the brass and the guards who are sworn to secrecy under penalty of death."

"Yup. Their secret covenant – I've seen it." With his phone back in his hands, Will sat down again.

"Wow. How much have you found out?" Adam crouched to pet Ralph.

"A lot. It's on their servers. If I can get to it." Will's eyes clouded over. "One of several quantum computers in the entire world is located here."

"Seriously?"

"Afraid so. The place is a tech mega-city, directly run by the US Military, and connected to CERN. Everything is on their servers – and I mean *everything*."

"What do you mean *everything*?!" Adam stammered.

"Everything they need for the blackmail operation is on there. If you know what I mean?"

"And how are you finding all this out?"

"Let's just say a little birdie had his wings clipped." Will guzzled half his cold beer in one swallow and followed it up with an impressive belch. "So, anyway, I've been watching for a while, and I know how I can to it."

"Do you want to risk getting caught? You've *seen* what they do to people whose opinions they don't like!" Jumping to his feet, Adam tried to keep calm. "What are they going to do to you if they find out!?"

"We're at war."

"But is it worth it? They'll call anything we get 'dangerous information' anyway."

"Of course, it's worth it. Only the guilty consider information dangerous."

Chapter 88

It was still before sunrise and Tessa's stomach told her it was late enough to follow the aroma of coffee to the kitchen. She jumped out of the warm bed, throwing Anna's floral robe on to cover the goosebumps all over her slender body. It went to her knees...where were fuzzy pajamas when you needed them? She dragged herself to the kitchen on the cold floor, barefoot and rubbing her eyes.

"Good morning, sleepy head!" Anna was at the stove cooking eggs. "I know it's chilly. I just started the fire. How did you sleep?"

"I crashed hard. May be the pure mountain air." Yawning, Tessa took her usual seat.

Anna set a steaming mug of fresh-brewed Nicaragua blend coffee and a full plate down in front of her guest. Poached eggs on bean bread, and canned fruit from the garden. "I hope you're hungry, my girl."

"A little." Tessa hadn't eaten the day before...since she'd sensed the premonition in her sunroom. *Had only one day passed?*

"Let's give thanks," Anna bowed her head. "Creator God, we thank you for the Earth Mother for producing this blessed food, and for the Great Spirit who dines with us at your abundant altar. In Jesus' name."

"Amen." Tessa made the sign of the cross. She dove into her food like she was one calorie short of starvation.

"Did you read the book I gave you?" Anna added a teaspoon of honey to her tea.

"I see what they're doing now, Anna." Tessa tried to sip her coffee; it was still too hot. "Cole told me that *my* great grandfather was a Klansman, when it was the other way around – it was them." She devoured her second slice of bean bread in four bites – she was hungrier than she thought, and Anna's raspberry jam was *so* good. "Is this the jam you were making when I was here?"

Recalling the encounter, Anna wagged her finger at her guest. "Good, isn't it?" With a satisfied smirk, she gathered the empty plates.

"Very." Tessa smiled, thinking to herself how fast Anna's inner mom could take over, despite never having any kids of their own. "How did you get that book?"

"I tracked down the author. He's in hiding – has been for years." Standing at the sink, Anna finished the last of her lukewarm coffee. "He fears retaliation for exposing the Fishers. All other copies have been nuked from the planet, and no publisher will touch it now."

"*All* the history is gone." Tessa helped herself to another cup of coffee. "I checked."

Anna filled the sink with hot, soapy water, the scent of lemon briefly overtaking the permanent aroma of ginger.

In the living room, Tessa pushed aside the pleated yellow drape in front of the bay window. "The weather is all over the place, isn't it?" Her eyes were directed toward the angry gray skies. "Climate change?"

"Ha!" Drying her hands on a tea towel, Anna joined Tessa in the living room. "The climate has been changing since the planet was formed. What is that... 4.3 billion years? If there *are* any manmade issues, the corporate media is blowing it way out of proportion."

"How can you be so sure?"

"Because they've been lying about it for decades. First, we were supposed to get into an ice age. Then acid rain was going to kill all the crops. Then there was a hole in the ozone layer. All the ice caps were supposed to be gone by now."

Realizing the doomsday clock had been ticking for longer than she'd been alive, Tessa suspected Anna may be right. "My friend Megan is always preaching about climate change, but she uses disposable diapers, so..."

Anna left and came back with a small black safe, placing it on the floor beside her chair with a thud. "This is a scary place when the media encourages rage." Click click. She pulled the door open.

"Anna, what are you doing!?" Tessa recoiled when she saw what was inside. "You know I hate guns! My father had a whole arsenal. I was *terrified*."

"Well, now you've got more to be terrified of than guns. You've cornered a dangerous animal. When people start going missing, you need protection."

"Look at that thing. Nobody needs assault weapons!" Tessa had one hand over her mouth while she took several steps back. "No wonder there are so many mass shootings."

"Don't be ridiculous, child." Failing to suppress an eye roll, Anna tried to pass the gun to Tessa. "It's a handgun. It's not loaded."

Tessa jumped back like Anna had shoved a live bug in her mouth. "Anna, I didn't even get one after the break-in! If I get caught with that thing, they'll arrest me."

Anna held up a well-worn, navy, hard-cover book. "It's called the Constitution."

"But Anna, they've already labeled me a raging alcoholic, schizophrenic, and racist terrorist. Red flag laws. Besides, the Constitution was written when people had muskets."

"Weak argument, child. It was written when people used quill feathers as pens and now, we have computers. You think the founding fathers didn't think about technology?"

"I guess," Tessa reluctantly admitted.

"That gun isn't just for your protection. It guarantees your right to fight back to maintain a free state: *A well-regulated militia, being necessary to the security of a free state, the right of the people to keep and bear Arms, shall not be infringed upon.*"

"Nice idea, but *this* government said that if we wanted to fight back, we'd need *actual* weapons of war. Like nuclear."

"Then you should know that when the government tells you that you don't need a gun, you need a gun." Anna pointed to the safe. "*That* lesson was passed on by my ancestors – Homeland Security since 1492."

"What if they –"

"Ask yourself this: Are you an outlaw if you dance around society's unjust rules?"

"Well, no."

"This government already has blood on their hands. They'll have to kill me to get my guns."

"Anna! Don't say that!"

"Adam is ex-military. He can show you how to use it," Anna pleaded.

The last twenty-four hours had been brutal; they were clearly gunning for her. No pun intended. And they were raging psychopaths. "You're probably right," Tessa sighed. "Okay. You win."

Another entire day passed before Tessa was ready to face reality. Watching the shampoo form streams of bubbles across her skin, she rinsed the stress of the world away, still having no idea how she was going to get out of her current situation.

Anna had washed the only set of clothes Tessa had – the ones she'd arrived in. Her favorite burgundy sweater accessorized by a wide gold belt was a dynamite combo with her attractive physical features and ripped blue jeans. Finally feeling refreshed, she stepped into the hall.

`Brrrrriiiiinnnnnng. Brrrrriiiiinnnnnng.`

"It's for you." Anna motioned to the black wall phone.

With a confused glance in Anna's general direction, Tessa studied the phone. What century were they in? She lifted the receiver. "Hello?"

"Tessa!"

"That's me." Tessa confirmed. "Who is this?" She glared at Anna.

"It's Jack Weber."

"Oh?"

"I heard what was going on. It's a terrible thing."

"Thanks." Tessa was confused. Yeah, her cellphone was dead, but why did he need to talk to her about the issues? Chris usually handled the glitches.

"I've got some money for you. If you can get down to city hall, it will be available for pick up from my assistant. It's a prepaid credit card and some cash." Jack cleared his throat. "A gift. No need to repay."

"What? Why? I don't understand."

"I have a charitable foundation that helps the men and women who defend the principles this country was founded on, and they will always have a special place in my heart." Jack paused, wondering if Tessa would put two and two together. "And so will their families."

A foundation for veterans and... families? "Wait." Oh my God! "It was ... *you* helping my mother?!"

"Yes." Jack's tone was flat; in addition to his hives, he'd been feeling ill for a few days with flu-like symptoms and general malaise.

"Holy... sh..." Tessa caught herself. "...mokes! Is the media lying about literally *everything!*?"

"The short answer is yes. You should know that by now." Judging by the tone of his voice, Jack was perturbed. "I'll give you the long answer another time."

Thinking it was too good to be true, Tessa hesitated. "I... I don't know what to say."

"Then don't say anything. I'll do what I can to support you through this. All I ask is that you keep fighting for this city and our country. Deal?"

"Deal." Avoiding Anna's eyes, Tessa hung up. "Hey, why don't you get into this century with technology? We have these things called cell phones now." She turned to face Anna with a playful grin on her face.

"Because our humanity must never lose our connection with Mother Earth, my girl." Knowing how the globalists purposefully got people addicted to tech, Anna's tone was soft and understanding.

"It's impossible to lose touch. We *live* on Earth."

"When phones were connected by wires, humans were free," Anna reminded her.

"Okay. But it's 2017."

"And humans are enslaved."

"I get it," Tessa sighed as she moved closer to Anna in search of her coat and scarf. "Now, where's my cell phone?"

"Where you left it?" The resignation in Anna's voice was discernable as she picked the phone up off the kitchen table.

Clothes shopping! "See you later." *So much for Mother Earth.*

By the time Tessa returned to Anna's, it was clear and sunny. With her breath suspended in the air and her cheeks rosy, she unloaded the cargo from her SUV.

Both arms laden with shopping bags and tugging a new suitcase up the concrete steps with her index finger, Tessa attempted to knock with her foot. One of the bags slipped from her hand, scattering the contents all over. "Bah!" Her white tam went flying when she leaned over to inspect the damage.

The door opened with a jolt. "You can take more than one trip, you know!" Anna folded her arms – her inner mom was back.

By the time Tessa got inside, Anna had moved her loot to the guest room.

"Retail therapy?" Anna's inner hippy had her hands on her hip. "Really?"

"Hardly. They have all my things, Anna." Tessa located the bag with the phone charger. "It's a few necessities."

"How many pairs of shoes did you buy?" Anna teased as she helped Tessa unload her cargo.

"Two. It's winter," Tessa sulked. *What was she now? An accountant?*

"How did you manage to not get kicked out of all those places?"

"I still had my disguise in the car," Tessa giggled. "Fake ID and I wear the stupid armband. It's the same way I get past the checkpoints."

"Perfect." Anna's fondness for civil disobedience twinkled in her smiling eyes. "Will you be here for dinner?"

"If it's okay, I'd like to stay another day – at least until Adam shows me how to use that *thing*."

"Good idea. That *thing* might save your life," Anna scolded.

When Tessa was done inspecting her day's purchases, she returned to the alcove. While her mouth watered from the tantalizing smells coming from the kitchen, she crouched to plug in her dead phone. "Oh, and there was a letter and another package from Jack. He's offering me the exclusive use of the guest house at his estate for as long as I need." Leaning on the stucco wall to balance herself, she got to her feet. "I guess I don't have to live under a bridge."

Anna set two steaming mugs down on the bamboo table. "There's a good man beneath that rough exterior."

Tessa picked up her tea while she sat down, trying to find the right words to suck up. "I'm so sorry, Anna. I should have known better than to trust them. It's just the …" She stared at the hoarfrost-covered trees sparkling in the sun.

"I know." Anna gazed upon the thawing lake, her thoughts drifting to a long-ago canoe ride and the haunting call of a broken spirit. "You're about to learn a whole lot more."

Chapter 89

Australian private eye, Jason King, was tired. He was tired of the unrelenting heat: 120°F in the shade. He was tired of fake people and their virtue signaling. He was especially tired of dumb saltwater crocodiles and everything else in his God forsaken country that wanted to kill him. In fairness, they didn't *want* to... but they would. The stuff of horror movies. He needed a holiday. Someplace cooler.

`Ping!` An encrypted text from Adam Logose.

> **Adam:** You need to get to Dormin, asap.

> **Jason:** What's up, mate?

> We're about to blow the case wide open. In danger.

> Whoa. I'll get there as soon as I can. Expect layovers.

> lol, I thought that said lawyers. Airport still closed. Rent a vehicle in Jackson.

> Roger that.

Well, well. Wyoming was certainly cooler, now, wasn't it?

Chapter 90

By the time a re-energized Tessa left the gun range, the heavy clouds had returned with a vengeance, rendering it almost impossible to see through the raging blizzard. Adam had just taught her how to use the handgun Anna had given her, and she was ready to call it a day.

White knuckled when she reached the security gates of Jack's estate, Tessa finally exhaled when the high-beam headlights shone on an A-frame guest house through the snow. Serene and private, it was nestled in a grove of mature vegetation out of sight of the massive main house.

The heavy storm activity triggered the motion light to stay on, illuminating the path to the front door from Tessa's SUV. With ice crystals flying in her face, the biting wind whipped at her matching ensemble, prompting her to hold her tam in place with one freezing bare hand. *One can't forego fashion, after all – even in a snowstorm.*

Stepping inside to set her luggage down, Tessa shook off the flakes that had pelted her on the way in, forcing the heavy door closed with her backside. The scent of combined essential oils immediately caught her attention; the place was quiet enough to chill one's bones. The floors were shiny hardwood with dimmed yellow wall lights eerily reflecting off them all around the spacious foyer.

As her eyes adjusted to the unfamiliar shadowy surroundings, Tessa took her high black boots off, carefully placing them on the vinyl mat in the entrance closet. To the right, brass-trimmed French doors opened to the colonial period living room, the two exterior glass walls perfectly angled to draw one's attention to the massive stone fireplace and the contrasting modern chandelier hanging from the high ceiling. The tasteful color scheme was black, ivory and wine-red. The totality was magazine stunning.

With the fire ready to go, Tessa lit the kindling, mesmerized by the high flames soon licking at the thick tar above them. It seemed the perfect contrast with the steady, howling gusts of flurries right outside the windows. Digging her feet into the wine-red area rug, she lit the votive candle on the black coffee table, inhaling deeply when the scent of apple pie wafted toward her.

With a sudden craving for cinnamon hot chocolate, Tessa found the fully stocked kitchen and a fruit bowl full of apples and oranges on the counter. Beside it was a note: "Need comparing. If anyone can do it, it's you. Smiley face." *Ha.*

Rap! Rap! Rap! Someone was at the door!

Her heart racing, Tessa got the handgun from her tote beside the elegant ivory sofa – thank *God* Adam had showed her how to use it earlier. Who could *this* be, though!? The estate was *crawling* with security.

Rap! Rap! "Tessa!"

With every nerve in her body at attention, Tessa moved to the door, the loaded gun raised in the air. "Who's there?!" she shouted; her voice strong and confident. She was prepared to use deadly force to defend herself at this point.

"It's Jack!" The unexpected visitor shouted over the roaring wind. "Don't shoot!"

Hiding the gun behind her stiff back, Tessa stopped holding her breath, ready to give Jack a good tongue lashing when she opened the door.

"I know. I should have texted, but we were driving by." Jack pointed to the tall guy beside him. "This is Dan. He'll be keeping an eye on the place tonight." Dan's security uniform showed off his bodybuilder frame and pistol on his hip. *Cool.*

Shivering, Tessa stepped aside to let the two men in, noting that the limousine was parked in the middle of the road with the back door open. Snow was blowing into the car, as well as into the house through the open front door.

"Oh, we won't come in," Jack said, his voice rising about the roar of the forceful wind. "Just wanted to let you know not to worry so you could get some rest. Everything is safe." He stepped away.

"Whoa. Thanks." With the two men gone, Tessa locked the door, wondering how she could have misjudged a person so badly? *Besides the boldfaced barrage of bullshit. Oh. Right.*

Trying to put the last three days out of her mind, Tessa prepared to get down to business. *Three days?* It seemed like it had been a month! She turned on her phone.

Tetracimia was the top story, as always, with an incessant push to take the antidote. People were dying by the minute, they said. Some scientists had noted that there was a correlation between those who had received more than one dose of the antidote and those who died suddenly. Alas, there was no causal link, and they didn't think it warranted further research.

Continuing to scan the headlines, Tessa became increasingly frustrated that schools and churches were still not allowed to open. *Great way for the state to say they weren't interested in feeding either the spirit or the mind.* Under immense pressure, small business owners surrendered their livelihood to a contrived authority, permanently shuttering doors and saying goodbye to their hopes and dreams; life savings; and blood, sweat, and tears. And in some cases – their lives. *Because of stupid, bureaucratic decisions.*

The social costs of the restrictions were becoming visible – *like bad neighbors who never cut their grass and get visitors at all hours of the day and night.* A shocking number of people were turning to drugs and alcohol to cope, with mental illness and skyrocketing suicide rates not far behind.

In related news, poverty, unemployment, domestic violence, and further destruction of the family unit followed – the tragic results of an epidemic response gone terribly wrong. *If thalidomide babies, the destruction of entire ecosystems, and historical massacres of innocent citizens were any indication, it was just business as usual.*

Meanwhile, the people making the rules were doing just fine, still getting paid for basically doing nothing and going to their exclusive parties – not an armband in sight. *Rules were for lesser beings.* Everyone in power was exempt from taking the antidote, and the pharmaceuticals were protected by the same power.

In the parallel world of the AltMedia Group, Tetracimia wasn't even a thing. It was all theater, and deep down everyone knew it – even those who believed the grand illusion.

Weird how alternative media had transformed into the model that the corporate media used to follow. As the voice of the people, Tessa was putting herself in harm's way, but she was *not* going to be silenced. The empire had gotten away with the lies for far too long.

Chapter 91

In Jack's Victorian themed study, he and Chris were trying to find a solution of their own. After travelling through the blizzard, he was chilled to the bone; limenade wasn't going to cut it. "How could anyone know what's going on in that plant?" He handed Chris a glass of cold water and a white plastic pill bottle.

"That's what they do – they sell reality." Holding his index finger in the air, Chris guzzled down two acetaminophens. "And they pay well for it, too – everything from production to anchors to tech... anyone involved in the information war is very well paid."

"That's what military leaders have always done – make sure the people who make the weapons of war are handsomely rewarded." Jack twirled a yellow pencil in his hand. "That's why TownSquare employees get paid over a hundred grand a year to not work. The feds run it."

"I know. It's David and Goliath." Chris picked up some colored marking pens off the desk and started juggling them. "But we have our own infrastructure. Now all we need is for alternative social media to take off."

Jack doused his dry hands with sanitizer, catching a good whiff of the alcohol while he rubbed it in. "What's the deadline?"

"Deadline is whenever they chose to pull the plug." Chris was now juggling four marking pens.

"Will it stop them?" Jack reached into the minifridge. "I'm having a tequila. Care to join me?"

"Huh?!" In Chris's shock, the marking pens fell to the floor one by one. "When did *you* start drinking?"

"We *need* them stopped," Jack set another broken pencil on the desk; how many was that now? "If we can't do that, maybe the booze will help to calm my nerves."

Stunned at the sudden change, Chris sat down to catch his breath. "No tequila," he mumbled before he found his voice. "The Bible says that no weapon fashioned against you will work. Are we gonna trust it, or what?"

With a swipe of his fingertips across the neck, Jack signaled the discussion was closed. "What do you have for me?"

"It's opposition research." Slowly and methodically, Chris set the thick report on Jack's antique desk. "All the data is there."

"Give me a quick rundown." With his sock feet on the desk, Jack clasped his stiff hands behind his head.

"Long story short: The empire subverted us from day one. Corporate media are part of the operation. Big tech censored, and continues to censor, opposition. Political violence is legitimized and encouraged. The court system has been weaponized against the empire's political opposition."

"Nothing we didn't already know." Jack's disapproving look didn't exactly hide his disappointment. "I'm living proof."

"True! But now we have *forensic* proof."

Near the door now, Jack turned to face his visitor. "Good point."

"Despite all their cheating, though, they still failed." Chris helped himself to another glass of water. "So, there's that."

"What difference, at this point, does it make? If they control everything behind the scenes, why do we even vote? And the people *still* can't see it?"

"Ha. Are you kidding me?" Not exactly looking forward to going back out in the storm, Chris joined Jack near the door. "Some of these people are experiencing a psychotic break from reality, literally admitting that they'll accept *the corpses of children* as collateral damage before they allow the people to govern their own affairs."

"I know. They don't even know what they're saying anymore."

"But it's for the noble cause of 'saving' democracy by destroying democratic institutions."

"And to stop an opponent from breaking all the rules by breaking all the rules," Jack chuckled. "Go figure."

"Poison ideology spreads fast with the right manipulation," Chris reminded him.

"Are you sure you want to head back out in that?" Jack pointed at one of the second-floor windows as it framed the blowing snow.

"I've been through worse." Chris was on Jack's heels as they descended the wide, curved staircase. "I've been investigating corrupt politicians and other powerful leaders for almost half my life, and I've never seen such a coordinated criminal conspiracy."

"Was there ever a time in history when the side guilty of censorship, prosecution of political opponents, and fraudulent elections were the good guys?"

"It's time to put Plan D in motion. Or is it E?" Chris turned to leave. "See you in the war room."

With the storm still raging outside, Tessa got unpacked in the spacious guest suite upstairs, changing into the white silk robe she'd purchased the day before. Jenny, maid extraordinaire, had prepared the hot tub for her earlier, and boy, did she need it. Before long, she was soaking in the hot bubbly water, completely nude, hair up, sipping sparkling wine, and listening to her favorite music. With her nagging phone upstairs, there was nothing to distract her – it was the perfect time to regroup and contemplate her next move. Ahh.

In Dormin, they really *were* at a crossroads. On one side, a fallen angel roamed – intent on making God's creation in his own image. Unsuspecting people with low vibrational frequencies attracted this dark side, opening themselves to demon possession. On the other side, high-frequency resonance prompted the journey to enlightenment.

Despite the temptation, despite being the involuntary main character in a science fiction-horror hybrid, Tessa couldn't quit. They *couldn't* lose this war for the soul of humanity. Zero hour was fast approaching.

Back upstairs, Tessa opened the door to the other room in the suite, unprepared for the shock that awaited her. It was converted to a studio – designed exactly like her old one with all new, state-of-the-art equipment! No expense spared for this gig.

After rinsing the chlorine from the hot tub off in the shower, Tessa changed into her fuzzy beige, hooded onesie – a gift from Stefan and Nettie Constantin and a reminder of her time in Maine, a thousand or so years ago, where the cold humid wind off the Atlantic cut right to the bone. Now that she was on the sofa with her laptop, she basked in the warmth of the dancing flames, the perfect companion for brutal Wyoming nights.

As Tessa began to scroll through her social media feeds, the bigger picture started to emerge; it was like trying to put a jigsaw puzzle together with no illustration on the box. Everything was related, but how? *Had the Holocaust occurred in isolation or was there something even more wicked than the banality of evil? Had they simply found another way to slip under the radar? What about the famines, ongoing proxy wars, disease, abortion, vaccines, sterilization, and poisoned skies, water, and food? Was it random or was it orchestrated? When did the entire world lose its mind?*

Turned out that the Greek philosopher, Euripides, was right: "Question everything. Learn something. Answer nothing."

Kyrie Eleison: Lord, have mercy.

Chapter 92

An irritating beam of ultrabright sunlight crept across Tessa's slumbering face until it was shining right in her eyes. Annoyed, she sat up, confused by the unfamiliar surroundings. Curved sofa. Laptop upside down on the floor. Gun on the coffee table. *Gun?!*

Tessa sat up like a jackknife. Jack's guest house. It was melting outside.

While she stretched, Tessa's vibrating phone jarred her out of her sleepy zone. She searched for it underneath the decorative pillows, getting to it just before it stopped ringing. It was Chris; he and Anna were on the way over and it sounded important. *Oh goody.*

Moments later, when her visitors were seated, Tessa brought in a full tray laden with fresh coffee and chocolate chip cookies that Jenny had baked the day before. A bowl of oranges added color and the heavenly scent of citrus. She set the tray on the coffee table to serve her guests.

With Chris on his phone, it was up to Tessa to get the meeting started, apparently, although she had no idea what they were supposed to be discussing. She took the opportunity to extract some more of Anna's infinite wisdom. "What's going on, Anna?"

"Currently, we're having a meeting with a grown ass woman in a onesie with messy hair." Anna's clear coffee mug was almost touching her lips when she laughed.

"Think of it as a grown ass woman in her comfort zone," Tessa retorted with a cheeky smirk. "I was talking about the cultural upheaval."

"Ah. Okay. Well, things aren't getting worse; they're getting exposed." Anna chose her words carefully as she set her coffee mug down. "It happens right before a civilization collapses."

"Wait." With her long, slender legs crossed, Tessa bravely peeled an orange with her manicured purple metallic fingernails. "This has happened before?"

"Take ancient Rome," Anna confirmed with a nod. "They were in moral decline while their founding principles, ideals, values and traditions were replaced by the idea that depravity was the norm."

"That's it, exactly!" Tessa gasped, the sunlight streaming in from the high angled windows drawing out the bewilderment in her eyes. "But how does it happen? How does a society become so depraved at the end?"

"Get them young, and they're yours for life." Teacher Anna was in the building. "Mold young minds to be immoral, and the entire culture follows. I'll call you when I get home to explain."

Without taking his eyes off his phone, Chris picked up two cookies and continued to scroll with his other thumb. "That's why Maria and I homeschool." *Multitasking at its finest.*

"I wasn't homeschooled, and I don't remember being taught stupid stuff. Useless, yeah, but not how to be a degenerate." Tessa's mind drifted back to the innocence and joy of her school years. "Gen Z will need *a lot* of deprogramming to bring them back to reality."

"It's too late to save Gen Z, child." Anna's soft voice was full of sadness and resignation.

"We can't give up on them, Anna!" Tessa was *not* having it.

"Gen Z is Gen Ocide." Anna finished the last of her cool coffee. "Convinced by wicked people in high places that they're doing the virtuous thing, they're killing themselves off through abortion, assisted suicide, attrition, sterilization, and transition."

"Don't forget the huge number of fentanyl deaths," Chris added, having been touched firsthand when his cousin overdosed. "It's a crisis that continues to be ignored, more deadly than the Tetracimia epidemic – *by far*."

"So, what do we do, then?" Tessa sighed, pouring herself another steaming cup of coffee from the gold and black carafe. "Let them die?"

"I was hoping you could tell us," Chris teased, his eyes still directed to his phone. "We've been trying." Finally turning his full attention to the conversation, he put his phone face down on the coffee table. "It's possible they're too far gone."

Anna accepted a coffee refill and an orange but passed on the cookies. "We need to fix the education system."

"Decentralization is the answer. Give the power back to the parents." Chris was now on his feet, pacing. "Then we can teach them practical things like gardening and civics."

"Nah. I'm sure I'll be using Pythagorean Theorem any day now," Tessa giggled.

"Ha. They should probably know how their government works better than they know the rules of baseball." Chris gazed out the window at the thick bluff of trees beside the guest house. "And while we're at it, teach them to get away from the university scam and get a trade – something that pays instead of sending kids into debt for eternity."

"Uh, I have a university degr..." Tessa stopped; she was talking to the back of Chris's designer jeans.

"A *law* degree, Tessa, not one of these harebrained *liberal arts* joke degrees." The playfulness in Chris's smooth voice when he turned around put Tessa at ease. "The world still needs trained professionals."

Smiling at the memory of her college days, Tessa confessed. "I still had blue hair, though. Ha ha."

"You came back from New York with a liberal arts attitude, too," Chris reminded her.

"I remember," Tessa reluctantly admitted. "Cringe. However, I did pay my own way."

"Unfortunately, the way the world has changed, many professionals have become mouthpieces for the dying empire." Anna stood up to stretch, moving her hips from side to side. "Doctors have turned away from their oath to do no harm. All I see right now are *dirty* doctors."

"Omigod, Anna! No kidding." Tessa tapped her feet to stop them from going numb. "Look what happened to the doctors during Tetracimia."

"Indeed. Good ones were marginalized, and bad ones are sell-outs." Chris grabbed three oranges to juggle. "And only the good ones are fighting back against medical transition, or as I call it – mutilation."

"And the teachers! My God! What happened to the teachers?" Anna was beside herself at what the profession had become since she'd received her certificate. "Kink and perversion are the new curriculum."

"Now they have the mamma bears enraged." Tessa thought about all the footage she'd been sent from school board meetings, the explicit material in libraries, and the erasing of gender. "And the empire is labeling suburban moms domestic terrorists."

"Tactical error on their part." Anna smiled; she loved watching an enemy hang themselves.

"Lawyers are as crooked as I've ever seen them, and that's saying something." Tessa burst out laughing at her visitors' shocked faces, both squinting in the sun.

"It's sick. It's the same reason awards and prizes these days are jokes. You're only eligible if you're in the big club and have the right politics." Tessa paused for a sip of coffee. "What happened to the Pulitzer? They give it to known liars now. And the Nobel Peace Prize to a war monger. Ha!"

"I know. Some of the world's best sports stars aren't in Halls of Fame because they're too outspoken about government malfeasance," Chris lamented. "Take baseball, for example."

"You can make anything about baseball, can't you?" Tessa's offhand sarcasm was curt, but an accurate mockery of an out-of-control, utterly lawless, morally bankrupt empire. "If I had a schilling for every time that happened, I'd buy the Arizona Diamondbacks."

When Chris winked, Tessa's stomach somersaulted. "Or maybe the Hall of Fame itself." He took a fake swing with an imaginary bat. "But enough baseball. I'm here to talk about Jack."

"What about him?" Tessa asked. "I just talked to him last night."

"So did I," Chris announced. "He poured himself a tequila and offered me one," Chris announced.

"What?!" Tessa and Anna spoke in unison. All discussion ceased for a moment.

"As long as I've known the man, he's been clean as a whistle. Doesn't smoke, drink, or do drugs," Anna confirmed. "He's a hardworking businessman."

"I know," Chris agreed. "That's why it's so alarming."

"Okay. It's not just me then." Tessa's cast her eyes downward. "I thought I saw him at Luigis's at Diablo Mountain Mall two days ago when I picked up the money he left for me at City Hall. He was at one of the slot machines." An uncomfortable silence descended on the room.

"He's obviously cracking under the pressure," Chris concluded.

"So, what do we do? We can't just let him sink in further." Tessa bit down on a cookie, using a napkin to catch the crumbs.

"How about we all handle him with kid gloves?" Chris looked back and forth between Tessa and Anna to seek approval. "Let him be his cocky self, and the real work will take place behind the scenes. That way we won't damage his ego."

Chapter 93

Tessa's phone rang as she was slipping into her jeans. She raced back downstairs where a roaring fire was waiting for her. "Tessa here."

It was Anna – right on time. "Hi my girl. Is now a good time?"

"Yes! I'm really curious how an empire collapses." Tessa sat on her usual spot on the sofa.

"Then have a seat, child. Let me tell you a story."

March 23, 2017

Anna: You've heard the word 'woke', correct?
Tessa: Yeah, but what does that have to do with the collapse of a civilization?
Anna: Well, dear child, woke is the communist revolution you wanted.
Tessa: Huh?
Anna: It begins with Marxist theory.
Tessa: Marx? That's applies to class, not this other stuff.
Anna: So, you know how he developed his views?
Tessa: During the Industrial Revolution. From watching the poor being exploited, child labor, the English workhouses.
Anna: When Marx was talking about seizing the means of production, he meant controlling how man produces himself.
Tessa: Clear as mud, Anna.

Anna: *It means that if thought is organized around private property, then society is divided by those who have access to private property and those who don't. It's a class conflict between the oppressors and the oppressed – the bourgeoisie and the working class.*

Tessa: *Right. So?*

Anna: *So, you awaken the consciousness of the underclass and remind them that they are historical agents of change.*

Tessa: *Right. The spark of a revolution.*

Anna: *But Marx was wrong. Free-market capitalism **does** work to make people better off, so Marxists had to abandon the working class as a means of revolution.*

Tessa: *I see.*

Anna: *Woke is Marxism adapted to decimate the West in the name of equity.*

Tessa: *Why is that a bad thing? I don't understand.*

Anna: *Because equity is communism, and Western culture repels it. People get too comfortable.*

Tessa: *What are you talking about, Anna? People in America are poor and suffering all over the place!*

Anna: *That's not the system of free-market capitalism, child. Why shouldn't people be able to trade goods and services among themselves?*

Tessa: *I think it's because of predatory capitalism.*

Anna: *If you grant the rights of an individual to a corporation, you end up with feudalism. That's what we need an end to – not the free market economy. What we want for a healthy society is equality of opportunity, not outcome.*

[Inaudible]

Tessa: *But –*

Anna: *After the Red Revolution failed in Hungary in 1919, the Marxists knew they'd have to infiltrate Western institutions to change the culture. That was the rise of Cultural Marxism.*

Tessa: *I thought that term was only used by extremists and nutjobs.*

Anna: *Of course, you did. We're not allowed to talk about it. It's been categorized as an antisemitic conspiracy theory – which means it's true. Their assertion is easily disprovable. People wrote books about Cultural Marxism and they're easy to find online.*

Tessa: *Is that why they attack us at our weakest points? They target everything about our culture that makes us good – openness, acceptance, tolerance, justice, generosity, etcetera?*

Anna: The guys that wrote those books knew that in a capitalist society, the working class can no longer be the base of the revolution. They turned instead to identity.

Tessa: I'm not following.

Anna: Marxism is a tree with many branches. Classic Economic Marxism. Radical Feminism. Critical Race Theory. Queer Theory. Post-colonial Theory.

Tessa: Uh huh.

Anna: Remember on your show when you talked about Black Fist Warriors being trained Marxists?

Tessa: I do.

Anna: Well, that's what this is. On each branch of the tree, there are twigs. Every twig is an identity, such as LGBT, race, etcetera, and they all think of themselves as a nation. They even have flags that they plant on Western buildings.

Tessa: That's why all the American flags have been replaced!

Anna: See, whiteness, and by default white privilege, is a form of private property. Their theory is that anyone who isn't white is oppressed because they don't have access to the means of production.

Tessa: But that's crazy! They **do** have social capital. A lot of it!

Anna: To them, a white supremacist is someone who believes that white people should control society. That's why they call black people wh –"

Tessa: But I don't believe that!

Anna: I know that, my girl. But you're white, and **they** use that as cultural capital.

Tessa: Oi.

Anna: Their reference to slavery isn't about slavery at all. That's just an excuse. It's about creating a class consciousness that's against this form of property called whiteness. Anyone who isn't white can come together to channel their resentment.

Tessa: So, calling everything you want to control 'racist' until you control it?

Anna: Yep. If it exists, it's racist. Now take queer theory.

Tessa: Do I have to? I'm probably going to be embarrassed, considering my recent history.

[Laughter]

Anna: Likely. Think about it. What does woke attack?

Tessa: Umm.

Anna: It attacks the idea of being traditional. Normal, so to speak. The status quo.

Tessa: You're right, but people who get to set the norms of society **are** privileged. What is a woman, anyway?

Anna: How would I know? I'm not a biologist.

[Laughter]

Tessa: Ha! Seriously, who gets to be considered normal, and who is a pervert or freak? Who decides? What is queer?

Anna: Queer theory is an identity without an essence. It's strictly opposition to the concept of the accepted mores of society. I describe it as anything goes theory as if sexual liberation will somehow heal society. It spells the end of absolute truth and the beginning of moral relativism. There's no place for God in Marxism.

Tessa: I've never thought about it like that.

Anna: Then it's time you open your mind. Now, as a Native American woman, this one is my favorite. Post-colonial theory. Ha!

Tessa: I can only imagine.

Anna: The West is the oppressor, and the Natives around the world must band together to erase every remnant of influence. Their activities are called decolonization.

Tessa: Ah. By George, I think I'm getting it.

Anna: In the UK, they are trying to decolonize Shakespeare! **Shakespeare!** They say that the artifacts of Western culture are oppressive.

[Inaudible]

Tessa: That's why they're getting rid of the statues!

Anna: Now, here's the kicker. Because they don't have to be responsible to the working class anymore, Marxists seeking power make friends with the corporations – no longer an enemy, they're an **opportunity**. 'Stakeholder capitalism' is the perfect vehicle for normalizing perversions.

Tessa: And that's why the corporations all started going woke! It's all starting to click!

Anna: The energy for a revolution in the West is in the racial and sexual minorities, feminism, the outsiders. They are against what they view as the oppressive patriarchal white system – on which all of society is based.

Tessa: That was me not too long ago.

Anna: I know. [Laughter] Marxists sell culture by seizing the means of production of the culture industry, then they transform it to sell racial, sexual, and gender identity as if it's **thee** appropriate culture. That's how we end up with concepts like cultural appropriation, cultural relevance, cultural everything.

Tessa: That's it, exactly! They say diversity is our strength, except white people aren't supposed to take part in the diversity. And what the hell is cultural appropriation, anyway? Every culture 'steals' from other cultures.

Anna: It begins in schools. First, they stripped out all references to communism. Kids don't learn about communism at all. Nothing about Mao.

Tessa: Wait. Now Mao? What does it have to do with Mao?

Anna: Identity politics was how Mao radicalized the youth in China. He created ten identities – five for communist and five for fascist. Five good, Five bad. Five red, Five black.

Tessa: So...let me guess. Those of us who stand up to the system are automatically labeled as bad and bad influences, and the empire can punish us if they decide they don't like what we're saying?

Anna: Yes. Worse, if **you** have a bad category, your **children** have a bad category, by default.

Tessa: So, that creates social pressure for the kids to transform. Wow. That's how they turned an entire generation into woke revolutionaries! Omigod. Those poor kids.

Anna: Right. And if they come out as transgender [inaudible], **that's** the point where they get a good identity – establishment approved. A life filled with confusion and pain.

Tessa: So, identity politics through the children in the schools is how it starts?

Anna: It starts at birth with pop culture – books, movies, TV. How else are they going to get away with telling kids that by being white you automatically hurt people of other races by your very existence? If you become queer, we'll celebrate you.

Tessa: That's how they do it!? They can create a radical army of people who hate themselves and their culture. That's why kids are identifying as gender and sexual minorities at seven years old! They want to be accepted by the gang that's turning them away from their family.

Anna: And lead them down the path of puberty blockers and so-called gender affirming care – all big pharma hears is cha-ching! We're now facing a suicide epidemic of young people who regret that they transitioned.

Tessa: Behind their parents' back no less. Every queer identity is a special occasion now! Who would want to miss out on trans-racial, poly-gender, asexual, non-binary multi-species day?

Anna: You forgot people who identify as cats. [Laughter] Now, we wouldn't buy into that nonsense in the West, so it's called inclusion.

Tessa: I think we've now talked about all of them: Diversity, equity and inclusion.

Anna: Exactly. They want to make everyone a global citizen under the DEI umbrella.

Tessa: What? That's nuts. There's no global sovereign. No ruler of the globe. We don't want one.

Anna: What they mean by a global citizen is someone who supports the United Nations radical agenda.

Tessa: What are the rights of a so-called global citizen?

Anna: They're not interested in rights. Only responsibility. Also known as slavery.

Tessa: [inaudible]

Anna: And remember, they use middle-level violence. They don't come at you with full-blown Bolshevik assault, very often. They provoke. They want you to react, so they can use militarized police and/or their street thugs like the Black Fist Warriors.

Tessa: We discovered that from our encounter in Old Town Square. Give your culture away, and they'll let you live?

Anna: Yes. By appealing to the best in us, like you stated earlier.

Tessa: So, what do I do, Anna?

Anna: Outsmart them, my girl. Stand firm in your principles. If you understand you're being provoked, that they want you to react, then you have beaten the provocateur.

Tessa: I guess. It's hard to cure what you don't understand.

Anna: If you don't understand that Woke is Marxism evolved to attack the West, you will not act correctly. You will not cure it, and it will conquer you.

Tessa: I never truly understood before how close we are to losing our culture. And the state has turned people against traditional Americans!

Anna: This is such a pivotal moment in history. Want to know what your future looks like if we don't stop the woke? Look at China. The social credit system. Disappeared for having the wrong opinion. Even a billionaire. Sounds crazy, doesn't it?

Tessa: Cuckoo for cocoa puffs.

Anna: Wokeness is both their sword and their shield. Ultimately, it is all they have, and they're not about to surrender it.

Tessa: How do you know all this, anyway?

Anna: I discovered a guy called Dr. James Lindsay. [cough]

Tessa: I think I'm getting it – the culture war divides us and distracts the public from noticing the shrinking middle class. The rich get richer. I should have figured that out during Occupy Wall Street.

Anna: Yes. They're tearing down the West and getting richer in the process. They use our open, loving, accepting nature against us until extremists are the only voices *left. It went from bake the cake, bigot; to use the pronouns, murderer; to legal kiddy porn in short order, didn't it? Drip. Drip. Drip.*

Chapter 94

When Tessa ended her call with Anna, she stayed motionless for a few minutes as she gazed out the window of Jack's guest house. Before she had a chance to process what she'd just heard, her phone was going crazy again. A notification from TownSquare – a townie had been removed for violating community standards: *Hate speech or some stupid thing. Did she tell a so-called journalist to learn to code, or something? Stupid boneheads. Account suspended because reasons.*

Tessa knew where this was going. MainStreet? Gone. U-Talk? Check. All her social media accounts had now been deleted. Quick and coordinated. Every way she had to reach her followers had been terminated. Just like that. Sounded like a government operation to her.

Still on the ivory sofa, Tessa put her head down on one of the cushions to cry. After several minutes, she got up and retrieved her laptop to call Adam via video chat.

"Hey, sweetheart."

"Adam. Hey."

"You've been crying."

"They're not done with me yet." Tessa dabbed at her eyes with a damp tissue. Now all my social media accounts have been shut down. I lost my channels," she sobbed. "My online donations were canceled. I can't bring in any revenue for AltMedia anymore."

"Wow. On top of what you told me earlier about the threats to your staff, that's a bit much."

"Adam, I'm public enemy number one." Tessa dabbed at her tears. "You know what would cheer me up?"

"Yup."

Ralph's sweet golden face came into the frame. "Woof!" Since she'd met Adam, Tessa and Ralph had become BFFs.

"Woof to you too, buddy!" Tessa blew Ralph a kiss.

Adam lapped it up while he watched. It appeared the package deal was in order.

"Let's see." Tessa prepared to rant. "We have a tyranny problem disguised as a safety issue. The city is literally crumbling, there are homeless people all over the place, the so-called lawmakers are lawless, violent criminals are free to burn, loot, and murder with impunity, there's a drug epidemic fueled by porous borders, they're indoctrinating kids with garbage. Political opponents and Christians are persecuted, free speech is a thing of the past, and our politicians never met a war they didn't like. Grown men are abusing young boys in plain sight, and they're trying to add sex with children to the alphabet string. And they have the nerve to tell us white supremacy is the country's most pressing problem?!"

"I'm a journalist watching my profession become a dumpster fire and radicalizing people in the process." Adam stared out the window at the mountain range in the background hoping he sounded convincing. "But I stay because I think maybe I can change it."

"Adam, are you kidding me right now? You work for New World Now! They're not going to change."

"I have *a job* with NWN," Adam reminded her – as if it made a difference. "Tessa, I...." He drifted off.

"You...what?"

"I don't really know how to say this. I know that's ridiculous for a journalist, I should always have the right words, but it is what it is."

"Oh, my God. This is bad." *Adam was crying.*

"I've been threatened."

"**What?**" Tessa shrieked, panicked. "Don't tell me, you're not supposed to associate with me, or they'll *ruin you* too?" Her voice was still high-pitched, and her heart was racing. Trying to calm the shaking, she rested her feet on the coffee table and rubbed her sweating palms on her the legs of her jeans.

"Bingo." Adam closed his eyes but didn't move, his legs still stretched out.

"Woof!" Ralph was at Adam's feet.

"Oh, hey buddy. It's all right. We'll be okay, pal." Adam rubbed Ralph's ears, this time *even less* convinced of his own words.

Wanting to know where their relationship stood, the back of Tessa's heels slammed into the coffee table. "So...where does that leave... us?" Her voice shook.

"Well, I'd rather cut off my left one than stop seeing you." Adam grinned. "I'm not giving you up. We'll keep seeing each other on the sly."

Sighing with relief when she heard the response, Tessa clutched her imaginary pearls. "A secret affair?"

"Why not?" Adam raised his eyebrows. "Want a visitor?"

"Yes!" Tessa loved the idea. "Are you safe to get here, though?"

"I have my ways, sweetheart." Adam prepared to sign off the call. "See you soon."

Ralph's adorable panting head came into focus, head cocked to one side, floppy ears bouncing. "Woof!" His bushy tail was twitching.

Tessa looked into the big puppy dog eyes and giggled. She felt better already. What would they do without Ralph?

Tessa found her new royal-blue midi-dress, off the shoulder and cut just right to hug her curves. She spritzed on a light sweet perfume, French-braided her hair and... her phone vibrated. Bzzzzzzt... Bzzzzzzt... It was Chris. "Talk to me, friend," she sighed.

"You know Cole Adams, right?" *Right to the point.*

"Well, I've *met* him. I wouldn't say I know him. Why?" Tessa asked. "A hottie from California, but kinda creepy. I met him at the centennial celebration."

"Well...he isn't who he said he was," Chris announced. "He has some connections to some very powerful people in the DC area."

"Beating around the bush is rather uncharacteristic of you, Chris. What are you talking about?"

"He's CIA. His real name is Gregory Gould. The guy has never been married. The ex-wife he told you about is pure fiction.

"I knew something was weird about him, but I couldn't figure out what." Tessa snapped her fingers.

"Tessa, you don't understand." Chris decided the best way to tell her was point blank. "He was spying on *you*."

Tessa gasped. "Why would he need to spy on me?"

"They got sloppy. They knew that if you recovered your memories, you could blow the whole thing wide open," Chris disclosed. "Max has been watching you for years, Tessa."

"Oh my God." Feeling faint, Tessa sat down on the bed. "Even in Manhattan?"

"Are you sitting down?"

"I am now."

"Okay. You getting recruited to work in that club wasn't random. You were selected."

Scenes from Tessa's time in New York as a teenager played in the theater of her mind.

"Remember Vince from Tito's club?"

"How could I forget?" Tessa exclaimed, recalling the relief when she got into the taxi after she'd won the money. "He saved my life!"

"In the early 2000s, Jack and I worked together on bringing down a child trafficking ring in New York City."

"I'm not following."

"We... were... working on bringing... down... a trafficking... ring," Chris stressed, annoyed.

"Yeah, so? I'm *still* not following."

"Tessa," Chris sighed. Did he need to draw her a picture? "It was Jack who saved your life... he was in disguise as Vince."

Tessa was dead silent as the scene at Tito's club played in her mind's eye – her divinely blessed escape from New York.

"Tessa, your artwork getting wrecked wasn't an accident. It was all planned. The gallery owner was working with them. Aamon Della Rossi was an alias. He's Iranian not Italian. Someday, I'll tell you what he was doing on his trips to Rome."

"My art was... what?" Thankful she was already sitting on the bed, Tessa laid her head back on her pillow.

"The guy you recognized at the Beehive Tavern?"

"Yeah. The bartender." Tessa scanned her memory. "I saw him the first night I arrived in Underville... then never again."

"He was one of ours. He followed you from New York." Chris paused to take a breath. "He was undercover as a dealer at Tito's."

More silence.

"Are you okay?"

"Yeah. I'm okay...just confused." Raising her trembling hand to her throbbing temple, Tessa closed her eyes. "Why did Max invite me to the centennial celebration?"

"You were easier to control here. They knew that one days your memories would surface."

"Those slimy bastards! I feel like I've been kicked in the stomach." Tessa paused. "Wait...*what memories?*"

"The time's not right yet. Just know that it's a *massive* cover-up."

"That's why they've been trying so hard to kill independent media." Tessa's rubbed her tired neck. "And probably all of *us* in the process."

"Exactly. And you're *still* not afraid to go against the grain and tell the truth."

"Ha. I barely have anything left to lose. I feel like I haven't done enough."

"Give yourself some credit. What you've done is revolutionary."

Chapter 95

The dying wind pushed heavy clouds across the pitch-black sky and Tessa was wide awake at the midnight hour. Adam had just left after a wonderful evening cooking dinner together and sharing a bottle of wine around the ambient fire.

Freshly showered and with her hair still wet, Tessa changed into her new pink and gray elephant-print cotton pajamas and got ready for bed. Sitting on the bed, she sat cross-legged to prop up her laptop. Even though she'd been erased from the internet; she could still browse.

An e-mail from Tessa's best friend in Manhattan was waiting! It had been a few weeks since she and Megan had chatted and so much had happened. She always looked forward to hearing about Megan's family life.

> **Subject heading:** I saw you on the news
> Dear Teresa:
> The real news. Not that conspiracy crap you talk about, what happened to you? What changed?
> So your hanging out with far-right haters' now? What happened to Hippies of the New Millennium? Diversity equity and inclusion?
> Either your racist, like they say, or maybe your just crazy...like your mother. Maybe it was all an act. Too bad you didnt make broadway.
> See a therapist, and dont contact me until you get some help.
> Megan

Tessa was stunned. Gutted. Betrayed. Absolutely blindsided. Concern trolling was her pet-peeve. *And the grammar was...yikes.* Megan was the last person Tessa thought would turn on her. Her *only* close friend in Manhattan and the best friend she'd ever had – someone who Tessa had poured her heart and soul out to many times, and vice versa. *Teresa? What the...*

What happened to me?! What changed? The world has lost its ever-loving minds! Not me, dammit! You went from opposing censorship to demanding it. You went from opposing war to overtly embracing it.

Tessa screamed into the darkness of the still-midnight hour while the laptop crashed to the floor. Never needing her mother more than right now, she dropped her head down on the pillow while wiping a tear away from her closing eye. The soft light of the lamp cast a shadow around her dark auburn hair, fanned out all around her head – like a halo.

With Tessa's sweet perfume all over his clothes, an aroused Adam drove away wishing she'd invited him to stay. Still tasting her full, luscious lips on his, he pictured her in all her God-given glory. Arriving home to a happy puppy after a dynamite date with his beautiful girlfriend was a recipe for contentment.

Turning on the backyard light, Adam whistled from the top step and readied himself as he waited for an excited Ralph to tackle him. His anticipation was met with an ominous silence.

As he went inside, a cold chill went up Adam's spine – there was some dark energy in the house. "Ralph! Ralphie?" he whistled. No reply. *So odd. Where was he?* Haunting nothingness screamed into the silence.

"Ralph. Ralphie." Adam's heart raced as he hustled down the basement stairs. "Daddy's home." "Ralph? Where's my Ralph? Who's a good boy?" he whistled. His gut was aching.

Did Ralph *escape*? Please tell me he didn't escape. Adam checked his phone to see if he had a message from the pound or the maid. *Nope. Thank God.*

With his mind in circles, Adam ran through the main floor to the backyard. Maybe Jenny had accidentally let him out when she was cleaning. Maybe he's sleeping in the doghouse and didn't hear the whistle.

Squinting, Adam shone his flashlight into the dark space on the cloudy night. As a feral cry escaped his lips he fell to his knees in defeat.

Chapter 96

Screaming, Tessa bolted up in bed in a cold sweat. Her head throbbed and her pulse raced. Somehow, she found comfort in the aroma of brewing coffee. *Thank God for timers.*

Bare feet on the cold kitchen floor prompted Tessa to build a fire. With her steaming fresh cup of java in hand, she took her favorite place in front of the glowing blaze. *Now* she could analyze her nightmare:

> *A red maple tree in Central Park. The Vatican shapeshifting in the background. A younger Tessa with a dark-haired mother of two, giggling together under the mid-summer ball of fire spiraling, opening a black hole in the center of the sun. Megan's face transforming into that of a serpent with glowing hell-fire eyes and a forked tongue dripping with venom...*

RAP RAP RAP!! Someone was pounding on the door.

Tessa jumped. *A visitor at 7 am? What the what? Dan, the security guy, maybe?* She hesitated in the foyer. "Who is it?"

"Tessa!" It was Adam's panicked voice on the other side of that door. "It's me. Open up!"

Tessa yanked the door open and moved aside as Adam bounded in, shoving his phone in her face. "Look!" Still in the same clothes he'd worn the night before, it looked like he hadn't slept at all.

The French doors to the living room were open, lemon scent emanating from the candle on the coffee table and blending with the coffee. The room was filled with the radiance of the corner fireplace in the dim light. The sun hadn't yet risen.

Tessa's entire body went slack. She was looking at Ralph's shattered skull, torn open – execution style. Adam caught her, the rage welling up inside him as he lovingly scooped her up and carried her upstairs to bed. She was still in her pajamas, so he gently tucked the covers up around her shoulders.

Tessa opened her mouth to speak – no sound came out. She knew what this meant...they were breaking up, again. They had no choice, the empire meant business.

Stroking Tessa's hair, Adam sat on the edge of the bed. "It's too painful for me to drag this out. Go see Anna." His voice was thick with emotion. He kissed her forehead and swallowed the lump in his throat. When he left, he locked the front door as hot, angry tears spilled down his face.

A whole day passed before Tessa even *thought* about getting out of bed – now she *had* lost everything. *She should have listened to her gut and not fallen for the guy.* The mobile and laptop were both turned off – it would just be more bad news. It was too much. She couldn't handle it. She couldn't cope with *anything*. Nothing made sense anymore.

On the morning of the second day, Tessa finally threw the covers off before she really *did* go crazy, trying to remind herself that she only *felt* crazy because she wasn't well adjusted to a profoundly sick society. Knowing she'd have to take her chances with the mob, she donned her disguise and her armband – she would never get past the checkpoints without it.

Thick smoke spewed from the chimney on Anna's house when Tessa pulled up.

The sun sparkling on the thick hoarfrost painted the backdrop for the icy bank hanging over the thatched roof. A pair of old snowshoes rested on the small landing beside an excited, tail-wagging Spike.

In Tessa's sorrow, the scene filled her with momentary gratitude. She still had so much to be thankful for – she hadn't lost everything. Tearing up when she knelt to pet Spike, a surge of divine magnetic energy passed through her. Maybe that was the lesson: If we treated other people the way we treat our pets, most of the world's problems would disappear overnight.

With her glove-covered fingers wet and stinging at −2 freaking degrees, Tessa could see her breath. *Come on Anna, open the door!* It was the beginning of April – it was like winter put on a pantsuit, ran for President, then wouldn't go away.

Sadness filled Anna's eyes at the sight of Tessa's tear-stained face. Without saying a word, she gestured for the troubled young woman to go to the alcove to wait for her. "Be right back." She disappeared down the hallway.

With images of Adam flashing through her mind, Tessa closed her eyes. Her drifting was interrupted only when Anna gently placed a steaming cup of cocoa in her hands, the mug warming her while she mindlessly gazed upon the thawing lake.

"Tell me what's going on, my girl." Anna covered Tessa with a warm plaid blanket and sat down in her cat-clawed chair, the healing sound of Puffball's purring momentarily giving them comfort in the near silence. Trying to discreetly move the top copy of the Dormin Times from Tessa's view, she encouraged Tessa to open up. "Do you –"

"Anna, what *is* that?"

"Nothing," Anna fibbed. "I need it to...swat a fly."

"A fly when it's this cold?" Tessa was exasperated. "Stop treating me like a little child, Anna! Why is everybody keeping things from me?! Whatever it is, I can handle it."

Reluctantly, Anna pointed to the headline tucked away in the bottom right corner of the front page: **REMAINS OF MISSING NORTH CAROLINA WOMAN DISCOVERED IN CALIFORNIA.**

Tessa took the paper and began reading. "Jennifer?"

Anna avoided Tessa's gaze.

"Noooo!" The newspaper fell to the floor. "I can't deal with any of this anymore," Tessa sobbed. Now, her childhood friend, too. *Who was next? Why was everyone close to her getting attacked?* "Anna?" *Omigod...* she felt sick.

"In a two-tiered justice system, murdered and missing Indigenous women don't take priority. Anyone with money or power gets preferential treatment, and the marginalized are dismissed as second-class citizens. White college girls..." Anna trailed off as she wiped a tear. "That she was a medical student and performing artist doesn't matter, I guess."

"What about people who cared about her? Do *any* of our lives matter?"

"Long ago, when the white man came, they said our ways were savage." With her eyes full of sorrow, Anna glanced up at her visitor. "They tried to beat the Indian out of us."

"What? Who the hell did they think they were?"

"They came with the bibles and started the boarding schools."

"What happened?"

Anna stayed silent for a moment while she thought about what she was going to say. "We had boarding schools where horrible things happened. Assimilation meant tearing our families apart and destroying our culture. My grandfather never wanted to set foot in a church again."

Why were humans so inhumane? Gripped by compassion for the plight of Anna's ancestors, the spirit of reconciliation moved Tessa to tears. "So, why are you a Christian, Anna?" she asked through the tears.

"The Cherokee way is a belief in both a higher power and the Great Spirit. The Earth Mother provides and must be respected. Family and community are our focus." Anna embraced the chance to talk about her proud culture. "The Creator made us all one – the physical and spiritual worlds are not separate."

"That still doesn't explain why you follow Jesus."

"It's simple: Jesus is the embodiment of peace and love." Anna's face began to glow. "In the '60s, we called them Jesus freaks... then I learned about Judeo Christian values... and it was who I wanted to be.

Chapter 97

By evening, Tessa was feeling well enough to return to Jack's guest house, but she couldn't get Jennifer out of her mind – an awful lot like her favorite auntie, Anna. Beautiful face, beautiful spirit. Sharp as a whip. Fun. Such a tragedy. May justice be served.

Meanwhile, there was *so much* contradictory information coming from the slimy corporate media about literally everything that nothing seemed *real*. *What was going on?* Tessa had to get onto other platforms that weren't affiliated with – or directly run – by the government.

Tessa could hardly believe that was happening – the government used the internet to control people. Information. Artificial Intelligence. Psychological warfare – its entire reason for existing. Anyone with a digital footprint had a digital doppelganger, and it was being used for nefarious purposes. *Like a sci-fi come to life.* That's why independent media had to crank up the building of culture even more. That's what a movement looks like: Don't just boycott. Build.

Before long, Tessa's research led her into a whole new rabbit hole. How deep did these wormholes *go*?

In 1984 *(ironically)*, a KGB defector penned a book called <u>Love Letter to America.</u> One quote immediately jumped out:

> We rarely use guns to kill people and take their country. The cleanest way is to blackmail, pervert, bribe, lie and intimidate the **POLITICIANS** and the **MEDIA**, and they will destabilize and disunify their own country for us. Then all we have left to do is to

arm the pro-communist or simply criminal factions and we have a coup.

Yuri Bezmenov

Bezmenov described using subversion to capture the ideological soul of a nation in four steps: Demoralization, destabilization, crisis, and stabilization. Public perception is fundamentally altered so that people are unable to defend themselves, their families, their communities, and their country. *In plain language, they do it through propaganda.*

That was it! To a T! That's exactly what Anna had been talking about with Cultural Marxism! They studied the culture for a generation, then put their long-term plans in place through stakeholder capitalism – corporations delivering their Marxist message.

So... the bad guys took over by convincing the public that they were the good guys, then told the actual good guys that it was a crime to question their authority? That's why everything was backwards! *Make it make sense.*

Tessa dug deep. She *had* to keep going. Somehow. Some way. *Real* people needed the truth! They had to hear this – **their own government was their enemy!**

Having to clear her head, Tessa donned her disguise and headed to Old Town Square – maybe a connection to her youth would elicit some answers. It was already dark as she drove through the scattered trees, her bright headlights and the full moon lighting the wide street. Parking near the curb beside the forest, she yanked at the door handle and stepped into the chilly air. The loud hoot of a horned owl startled her.

Where was that tree? Somewhere in here, at the edge of the forest...there it was! The elm tree with something etched in its trunk, surrounded by a heart: TNT Forever: Tyler and Tessa in love forever. Her first love, the tree where they'd first kissed. A triangular light shone down upon her from the nearby streetlamp as if to illuminate a harsh life lesson.

Covering the carved heart on the rugged tree bark with her outstretched palm, Tessa's memories came flooding back. Her bottom lip quivered while she tried to stay strong. Do you ever *stop* loving them, even after they tie a rope around the branches of *your* tree and dangle from a noose? When Tyler's pain exceeded his ability to cope, he ended it the only way he knew how. She'd selfishly wanted him alive to alleviate *her* suffering. Now that she'd experienced *his* suffering – she understood.

A noise broke Tessa's contemplation! Was that someone rustling in the bush!? She'd been so zoned in, she'd ignored her surroundings. The hair on the back of her neck stood up as she scanned the forest in the moonlight, bracing herself for the worst.

An acorn fell from the tree. Tessa looked up and giggled. Framed by the full moon, an adorable bushy-tailed squirrel was on a thick branch, tossing another acorn. If she didn't know better, she'd say the little bugger was aiming at her! *Better luck next time, cutie*!

A twig snapped. A cold chill moved through Tessa's whole body. She squinted to peer into the thick brush... a sudden movement! A pair of red, glowing eyes appeared in the dark...then, just as quickly, they were gone.

Tessa exhaled with relief, certain that she was letting her imagination get the better of her. Then the red eyes were back – a wolf was watching her from behind a fir tree. Remembering that if you run from them, you become their prey, she decided to face him, stare him down. She had to be fearless.

A man walked out of the forest, his hair turning from bushy to slicked back right in front of Tessa's eyes. When he smiled, two of his teeth were filed to points and dripping blood.

Tessa gasped.

"Did I ssstartle you?" The stranger was soft-spoken and had a Welsh accent.

Although flustered, Tessa quickly regained her composure. "No. Of course not."

"We've been watching you."

"Who *are* you?"

"We are legion, Tesssssa." The man flicked his tongue. "We know all about your inner demons. Your toxic relationship with your mom was *your* fault."

Horrified, Tessa stepped back, screaming when his piercing blue eyes cut right through to the depths of her soul.

"God is a lie. There *is* no Holy Spirit."

"How do you know all this?!" Tessa shouted.

"Your past will always haunt you, no matter how much you meditate." The look of evil on the man's face was enough to cause nightmares. "Do you think you're Jesus, wandering in the desert?"

"No, I –"

"You're not crazy. You are *evil* – possessed by a demon."

Tessa covered her ears with her hands.

"You will always be under our control." The man's laughter rang out as he vanished in front of her eyes.

Chapter 98

At Atluko Industries, Cole Adams/Greg Gould left the control room and sprinted up the back concrete stairwell two steps at a time. Though he wasn't included in the Circle of Thirteen (League of LIES), he was one of Max's two remaining insiders, a title that granted him free reign of the place.

Emerging a short distance from Max's office, Cole slowed down when he heard the raucous laughter and loud club music inside. With his burgundy suit jacket slung over his shoulder, he smoothed his already perfect blonde hair and loosened his black tie. He nodded at the two stony-eyed guards stationed in the arched hall. "Gentlemen."

Pulsating lights kept time with the music as Cole moved through the overcrowded room to the stage. His nostrils caught the combination of sweat, sex, and perfume. The dancer looked familiar. *Trixie? We meet again.* Gyrating around the pole, the young seductress licked her lips while her mother watched from the shadows – mommy dearest and her ten-year-old daughter.

Pouring a shot of top shelf whiskey, Cole scanned the guests. Except for the late Miles Malone, the Dormin Group was all there. With the absence of one of the thirteen, and the diminished strength of another, the power of the circle was damaged, but they carried on with their magical thinking.

Max was present, but only in body. He had passed out in an armchair somewhere in the suite, coming to life periodically to mumble some incoherent gibberish. The chief of police was falling-down drunk with a loose woman on his arm. The President of the local university looked like he had one mission – money. Now having an abundance of spare time, an excommunicated high-ranking member of the royal family was also in attendance in the company of pre-teen girl.

Emerging from the crowd near Max's workstation, Cole was alarmed. The monitor beside the desk was off! Racing back down the stairs to the control room one floor below, he tried his key card to gain access. *Damn!* The power to the room had been cut. He pulled his old-fashioned metal master key out of his pocket and pushed the door open with his shoulder.

With a pout on her full, red lips, a dolled-up girl turned her seductive gaze toward Cole. *So, **that's** why Lou ignored the monitors.*

Cole kept his eyes trained on her, lapping up the underdeveloped body of the twelve-year-old with the low cut, scarlet red mini dress and stiletto heels. "Lou, go down to check on the power supply for the monitoring system. I've got some business to take care of." He kicked the door closed with the back of his foot, reaching behind him to lock it. "Are you one of Johnny's girls?"

She began unbuttoning her dress. "In the flesh. Lady M. sent me."

The lock just above his head would grant Will Garcia access to a room labeled **Unauthorized Personnel Strictly Prohibited**. He was five floors below ground, crouched down, and fishing in his dark green maintenance uniform pocket for the stolen key card. The only illumination in the wide, institutional hallway was a dimmed fluorescent light. Footsteps were coming around the corner!

Will scrambled across the hall, holding his breath as he crouched beneath an abandoned metal desk. The beam of a flashlight shone into the opening, stopping just short of his rear. The footsteps continued echoing until the double steel doors clanged shut.

Once inside the room with the servers, Will popped a mini flashlight into his dry mouth as the thick metal door closed automatically behind him with a loud thud. What seemed like an hour had taken him a little less than four long, unnerving minutes, but now he had the data on the thumb drive. Every noise sent chills up his spine.

Will had to get to the room across the hall, and quickly. He was standing and unlocking the door to the Boiler Room B5 when a rushed guard stepped around the corner.

By all accounts, the white-haired Lou had passed his best-before date, often nodding off during his monitoring shift. Alarmed, he took a step back. "You startled me, Willy. I wasn't expecting to see anyone in this part of the plant."

"Just finishing my shift, Lou. Got booked to work late tonight," Will lied. "I've got one thing left to do in here, and I'll be on my way."

"Can you check on the power to the monitoring system?"

"Sure thing." Will clanged a wrench against a pipe, flipped a switch, and retrieved his travel mug. "Looks like I accidentally bumped it when I was adjusting one of the pipes earlier. Should be back on now."

Lou attempted to make small talk while he escorted Will to the employee exit. "There's a big party going on with the big wigs tonight."

"Really?" Will pretended to be surprised. They had reached the exit, where he passed through security with ease. With a smile, he tipped his white Atluko ball cap on the way out.

Alone in his car, away from the prying eyes of the gestapo, Will unscrewed the center of his travel mug. *There it was!* Safe and sound, and free from detection by the machine through the metal. He wasted no time dialing from his burner phone.

"Adam here."

"I got it. It will be delivered by a... cough...cough ...saleslady. Look inside the cup and unscrew the middle." True to Will's word, the 'saleslady' arrived within twenty minutes.

"Hey, Adam." Molly Jacobs, in disguise, stepped inside.

Adam wasted no time on niceties. "Why did you kick Tessa out of the café?"

"Because if she'd stayed, it would have blown our cover. My kitchen staff, mostly minorities, were convinced she'd founded the KKK." Adam's visitor, as a method actor, had gin on her breath. Her role as a recently widowed floozy was all an act. Once the team got access to the tunnel under PJ Bar and Grill, she and Will Garcia began studying the tunnels. The tunnels were their golden ticket.

"Fair enough."

"Did you find out who murdered Ralph?"

Adam led Molly to the kitchen table. "He left this note on Ralph's doghouse."

Setting her briefcase down, Molly squinted to inspect the handwritten note: *'You were warned. She's next.'*

"Whoa." Molly stuffed the note into the briefcase and took out the thumb drive. "Here's what you've been waiting for." She handed the file to Adam and made her way back to the door.

Once Molly left, Adam wasted no time getting the drive into his computer – he'd been waiting for this! When he started scanning, his jaw dropped. It made sense now... the depths they went to to deceive. To be enlightened, to belong to this secret society required 100% compliance, and a sacred oath of secrecy. Or a fate worse than death. It was all in their covenant, like Will had said.

The Fisher clan was the Fisher Klan. The Klan. The literal Klan! *Literal* white supremacists had developed the city from the ground up away from the prying eyes of the slave police after the Civil War.

Then, it got worse. *Oh my God! Way worse.* They'd been hiding in plain sight. It had worked like a charm.

Chapter 99

In the dim light of Max's office, the music was off. The guests were gone. The party was over.

Under the glow of the silver moonlight, a group of twelve intoxicated men meandered their way to a clearing in the forest. There, a giant stone owl, hidden from public view, had a fire burning in its belly.

Covered in blood-red robes, their faces masked, the men began to chant in a circle, their voices united to summon Lucifer from the depths of Hell.

They worshipped one leader, draped in a black robe, and it pleased Ba`al.

Promiscuity abounded, and it pleased Ishtar.

A bloodcurdling scream echoed throughout the forest and it pleased Moloch.

The ancient gods had returned.

Watching from the cover of the thick forest, Dmitri Petrov moved away from the others. It was time.

Chapter 100

Saturday morning was overcast, the low-hanging gray clouds reminding mere humans of Mother Nature's awesome power.

With the brisk wind whipping at her navy hoodie and jeans, Emma Langford raced up the cracked and chipped concrete steps to the boarded up double glass doors at city hall.

Jack was waiting on the other side. "Emma! Great to see you." He sounded more enthusiastic than he felt.

Greeted by the harsh scent of bleach, the smile disappeared from Emma's face. "Thanks for meeting me so early."

Still trying to recover from the Black Fist Warriors' night of love, a maintenance worker in a dark green uniform was mopping the floor in the otherwise silent building. Not *one* of the perpetrators from that night had been arrested.

In his office on the 4th floor, Jack gestured toward one of the duct-taped, padded green chairs now pulled around the meeting table. *The bastards had taken everything when they looted city hall.* "Sorry about the chairs. We found those in a storeroom. We're still trying to free up some money for recovery. But at least we're starting to find the records they tried to hide."

Emma draped her jacket across the back of the chair. "This is going to blow your mind." She pulled a thin file out of her turquoise-paisley satchel case and sat down.

"Try me." Jack urged her to continue. "Nothing could surprise me at this point."

Emma pushed her signature white cat-eyeglasses up the bridge of her nose with her index finger. "It's a sophisticated military psychological operation – as

General Fowler told us months ago. Hitler could only dream of having this type of mind control – he would've conquered the world."

"Scary."

"Well, now the empire *does* have that kind of control. Dormin was the perfect population to experiment on, to apply MK Ultra on a broader scale."

"No way."

"Jack." Emma stood up. "Listen closely." With a spring in her step, she closed the gap between her and the whiteboard.

"Oh no." Jack winced. "Am I getting a lecture?"

Turning her back to Jack, Emma wrote: 1. Poison the municipal water supply, the food, and the air to ensure compliance. 2. Erase memories through trauma. 3. Emit a low vibrational frequency throughout the city to lower resistance. 4. Fill the washed mind with propaganda.

Scanning the list, Jack glanced sideways at the water cooler. *That's how they'd done it!*

"People think they're in control of their own lives. They're not." Sitting sideways with her knees together like a royal, Emma fanned her face with the paper she was holding.

"Do you want me to open the window?"

"Yes, please." Catching the cool breeze on her flushed face, Emma was quickly reminded of the homeless encampment from the stench.

"Allow me to summarize." Jack leaned over to get a glass of cold water from the cooler. "The world has gone *cahrazee.*" He winked as he handed the glass to his visitor. "That's imported water," he assured her.

Holding her index finger in the air, Emma paused to drink the water all at once. "Madness has become the norm. It's socially acceptable, and in fact – encouraged." She handed the glass back to Jack.

"The lunatics are running the asylum. Is Mercury in retrograde or something?" Jack couldn't help but grin. In fact, he could barely wipe the smile off his face. *Nice, but...odd.*

"General Fowler told us that the military has an entire branch dedicated to psychological warfare. Remember?" Emma handed some handwritten notes to Jack. "This is based on the work of the French psychologist, Gustave Le Bon and popularized by Dr. Mattias Desmet. It's crowd theory."

Mass Formation Psychosis:

1. **A lack of social bond, a lack of connections with others.** Digital age bombards us with too many stimuli, separates people in the real world.

2. **Lack of meaning and sense making.** Information overload and the absence of spirituality leads to lack of meaning, depriving humanity of the need to make sense of their world. One of the reasons for the increase in anti-depressants.

3. **Free-floating anxiety.** A constant state of panic with no known cause, and possibly the greatest cause of psychological pain known to man.

4. **Widespread free-floating frustration and aggression.** A passive-aggressive energy waiting for a unifying cause to ignite it.

Jack scanned the list. "Explains a lot." With his hands clasped behind his head, he put his feet on the desk, the overhead light reflecting off the shine of his shoes.

"It's like Pavlov's dogs. The people *think* they're rational beings – making decisions based on thought."

"What are you talking about?" Jack guzzled his limenade.

"The world has been divided into two groups." Emma formed two columns with her hands as she spoke. "The rulers and the ruled. A handful of self-appointed saviors vs the people of the world."

Jack stroked his beard. "That old game again – just like in the comic world."

"Except in *our* universe, the good guys are the bad guys, and the bad guys are the good guys."

"So, why –"

"Victims lose the ability for rational thought and judgment. It's like Stockholm Syndrome – they side with their captors."

"Can I get a word in edgewise?" Jack grinned.

"Of course." Emma paused. "What do you have?"

"Nothing. I just wanted to hear my own voice."

Relaxing a little, Emma returned the smile. "Don't be a cheeky monkey."

Jack chuckled. "Whatever that is."

"Now, at this point, an interesting thing happens   society begins to hate the truth tellers." Searching through her faux-leather purse for something, Emma squinted then raised a small tube of balm to her lips. "Instead, they'll worship anyone who feeds their delusions."

"I know," Jack replied flatly as he started out the window.

"Mass formation psychosis isn't fiction, either. Think of the Salem witch trials."

"What does *that* have to do with anything?"

"The political leaders of the day convinced the public that innocent women were witches. Those same people then *cheered* as the women were brutally murdered – burned alive at the stake. Can you believe that?!"

Jack poured hand sanitizer into his palm, its strong smell of alcohol temporarily overcoming the permanent stench of a society in decay. The golden sun disappeared behind heavy cloud cover just as the wind picked up. "The Third Reich did it too – they dehumanized their opponents to make it easier to kill and imprison them. Everyone piled on."

"Yes. And right now, all over the world, the people are in a classic abusive relationship with their own governments. Walking on eggshells. Always waiting for the other shoe to drop." Emma took a sip of tea from her travel mug while maintaining eye contact. "It's –"

"A situation worthy of a lot of clichés?" Jack's mischievous smile emitted a strange energy.

Emma ignored his smart-ass remark; she'd never seen him in such a giddy mood. "As is often the case with battered spouses, emotion trumps both logic and reason. In their confusion, morality becomes less of a priority. They just want to put an end to the mental anguish."

"Are you talking about Tetracimia?"

"Jack." A dramatic pause followed as Emma shifted in her chair. "There *is* no physical illness. It was 100% psychological. Television is tell-a-vision. They broadcast their spells."

"I know that," Jack stressed, "but how are they explaining the symptoms and the deaths?"

"Once the newscasters gain the trust of their viewers, they can convince them of *anything*. It's all done through the power of suggestion."

"You're kidding." Jack's declaration was flat and monotone.

"Would I kid you about something like this?? The symptoms are psychosomatic." Emma stood up, her small frame partially blocking out the daylight from the window. "As for the deaths, they simply manipulated the cause of death and played with the numbers."

"So, big picture?"

"Half the population doesn't even know we're in a spiritual war. The status quo feels better to them, so they avoid digging deeper, instinctively knowing what they'll find."

"Good thing we don't all take the coward's way out," Jack added, annoyed.

"Indeed. It was bound to happen, though. When people are in a safe and comfortable society for too long, they get soft and lazy." Emma stood up to put her jacket on. "Is now a good time to remind you that if we can broadcast *our* frequency to the world *while* telling the truth, their spell will be broken."

"Yep. Wood of the holly tree, the casting, the channels, the programming. Even *the language* was telling us that they were doing." Jack glanced down at Emma's fastened jacket. "We're done?"

"For now." Emma moved toward the door. "I'll have more for you this afternoon."

"How do we fix this?" Jack asked again, swinging his chair around.

"I'm meeting with Chris when I leave here. I have an idea." Emma opened the door. "It's a dangerous time – they know they're losing. See you at the war room."

Chapter 101

Tessa's head was pounding when she awoke on the colonial sofa in Jack's guest house; an empty wine bottle and a dirty wineglass were on the black coffee table beside her. Still in the crumpled clothing she'd worn the night before, she swung her legs to the floor as she recalled the creepy encounter in the park. Was it real? A dream? Was *anything* real? Was *she* real?

Every statue was gone. Every book burned. Every truth teller censored. Every liar exalted. Good was called evil, and evil was called good. Every truth was a lie, and every lie was the truth. Liberty had been replaced by slavery, and the slaves didn't even know they weren't free, imprisoned as they were in their own minds. Everything was stupid, upside down, and backwards. And there appeared to be no way to fix it.

Completely deflated and devoid of feelings, Tessa dragged herself up the wooden stairs in dead silence, the cold steps on her bare feet barely registering. Skipping her comforting routine of coffee, she stopped to relieve herself in the half bath on the way to the guest room and quench her insatiable thirst with several glasses of cool water. Without getting undressed, she pulled the heavy covers over her head and curled up in a fetal position, crying herself to sleep in defeat.

By dusk, the morning's dark skies had turned angry, a blustery storm beginning to rage in the nearly deserted streets. Would April showers bring May flowers, or had the simulation done away with crocuses too? Tessa forced herself to get up; she had a meeting to go to.

The striped green and white awning of the Near and Far Café was torn and fluttering in the brisk wind. After decades of use, the double doors were worn down on the wood surrounding the handle.

The bell on the ceiling clanged when Tessa entered – it was the first time she'd gone out in public without her disguise since... the incident... when they got kicked out of PJ Bar and Grill. Inside, new paintings graced the walls: Canvases with triangles, circles, and hearts. The entire dining area smelled like grease.

Jack was in his favorite booth beside the window with Chris and Anna. He greeted her with a warm smile as she approached. "You look like hell."

Avoiding eye contact with Jack and without changing her blank expression, Tessa removed her raincoat. Still in the same crumpled clothes, not showered, and her hair a mess, it was a fitting frame for her bloodshot eyes. She did indeed look like hell. She didn't return the smile as she stayed on her feet.

The assistant manager was suddenly beside the table, his intimidating presence crowding Tessa's high-security social space. "You have to wear an armband when you're standing."

Tessa stood up, took her armband out of her pocket, dropped it on the muddy floor, and stomped on it with her boot. "Try me." She sat down.

Everyone in the suddenly silent café was staring; unsure how to react, the assistant retreated to the kitchen. The slovenly, middle-aged server approached the table, clearly annoyed. She made venomous eye contact with Tessa as she filled the other coffee cups.

Batting her long eyelashes, Tessa glared back. "I know. I'm a white supremacist." Her words dripped with syrupy sugar and were followed up by some inaudible profanity.

Exchanging glances, Anna and Chris burst into laughter. Keeping his eyes trained on the server, Chris pointed at himself, then Anna. "Hello?" he stated sarcastically. "Do we look white?"

"That makes you black on the outside and white on the inside," the server snapped. "Are you proud?"

Ignoring the server's implication, Chris flipped Tessa's mug upside down. "I need a fresh cup. There's a fly in my other one."

Scowling at Chris, the server filled the empty cup. Dark energy seemed to vanish as soon as she walked away.

With a full cup of fresh hot coffee in her hands, Tessa glanced around the half empty café while the conversations faded into the background. Rumors had been swirling that the iconic Near and Far Café was going out of business. With the lock downs, the fires, the vandalism, the theft, the retrofitting – they were done. *Almost like it was planned. Another link to Dormin's past severed.*

A distant male voice broke through Tessa's contemplation, then a big hand waved in front of her face. "Calling Tessa. Earth to Tessa. Breaker 1-9. Hello??" It was Jack.

"Sorry." Tessa mumbled, redirecting her attention back to the conversation.

"I was asking you why you didn't show up at the war room this afternoon. Emma wanted to talk to you."

"I'm dead inside Jack." Finally accepting defeat, Tessa made eye contact with him. "There is no reaching these people. They can all go straight to hell as far as I'm concerned. They deserve everything that's happening to them – we tried to warn them."

"Tessa, I don't think that's true." Jack scolded. "Our Creator is counting on us to save them, too. Forgive them Father, for they know not what they do." With a loud buzz, one of the fluorescent lights in the café flickered in the storm.

"What the hell –"

While the others tried to figure the electrical issue out, Tessa watched a young couple running in the heavy drizzle through the parking lot. "My decision is final. That's the only reason I came here tonight – I wanted to tell you in person."

"Come on, Tessa," Chris pleaded. "You're a strong woman. You were chosen for this mission."

"Chosen?!" Tessa glared at Chris with anger flashing in her eyes. "Do you have any idea what it's like? To be canceled and erased simply for having an *opinion*?" she seethed. "To lose everything? To not be able to access your own money?"

Chris ducked out of the way of Tessa's waving arms.

"Oh Tessa, think –" Jack began.

"I wasn't finished." Tessa snapped. "I couldn't go... I couldn't... my entire life was ruined."

Anna gently placed her warm hand on Tessa's forearm.

Shooting daggers at Jack, Tessa jerked her arm away. "Do you know what it's like to have everyone close to you a target of harassment?!"

Jack grinned.

Her bottom lip quivering, Tessa's eyes filled with stinging tears. "You think this is funny? Do you know what it's like to lose friends?" Her voice was shaking. "The lo...lo...love of your life?" The tears snaked their way down her numb face. "*Chosen!?*" she wailed.

Jack watched her animated moves with amusement. "Ah, Tessa. I ran for public office against the most organized, corrupt, and powerful empire of psychopaths in the world. And we're winning, despite their cheating." Jack shrugged. "There is nothing they haven't done to me and my family – and I knew it would happen."

"If you're trying to guilt trip me, it's not working. I can't do it." Irritated, Tessa frowned at Jack. "I'm broken, okay? I give up. Complaining on the internet isn't working. We're *not* winning."

"Complaining on the internet is an interesting characterization," Jack muttered.

"Whatever. I'm going back to New York. To hell with all this." Tessa rose to her feet. "What a colossal waste of time."

Jack slammed his coffee cup on the table.

With a golden rosary dangling from her shaking hand, Tessa's bottom lip trembled as she walked off into the stormy night.

Part VI

Redemption

"Some of the greatest battles will be fought within the silent chambers of your own soul."
~ **Ezra Taft Benson**

Chapter 102

Only one other vehicle was parked on the soaked grass beside St. Theresa's Roman Catholic Church when Tessa arrived. With the brisk wind and heavy rain whipping at the windshield, she reached into the back seat of her SUV for her floral-patterned umbrella, reluctantly stepping out into the eye of the storm. After this quick stop, she'd head back to Jack's to pack and find a flight.

Next to the decorative black metal fence around the graveyard, the sky's fury splashed in the maze of puzzles in the gravel, an obstacle course Tessa hopped around like a one-legged frog. *Poor frog*. The weathered wrought iron handrail seemed like a guidepost in her hand as she climbed the familiar cracked concrete steps, the earthy scent of rain giving her a temporary moment of calm.

With the ground shaking from deafening thunder, a brilliant flash of lightning illuminated the midnight-black church bell and the silhouette of a young woman in a trench coat as she climbed the crumbling stairs. The painted white double doors were faded and peeling, a parabolic portrayal of the state of the Christianity itself, it seemed.

"Whooo... whooo..." a great grey owl cried out into the darkness.

The 110-year-old building was small, but ornate, with wood-carved stations of the cross between the old pews and marble statues of Mary in the corners. Above the altar, Jesus hung on the life-size Cross, his arms outstretched as if he were welcoming home a lost child. Gregorian chants, familiar yet creepy, played softly on the outdated stereo system amid the residual, acrid aroma of burning incense.

With rolling thunder as her soundtrack and lightning creating the special effects, Tessa made the procession to the front of the old, familiar church. In the hidden crevasses of her mind, buried memories began to emerge from beneath layers of debris. Reaching up for a white-gloved hand to lead her. Tyler's celebration of life all those long years ago, such a sad day for all. Catechism in the basement – a bare concrete burrow with the distinct aroma of mildew.

Full of racing thoughts and mixed emotions, Tessa shuddered and lit a candle near the altar. Dropping her knees to the cushioned kneeler in the first pew, she placed her trembling hand on the spot where her mama always sat, bowing her head to say a silent prayer. Closing her weary eyes, she made the sign of the cross.

In the name of the Father, and of the Son, and of the Holy Spirit.

> *Heavenly Father: I'm lost again, Lord. So alone. My soul is empty and crying out for answers to so many questions like that night long ago in Manhattan, yearning to be filled with Your Grace. I ask for Your forgiveness in turning away from You again, and for Your mercy now in my hour of need, and I pray, Lord, for the soul of humanity that's crying out for a Redeemer. Show us what's real, Lord. Show us the way, the truth, and the life. May we carry the Holy Spirit within us as a beacon to the world. Guide us to speak the truth to ears that will hear and show it to eyes that will see.* ***Your*** *will be done. I ask this in Jesus' name. Amen.*

The raucous thunder moving through the valley prompted Tessa to open her eyes. She watched in horror as her clammy skin took on an odd, grayish-green kind of...aura, then morphed into a golden glow? As suddenly as it started, her skin returned to normal, leaving her with a tingling sensation. *Good thing, too. If she'd started to sprout scales or something, she was so outta there!* Presently, the tingling surrendered to a joyful sorrow as her soft sobs ominously echoed throughout the empty church.

A message *was* coming through to Tessa with the clarity of aluminum-foil rabbit ears on an old black-and-white TV. The voice grew louder...the voices? With her eyes closed, the picture became clear. It wasn't external voices – it was *her* voice, her own inner wisdom:

*Have faith. It doesn't matter what you call it, or what religion you practice, there is only one Creator who **must** exist for the universe to exist; only then can the laws of physics exist. Religion did not create God, but Man created religion – not as a means of worship, but as a means of control. As all empires do, civilization will collapse under the weight of its own decadence. Put man first, the world suffers. Put God first, and the world heals.*

When Tessa opened her eyes, a sudden flash of bright light appeared in front of her as the material world faded into nothingness. In its place, a circular pitch-black portal rimmed with the shimmering golden essence of the spirit world was spinning counterclockwise. When it swallowed her up, she was no longer limited by earthly senses or ego. There was no time or space.

The nature of reality became crystal clear: *Everything is energy. Manmade divisions are a lie. All life is one in the universal consciousness – the collective thought frequencies that create reality. Humanity must raise its vibration to exist in the five-dimensional world, also called the New Earth.*

A sudden shift in Tessa's universal awareness manifested faint golden symbols that appeared in a light breeze, falling like snowflakes until a loud noise on the altar startled her. Upon lifting her heavy eyelids, she met the gaze of the elderly, balding priest, watching her with his virtue-signaling armband.

With a scowl, the priest made it clear that he wasn't a fan of her disheveled look or missing identifier. *What a ray of sunshine.* Who'd have ever thought that all these men of the cloth would turn into such hateful zealots and douchebags?

Just after *Reverend sunshine* left, a sudden movement to the left of the lectern caught Tessa's attention – visible, pulsating energy began to surround the Cross handing on the wall. The golden glow reflected off the fresh blood dripping from the gaping wounds on Jesus' feet, droplets splattering on the ornate darkened altar beneath Him. Dancing shadows cast a slow-motion hypnotic spell from the flames of a dozen flickering candles, the eerie ambience and a flash of lightning revealing the bloodied crown of thorns.

The nearby statue of Mary, with outstretched hands, toppled and crashed onto the shiny marble floor, shattering into a hundred pieces in the stillness of the night.

At once, a grotesque dark-green demon appeared directly in front of Tessa's eyes. Cloaked in a thick blanket of black smoke and reeking of the underworld, it moved closer.

Still on her knees, the terrified Tessa froze, unable to move and unable to scream.

A hooded dancing cobra swayed beside the demon, his eyes as blood red as his keeper's.

With her heart pounding out of her chest, a wide-eyed Tessa screamed into the hideous face of evil while she found her footing.

"It doesn't matter what you do, Tessssa," the demon hissed with a growl, obstructing her view of the tabernacle. "We own your sssssoul."

To keep her eyes on the surprise visitors, Tessa retreated backward, stumbling over the patterned rug and falling on the hardwood in the wide center aisle. The dastardly duo disappeared in front of her eyes. Sighing with relief, she scrambled to her feet, anticipating the salvation of the cool night air as she turned around to run to the exit.

The Gregorian chanting had stopped; the church was dead silent. Expecting to be greeted by the storm, Tessa reached the weathered double doors.

"You can't hide from usssss." The wicked demon had reappeared, blocking her exit, a bolt of lightning illuminating his monstrous outline in the open doorway.

Grasping the Holy water font in the entrance of the church, Tessa approached the beast, careful not to spill the blessed cargo before she reached him. "You can't scare me!" Her powerful words rang out into the stillness of the night.

The demon didn't budge.

"I rebuke you in the name of Jesus Christ and command you to be gone! Never to return!" Tessa splashed the evil entity with the Holy water.

With a spinetingling scream and a small sizzle, the hideous beast vanished, leaving nothing but a faint mist and the opaque skin of a snake in his wake.

Back at the front of the church now, Tessa fell to her knees in front of the altar. There was no blood. No shattered statue. *"Thank you, Lord,"* she whispered. The peace she felt within was reflected in the eloquence of her movements as she returned to the old, familiar wooden pew. On the padded kneeler, she closed her eyes. A big picture of some random dots began to emerge in her mind's eye. *Random dots? What if... connect...the...dots!*

It's fear! Fear and other negative emotions are low vibrational frequencies that attract the dark side. When Tessa faced her fear by calling on the name of Jesus Christ of Nazareth, the God frequency replaced the devil's dark energy.

They were, *quite literally*, in a spiritual battle for the soul of humanity.

Still on bent knees in a meditative trance, an alluring familiar scent stirred Tessa's senses. Next to her, Adam was sitting on the pew, his head bowed in prayer. Sensing he was being watched, he turned to meet her dreamy gaze – they locked eyes.

Reminding herself how she'd tried so hard not to fall in love, Tessa's stomach did a somersault. With him now peering into the depths of her soul, she was released from the devil's persistent lie. Love is patient and kind, *not* pain and betrayal.

Without a word, Adam led Tessa outside by the hand, shielding her from the pouring rain with his camo umbrella as they descended the old, familiar steps. A few feet away from his car, he stopped.

Rather than opening the car door, Adam tossed the umbrella to the ground. He turned to Tessa, and overcome with passion, crushed her in his arms. "I can't live without you," he moaned as he brushed her ear with his lips. When her knees buckled, he caught her and found her luscious lips.

Tessa threw her arms around Adam's neck while his sturdy hands explored her body through her soaked clothing. The couple shared an intense, lingering kiss with abandon, getting drenched in the downpour. Behind them, spooky shadows danced on the tombstones that disappeared when a jolt of fork lightning illuminated the peculiar romantic scene.

With her eyes closed, Tessa rested her weary head on Adam's shoulder. "What are you doing here?" she whispered.

"I'm worried about you." Adam guided her to the passenger seat of his car. "Let's go."

The interior of the car was dry and spotless. Enjoying the scent of the new car, Tessa basked in the warmth of the heater and a newfound sense of peace. Soft classical music played, the perfect soundtrack for her reflective, post-epiphany silence.

Reaching across the leather center console, Adam grasped Tessa's hand. "We're going to get you through this," he assured her. The couple rode in comfortable silence for the remainder of the trip.

"Did you find out who killed Ralph?" Tessa asked softly as they approached the welcoming lights of Anna's house in the violent storm.

"Not yet, but they pissed off the wrong guy." With the reminder of losing his prized canine, Adam slammed the car in park. "It's payback time!"

Chapter 103

Seated at her kitchen table, Molly Jacobs, 'owner' of PJ Bar and Grill, undercover officer, and brilliant method actor pulled the note from her briefcase. Examining it closely, she ordered her phone to "Call Cliff."

The call was answered after one ring. "General McNab here."

"Hi Cliff. It's Molly. I've got something I think you should take a look at."

"I'll be there in fifteen minutes."

Chapter 104

Still a little rain-drenched from their intimate moment beside the church, the couple held hands as they walked up the cobblestone path. The front door opened before they reached it.

"I've got a nice fire going," Anna greeted them, moving aside to let them pass. "Go on and dry yourselves. I'll get some blankets."

In the cozy kitchen, Anna put the tea kettle on the stove, temporarily blinded by the lightning flooding the entire house. "My God." The lights flickered while rolling thunder shook the foundation. The fine China tea set on the corner shelf rattled. Fresh baked apple pie was on the counter cooling, a Stevie Ray Vaughn record playing softly on the old-school stereo.

Pulling up a wooden captain's chair from the dining set in the kitchen, Adam massaged Tessa's tense shoulders. "You're wound up, sweetheart."

"I wonder why," Tessa teased as she watched shades of purple and orange dancing in the flickering flames.

Placing two fuzzy plaid blankets on Adam's lap, Anna handed a large golden envelope to Tessa. "Jack asked me to give this to you."

"What is it?"

"Open it and find out, child!" Anna suggested, not so patiently.

A faded scarlet velvet bag landed on the bamboo coffee table on top of the stack of newspapers. Opening the tightly pulled drawstrings, Tessa gasped. Inside was a dazzling, exorbitantly expensive diamond necklace. "It's the necklace! The family heirloom. The one that went missing in New York!" She pulled it out to show Adam.

"There's more." Turning the music off, Anna pointed to the golden envelope. With the hum of the refrigerator off, the steady rhythm of the rain accompanied the ticking of the kitchen clock and the snapping of the birch in the fireplace.

A small white envelope was tucked in the corner of the package, and inside the envelope was a thin piece of floral stationery, folded in four. Tessa hesitated before raising the letter to her nose... her mother's scent lingered.

"Come on, my girl. You're keeping us all in suspense," Anna urged.

Tessa unfolded the paper in her hand, instantly recognizing the shaky handwriting from beyond the grave. She read the words to herself:

> September 2016
> My dearest Tessa:
> You must have so many questions.
>
> The doctors told me I couldn't get pregnant, then they told me you would be born with Down's Syndrome because I was almost 40. Your father was Roman Catholic, and he wouldn't hear of an abortion. A few months later, I gave birth to a beautiful, healthy baby girl.
>
> On the day your father died, I was upstairs sewing when I heard the shot. When I came downstairs, he was slumped on the kitchen table, and the gun was still spinning on the floor. He was gone.
>
> I picked up the gun and lit a fire to keep your father warm. Then, I don't know what happened. Somehow the fire got out of control. When the police showed up, they arrested me. Tessa, they thought I killed your father! This time I really did feel like I was going crazy. I couldn't cope.
>
> When your great aunt hid the necklace from the gestapo, they never thought it would get that bad. But it did. Ordinary people turned on other ordinary people until millions of innocent citizens were dead. They tricked everyone until they were screaming and clawing on the gas chamber walls.
>
> Your grandma always said that the devil uses fear and deception to conquer his enemy. When your great-grandmother tried to warn the people, they didn't believe her. They said it was just the rantings of a crazy old lady.
>
> Never be afraid to speak out, even if you are the only one. One person can change the world just by speaking the truth.
>
> You have the spirit of your ancestors within you, my dearest daughter. You are a light warrior. Truth will always win over lies. Good will always win over evil. Love conquers all.
> Mom.

Tessa looked up with a blank stare on her face. Anna quickly turned her head away and left the room. While she was gone, Adam cradled Tessa in his arms while she softly cried, pulling the blanket up around her shoulders. Despite the radiant heat from the fire, she was shivering.

A full tray of cinnamon tea and apple pie appeared on the coffee table to rip Tessa out of her trance. "Why did it take so long for me to receive that?" she sniffled, still resting her head on Adam's shoulder.

"It took until now for the will to go through probate. Jack wanted to give it to you at dinner, but you were too upset." Anna handed a plate to Adam.

Sitting up, Tessa nodded. "I'm still upset," she wailed, holding up her hand to refuse the pie.

As Anna sat down, she reached for her weathered bible. *"Put on the full armor of God that ye may be able to stand against the wiles of the devil."* (Ephesians 6:11 KJV).

Adam and Tessa exchanged confused glances as violent thunder galloped across the heavens like God got up on the wrong side of the bed. Sheet lightning lit up the gloomy sky in the distance as the storm system moved further down the valley.

Anna continued.

> *No weapon that is fashioned against you shall succeed, and you shall confute every tongue that rises against you in judgment. This is the heritage of the servants of the Lord and their vindication from me, declares the Lord.* (Isaiah 54:17, KJV).

In Tessa's vulnerable state, her spine tingled upon hearing the words, 'servants of the Lord'. It was a kick in the gut, a reminder that she wasn't a servant of Tessa. "Amen," she whispered. "We got this."

Chapter 105

With the golden rays of the early morning sun poking over the mountainous horizon like a shiny crown, the Arem River Valley awoke to a bright, new rose-colored day. In the aftermath of the storm, any remaining snow was gone, leaving only a light wind that tantalized one's skin like a feather.

By midafternoon, Tessa knelt beside her parents' tombstone in the graveyard, getting chills when she placed her hand on her mother's name beneath the concrete cross. Covering the full cost of the funeral, Jack had spared no expense for the photo – a likeness captured before she'd involuntarily abandoned her only child. It reminded her of a younger, more vibrant Cecilia.

"I got your letter, mama," Tessa whispered. "I came to say goodbye. I wish you were here so I could tell you I love you." She struggled to keep her emotions from overwhelming her. "We b-brought your favorite f-fl-flowers."

Adam placed his warm hand on Tessa's shoulder, softly massaging the tight muscles around her neck while she gently wept. With the other hand, he placed a bouquet of daisies across the grave, their citrusy scent rising in the air.

"I'm sorry," Tessa continued. "It wasn't your fault. It wasn't my fault," she wailed, still trying to come to terms with what she'd put her mother through. "We didn't understand each other. We both did our best."

A dog howled in the distance as Adam dropped to his knees beside Tessa. "I'm here, baby."

"I forgive you. I hope you'll forgive me." Tessa's voice shook. As Adam helped her to her feet, she stared at her father's side of the grave. It left her cold, and she had no idea why; she'd had such fond memories of him – the way he doted on her. Now, nothing. *Strange.*

"Look." Adam pointed to the tombstone where a beautiful mourning cloak butterfly had landed, dazzling them with its deep purple-brown wings enclosed in borders of bright yellow. Inside the black band that rimmed the edges, spots of vibrant royal blue jumped out.

"Thank-you, mama." Tessa's voice was full of love and forgiveness. "Message received."

By the time the couple left the church grounds, it was late afternoon, calm and sunny with a gentle breeze. They arrived at magical Saboro Point in time to enjoy the spectacular dimming of the day.

In the picturesque picnic area, a few other parties had gathered, including a family with two small children. Their laughter filled Adam and Tessa with delight as they passed by their table.

Near the entrance to the campground in the pine forest, Tessa spread out a red and white checkered blanket on the thick grass. She'd thrown some ham and cheese sandwiches together before Adam picked her up. Smiling to herself, she removed the wicker basket from the back seat. As she pulled a bottle of red wine out of the trunk, she glanced at her beau – he was on the blanket watching her like a lovesick puppy dog.

During dinner, Adam cracked jokes until Tessa had a giggling fit, then he just sat back and smiled at her joyful laughter. Afterwards, they laid on their backs in silence watching puffy white clouds forming cool shapes in the late-afternoon sky.

Tessa mulled her mother's words over in her mind. "Adam, why was I chosen? I'm just an ordinary person. There are so many people more deserving, more righteous than I am." She hadn't taken her eyes off the sky.

"You're a light bearer, leading the way for others with a torch." On one elbow now, Adam stroked Tessa's hair as he spoke.

"That's not what Chris said when he was sucking up to me," Tessa giggled. "Trying to find people in dark places with a lousy lantern isn't all it's cracked to be – *especially* when they don't want to be found."

"Why do you do it?" Adam asked softly.

"Ha. Good question." Gently coaxing Adam to lie down again, Tessa placed her hand on his warm chest so she could feel the beat of his heart. "I don't do it for the money, *that's* for sure. Even if I got rich, you can't buy the feeling of being divinely inspired."

"Now that's a flex," Adam laughed.

"I wish I could laugh too, but I know what's facing me. I'm taking the big stage."

With the sun starting to sink behind the mountains, the sky filled with magical colors, swirls of dark orange and violet surrounding flames of golden fire. It was the perfect ending to their romantic afternoon as the couple connected on a deeper level. They sat on the same red metal bench at the apex of Saboro Point where they'd begun their journey. Tessa rested her head against Adam's sturdy shoulder, reminding herself how lucky she was to have met him and how she'd finally let go of the past. Taking his hand, she thought about how this would always be their special spot.

"Tess," Adam broke the silence. "I have something to tell you."

Tessa's dreamy mood was suddenly interrupted. "Mmmm," she murmured. Was this the part of the romance blockbuster where he professed his undying love for her? Where he got down on...

"I have to come clean on something."

"Way to kill the moment." Tessa didn't move. "You gonna tell me you're having an affair or you're a spy like Cole, or what?" she pouted.

"Funny you should mention that." Adam smiled. "Tess, I *am* a spy."

In shock, Tessa picked her head up. "No way!"

"But I'm not spying on *you* – like Cole was." You had me at 'fuck the system'."

"Okay. I'm awake!" Tessa caught the twinkle in Adam's eyes.

"I'm undercover at New World Now. *Now* I can tell you that you had me at 'fuck the system'," Adam laughed. "I work for Envisage and we're ready to go public."

Chapter 106

Awakening to the heavenly, familiar aroma of fresh coffee, Tessa stumbled down the stairs in her bare feet. Today was the day.

Still leaning against the kitchen counter as she finished her first cup of breakfast blend, Tessa jumped when the loud ringtone next to her broke the morning silence. After a minute of listening to the two voices on the other end, she swiped to end the call. It was `7:06 a.m.` "Meh. It's five o'clock somewhere," she mumbled, tossing the second cup down the drain.

Moments later, Tessa replayed the conversation in her head. She was now in a padded lounge chair on the back patio with a glass of red wine and the warm morning sun on her face. She'd forgotten she gave her number to her old school friends, Kaitlin and Amy, the day she ran into them at the mall. *The odd couple apparently weren't fans of her work.*

The vitriol was more than disturbing, the emotional turmoil almost *supernatural*, like they were possessed by an unexplained dark energy. It was as if Tessa's very *existence* would kill them, her words of truth sizzling on them like holy water on a demon. It drove them *crazy* that she was immune to their absurd rantings, thinking that all they had to do to gain control was call her racist. Those days were over. *Game on.*

Rap! Rap! Rap! "Tessa, open the door! It's Jack."

Tessa raced through the open patio door and across the house to the front entrance. She wrenched the door open. "Hi?"

"Got something I thought you might want to take a look at." Jack held up a thick brown envelope tied with graying white string. "You might need it soon."

"Come on in." Tessa stepped aside.

"Not likely," Jack held up his hand to refuse the invitation. "We're under a time crunch."

"I know," Tessa acknowledged as she thought about her impending noon assignment. "Alright. I'll catch you later at the theater."

As soon as Jack was gone, Tessa ripped into the package. It was a pile of paperwork and notes from an unknown source. *Hmmm.* The handwritten sticky note on top simply said, 'Found in the back of a locked closet at city hall'.

Rifling through the thick stack, Tessa discovered a workbook called <u>Rebuilding Community: A Practical Approach</u> from April 2001 when old man Fisher was still mayor. Setting the primer down on the patio table, she fetched another glass of red wine along with a notepad and pen from her new floral satchel. With a bit of a chill in the air, she rested her white cardigan on the back of her patio chair in case a sudden wind came up. *All set.*

As Tessa leafed through the material, she learned that community development seeks to empower local citizens with the tools they need to find solutions to common problems. *Cool!* Why had it been hidden away instead of applied? *Of course, that would require political will. 'Nuff said.* Well, too bad for the powers that be, Dorminians were no longer willing to participate in a rigged game – they were creating their own rules.

With her feet resting on another patio chair, Tessa tapped her lips with her pen. *Okay.* They'd need to get out of the ivory tower and back to the grassroots. *Decentralize. Where to start? She turned to the next page.*

<u>Recapturing Legislation from Corporate Control.</u>
Checklist:
- Initial Volunteer comes forward and brings two friends.

- The volunteers recruit community leaders for the initial organizing committee.

- The organizing committee initiates fundraising and establishes subcommittees:

    ◦ The fundraising committee launches a campaign to secure operating funds.

    ◦ The outreach committee generates interest in civic elections: Door knocking, leaflets, posters, community nights at the local churches and schools. Neighborhood cookouts. Advertising. Billboards.

- The education committee provides training for new employees and informs citizens that decisions that govern day-to-day life are made at the municipal level – police, fire and ambulance. Road maintenance. Snow removal. Garbage collection and utilities. Parks and recreation. Etc.

- The media committee attempts to restore faith in the media by implementing the independent media model. **NO** corporate sponsorship – 100% audience funded.

- The elections committee attempts to restore faith in the electoral process. **NO** political party affiliation for candidates. **NO** corporate donations. Crowd funding only – it ensures service to the right people.

- The HR committee delivers pink slips to everyone in civic administration and suspends city services until a new council can be elected. They hire community consultants.

- The Election Day committee organizes an autonomous, people-run election to select leaders for community associations. One day. In person. Paper ballots. Voter ID. No machines. Adequate oversight of the entire process. Checks, balances, and collective resolution of issues are the way forward.

• Elected officials are the new council – they re-establish the Constitutional rule of law and develop infrastructure.

• Qualified community consultants are hired to form active community associations.

• Community associations get to work.

Next page: United Nations International Standards for Community Development Practice? *Good Lord! Everything doesn't have to be centralized!*

Tessa guzzled half a glass of red wine while she thought about what she'd like to say to the globalists:

> *Nobody elected you. Get out of our communities and pound sand! International governing bodies have **no authority** over Americans. I am not your subject, and you are not my ruler; so kindly take your mandates, your decrees, your executive orders, and your armbands, and shove them up your collective nether regions. To anyone who would see our city, country, and world burned to the ground just so you can rule over the ashes: you're going down, Mother Hubbard!*

Now that she had *that* out of her system, a tipsy Tessa wondered how they would apply the checklist to a broken Dormin. By the time she was done, she had a first draft of potential action items written on her yellow legal notepad.

Memorandum *(draft)*

Date: To be determined
Attention: Community Consultants
Goal: Develop a parallel society with self-governing economies, culture, law enforcement, etc.
Enclosed: Potential Action Items for discussion with citizens

- Start with simple, bitesize tasks to not get overwhelmed.

- Shop local, organic and ethically sourced. Buy direct from farmers. Patronize farmer's markets. Support small business. Develop a directory of parallel goods and services. Fill niches as required.

- Reduce reliance on corporations and rethink consumerism. Do you really need eighty towels if you only use ten?

- Use or start local credit unions instead of centralized banks. Use cash wherever and whenever possible, then you don't need a credit score.

- Support or start member owned coops. Barter for goods and services.

- Get to know your neighbors, volunteer as a block parent, have block parties and neighborhood potlucks. It will lead to a reduction in crime and a resurgence of families.

- If you don't practice faith, start a social group to discuss issues of spirituality and faith, the decline in morality. The world needs a moral reckoning, a return of Creator God.

- Rebuild families as the foundation of society.

- Take an interest in educating future generations whether you have children or not. They'll be running the world someday.

- Home school or start teaching pods. Get the children outside, teach them to play again. Their books, games, and entertainment are vitally important.

- Get information from independent media sources who aren't beholden to corporate messaging.

- Start campaigns.

- Run for city council.

- Teach each other skills through workshops.

- Learn social psychology to avoid mass brainwashing.

- If you can, get a plot of land. Raise chickens. Grow a garden. Cook, sew, chop wood.

- Create and shape culture. Write books, make films, start a podcast, comment on social media, wear a t-shirt, etc.

- Whatever you can do, do it.

- Add to and rework list as needed.

Before long, the emerging video streaming platform, Thunder, had a new user: TDR Report. Tessa literally had no followers but was going to record a show anyway. Maybe it would get shared if someone stumbled upon it. The show must go on.

File Notes: TDR Report (transcribed):

April 11, 2017

Once upon a time, I was lost.

What changed? The solution was simple, but not easy. I had to admit I was blind. And I was wrong.

When I stopped talking and started listening, I began to learn about the Marxist coup that happened right under our noses. Marxism, also known as wokeness, is a new religion where individual identity is supreme and must not be questioned, where the material world is the best they can ever hope for.

When they came up with the term hate speech to protect certain identities, dissident thought became a crime, and...freedom – was over. The policing of language, the policing of speech is ultimately the policing of thought and behavior.

It only takes one generation to destroy a culture. Things that are accepted by society **now** *would have been considered preposterous just a few short years ago. In America, it's perfectly fine to burn a bible or the Stars and Stripes, to mock Jesus and jail traditional Americans, but if you burn a rainbow flag or misgender someone, you go to prison for a hate crime. Without propaganda, it can't be done. Without programming, people will not hate their own country. No matter how much you think you hate the corporate media, it's not enough.*

What they won't tell you is with heightened racial and other tensions, we defeat ourselves. A truly egalitarian society is impossible when the love of power is stronger than the power of love.

I blame myself. I got sucked into thinking I was superior to the other guys because that's what the corporate media said. I wasn't.

So... my friends, cling to your steadfast morals and carry on with love in your heart. God bless America.

Today, I want to close with scripture.

"Create in me a clean heart O God; and renew a right spirit within me." (Psalms 51:10 KJV)

Hold the line, fearless patriots. We got this.

This is Tessa Ryan, signing out.

Chapter 107

By the time Tessa signed off her spur-of-the-moment broadcast, Adam Logose was winding his way through the deep woods on Diablo Mountain. A narrow trail led him to an isolated clearing near the uninhabited Lake Abigor where he parked his black rental 4 x 4 and left the vehicle idling to stay warm.

As heavy gray cloud cover swept away the warmth of the morning sun, huge snowflakes began to fall from the sky like tiny parachutes looking for a landing. They accumulated on the windshield and mostly-thawed lake to signal the long winter wasn't quite done with them yet.

In the rear-view mirror, a beam of bright headlights flashed in and out of view through the birch and pine on the trail. A maroon-colored rental SUV pulled up and a slender, pasty-white, clean-shaven young Aussie exited the vehicle. At thirty-eight and not a thick blond hair out of place, the handsome Jason King opened Adam's passenger door, letting himself and noxious exhaust fumes in. He set his souvenir travel mug down in the center console so he could shut the door. "G'day, mate."

"Hey, Jason!" Adam pulled his new leather briefcase out of the backseat and polished the handle with a tissue.

Jason saluted. "I came all the way from Queensland, so this *better* be good." His sky-blue eyes contrasted with the backdrop of the dreary day.

While Adam rifled through his briefcase, he killed the ignition on the vehicle. "Tyranny, like hell, is not easily conquered." He pulled out a thumb drive and a thick paper file.

"Thomas Paine," Jason acknowledged, reminding Adam that he was an American history scholar.

"Okay." Adam returned the briefcase to the back seat. "What if I told you that what is really going on is that a group of reptilian, cannibalistic devil-worshiping aliens live inside the Earth under Antarctica where they eat kids?"

It took Jason a moment to compose himself after warm coffee dribbled from his mouth when he laughed. "I never took you for the crazy conspiracy theorist type." Grabbing a napkin from the center console, he wiped coffee from his chin. "Did you read that on the internet?"

"Okay, then." Adam paused for dramatic effect. "What if I said that a small group of unelected bureaucrats performed a global coup, and their agenda is depopulation. Call it whatever political system you want. I just call it tyranny."

"What are you... what?" The shadows from the rapidly moving clouds danced on Jason's face while he tried to make sense of what he had just heard.

"It's true," Adam replied. "I have the receipts." He held up the thumb drive.

"How could they possibly do that, though, Adam?" Jason's expression morphed from contemplation to disbelief. "It sounds absurd!"

"For reference, 'they' are operating out of the base they have right here in Dormin. It's the head of the snake, and it goes way back."

"How far?"

"Far enough so that they founded the central banks then took over all the institutions. Left and right political parties are a joke. People think they have a choice. Ha!"

"New boss, same as the old boss?"

"Exactly. They infiltrated churches and started both world wars." Adam slammed his palm against the steering wheel. "They overthrew governments and destroyed countries who stood in their way."

"Oh, you *are* serious!"

"Yeah. And they don't *just* want to depopulate. They want us to *be* evil and perverted. Like them."

"Here I was thinking you'd find some good old-fashioned run-of-the-mill corruption," Wondering why he'd chosen investigative journalism as a career path, Jason shifted in his seat.

"It's like that song... the Skeleton Dance, but except for the foot bone connected to the leg bone and the leg bone connected to the hip bone... doing the skeleton dance." Adam moved his head and arms around while he sang the lame version, much to the delight of his companion. "Global Intelligence is connected to Johnny. Johnny is connected to the Congress. Congress is connected to the Media. Doing the blackmail dance."

"Blackmail? What do you mean?"

"Lots of incriminating evidence. Humans are trafficked from all over the world to serve the wealthy and powerful. Countries in Eastern Europe are goldmines for these sickos." Adam thought about all the evidence they had against the ruling class. "Young girls – and boys, are ordered to give the men anything they want. It's all recorded."

"So... that's how they control governments?"

"It is, indeed." Adam added a nod for emphasis while he passed the folder to Jason.

Without looking at it, Jason put the paper file on his lap and the thumb drive in the pocket of his light blue golf shirt. "So, who's running the whole thing?"

"The Pentagon."

"The *Pentagon*?! The US military?"

"The *global* military."

"Crikey! I don't get it," Jason admitted. "In Dormin?!"

"With the infrastructure they've spent so long putting in place, this location has always been critical to DC powers," Adam explained. "Old man Fisher had a reckoning. The people loved him, and he felt the same way about them. He was going to come clean and give the town back to the citizens. Then *he* disappeared. He's been gone for sixteen years, missing and presumed dead. It's unlikely to ever be solved."

"You watch too much TV." Jason wiped his chin.

"And that's why they're trying to destroy not just *Jack*, but his movement as well. My girlfriend is...*was*... the star anchor for alternative media, so they had to bring her down."

"What did they do to her?"

"What *didn't* they do to her? They used to assassinate their enemies, but it got too hard to cover up. So, now they assassinate their characters to avoid creating martyrs."

"Right." Trying to cope with jet lag, Jason suppressed a yawn.

"It's the same thing they do to *any* threat to established power. They infiltrate and destroy movements. They brought down Nixon."

"Nixon? But –"

"But nothing. The empire's crimes make Nixon look like a boy scout. I saw pictures of a *literal* concentration camp under the plant, Jason. This is some serious shit."

This time, Jason was unable to suppress a yawn. "Sorry. I'm so buggered."

"Stop it. That's contagious." Adam yawned. "Way back in the 1970s, the empire started to train world leaders on how to implement this global coup."

"Can you prove any of this?"

"Yeah. Thanks to a man named Will Garcia. He risked *everything* to get me the information. We have it all."

"Talk to me, mate."

"Considering the US harbored Nazi war criminals and recruited them for the highest positions of power, they're all on the same side, always have been. The Vatican helped war criminals escape Europe, for God's sake! It's all for show. The established power vs the people of the world. The League of Nations became the United Nations which became the League of Lies."

In shock, Jason gasped. "But again, why *here?*"

"The place was settled by the Klan after the civil war – far away from prying eyes." After a brief pause, Adam continued. "They hid Hitler here – he never killed himself." He sipped his lukewarm coffee. "The entire town is a fraud – the Fourth Reich has been experimenting on the citizens here for several decades. Atluko Inc is fake."

"Then, *what the hell* is going on?"

"The plant is a cover for a massive studio where they produce the news. It's all a movie." Adam grabbed a tissue to sneeze. "And that's just the main floor. It used to be a meatpacking plant but hasn't been since the 1950s."

Jason reached into the center console for another napkin. "They'd need *a lot* of advanced tech for that, no?"

The snow had stopped. "Seriously, Jason? What do you think we're dealing with here? It's the most sophisticated psychological and technological warfare the world has ever seen. Below ground, the plant is a massive cybercity with an elaborate system of tunnels that connects to the ranch and businesses all over the county."

"Son of a... no way!"

"My girlfriend discovered one under an art gallery, so we started looking for the map – we found one, thanks to a surprise double agent." Adam's stretch coincided with the sun's return. "They have their own landing strip and a back entrance through a passageway."

"What!?"

"That was part of the trillion-dollar project – it's all hidden from public view. Think Jonestown or a secluded island."

"Oh my God."

"Believe it or not, they have a wing with political prisoners who are being tortured to death and sacrificed for their sadistic pleasure." Trying to keep the emotion down in his voice, Adam continued. "They have a temple, too. It's where they do the sacrifices."

"No way!"

"Yes way." Adam nodded, channeling a teenage stoner. "They're not just evil. They're Evil Inc. Organized Evil. Big Evil. The Evil Industrial Complex. St –"

"I get it, Adam. They've developed a global corporation out of it."

"Bingo." Adam glanced sideways to make sure he had Jason's attention. "The movie that was filmed here in the 1950s was predictive programming."

"You mean Bell Hound?"

"Yeah. It's about a dying dog called Bell who dies... a real tearjerker." As the day was warming, Adam removed his jacket. "It was code for killing God! Everything is backwards, they were trying to tell us we were all hell bound." He slammed his palm against the steering wheel.

"They weren't lying. Crikey!"

"When the filming was finished, a staff member at the chateau discovered a satanic altar with swastikas in the attic." Adam's speech was rushed like a sketchy visit in a bad neighborhood. "They've been holding rituals all over the forest for decades. So many celebrities are involved with the dark arts."

"*How?*"

"It's part of the contract. They sell their soul for fame and fortune."

"Get out of here."

"No. For real. They think Lucifer is a good dude, and they worship him. Look into spirit cooking."

"How do they get away with all this?"

"They hide universal and natural law from the people so they don't know they're being manipulated." Adam scratched his goatee. "Secret societies are alive and well, it's not a conspiracy theory."

"I'll be damned." With so much new information, Jason's mind raced. *No wonder he needed to get to Dormin.*

"The Delicacy brand they boast about?" Adam settled his gaze upon the lake. "Yeah, that's human bacon, the only part of the plant that still operates as a meatpacking plant."

Gagging, Jason opened the door and retched until his breakfast was all over the ground. When he was finished, he took a moment to lean back and recompose himself while he wiped the spittle from his chin. "Adam! How did you end up doing *this* kind of work?"

"I grew up in Saskatchewan." Adam paused, trying to remember how much Jason knew about his home province. "Saskatchewan was a hotbed of unethical experiments in the '50s and '60s. CIA trauma-based mind control. MK Ultra. LSD experiments."

"I knew that." Jason confirmed he had, in fact, done his research.

"Right. So, then I stumbled upon a case involving an entire family being shot by a random stranger in the night."

Jason raised an eyebrow. "That's horrific, but what does *that* have to do with it?"

"It's too similar to the lone gunman mass shootings in the States." Adam gripped the steering wheel tightly.

"How!?"

"Consider this: The killer had been a patient in a mental hospital, diagnosed with schizophrenia, had no memory of the event, and the CIA doctors just *happened* to be running experiments at the time."

"Oh...."

"I've been fascinated by psychological warfare ever since." Adam rubbed his eyes. "When I found out about the experiments, my Mengele radar went off."

"What experiments were they doing?"

"During Operation Paperclip, a former SS war criminal took over as head of one of the biggest pharmaceutical companies in the States," Adam reminded Jason of how deeply entrenched fascist philosophy was throughout the North America. "Decide for yourself."

"At one point, I'd have said that while the US government wouldn't do that, but we *know* that the feds took out President Kennedy and sent suicide letters to Martin Luther King Jr."

"Indeed." Adam's noticeable pause put Jason on alert for the next bombshell. "Hey, do you remember when the globalists performed that satanic ritual at the Goddard Tunnel last year?"

"Vaguely," Jason acknowledged. "I don't believe in Satan, mate."

A wolf emerged from the thick forest. Stopping just outside the tree line, he turned his head to meet Jason's eyes.

"I don't care what you believe." Adam shrugged. "Through that ritual – which was attended by power players all over the world, they opened a portal to hell. *Literally.*"

Still unsettled by the powerful canine energy, Jason rubbed his eyes with his palms.

"The world has been under a demonic frequency-induced spell ever since."

"Is that even possible?"

"Obviously. But the spell is losing its power. Now, they're trying to make the Earth a permanent hell." Adam turned to Jason. "And we're running out of time."

"Get real. This isn't a science fiction movie." Jason laughed nervously.

"People in a hypnotic trance are highly susceptible to suggestion. Have you ever investigated the Mandela Effect?"

"I'm familiar with it." Jason nodded while he dabbed at his pants with a napkin.

"They've been messing with our minds for a very long time."

"A psychological operation. Who knew? And all this time, I thought those people were crazy." Jason turned to face Adam. "Good on ya, mate."

"Centuries of propaganda will do that to a person." Avoiding Jason's eyes, Adam hugged the steering wheel like an anchor. "They're a death cult. This is a spiritual battle for the soul of humanity."

"And now, we bring their whole rotten system down."

Chapter 108

Day was breaking when Chris Simon arrived at the Weber residence the next morning. With his headlights shining on the early morning dew, he pulled his van into the circular driveway. The warmer air had returned and melted the previous day's light snowfall.

"He's upstairs in the study, Mr. Simon." Jenny was sweet, though heavyset and somewhat masculine in her features and mannerisms. "Go on up."

Chris sprinted up the carpeted stairs in his sock feet two at a time, knocking on the door of Jack's study when he reached the top. Today was the day.

"Come in." Jack yelled. "It's open." Seated in his favorite wing back chair, Jack gestured for Chris to join him. "I wasn't expecting you this early."

"Couple of things." Chris skipped the niceties. "Jenny, your maid, is working with them. She's the one who shot Adam Logose's dog."

Jack's face turned ghost white as the bombshell hit him. "How do you know that?"

"Jenny was Logose's trusted weekly housekeeper. His people did handwriting analysis."

"I'm surprised there was anything to clean," Jack quipped, thinking about Chris' cleanliness obsession. "So what to we do?"

"For now, we don't do anything so she doesn't suspect we're on to her. She'll go down in the raid."

Still speechless, Jack gestured to Chris to continue.

"The kicker? That ain't no woman." Chris drew an outline of the feminine form with his hands. "That's gender bending." He grabbed his crotch.

Jack's eyes grew wide. *She... he was trans! Oh, man. That's a connection to Johnny Eden right there if ever there was one.*

"You have to hear this." Chris remained standing.

"If we had a smart dictatorship, we could manage eight... or maybe nine billion on the planet. But dictatorships are always stupid, and it's too difficult to limit consumption...we can have a billion, maybe two for the available resources, so we need to liquidate six billion within the next five years. Civilly. Peacefully."

"Who... who is that?!" Jack stammered. "Kill p...people civilly? Huh?"

"But wait. There's more."

"The people will willingly fund their own extermination – much less costly and messy than crematoriums and gas chambers. They will just fade away quietly. It is the final solution to the overpopulation question."

"Holy Mother of God." The blood drained from Jack's face again. "Who *is* that?" he reiterated.

"That's one Wolfgang Hertzig – evil genius and founder of the Global Dormin Group and the League of LIES. The antidote is a bioweapon. Manufactured right here in the Arem River Valley."

"What are you talking about? These people are evil but... come on." Jack loosened his tie.

"It's poison. It's weakening the immune system." Chris paused. "We tested it. It's synthetic King Cobra venom mixed with human blood and a deadly chemical. Some people got the placebo. Others literally drank the devil's potion."

"Get out of here!" Jack retrieved some limenade from the brown mini fridge.

"No. Really. Where they get the blood is going to curl your toenails."

"Again, how do you know all this?" Jack returned to his chair. Swirling the slice of lime in his limenade with his straw, he raised the glass to his mouth. And stopped. "Wait. Where do they get the blood?"

"Human sacrifice."

Jack abruptly stood up. "That's preposterous." He slammed the glass down.

"Dmitri Petrov has been feeding us information for months." With the morning sun on his face, Chris rested his back against the wall. "He's the one who slipped the note to Adam at the plant. He was in disguise when he introduced himself as Boris."

As he tried to place Dmitri, Jack's eyes swept around the room. "You mean..." He frowned. "Fisher's personal assistant?"

"None other. I guess he got sick of being treated like a slave in a monkey suit. He was our mysterious Mr. X. And it gets even worse than that."

Jack's jaw dropped even more. "Are you kidding me? How does it get worse than mass murder?!"

"They're starving millions of people to death, using climate change as a ruse. They've declared that farmers are their enemy." Chris stared out the window with his back to Jack, his ripped jeans and long-sleeved, black t-shirt showing off his muscular physique. His light cologne overpowered the scent of the freshly brewed coffee Jenny had just delivered.

"It makes sense now. It makes sense why they don't care about the fentanyl crisis or poverty or homelessness or mental health. They *want* people to die." Jack sat down. "Soon they'll find out that their time is up."

"And soon the people will discover that they can challenge the guys in white coats. Experts say, studies show, blah blah blah."

With his eyes misting over, Jack leaned back in his chair to put his ankle on his knee. A moment passed before he spoke again. "When Anna told me what was happening, I knew I needed you on the case. I didn't think we'd cross paths again after Manhattan, yet... here we are."

"Is that a bad thing?" Chris replied with a half-smile.

"You're the best damn detective in the country. It was you who brought down Johnny's trafficking ring."

"Jack." Chris leaned back. "When you found me, I felt like something was missing, like the world we were living in was a lie."

"You weren't wrong," Jack concurred. "They're worse than their mentor – one Adolph Hitler. *He* never pretended to care about the people *he* was killing." Jack grabbed his suit jacket as the two men headed out to their vehicles.

"Let's get ready to rumble." Chris led the way down the stairs.

Just outside the double front doors to the entrance, Jack stopped. "I'm afraid I can't do that, Chris."

Startled by Jack's deep, distorted voice, Chris turned around to face his host. His blood ran cold.

Chapter 109

One of only several quantum computers in the world, the one underneath Dormin communicated in real time with the Large Hadron Collider at CERN – the most sophisticated technology to ever exist on Planet Earth. If the empire succeeded in their mission, humanity would be enslaved to the devil for eternity. There was no turning back.

In the hectic war room at the old Moreno Theater, distressed scientists and technicians were still attempting to commandeer the globalist-controlled airwaves for the looming noon deadline.

Upstairs, in the seating area of the theater, Emma checked her watch. It was just after 9 am; it wasn't like Chris to be late. When the microphone screeched, the noisy main floor of the theater fell silent. Emma began.

> **File notes: Emma Langford, Moreno Theater** *(Transcribed)*
> *Scratching the surface of Psychological Warfare*
> **April 11, 2017**
> *Good morning.*
> *What happens when we can't socialize? Much like solitary confinement in prison, isolation is designed to break the spirit. When isolation is forced on the global population, society loses the voice of reason in lucid people – the people who remind us when things have been taken too far.*

Alone and confused, the empire can convince us of anything – no matter how anti-science or delusional it is: The air we breathe is going to kill us. Climate change causes heart attacks. Women have penises. When nothing makes sense anymore, the people panic. Amid our turmoil, all we want is a return to a more ordered world.

The rulers step in with an answer that's layered with flattery and bribes. We are all part of the solution to keep the collective safe. Anyone questioning the solution is therefore the enemy of humanity.

Once the soul is destroyed and the victim is out of touch with reality, the rulers can do anything they want to them to break the mind: Amnesia – loss of memory; abulia – loss of will; and apathy – loss of interest. **These** *are the outcomes of an effective psychological operation.*

Folks, that's why perfectly reasonable, intelligent people have lost their way. It doesn't matter how much data you show them – they have now been **turned against** *rational people. The rulers reveal the deception after the fact, but by then, nobody cares.*

Far-fetched, you say? So was the Third Reich slaughtering millions of innocent people in World War II. After all, they were a duly elected, legitimate government. Yet, an advanced society full of intelligent people believed them.

Do you think the criminal cartel is going to announce on the six o'clock news that we're a fascist country now? They're not going to send storm troopers to flood the streets. No. Fascism, communism, the isms... they creep up on us. The tyranny crawls quietly like a cute little turtle until we find ourselves living alongside roaring lions in a police state. By believing lies, we fall right into the trap.

Modern man thinks he is too smart, too developed to fall for mind tricks. Think about it for a minute. Has our species somehow evolved beyond psychopathy? Is that why we treat the authorities like some kind of gods whose judgment can't be questioned? Are they, and they alone, the arbiters of truth and morality? Have we forgotten that human beings are easily corrupted by money and power? Would an evolved species believe in the concept of mass mind control? Based on our history, I think it would.

It's time to put things back into perspective. Governments are run by people. They're... just... people. They're evil people who recruited hundreds of millions of innocent people to manifest the dark awakening, sleeper demons who will turn on their fellow humans in an instant. Now they want to make that permanent.

As we go forth, remember: Strong men make good times. Good times make weak men. Weak men make hard times. Hard times make strong men.

The cycle continues. Stay strong.

Chapter 110

Chris Simon took a step back. Blindly searching for his van behind him in Jack's circular driveway, he couldn't tear his wide-eyed gaze away. The demonic evil in Jack's shadow-rimmed eyes was matched only by the visible dark energy that surrounded him. He flicked his forked tongue. "Did I ssscare you?" he hissed Satan's catchphrase with a dramatic flair.

That's when Chris noticed the ouroboros on Jack's left wrist – he was wearing the devil's cross. He sped away.

By the time Chris returned to the estate, forty panic-stricken minutes had passed. It was already after 10 am when he pounded on the door of Jack's guest house.

On the other side of that door, the hair on the back of Tessa's neck stood up. "Who is it?" she yelled from the sofa, not daring to approach the door. She tossed the notes for her broadcast onto the coffee table.

"It's Chris." `Rap! Rap! Rap!` "Open the door!"

The alarm in Chris's voice sent shivers down Tessa's spine. She wasted no time.

Chris was breathless as he stumbled in. "We... have a... problem."

"What?" Tessa gasped. "What's going on?!"

"It's... Jack." Stopping to catch his breath, Chris leaned his back against the cedar wall. "Get over to the main house as soon as you can." He was gone as suddenly as he'd appeared.

Ten minutes later, Tessa's mind was on fire as she closed the short gap from the guest house to the main house on foot. A cluster of vehicles were hastily parked around the dormant fountain on the driveway.

Tessa was unprepared for the scene that awaited her at the top of the landing. Odd screeching sounds were coming from inside the study. From the open door, she watched Jack thrashing violently on the sofa. He was bound with a thin rope and being held down by two men she didn't know.

Anna and Chris stood a safe distance away on either side of Jack's sobbing wife, Abby. Her long, light brown hair was soaked with tears and mucus.

Still constrained and foaming at the mouth like a rabid dog, Jack rotated his head at an unnatural angle until he was leering at the new arrival. When he recognized her, the afternoon sun highlighted the dark clouds in his eye slits. "Tesssa..."

Draped in a bright purple stole with a large wooden crucifix in one hand, Father Del Rosario called on the Apostles and Saints to expel the demon. Using consecrated oil, he made the sign of the cross on Jack's forehead.

With two strong men straining to hold him down, Jack violently broke free from the thin rope. He began to levitate.

Father Del Rosario sprinkled holy water over a squealing Jack, who was now growling and thrashing in midair. "Our Father who art in Heaven." Renewed energy whirled through the room like a tornado. "Hallowed be thy name. Thy kingdom come –"

Everyone in the room jumped when Jack let out a bloodcurdling scream, interrupting the Lord's Prayer.

"I **command** you to retreat in the name of Jesus!" Speaking with authority, Fr. Del Rosario made the sign of the cross and held the crucifix up to Jack's flushed face. "You have no dominion here!"

Dropping to the sofa, Jack's projectile vomiting shot in the air, landing all over his clothes, the sofa, the priest, and the surrounding area.

Fr. Del Rosario continued praying.

From across the room, Chris approached Tessa and pulled her into the hall. When he spoke, his tone was hushed. "Get down to the war room as soon as you can. This is going to take some time."

"What do you want me to do?" Tessa whispered.

"Stall. If Father can expel the demon, we'll be able to get into their system. That's what's stopping it." Chris checked his phone for the time.

"What happened before I got here?"

"Jack freaked me the F out is what happened. I've seen this before. I knew what it was."

"That explains his erratic behavior! It wasn't overwork."

"Before we could begin, I had to get permission from the bishop. A psychiatrist had to rule out psychosis. They're the guys holding him down."

"What did the shrink say?"

"Jack is perfectly lucid; he's not delusional." Chris accompanied Tessa as she descended the stairs to the entrance. "The bishop thinks it might be demonic influence rather than a full possession. Like someone put a curse on him."

"Okay," Tessa opened the front door to leave. "I'll get down to the theater to brief the others. When will you get there?"

"As soon as I can." Chris rubbed his bloodshot eyes with both hands. "Jack's not going to make it today."

On the way to the Moreno Theater, Tessa contemplated what she'd just witnessed and how the Catholic Church had been under attack for so long. Multiple scandals didn't help. But the flock wasn't guilty; it was all on church leadership.

When the Pope embraced Marxism and postmodernism, it was like a postmortem on a dying culture. Fifty miles of secret archives lay beneath the Vatican. What were they hiding? Could it be the true history of the world? Evidence of aliens? Or perhaps...it was how to summon Satan.

Chapter 111

Out of the clear blue sky, a massive white cloud formed over the peaceful valley, its shimmering rim of pitch-black outlining it like a coloring page.

In a bunker deep beneath the sham meatpacking plant, a dozen demonic entities in hooded garments gathered around a bloody altar. Each of them wore a scream mask. Crimson robes swept the floor when they moved, drapery that hid their matching bloodstained shoes.

The thick metal door opened; a man shrouded in a black robe entered, his face hidden by a leather mask. Chanting, he dispersed incense from a metal censer.

The triumphant Global Dormin Group were ready to celebrate.

Soon, they would make a human sacrifice to Moloch. Soon after, they would become gods.

Chapter 112

The old school popcorn machine at the Moreno Theater was going full tilt. Overflowing buckets disappeared from the greasy counter as quickly as they appeared.

Inside the seating area was a century-old charm with bygone deep burgundy décor and traditional stage. Three rows of balconies surrounded the spectators. In contrast, the huge digital clock on the side wall displayed the current time plus the remaining time until Zero Hour – a little over an hour.

From the podium, Tessa scanned the room with a newfound appreciation of how many people had been working with independent media – standing room only. She tapped on the microphone to get everyone's attention. "Good morning!" Her warm smile exuded a peaceful energy as it lit up the room. "Chris has been temporarily delayed but rest assured...we're still going ahead as planned. Relax and have some more popcorn. I'll be back." Tessa raced home to change.

Fifteen minutes later, a shrill whistle pierced the noisy air when Chris jumped onto the stage to grab the microphone. A nails-on-a-chalkboard squeal was followed by "Testing, testing. One. Two. Three." The screen behind him was blank. It was 11:34 a.m.

The only illumination in the hushed theater were the exit lights and the red, white, and blue spotlights moving around the stage. At the top of one of the aisles, a silhouette appeared in the frame of the open door.

His tall frame was much slimmer now, but his 91-year-old presence was just as imposing. Moving with the gait of an elderly man keeping time with his cowboy boots and cane, he carried his white cowboy hat in his other hand to reveal his balding head.

A collective gasp sucked all the air out of the room when the man's identity was revealed in the spotlight. No one was prepared to see a ghost. Old man Fisher slowly climbed the three steps to the stage to approach the podium.

The microphone already on, Graham Maxwell Fisher III cleared his throat to begin. Several seconds of silence passed. "When a man's been gone for sixteen years, he certainly has a story to tell." His voice was faint and shaky. "But that can wait." He flashed his characteristic wide smile, his charisma instantly filling those assembled with a sense of calm. "We're running out of time."

Nodding to old man Fisher as he exited, Chris took over the podium again. "We're in a very dark time folks, but we stand on the shoulders of giants. Thanks to them, the supreme law of the land is called the Constitution." He held up a worn book to show the crowd as the colors of America danced in the background.

In the war room beneath them, the signal was fading in and out. At 11:52 am, panic set in – they weren't going to make the deadline.

Chapter 113

In the celebratory war room of the plant, meanwhile, the champagne was chilling. The music was on. The sacrifice was waiting. Today was the day.

11:57 a.m. In three minutes, every unsuspecting innocent soul on the planet was theirs – the black awakening.

Welcome to hell.

When the blood drained from his face, Jack turned as white as prairie snow. The bishop and the psychiatrist carried him to the master bedroom.

Once Abby began wiping his face with a cool cloth, Jack sat up, his eyes expanded, his index finger pointing to a blank space near the ceiling. As the life returned to his eyes, his face began to glow.

Abby checked the time. It was 11:59 a.m.

At the plant, the League of LIES had begun the countdown with blood lust on their minds: Thirty... twenty-nine...twenty-eight...

Chapter 114

At the Moreno Theater, the AltMedia Group waited. The digital clock began to flash – they had under thirty seconds left. Nobody dared to make a sound.

Then... from the war room came a jubilant roar!

Still at the podium, Chris had an ear-to-ear grin on his face. "We're in, folks. The spell has been broken." The room erupted in boisterous applause.

After the noise died down, everyone was drawn to a feather-soft feminine voice coming from the back of the room. "You sure about that?" All heads turned to watch a luminous Tessa Ryan gracefully make her way down the aisle. Her off-the-shoulder, silk, ivory blouse and the French twist in her mahogany-brown hair were enhanced by the exorbitantly expensive diamond necklace she wore around her neck. Her look was completed by a black pencil skirt and black pump heels that clicked on the wooden stage as she gracefully crossed it.

Chris turned to face her. "Yes. I'm sure. We've been expecting you." As he left the stage, the jumbo screen displayed a red, white, and blue flag waving in the wind next to the statue of liberty.

Zero hour had arrived.

On bustling city streets and in private living rooms, from busy shopping malls to gloomy nursing homes, in flashy Times Square and demon-possessed Brussels, they stopped what they were doing. With an unusual energy in the atmosphere, the entire world was inexplicably drawn to their screens.

In place of their videos, television programs, podcasts, electronic billboards, radio announcers, and every other medium on the planet, a beautiful, young woman with her mother's olive skin and her father's piercing baby-blue eyes stood at a podium. Though she spoke the words in English, they were translated to each person in their own language. Hi-tech warfare.

GLOBAL GOVERNMENT AND THE OCCULT:
Not today, Satan (Transcribed)
April 11, 2017

Let all bitterness, and wrath, and anger, and clamor, and evil speaking, be put away from you, with all malice: And be ye kind one to another, tenderhearted, forgiving one another, even as God for Christ's sake hath forgiven you. (Ephesians 4:31-32, KJV).

Hello world. My name is Tessa Ryan, coming to you live from the classic Moreno Theater in beautiful Dormin, Wyoming, USA. Unscripted, and most important of all – unafraid.

*Imagine a small island in the South Pacific where a beast called Evil reigns. It's an entity unlike anything you've ever seen. This is an evil **so vile** that it's capable of training an intelligent species to passively accept their own demise.*

On the other side of the world, a global war is building in which truth and lies are the weapons. The enemy of humanity has flipped the script – evil is called good and good is called evil. They fire missiles called war, pandemics, and climate change. Like the masters of illusion they are, they divide the people to diminish our strength.

Now imagine a tsunami barreling toward the island, picking up strength at it draws near. The roar of the ocean builds until the crashing waves destroy everything in its path. The land remains – barren and uninhabited.

*We need to ask ourselves... are **we** on the wrong side of history if we're against Evil? Are we the enemies of humankind if we ARE humankind?*

Today, we are called to remove the divide. Today, we are reminded that you are not my enemy. I am not your enemy. Other than the Creator, there is no force more powerful than a united humanity – unity we can achieve simply by speaking the truth. When we speak the truth, we become incredibly powerful. The truth will always come out in the end – it's the iron will of the universe. As long as we can hear the words, there is hope.

*While we've been waiting for a savior, we discover they are much closer than knew. Folks, we are the saviors. WE are the tsunami barreling toward the evil island. **We** are the ones we've been waiting for. **We** are the people – united, we will never be defeated!*

[Loud applause, whistles, cheering]

My friends, let's remember who we are and what we've sacrificed. It's what our founding fathers knew. It's what many great leaders throughout history

have died for. It's why revolutions are waged, wars are started, and economies are crashed. Perhaps Braveheart said it best: FREEEEEEEDOM!!
[Loud crack from the unoccupied top balcony]
God didn't turn his back on us. We turned our back on God and now we're living in a world without him. When Man worships Man, we suffer. Do you think it's time to welcome Creator God back? Whatever religion you practice, whatever God it is you worship, let's join our hearts and minds to raise the collective frequency to one of love and forgiveness and beauty and truth.

As Christians, we are called to drop the ego and live as Jesus did. It's not easy. It's not easy to turn the other cheek. It's not easy to forgive. It's not easy to love your neighbor as yourself. But when did anyone ever say that it would be easy to defend the soul of humanity?

Please bow your heads now as we pray for redemption.
In the name of the Father, and the Son, and the Holy Spirit.
The enemy fights hard against us because we're making a difference for Your Kingdom. Today we remember that the battle is Yours, Lord, and that You can take them down in one fell swoop. Fill us with the Holy Spirit as we strive to do your good works. We ask this in Jesus' name.
[Amen by crowd]
Be not afraid, patriots. The truth has set us free.
This is Tessa Ryan, signing off.

As Tessa spoke, a golden light appeared in a gentle breeze. The people, enraptured by this girl's speech, looked up into the sky – the light was manifesting in the physical realm. In front of every person, the sick, the poor, the disabled, the vulnerable, the rich and poor, the black and white, and the old and young appeared a golden symbol – the Ancient Sumerian Symbol of Peace and love. A four-pointed star, surrounded by circles and waves carried with it a message. They were going to be okay now and they didn't even need a safe space.

Across the valley, a loud cheer was heard in the festive streets.

While the charismatic Tessa Ryan captured the hearts and minds of people across the globe, the people's law enforcement set their plan in motion to arrest the perpetrators. Adam, Jason, Molly, and the military were closing in on the plant to execute their plan.

As Tessa exited the stage, the victorious cheers continued. The screen morphed into the image of a dove. Standing in the first row, Anna Hale began a spontaneous rendition of <u>Amazing Grace</u> (John Newton). She had the voice of an angel.

Amazing grace, how sweet the sound that saved a wretch like me
I once was lost, but now am found. Was blind, but now I see...

The entire Theater joined in:

'Twas grace that taught my heart to fear and grace, my fears relieved
How precious did that grace appear the hour I first believed
When we've been there ten thousand years bright shining as the sun
We've no less days to sing God's praise than when we've first begun

Completely captivated by the magical moment, Dorminians were compelled to lift their spirits in prayer. The streets filled with celebratory song.

Amazing grace, how sweet the sound that saved a wretch like me
I once was lost, but now am found. Was blind, but now I see

By now, people all over the world lifted their voices in praise, a harmonious and victorious tribute sent to the heavens.

Amazing grace, how sweet the sound that saved a wretch like me
I once was lost, but now am found. Was blind, but now I see

By the time the song ended, an unexpected wave of joy and relief swept across the globe like a ball of pure loving energy. Everyone who was open to the gift of the truth joined their hearts and hands in prayer as healing tears flowed.

This was a special moment – anyone who had eyes to see, and ears to hear was overcome by what they had just witnessed. It was the day that time and space stood still. It was the day they slammed the door in the face of Satan.

Chapter 115

Inside the plant, everything went black. An eerie silence followed.

At Mystic Manor, the window of Max's study was open, the sweet sound of birdsong filling the room with harmony. Rays of sunshine poured in, the casement windows casting tic-tac-toe patterns across the dark floor.

Smoke from Max's cigar drifted while he locked the door. He stubbed it out, moving to the window to watch his wife tending to the vegetable garden, oblivious to what was about to happen.

Footsteps on the stairs echoed like thunder.

A single gunshot rang out.

Chapter 116

Six months later

With the sweet melody of birdsong in the air, the warm autumn sun peeked through the barren trees and projected beams of light onto the jutting headstones. A thick carpet of orange and brown covered the graves and the still green grass that surrounded them.

The leaves crunching under Tessa's boots reminded her of the intuitive calling she'd received a year earlier. She'd been so isolated in her little bubble that it never occurred to her that she was living in a make-believe world. Kneeling, she placed the bouquet of fresh daisies on her mama's grave.

On the one-year anniversary of Cecilia's death, Tessa regretted that she didn't have a chance to say goodbye. Now, she wanted to tell her that she got it, that she understood. There's so much societal pressure on mothers to be perfect. So many people of her generation disowned their parents... further disintegration of the traditional family.

"Those daisies must be captivating, Tess."

"Adam!" Tessa was startled out of her reverie. "You scared me half to death!" She still loved the way her name sounded on his lips.

"Then I'll be careful not to do it again," Adam joked. "At least we're in the right place."

Tessa jumped to her feet. "Ha. Funny man."

"I've got good news," Adam drew nearer to Tessa.

Behind the couple, someone cleared their throat. They both turned to welcome the new addition to their little impromptu meeting in the graveyard.

"Anna!" Tessa beamed. "Adam just told me he has some good news."

"Mystic Manor is now city property." Adam's eyes darted back and forth between the two women. "The plan is to convert it to a community center and event venue."

Anna and Tessa exchanged glances, the latter seeking clarification. "So, you mean... community owned?"

"Yep. Are you still looking for a place for that gallery?"

"Oh my God!" Tessa covered her gaping mouth with her hands. Throwing her arms around Adam's neck, she couldn't suppress a cheer. "Yeeeah!"

"I hear that place is haunted," Anna added.

"Ooh. This should be interesting," Tessa grinned and rubbed her hands together.

"I've got a meeting to get to." Adam pecked Tessa on the lips. "I wanted to deliver that news in person." As head of the new community owned and citizen-driven news organization in town, he was a busy man.

As Adam drove away, Tessa turned to Anna. "There's something I need to talk to you about. I wonder if we can find a better venue than the graveyard."

Anna pointed in a random direction. "I'll meet you at your house in half an hour."

On Maple Street, Tessa parked her white SUV in front of a mid-20th century country-blue two-story house. Only three blocks away from her childhood home, it was similar in layout, still boasting original hardwood floors, curved banisters, and a beautiful stained-glass window. While it had retained most of its character, it had fallen into disrepair during the forsaken city's darkest days. Despite the devil's attempt to rewrite history with haunted tales of defeat, these old houses told vivid stories of the before times and hosted memories that no one could steal.

While she waited for Anna, Tessa lounged on the back deck. Surrounded by autumn flowers, a glass of red wine in hand and the radiance of the sun on her face, she reflected on returning to Dormin a year earlier. At that time, she'd have thought you crazy if you'd suggested she'd be back in Dormin and living life to the fullest with the man of her dreams – yet here she was.

When she first arrived, Tessa had had an entirely different worldview. How was she to know everything was an illusion? 'The science' can be bought and sold, universities are Marxist echo chambers, corporate media is evil, the entertainment industry is a propaganda machine, the justice system is the 'just us' system, and uni-party politics only serve the oligarchy.

"The flowers smell amazing." Anna had come in through the back gate.

The soft voice startled Tessa back to reality. "I'll get tea," she announced while she disappeared through the patio door.

A few minutes later, Anna inhaled the steam rising from her cup of peppermint tea. "This tea smells amazing too."

"Anna," Tessa sighed. "We both know you're not here to talk about flowers and tea. Can you finally tell me what was going on with my dad? Please? You've been dodging it for years."

"Out of love..."

"I'm all grown up... I think I can handle it." Tessa sat up in her lounge chair. "I'm trying to figure out... why I feel so... cold toward him."

"... Okay," Anna sighed. "One time... when you and your father went out to the Fisher ranch, well... it was just before your tenth birthday." She was treating her young friend like she was fourteen years old – the age she'd been when her mother was taken away by the paramedics.

"Enough suspense, Anna. Get to the point."

A moment passed before Anna continued. "You know all about the blackmail scam... the tunnels... the elaborate underground city to attract power players from all over the world."

"I know that, Anna! Quit stalling."

"Well, on one of the visits you and your father made to the ranch, you were lured into a shed." Anna's eyes clouded over as she recalled the dark days. "Max said he wanted to show you some art supplies."

"I have a feeling I didn't get any art supplies." Tessa lamented in a monotone.

"Once you and your father were in the shed, they drugged you both. The shed was a façade...one of the entrances to the tunnel. The rooms all had cameras."

"So... my fath... what?

"The drug they gave you removed any ability to resist their commands – they ordered him to rape you." Anna wiped away the tears that had spilled from her eyes. "I'm so sorry, child."

Speechless, Tessa gestured with her hands for Anna to continue. In denial, her mind and body were both numb.

"They recorded it, of course."

"I don't understand. Why didn't I remember?"

"Trauma. And the drug... it was designed to repress memories."

"But we were just a normal family. We had no money. No reputation to protect. What were they going to do to him if he didn't go along with whatever it was they wanted from him? What could they possibly take away from him that meant so much?"

Several seconds passed before Anna answered. "His... his only... precious child."

Tessa gasped and clutched her stomach. "Omigod. That's how they did it!" She grabbed Anna's hand.

"Then they told you he couldn't take care of you when they took your mother away. They made up an excuse. He was really in jail taking the rap for someone else."

Tessa's mind raced back to that night her mom was taken away.

"He couldn't live with the guilt, so he took his own life. These psychopaths get off on that kind of stuff. Johnny Eden. Do you remember him?"

"Yes." The New York tunnels flashed before Tessa's eyes. The kids in that den. She was nauseated.

"That day, when they tricked you and your father, Johnny was there. He and Max were key players in the global blackmail operation, an unholy bond that tied them together through secrets and an unlimited league of lies."

"So that's why they tried so hard to cover it up," Tessa whispered. When her jaw dropped, she stared into space, trying not to think.

"Remember when I told you that sometimes you had to be shown things, to feel them, that they can't be explained?"

"Yes. Of course. That was the day my mom died. That whole day was weird. Felt like I was in a dream. Losing my mind."

"Do you understand now?"

"It couldn't be easy, or I wouldn't have learned anything."

Anna gazed at Tessa with motherly love shining in her eyes. "What you went through, child, is called the Dark Night of the Soul."

"It was a long-ass night," Tessa giggled.

"Indeed. It started in New York. The demons wouldn't let you alone. But we are on the new Earth now." Anna's eyes misted over. "Those dreams, child... always telling you something."

Tessa's mind reeled. The dreams. Not being able to distinguish them from reality. The time her mind went missing for five days...

"Everything you think you learned; you already knew. All those visions were parts of your psyche trying to come to terms with your past."

"Wait," Tessa turned her head to catch Anna's eyes. "So, I was in a parallel universe?"

"Or many. There were similar scenes playing out elsewhere in the cosmos."

"Whoa."

"Those who could not or would not receive the gift of the truth remained on the old Earth, and it played out very differently. They didn't stop the global government takeover and every dystopian story you've ever heard of manifested."

"Why is it that some people can see what's going on and others can't?"

"Oh, dear! How much time do you have?" Anna laughed.

"How complicated is it?"

Anna leaned back in her chair, a gesture that put Tessa at ease. "Those who can see the big picture can see connections and patterns. they can connect dots. Imagine having a bird's eye view in the proverbial rabbit hole," she laughed. "It's called insight."

"So –"

"Tribes can form quickly when one side craves a return to traditional values and the other is founded on, 'Do what thou whilst be the whole of the law'. But there is only one truth and only one way to the truth. When we pushed Him away, the world fell."

"You mean God?"

"Yes. It's like Jonathan Cahn wrote about in his book, Return of the Gods," Anna began. "It started in the `60s when Ba'al, the false god, replaced God with sex and money and took over leadership of the church."

Fixated on a spot of grass on the lawn, Tessa didn't respond.

"When Ishtar, the goddess of fertility and sexuality arrived, the sexual revolution was upon us. It was the beginning of the breakdown of the traditional family."

Glancing from side to side, Tessa realized things were starting to add up.

"Finally, Moloch, the god of human sacrifice, moved in and abortions exploded. The ancient gods had returned."

"Omigod. That makes so much sense."

"But like a long symphony that ends on a sonorous note, Jesus had the last word." Anna stared off into the distance. , 'I am the way, the truth, and the light; no man cometh unto the Father but by me'." [1]

---

1. John 14:6 KJV

"And ye shall know the truth, and the truth will make you free."[2] Tessa was unable to suppress a smile. They had taken on the most powerful people in the world – and won. Their gods had failed them.

---

[2] John 8:32, KJV

Chapter 117

As Dorminians reclaimed their city through grassroots organizing, they'd developed parallel structures outside the mortal foe's twisted idea of morality. Before they knew it, a second, spontaneous society had emerged. Unlike direct political action, it gave power to the powerless. *These* are the structures of humanity: Pot roasts and lilacs. Children's laughter and church bells. Faith. Freedom. Family. Judeo-Christian values.

Tessa now understood why she'd been called back. She was just an ordinary girl in the wrong place at the right time, who'd taken an extraordinary journey beyond the façade. One day, she would tell her grandchildren about her battle scars from the great meme war – the Second American Revolution.

In the end, God wins.

The end

Epilogue

It was 1776 all over again – the Second American Revolution had begun.

Unlike 1776, the war wasn't over land. This time, the stakes were much higher – it was an epic battle for the soul of humanity in which everything was once again at stake: Life and death. Freedom over servitude. Neighbor against neighbor.

Vastly overpowered, out resourced, and unorganized, courageous patriots worldwide stood shoulder to shoulder and boldly stared into the face of the globalists, willing to sacrifice everything for an immortal passion. Ordinary truckers and farmers and nurses and working people of all stripes and colors and flags stood together for an idea – that they could be freed from the clutches of an evil empire. Their quest for liberty would never die. They would never surrender.

The American spirit lived on.

The revolution continues.

"*The Founders never intended for Americans to trust their government. Our entire Constitution was predicated on the notion that government was a necessary evil, to be restrained and minimized as much as possible.*"
~ Rand Paul

COLLECTIVE PRAYER FOR HUMANITY

---

*D*ivine Creator, gods of many names, be in our hearts and minds as we come together as one people. We acknowledge our differences while we seek common ground. You are the light that destroys the darkness. Illuminate us, Great Creator, so we may light the way for others. We thank You for Your mercy as we strive to be the good we desire to see in the world.
Amen.

Acknowledgments

I acknowledge Creator God, the Great Spirit, and Supreme Beings of all faiths and Abrahamic religions. Though we walk different terrestrial paths, we share one divine destiny. King of Kings, our Redeemer Jesus Christ – I am humbled before You, Lord; for You are the author of my life.

Bryan Herlen: My best friend and partner in life, my sounding board, my reference library, my beta reader, my critic, and my daily support; thank you for being part of my life.

AJ Adams: Your editorial expertise, keen insight, creative contributions, visionary genius, and endless patience brought the story to life. Through all the laughter and tears, frustrations and reflections, and nights of endless coffee, you never abandoned me when the going got rough. You only encouraged me – that is true friendship. You are truly an angel sent from Heaven. Kyrie Eliason, my friend.

Steph Cooley: For everything you've done, for your steadfast determination to make the world a better place for others, and for being the wind at my back – you are the woman I wish I could be. Thank you.

Michelle Lewis-Robertson: Over the years, the love and understanding you and Mark afforded me wasn't always easy on you. You selflessly did it anyway and it made all the difference for me. Thank you.

Lill Morenz: You always knew when I needed a push. Thank you for understanding that life is messy. Your compassion is a gift.

Myrna Robb: For the gifts, prayers, encouragement, and support. They did not go unnoticed and are very much appreciated.

Ruth Lees, Chris Shuya, Helen Jacobsen, Jeanne Fetsch, Anita Burnett, Shane Pooler, Derian Cooley, Damon Read, Aaron Waddington and **Autumn Clark**: Thank you for the feedback and for keeping me humble. You all did your part to get me through the process.

Rosemarie Nixon, John Donlan, and Sean Cummings: You are the wordsmiths and poets who helped me hone the craft and from whom I learned so much. Thank you for your time and patience.

Gordon Tolton: Without your friendship and mentorship, this book would not exist. I've never forgotten the words you said to me all those years ago. "Everybody wants to write a book. Don't just talk about it. Do it." Thanks, Gord.

Jimmy Dore: Thank you for using your platform to make a difference. All the while, your integrity was unshakeable – that's a difficult feat in today's world. Who knew that a jag-off comedian in his garage would be more of an inspiration than many spiritual leaders?

Tim Pool: Without you reminding common people, like me, to create culture, so many artistic endeavors would not be realized. Even though you are, most assuredly, the proverbial milquetoast fence-sitter, thank you for keeping me motivated to make a difference.

Larry Hubich: Everything I know about collective bargaining; I learned from you. Thank you for setting the example.

Joe Rogan: Your powerful and rational voice has been critical in today's culture of deception. There aren't enough superlatives in the English language to describe what a difference you've made. Thank you.

Oliver Anthony: Thank you for the music and for showing us that the people have the power.

Laura-Lynn Tyler Thompson: Your steadfast faith is a source of an ongoing source of inspiration to me. Thank you for the chance to meet you when you were in Saskatchewan.

Glenn Greenwald, Matt Taibbi, Catherine Herridge, Bari Weiss, Michael Schellenberger, James O'Keefe, Tom Fitton, Max Blumenthal, and **Tucker Carlson**: You are examples of what journalism used to be – holding power to account. Thank you for representing the people as you navigate through the stormy seas of propaganda. Please don't learn to code. (Note to other journalists: The aforementioned names are not an exhaustive list of good journalists. I know there are many more of you.)

Elon Musk: Thank you for using your resources to restore whatever sanity we can get to the Western World.

To all independent, citizen-driven media: The role you have played and continue to play in sharing the stories that matter to the people, rather than the corporations, is what is shining a light of truth in a dark, deceptive world. While there are way too many of you to list, just know how much you are appreciated.

To the people: Last, but not least, a sincere, heartfelt thank you for your part in shaping the global narrative. You are the hero in the story; it is both for you, and by you. Hold the line, patriots. You got this.

"Never doubt that a small group of thoughtful, committed citizens can change the world. Indeed, it is the only thing that ever has."
~ *Margaret Mead*

Author's Note

Attempting to understand the wonderful, fragile, submissive, creative, malleable, and vastly complex human psyche has been an extraordinary journey. <u>League of Lies</u>, while a fictional story, is based on my opinions and interpretation of academic teachings and current events. History and psychology are explored in this story only insofar as they encourage the reader to think beyond the surface world.

Twenty years of extensive research have gone into the creation of this book. While every effort has been made to credit others for their work, it's impossible to either list or remember all the sources I've used. If you spot anything I've missed, please visit www.elliepool.com to send us a message.

I hope you enjoyed reading <u>League of Lies.</u>

Namaste.

BIBLIOGRAPHY

Alinsky, Saul. *Rules for Radicals: A Pragmatic Primer for Realistic Radicals.* Vintage, 2010.

Black, Jeremy. *Rethinking World War Two: The Conflict and Its Legacy.* Bloomsbury Publishing, 2015.

Bloom, Harold. *George Orwell's 1984.* Chelsea House Publications, 2007.

Borch, Christian. *The Politics of Crowds: An Alternative History of Sociology.* Cambridge University Press, 2012.

Cahn, Jonathan. *The Return of the Gods.* Charisma Media, 2022.

Crawford, Jarret T., and Lee Jussim. *Politics of Social Psychology.* Psychology Press, 2017.

Desmet, Mattias. *The Psychology of Totalitarianism.* Chelsea Green Publishing, 2022.

La Vey, Anton. *Satanic Bible.* Harper Collins, 1976.

Lindsay, James A. *The Marxification of Education: Paulo Freire's Critical Marxism and Theft of Education*, 2022.

Marx, Karl. *Das Kapital: A Critique of Political Economy.* Simon and Schuster, 2012.

Publishers, Thomas Nelson. *The Holy Bible, KJV*, 2014.

Schuman, T. *Love Letter to America,* 1984 (Yuri Bezmenov).

Schwab, Klaus. *The Fourth Industrial Revolution*. Penguin UK, 2017.

Tzu, Sun. *The Art of War*. Courier Corporation, 2002.

About the Author

Ellie Pool was born and raised in the Canadian prairies where she learned to value faith, family, and freedom. As Western culture began its downward spiral into a spiritually bankrupt dystopia, she made it her life mission to understand how and why civilized societies collapse. Her first novel, League of Lies explores the idea that the enemy of humanity is humanity. Retired from her professional career, Ellie enjoys the quiet life writing, gardening, and spectator baseball. She resides in Saskatchewan, Canada with her husband and two feline fur babies, (half-brothers) Thor and Loki.

SF Photos

Manufactured by Amazon.ca
Bolton, ON